THE COMBAT KNIFE WAS POISED
FOR A KILLING THRUST

Schwarz slipped a hand across the sentry's nose and mouth, then jerked the guy's head back sharply, baring his throat to the knife's blade. One slash was all it took.

He wedged the body underneath a nearby cypress root and sheathed his knife, unslung the M-16 and flicked off its safety. Lyons and Blancanales waded through the swamp, speed and caution running neck and neck.

"I'd say another twenty, thirty yards," he told them, nodding toward the sound of voices and the fragrant smell of wood smoke on the breeze.

"Fan out," Blancanales said. "Say, five minutes to position. Wait for me to start the fireworks. When you pick your targets, make it count."

They separated, slogging through the hip-deep water on divergent courses, closing on the enemy. Five minutes later, Schwarz was huddled in a mangrove thicket, staring through a screen of hanging vines and Spanish moss across a clearing where two dozen men in paramilitary dress were eating out of army-surplus mess kits. The Able Team warrior brought the rifle to his shoulder, choosing a preliminary target and waiting for the signal.

War was about to break out in the Everglades.

D1012814

DON PENDLETON'S
MACK BOLAN®
STONY MAN™
TARGET AMERICA

A GOLD EAGLE BOOK FROM
WORLDWIDE®

TORONTO • NEW YORK • LONDON
AMSTERDAM • PARIS • SYDNEY • HAMBURG
STOCKHOLM • ATHENS • TOKYO • MILAN
MADRID • WARSAW • BUDAPEST • AUCKLAND

If you purchased this book without a cover you should be aware that this book is stolen property. It was reported as "unsold and destroyed" to the publisher, and neither the author nor the publisher has received any payment for this "stripped book."

First edition July 1994

ISBN 0-373-61895-6

Special thanks and acknowledgment to Mike Newton for his contribution to this work.

TARGET AMERICA

Copyright © 1994 by Worldwide Library.

All rights reserved. Except for use in any review, the reproduction or utilization of this work in whole or in part in any form by any electronic, mechanical or other means, now known or hereafter invented, including xerography, photocopying and recording, or in any information storage or retrieval system, is forbidden without the permission of the publisher, Worldwide Library, 225 Duncan Mill Road, Don Mills, Ontario, Canada M3B 3K9.

All characters in this book have no existence outside the imagination of the author and have no relation whatsoever to anyone bearing the same name or names. They are not even distantly inspired by any individual known or unknown to the author, and all incidents are pure invention.

® and TM are trademarks of Harlequin Enterprises Limited. Trademarks indicated with ® are registered in the United States Patent and Trademark Office, the Canadian Trade Marks Office and in other countries.

Printed in U.S.A.

TARGET
AMERICA

PROLOGUE

The worst part of dying, Jaime Sanchez decided, was all the blood. He felt no pain to speak of—still in shock, perhaps—but he was bleeding steadily and had been for the past half hour, since a pistol bullet had drilled his abdomen from front to back. His shirt had been a floral print, but you could only make the pattern out above his armpits now. The rest was dark with blood, and crimson blotches stained his khaki trousers from the waistband almost to his knees.

It was incredible, the sheer amount of blood a human body managed to maintain. How much of it had he lost by now? Sanchez couldn't tell by simply looking at his sodden clothes and didn't care to try. He was dying, but he still had work to do.

Things change, and Jaime Sanchez had been changing more or less nonstop for the past two years. If he had known that it would come to this, he could have done things differently, but that was wishful thinking and a waste of precious time. Whatever else was true or false tonight, he knew that he had little time to spare.

They would be hunting him, of course. Despite the fact that he was wounded, clearly dying, they couldn't afford to let him slink away and find himself a place to hide. It was imperative that he be silenced now, at any cost, before he could disrupt their plans. In recent days the irony of that had alternately made him laugh and sent him to the bottle for a jolt of liquid courage, but he wasn't laughing now and alcohol would only set his guts on fire.

No time.

The meeting had been scheduled two days in advance, with ample time for him to fabricate a story, double-check security. His former comrades didn't seem suspicious. They behaved as always, smiling to his face and chuckling when he spoke about the new *mujer* he had discovered in a club on Fortaleza Street. They wished him well and sent him off with sage advice on how to make the most of the experience.

In retrospect he couldn't fathom where the plan had gone wrong. Had he been too specific in his reference to the club? It was an easy thing to check, but he had made a point of stopping in three times before the scheduled meeting, tipping heavily enough that he would be remembered by the barmaids if it came to that. Of course, there was no girl—no special girl—but how could anyone discover that without interrogating every dancer in the club?

A leak, perhaps, and that meant he was finished from the moment he decided on a course of action, opting to betray his comrades when their plotting went too far. If they had eyes inside the Federal Bureau of Investigation, how could Jaime Sanchez ever hope to frustrate their designs?

And yet he had been honor bound to try.

A blaring horn roused Sanchez from his stupor, and he swerved the old VW Beetle back into its proper lane on Avenida Ponce de León. A chill was creeping over him, bone deep and growing colder by the moment, urging him to stop and rest. It was a sleep that he would never wake from, but it seemed inviting, even so. But not yet.

There was a crucial job to finish, if he only had the strength.

It was ironic how things had changed within the past few weeks. In the beginning he had been among the most en-

usiastic members of his clique, devoted to the cause. The
otherhood had given meaning to his life, direction that
as previously lacking. He had found a group of men and
omen he could feel at home with, patriots he could re-
ect for their determination and self-sacrifice. It was a
use worth dying for—and shedding blood, if need be.

He had participated in the revolutionary actions of his
dre to a point, including acts of violence, but he always
t the risks and pain involved were justified, that there was
mething to be gained. The final goal of liberation might
years away, but they were making strides. Success would
me within his lifetime, surely, if he only did his part.

But there was madness in the movement now, a new wind
owing through the ranks, and Sanchez had begun to
ther from its chill. At first the signs were barely notice-
le, overlooked in the excitement of the moment, but he
asn't blind. In time he found that he couldn't ignore the
idence of something new and sinister at work within the
dre, driving toward a goal that would destroy them all, the
ry land they fought to liberate.

The choice to cut and run hadn't been easy, and harder
ill was the ultimate decision to betray his comrades and the
ovement he had sworn to honor with his life. It was a
estion of priorities and conscience in the last analysis. He
uld proceed on schedule with his portion of the plan or
ke himself away and leave the others to continue on their
vn. The third alternative meant certain death for Sanchez
his treason was discovered, screaming death to countless
hers if he failed in his determination to resist the plan.

No choice, then, when he thought about it in those terms.

His first approach had been oblique, a phone call from a
blic booth, untraceable and vague in terms of subject
atter. He had spoken to an FBI agent, hinted at the sort of
owledge he possessed without revealing anything of sub-
nce on the open line. Unless he could convince the FBI in

person, they would laugh his warning off, dismiss it as paranoid delusion or deliberate lie.

He couldn't take that chance, with so much riding on the line.

A meeting was arranged, and Sanchez followed orders to the letter, stopping at a small café in Miramar and waiting for the agent to approach his table. Sanchez had expected someone from a television program, neatly barbered, with a suit and tie, but they had sent an undercover agent who could mingle with the neighborhood. It was the first sign that they took him seriously... or perhaps were giving him the rope required to hang himself.

Had he been followed to that meeting? It hardly mattered now that he was dying, but the thought repeated in his mind, a question begging for an answer but meeting only silence. He would never know, unless there was an answer waiting for him on the other side, and Sanchez had no great faith in the afterlife.

Initially his dealings with the FBI had been restricted to establishing a sense of trust. He told the agent things about himself, and they were verified through channels. At the second meeting Sanchez felt an urge to spill his guts but managed to restrain himself. The deadline was approaching, but he still had time. It was important that the federal men believe him, take him seriously. If he spoke too quickly, aired too much at once, they still might think him mad.

Tonight had been his fourth meeting with the agent in eleven days. They had been pushing it, but Sanchez watched his back and stayed alert for any hint of suspicion evident among his comrades. There was nothing he could point to in their words or attitude, no hint that they had found him out and marked him as a traitor fit to die.

It only went to prove how blind a man could be.

The meeting had been set for midnight on the beach at Ocean Park. It was a public place where either one of them would know if he was being followed by an enemy.

This time something had gone horribly, irrevocably wrong.

His contact had been waiting by the time Sanchez arrived, ten minutes early for the meet. That should have been a tip-off in itself, but he was eager to unload the burden of his knowledge, pass it on to other, stronger hands and spare himself the pain of bearing it alone. Once he had told them everything, the government would find him somewhere safe to hide while they took care of all the dirty details. Later, when the streets were safe again, he could emerge...or maybe find a better place to live in peace. The mainland possibly, or someplace altogether different. He could solve the problem for himself by simply leaving it behind.

Not now.

His contact had been seated on a wooden bench and facing toward the surf when he arrived. There was no sign of recognition from the agent as he'd moved in close enough to speak, words dying on his lips as Sanchez saw the crimson slash across the dead man's throat.

It all came down to blood.

He was recoiling from the body when a voice cried out his name. It was a voice he recognized, but Sanchez had no answer for his one-time comrade. Their friendship was as cold and dead as the unlucky agent on the bench. Three men were rushing toward him from the public rest rooms fifty yards away, and as he turned to run, the headlights of a car flared across the parking lot. There was a crack of gunfire at his back as he began to run, the impact of a giant fist against his side, but Sanchez somehow made it to his car, climbed in and fumbled the ignition key into its slot.

Adrenaline and fear were all that saved him in the early moments of the ambush. He had a pistol in his belt and he had used it, pumping three rounds at the other car as he began to pull away, but he would never know if any of them found their mark. It might be pure dumb luck that he had managed to outrun the hunting party, lose them in a maze of darkened streets that led him north and west, with no clear destination in his mind.

A pair of headlights fell in close behind him, and he felt the short hairs bristling on his nape. It had to be coincidence; there was no reason he should have the streets all to himself regardless of the hour. Still, he would feel better when he took the next left turn and lost the other motorist. He needed time to think, decide where he was going, what he had to do.

The FBI would have to be informed about their agent, for a start, but that was someone else's job. Presumably the uniformed police would find him and report his murder in the morning. Someone in the agency would know that he had gone to meet with Jaime Sanchez, and the manhunt would begin. But where could Sanchez hide while he was waiting for the federal men to save him? Would he even be alive tomorrow morning, at the rate that he was losing blood?

There was a number he had memorized for use in the event of an emergency. It came back to him now, and he felt like an idiot for wasting so much precious time. Of course, he had been running for his life, without a chance to stop and think of what came next, but he was thinking now.

It might not be too late.

The FBI had doctors, places he could hide while they were checking out his story and rounding up his former comrades. Even if they thought his story was bizarre, improbable, they would be motivated by the murder of a fellow agent, sparing no expense or energy to bring the killers down.

He reached the intersection, made his turn without a signal, cursing as the headlights in his rearview mirror fol-

owed. One more block, another try, and still the second car
was on his tail. At half-past midnight, in a neighborhood
where all the shops were closed, he dropped the notion of
coincidence and started thinking of a way to save himself.

He stood on the accelerator, shifting into fourth as he
swung left into a cluttered alley. Trash cans tried to block
him, but he mowed them down, their contents scattered in
his wake.

Emerging from the alley onto Calle San Sebastian, Sanchez aimed his car downtown and gave it everything he had.
He wanted witnesses—late diners, the valets in charge of
parking flashy cars, perhaps a prostitute or two. If he was
truly dying, which seemed almost certain now, at least he
wouldn't let the bastards trap him in the shadows by himself. If nothing else, his death would be observed, and when
the FBI came looking for him they would know that he
wasn't responsible for murdering their agent at the beach.

He didn't see the second car in time to swerve. One moment he was racing through an intersection, seeing people
on the sidewalk to his left, and then a vehicle erupted from
the alley on his right. They had to be using two-way radios,
Sanchez thought as he gave the Beetle's steering wheel a vicious twist and bounced across the curb, colliding with a
mailbox, rolling on to smash the plate-glass window of a
small boutique.

At that, he barely registered the impact. When the squat
VW's engine stalled, he didn't bother trying the ignition key.
Instead, he drew the automatic pistol from his belt and
fumbled with the handle of the driver's door. He got it on
the second try and swung his legs out, feeling giddy as he
drew himself erect and leaned against the car to keep his
balance.

They were coming for him, faceless shapes in the glare of
headlights, armed with automatic weapons. Sanchez raised
his pistol, sighting on the nearest silhouette and squeezing
off in rapid fire. He didn't count his rounds, conserving

ammunition. His final gesture should be grand, flamboyant. Let the bastards feel his wrath.

Incredibly he saw his target stumble, reeling, going down. A hit. He swung the pistol to his left, already tracking into acquisition of his second mark, but all of them were firing now, the muzzle-flashes winking at him, angry hornets swarming in the air around his ears. He felt the bullets striking him, but it was someone else's body twitching, jerking, toppling backward in the ruin of a lacy underwear display. He tried to keep on firing as he fell, uncertain whether the commands were actually transmitted by his brain. But there was no feeling in his arms by now, and he couldn't pick out a single weapon in the midst of so much firing.

Stretched out on his back, he heard another sound—the wail of sirens drawing closer by the second. Someone had alerted the police. He hoped they would be quick enough to catch his killers at the scene, but it wasn't a crucial point to Jaime Sanchez anymore. Instead, he focused on the ornate ceiling fixtures, dark now, wishing he could see them come alive.

There had been something on his mind, a bit of information he had wished to share with someone, but he couldn't focus on it now. What did it matter when his life was measured out in microseconds?

So much blood.

He knew the squad cars had to be getting closer, and it puzzled Sanchez why the sirens sounded fainter, dwindling in his ears. The ceiling, twelve or thirteen feet above him, suddenly seemed miles away. It felt like crouching at the bottom of a well and staring at the sky.

And when the darkness settled over him, it came as a relief.

CHAPTER ONE

The file reached Hal Brognola's desk at the Justice Department on a Monday morning, eight days after the events in Puerto Rico had transpired. The intervening week had been consumed with meetings, conferences and phone calls, memorandums and analyses. The problem had been passed from hand to hand by bureaucrats who either felt themselves inadequate to cope or simply didn't understand the stakes involved. It took some time for any case to reach the court of last resort.

On the morning following Sanchez's death, it had been the San Juan office of the FBI that started picking up the pieces, trying to decide on an appropriate response. They had an agent in the morgue, along with an informant, but the officer in charge of "running" Jaime Sanchez still wasn't convinced of any national-security considerations riding on the line. His first concern had been with the murder of a federal agent in the line of duty, and he started from the premise of a standard homicide investigation, running leads within the dead informant's circle of acquaintances. He got precisely nowhere for his pains.

The murder of a federal officer wasn't an everyday occurrence. Washington was notified at once, the FBI's director summoned from a champagne brunch in Arlington, Virginia, where he was preparing to address three hundred law-enforcement officers on modern terrorist techniques. The slaughter of a G-man in San Juan became the brand-new introduction to his speech. He also ordered personal advisories on every phase of the investigation as it ground along.

Because of Puerto Rico's status as a commonwealth controlled by the United States, the CIA was also interested in any acts of violence linked to separatist guerrillas on the island. While the Company was legally prohibited from practicing its craft on U.S. soil, Puerto Rico had always been considered a "gray area," neither domestic nor foreign, ever ripe for exploitation by seditious radicals and other enemies. That vested interest clashed with Langley's age-old adversarial relationship to the FBI, prompting one deputy director to suggest that the Bureau should be left to sink or swim in San Juan. Whichever way it went, at least the CIA wouldn't be blamed, and if they had to save the Bureau's butt at some point down the line, the order would include carte blanche to operate on Puerto Rican soil. It was a no-lose situation if they had the patience to sit back and wait.

At the State Department the diplomats involved with Puerto Rico were concerned. San Juan had been less strident in its dealings with the mainland during recent months, the militants less vocal in their calls for independence. The execution of a federal officer could swiftly shift the balance back toward something like the bad old days when Puerto Rican bombs were blasting targets from Chicago and Miami to New York. By Monday afternoon it was determined that the White House should be kept informed.

At that, it should not be supposed the President was ignorant of what had happened in San Juan. No man on earth paid more attention to the daily news than one who occupied the Oval Office, and that interest wasn't confined by any means to partisan politics. Barring heads of state and family members, any person's death could only occupy the President's attention for a passing moment, but the latest murders in San Juan were like a pebble dropped into a murky pond. When taken in conjunction with the late informant's hints and accusations, a disturbing picture started to emerge.

It was disturbing enough, in fact, that over Thursday's breakfast a decision had been reached to bring in Hal Brognola and his special team. The call was made at 9:15 a.m. It took another hour and a quarter for the necessary documents to be collected, copied and relayed by courier to Brognola's office at Justice, midway between the White House and the U.S. Capitol on Pennsylvania Avenue. Brognola spent an hour reading and digesting the material before he started making calls.

And so the deadly game began.

Trinidad, Colorado
Monday, 1115 hours MST

MACK BOLAN HAD a rest stop coming after Albuquerque. It had been a down-and-dirty mission—dirtier than most, in fact, with drugs and child pornography combined to give the syndicate a stronger foothold in New Mexico. The heroin came north from Ciudad Juarez, along with children from Chihuahua and Durango. Street talk also said that Anglo kids went south from time to time, procured by "talent scouts" who ranged as far afield as Oklahoma City, Denver and Las Vegas in their search of blue-eyed blondes to keep the hungry buyers satisfied.

It would have been enough for Bolan to just trash the heroin connection, but the rest of it was icing on the cake. Two days in Albuquerque had told him everything he had to know about the racket and its principals, their base of

operations and delivery routes. By sundown Saturday he'd
had his targets spotted, marked for brisk annihilation by the
numbers. There was nothing they could do or say to save
themselves.

And it had almost been a pleasure, slicing through their
ranks like the avenging sword of justice, laying waste to
everything they had accumulated over twenty-seven months
of trafficking in human misery.

Almost.

Except that Bolan always seemed to come up short on
satisfaction where the killing was concerned. Of course, he
recognized a job well done and knew the world would be a
slightly better place without the savages he removed. There
was no question of remorse at taking down narcotics dealers, child molesters and their ilk. He couldn't lose a wink of
sleep over the death of animals who preyed on helpless in-
nocents.

But it was still a job—a mission, if you will—and he could
take no pleasure in the scorched-earth remedy that seemed
to be the only answer for a plague of crime and violence in
the land. Sometimes the warrior felt as if he was putting out
a fire with gasoline; most days he simply buckled down and
did his job because he had the necessary skills and someone
had to do it, after all.

Trinidad was a deliberate choice, positioned in the eastern foothills of the Sangre de Cristo Mountains, on the
north bank of a river called the Purgatoire. He didn't plan
to spend much time in town, just enough to buy some
camping gear and strike off for the woods, a few days out
of touch with the chaotic madhouse known as civilization.
The rest would do him good, but first he had to make a call.

It was routine, the check in with his brother out in San
Diego. Johnny was his only living relative, a warrior in his
own right, and they kept in touch by choice, as well as by

necessity. If anyone with clear priority had tried to contact Bolan in the past three days, his brother would be keeping tabs and he would pass the message on. If not, then they could spend a pleasant ten or fifteen minutes on the telephone before he went to find himself a piece of wilderness.

The San Diego number was an automated cutout, specially designed to frustrate traces on the line. It shuttled calls from Johnny's vacant downtown office, rented in a phony name, to Strongbase One, where Johnny held the fort between engagements of his own. An answering machine screened calls around the clock, but there were ways to beat the system if you had a friend on the inside.

"It's Striker," he informed the distant tape deck once the tone had sounded in his ear. A heartbeat later Johnny's voice came on the line.

"What's shaking?" His tone was nice and casual, against the outside chance that someone might somehow have tapped the line.

"I met those salesmen you referred me to," Bolan said, facing toward the street and watching traffic as it passed the public booth. "I guess they're having trouble in the market. What I hear, they won't be taking orders for a while."

"They should have taken out insurance."

"Maybe next time."

"Anyway, I'm glad you called." His brother's voice had taken on a different tone, communicating subtle urgency. "I got a call from Shenandoah Industries this morning."

"Oh?" The Executioner was instantly alert. "What's shaking over there?"

"Some kind of flap on foreign sales. The man was hoping for a face-to-face, ASAP."

"I'll check it out," Bolan said. "That's a wrap?"

"It's all I have."

"Okay, I'll be in touch."

"Stay frosty, will you?"

"It's the only way to go."

He cradled the receiver, frowning as he put the Sangres out of mind and let his thoughts range eastward, toward the Blue Ridge Mountains of Virginia. R & R would have to wait.

The Executioner was moving on.

Terrebonne Parish, Louisiana
Monday, 1140 hours CST

THE SNAKE WAS ROUGHLY six feet long, its dusky color drab enough to mingle with the Spanish moss that draped the overhanging cypress branches like a heavy shawl. Crouched in between the arching roots, waist deep in muddy water, Hermann "Gadgets" Schwarz was watching it descend, the reptile's pale tongue darting in and out to test the atmosphere for any trace of food or foe.

It was a cottonmouth, among the largest Schwarz had ever seen. Its fangs would be an inch or more in length, the glands behind each eye containing venom that produced internal hemorrhaging and death through loss of blood. A grown man could survive the bite of such a reptile if he kept his wits about him, utilized first aid and found a source of antivenin soon enough to counteract the poison in his body.

Or he might run out of luck and die before he made it to the nearest highway, seven miles due north through trackless, stagnant swamp.

Schwarz drew his Ka-bar fighting knife and waited for the cottonmouth to chose its new direction. It was draped across a mossy limb, some eighteen inches from his face, and Schwarz remembered that an average snake could strike across one-third its body length. Add altitude and gravity to the equation, and he reckoned he was well within the viper's killing radius.

How long before the pits beneath each eye picked up his body heat and telegraphed the message of a threat to the brain inside that flat, triangular head? Had Lyons and the Politician reached their destination yet? Would they be waiting for him even now?

Their sojourn on the bayou was a no-holds-barred survival exercise. The men of Able Team had been dropped off at different points, some miles apart, with orders to rendezvous at predesignated coordinates, making their joint way from there to an extraction point at Sweetbay, thirty miles due north. They had no firearms, food or drinking water to alleviate the rigors of their trek. Each man had started equal, in his boots and camouflage fatigues—one knife, one compass, and a first-aid kit that would be useless in the case of anything beyond a superficial injury. The compact Handie-Talkie each man carried was reserved for use in life-or-death emergencies.

That much was standard.

They were also being hunted by a team of Navy SEALs, and while the trackers would be firing blanks, a "kill" meant starting over at the drop-off point, however many times it took for them to get it right.

Schwarz had been lucky so far. He had "killed" a SEAL two hours earlier, relieved his victim of an M-16 A-1 and two canteens before continuing along his way. The water helped, but he would have to save the rifle and its magazine of blanks for confrontations with the stalking enemy. Unless he swung the rifle as a club, it would be useless as a means of self-defense against the predatory creatures of the swamp.

He was prepared to give the snake a chance, but Schwarz would only go so far. The cottonmouth could crawl away and save itself, or it could hang around a few more minutes, slowing his pace, and thereby seal its fate. Another moment, give or take, and he would have to use the blade.

At first he thought the voice was part of his imagination or an echo from the trackers getting careless. Schwarz's victim was prohibited from giving any information to his friends—the dead were silent, after all—but it wasn't beyond the SEALs to pick up clues around the kill site, something he had missed or failed to cover in his haste to slip away.

Schwarz did a double take as the quality of sound persuaded him that this was something else. For one thing, he decided that the voice was airborne, drawing closer at a pace impossible for any man compelled to slog his way across the bayou. It was also coming from a speaker, since there was static in the background, and he soon picked up the sound of helicopter rotors chopping at the air.

The message got his full attention in a flash.

"Team Able scrub your exercise. Repeat, this is a scrub. You have new orders in the pipe. Present yourself for lift-off soonest, sector Tango-niner-three."

Schwarz knew the zone by heart, a midway point selected for extraction if the exercise went sour and some member of the team was maimed or worse. The drop zone designated Tango 93 was two miles from where he stood, and Schwarz could be there in an hour's time, with any luck.

But first he had to get around the cottonmouth.

"Tough luck," he told the viper, watching it begin to turn that lethal head in answer to his voice. The snake was deaf, of course, but it could sense vibrations, and its pale eyes picked out the mortal threat as he began to move.

The reptile's mouth opened, snowy white within, the wicked fangs erect. Schwarz waited for the strike and met it halfway to the point of impact, dodging to his left and hacking with the Ka-bar, deadpan as the severed head splashed six inches from his groin. The headless body took a moment longer, squirming on the mossy branch before it lost its grip and fell into the water, thrashing on the surface for a moment, finally surrendering to gravity and sinking out of sight.

Schwarz palmed his two-way radio and thumbed down the transmission button. "Able Two, acknowledge. Tango niner-three."

He didn't wait to hear the others chiming in. It was the chopper pilot's job to find them and relay the message. All Schwarz had to do from this point on was find the lift-off point and make himself available.

Along the way there would be time enough for him to wonder what the hell was going on.

Ramsey County, North Dakota
Monday, 1320 hours

WHEN JACK GRIMALDI HEARD the summons, he was skimming low across the North Dakota prairie east of Devil's Lake. On loan to DEA, he had been making runs across the border for the past eleven days, cooperating with an outlaw motorcycle gang whose leaders made their living smuggling contraband—most of it pharmaceutical—from Canada to the United States. Grimaldi's first three runs had cinched the case on ten or fifteen small-fry operators, but the leaders were supposed to be on hand this time. At an open field near Doyon, they were to accept delivery of a shipment that included seven pounds of uncut China white and forty keys of pure cocaine.

The sudden crackling in his earphones set Grimaldi's teeth on edge. A message this close to the finish line meant trouble any way you ran it down.

"Attention, Shrike. You have an urgent message out of Shenandoah for a comeback yesterday."

Goddammit! Who would air a call like that when he was winding down a mission and his mind was focused on the goal? Grimaldi made a mental note to kick some federal ass if he had the time and inclination once the dust had settled on his present mission.

Someone else was smart enough to let it go with one transmission, and he kept his fingers crossed that no one on the ground was listening, or else they would assume the message had been meant for any one of several hundred other radio receivers in the northeast quadrant of the state. There was no question of his pigeons understanding what it meant, but any hint at all could set them off at this point, turning simple into suicide.

He didn't need to check the mini-Uzi tucked beneath his leather jacket in a special armpit sling. The little stuttergun was cocked and locked, just waiting for a thumb to flick the safety off, an index finger on the trigger. Grimaldi wore two spare magazines in pouches underneath his other arm, but if he had to use the stubby SMG, there would be precious little time to spare.

Another moment and he saw the landing field ahead. At least they got the "field" part right, Grimaldi thought. A van, two motorcycles and a dark sedan were lined up with their noses facing toward the nearby highway, ready to evacuate at speed if anything went wrong. Grimaldi counted eight men on the ground, all staring at the chopper as he circled once, then brought it back to hover, slowly settling down.

The fallow ground they had selected for their makeshift heliport was overgrown with weeds, but it was flat and relatively smooth. He almost left the engine running, just in case he had to lift off in a hurry, but he reckoned that his welcoming committee would be paranoid enough without another boost.

Three of the faces he recognized from federal mug shots as the ranking officers of Satan's Nomads. That left five for muscle, some of them in greasy denim with their colors on the back, the others dressed like John O. Citizen to pass without a second glance in any crowd.

Grimaldi killed the helicopter's engine. He was reaching for the door latch when his radio came back to life.

"Attention, Shrike, in case you missed that bulletin—"

He cursed and switched off the two-way, disgusted with his so-called backup. Stunts like that could get him killed.

He popped the door and stepped down. Nobody offered hands, which suited Jack Grimaldi fine.

"You've got the shit?"

Grimaldi recognized the man who spoke as Bard Wardine. His nickname, "Ax," referred to the occasion several years ago when he had hacked three members of the rival Outlaws motorcycle gang to pieces in a fit of rage.

"Inside."

"Let's see it, man."

The order came from Wardine's number two, Grant Bottineau. His cronies spoke of Bottineau as "the Apache" for the joy he took in scalping enemies alive.

Grimaldi turned and reached behind the pilot's seat, where three athletic bags lay side by side. He chose the one with heroin inside and passed it out to Bottineau, returning for another. Wardine had his hand out now, accepting ten keys of cocaine. The grimace on his face was clearly meant to be a smile.

The federal spotters had already seen enough. A wail of sirens started from the prairie highway, and red-and-blue lights flashed as a line of squad cars closed from each direction, cutting off retreat. Grimaldi had his mini-Uzi out and aimed at Wardine's chest before the biker knew exactly what was happening.

"Don't try it," he advised.

"Fuck you!"

Wardine swung at Grimaldi with the gym bag, his left hand digging for a weapon underneath his coat. Grimaldi shot him in the chest, a 3-round burst that punched him over backward in a lifeless sprawl.

The others stood and stared, without a word to say.

Ten minutes later, when the other Nomads had been searched, disarmed and cuffed, consigned to waiting cars, one of the Feds approached Grimaldi with a cautious smile. The guy was trim, clean-cut and all of twenty-five years old.

"I don't know if you caught that message from your pals back East or not." The agent grinned. "They sounded pretty hot to trot—"

Grimaldi hit him with a looping right that dumped him on his backside in the dust.

"I read you five by five," he said before he turned and walked away.

Encinitas, California
Monday, 1650 hours PST

GARY MANNING WAS considering the prospects of a six-pack and some shade, perhaps a casual approach to the athletic blonde he had been watching for the past half hour, when his beeper sounded the alarm. He frowned and reached beneath the folded beach towel and switched it off, already speculating on the kind of problem that would face him when he found a public telephone.

So much for taking off on holiday, putting the wars behind him for a while. Two weeks without a trouble in the world, and he was barely three days into R & R when grim reality came knocking—or, in this case, beeping—at his door.

The tall Canadian had no illusions that the signal might be a mistake or anything besides an urgent mission from the Man. No one would call for Manning if there was no trouble to be dealt with, problems to be solved. Katz wouldn't bother him unless they had a job that couldn't wait.

He stood up, shedding sand, the sun warm on his back and shoulders. Scooping up the towel and beeper, Manning made his way back toward the parking lot and the concession stands where sunburned men and women stood in line for soft drinks, beer and ice-cream cones. It was a kind of ritual, the way they came to show their bodies off and bake beneath the California sun while making every effort to stay "cool" in all respects.

He found a pay phone, dug a quarter from the pocket of his trunks and dropped it in the slot. The operator took his name—the one he chose to give, at any rate—and made the call collect. It would be relayed out of San Diego to a blind in the Midwest, and on from there to Katz, wherever he might be. The miracle would be that Manning's call went through in forty seconds flat.

"Hello?"

He recognized the voice of Yakov Katzenelenbogen, hedging in the knowledge that their conversation was restricted by the open line.

"I'm checking in."

"We've got a squeal," Katz said. "I've spoken to the others. Can you book a flight tonight?"

"No problem." There were airplanes leaving Southern California around the clock.

"Tomorrow at the Farm. Familiar faces."

"Right. I'll see you there."

The line went dead, and Manning cradled the receiver, waiting for the telephone to give his quarter back. It ate the coin instead, and Manning gave the phone a solid backhand. It wasn't the kind of omen he would choose for the beginning of a mission, but he shrugged the childish superstition off and turned away.

Familiar faces.

So the call hadn't gone out for Phoenix Force alone. He felt a quickening inside, a new spark of excitement. If they needed everyone, it meant a major rumble coming down. That kind of action had its downside, in the area of risk, but it would also mean a challenge and the prospect of achievement. Something real.

The rest of it could be accomplished from his room, arranging eastbound flights and packing his civilian gear. So much for a vacation in the sun.

Instead of disappointment, Gary Manning found that he was looking forward to the chase.

Stony Man Farm, Virginia
Monday, 1930 hours EST

"THEY'RE ALL accounted for," Barbara Prince announced.

"How long?" Aaron Kurtzman asked, turning from his horseshoe console in the Stony Man computer room.

"With any luck, we should have everybody here by noon tomorrow."

"Why the long face, Barb?"

"You have to ask?"

"It might not be that bad."

"Who's kidding who?" she asked. "It's always bad."

"Okay."

"I don't like sending anybody in on sketchy information, least of all—"

She stopped herself and left the rest of it unfinished, feeling sudden color in her cheeks. She turned away from Kurtzman, shuffling papers on a nearby desk. It was a stupid slipup, and she cursed herself for being so damned careless with her tongue.

"Let's wait and see what happens," Kurtzman offered.

"Right. Are you expecting Hal tonight?"

"First thing tomorrow," Kurtzman said, relieved to change the subject. "Leo's coming with him. May be here by breakfast if they get their act together."

"I'd be more at ease with this," she said, "if we had something solid."

"That's what Striker and the rest of them are for. They'll sort it out."

"For all we know, it's just a fishing expedition."

"Tell that to the Man."

She frowned and shook her head. "No, thanks."

"Me neither."

"So that's it, then."

"For today that's it."

"Tomorrow takes care of itself, I guess."

"With any luck at all."

But Kurtzman wondered whether this was strictly true. Tomorrow often had a way of going wrong when it became today, and yesterday was here before you knew it...if a soldier lived to see it come around.

"I'm getting hungry. Have you eaten yet?"

"No appetite," she answered. "You go on. I think I'll have another look at those dispatches from San Juan."

"Don't burn yourself out in advance," he cautioned her.

"I won't."

The wheelchair was a manual, preferred by Kurtzman for the exercise it gave him, though he also kept a more sophisticated model on the premises. Instead of chiding Price for her doubts about the latest job or prodding her for answers both of them already knew, he wheeled away and coasted toward the coded-access door.

He didn't like the mission, either, and the vague preliminary data from San Juan was only part of it. The whole thing had a smell about it, putting Kurtzman off. He wanted to retreat and give the whole damned thing the widest berth he could, but there was no such option on the menu.

And he recognized that smell, beyond a shadow of a doubt.

It was a reeking whiff of death.

CHAPTER TWO

Stony Man Farm
Tuesday, 1300 hours

The basement War Room's giant conference table seated twenty-five, but only thirteen of the sturdy wooden chairs were occupied, with Aaron Kurtzman's wheelchair making it an even number. Hal Brognola occupied the hot seat at the table's head, with Kurtzman on his right and Barbara Price immediately on his left. On Kurtzman's right sat Leo Turrin, down from Washington with Brognola for the occasion. Filling up the seats on Turrin's side, the men of Phoenix Force included leader Yakov Katzenelenbogen, Gary Manning, Calvin James, David McCarter and Rafael Encizo. Mack Bolan sat directly opposite Turrin, next to Price, with Jack Grimaldi at his elbow. Able Team—including Hermann Schwarz, Carl Lyons and Rosario Blancanales—completed the assembly of Stony warriors summoned, in McCarter's case, from points as far away as London.

All the standard catching up and small talk had been dealt with over lunch. Four members of the circle had already thrashed the basic problem out among themselves; the other ten, all front-line troops, were waiting for the word to filter down.

"We might as well get started," Brognola said, shifting papers on the tabletop in front of him. "We have an urgent rumble coming out of Puerto Rico, and it's reached the White House."

"What kind of rumble?" Bolan asked.

"For openers the FBI thought it was dealing with an off-shoot of the former national-liberation organization, the FLN—some drive-by shootings in San Juan, Fajardo, Humacao, some arson fires on the plantations in Guayama province, a bombing on the northwest coast at Amey Air Force Base. Last month somebody left a package at the Bank of Caribbean Commerce in Miami Beach that contained three pounds of C-4 plastique. Metro-Dade defused it, but they're still on edge. A caller claimed credit for the Army of National Independence, the same name we've been hearing in Puerto Rico."

"Suspects?" Katzenelenbogen asked.

"The usual. Between the FBI and Puerto Rican Feds, we've questioned all the FLN alumni we could find. Most of them love what's going on, but they deny involvement. From surveillance and informants, it appears the ANI might be a new kid on the block."

"Outstanding." Jack Grimaldi's tone was thick with cynicism.

"Anyway, it's not a total washout," Brognola stated. "Right after the Amey bombing, federal officers in Bayamon took down an arms cache. No arrests, but they came up with automatic weapons, ammunition and explosives. Here's the kicker—all of it was heisted from the San Juan naval base within the past three months or so."

"A leak?"

"It's looking that way."

"Sounds like something for the FBI and Langley to coordinate," Carl Lyons said.

"The Company has doubtful jurisdiction," Brognola replied. "I know that's never stopped them in the past, but this time it's convenient to observe the rules and save themselves a headache.''

"What about the Bureau?" asked McCarter.

"That's another story. Can we have the slides?"

A switch on Kurtzman's console dimmed the lights and brought a large screen humming down from the ceiling at the far end of the room. Seconds later a projector blazed to life and cast the giant likeness of a man across the screen. He was Hispanic, in his twenties, smiling through a trim mustache. He wore dress whites, the emblem of a naval ensign on his collar tabs.

"Meet Jaime Sanchez, two years in the Navy, posted in San Juan. Age twenty-five, a Puerto Rican national, no record of arrests or radical behavior in his jacket with the Feds...until last month, that is. Five weeks ago he phoned up the Bureau and told them he had inside information on the ANI. He wouldn't spill it all at once, but there were hints about a tell inside the San Juan naval base and contacts on the mainland, some of them in uniform. No accident about the missing arms, if what he said was true."

"The Bureau checked it out," Encizo said. It didn't come out sounding like a question.

"They were trying, anyway," Brognola said. "Until last week."

On cue another giant face replaced the smiling ensign. More Hispanic coloring and features, black hair combed back from a seamless forehead over piercing eyes. No smile this time. The shot reminded Bolan of a driver's-license photo, or the kind often found on government credentials.

"Special Agent Tony Camarena. Twelve years with the FBI, the last four in San Juan. He was assigned to Sanchez, milking him for information, but he couldn't seem to rush the pace. They had three meetings, Camarena getting bits and pieces of the story, nothing he could hang indictments on without corroborating evidence."

"No names?" Grimaldi asked.

"We're getting there. They had another meeting scheduled in San Juan for midnight, Saturday the twelfth. The way it looks, somebody else was waiting for them."

A new slide clicked into place, showing a close-up of a dead man sitting on a bench, his head thrown back to illustrate the yawning chasm of his throat. Blood soaked his shirt, obliterating any pattern of the fabric with a solid rusty brown. The angle made it difficult, but Bolan made out Tony Camarena's lifeless profile, ashen with the combination of his blood loss, flashbulbs and the first gray light of dawn.

"Sanchez?" Grimaldi asked.

"He didn't do the cutting," Brognola replied. "From evidence recovered at the scene—including bloodstains, brass and skid marks—it appears he kept the date, found Camarena dead and split when someone started shooting at him from a nearby block of public rest rooms. They were meeting at the beach, a place called Ocean Park. It gets a little hazy after that, but Sanchez ended up downtown. The shooters found him there."

There was another muffled click, and they were looking at a crazy street scene, the rear quarters of a VW Beetle protruding from the shattered display window of a once-stylish boutique. Mannequins lay scattered on the floor around the car, but two bodies were clearly male, decked out in street clothes the boutique would never advertise.

A close-up showed Jaime Sanchez lying on his back beside the old Volkswagen. He was dead, his eyes locked open, dark blood soaking through his chambray shirt. The fingers of his right hand clutched an automatic pistol with the slide locked open on an empty chamber. He had plainly gone down fighting.

The next slide showed another dead man crumpled on his side. The stiff arm of a mannequin protruded from beneath his body, giving him the aspect of a mutant from a science-fiction movie. He had stopped at least two bullets in the chest and emptied out his Ingram submachine gun in a dying burst. The floor around his corpse was bright with blood and brass.

"The shooter's name is Manuel Uribe," Brognola said. "Prior affiliations with the FLN and Macheteros, fingered as a suspect in at least a dozen acts of terrorism, but the prosecutors never made it stick. He went away for three years on an arms-possession rap from 1981 to 1984. It comes as no surprise to anyone that he'd be mixed up with the ANI, but he escaped surveillance somehow, up until the night he died. That's one colossally black eye for the Puerto Rican Feds. It makes them look like idiots."

"The Bureau should have picked him up," Calvin said.

"They should have, but they didn't. Make that black eye number two."

"Was he the only shooter on the Sanchez hit?" Bolan asked.

"Negative. Ballistics says at least three weapons scored on Sanchez, one of them Uribe's Ingram. That leaves another parabellum round and a .45 still unaccounted for."

"About those names," Grimaldi prompted.

"Right. Before he bought it, Sanchez told his Bureau contact that the ANI had men inside the San Juan naval station. He was one of them, in fact, but something on the drawing board had scared him off. He wouldn't spill the details right away, just kept on saying it was big. My guess would be he didn't fully trust the FBI to start with. He was working up to something, but he never got there."

"But he named the others?"

"Two of them," Brognola said. "Supposedly the brass. He never got around to ratting out the rank and file."

Beside him Kurtzman keyed another slide, this time a naval petty officer, his features solemn, disinclined to smile. The eyes were dark, intense. The longer Bolan stared at them, the more he came to see them as the eyes of a fanatic, windows on a blighted soul.

"Miguel Albano," Brognola announced. "He's another Puerto Rican national and six-year Navy man, no black marks on his record, nothing hinky when the Bureau ran his name through ONI."

"Assignment?" Bolan asked.

"He's had a desk job at the base the past six months. Before that, three years in the submarine corps."

"Why the change?" Grimaldi asked.

Brognola shrugged, his broad shoulders rolling underneath his jacket. "Maybe he got claustrophobic, or he might have wanted something close to home. He sent the paperwork through channels, and they let him have San Juan. If Sanchez had him made, the move makes sense. He's in position to facilitate the arms leak, but he needs accomplices on the base."

"The unnamed rank and file," Calvin James said.

"Affirmative. It wouldn't take a crowd, say two or three subordinates, including Sanchez. Someone from the ANI whips up a shopping list, Albano's people go to town."

"In theory," Yakov Katzenelenbogen said.

"In theory, right."

"He's navy," James put in. "You mentioned ONI. Why don't they brig his ass and sweat him till he squeals?"

"Two reasons," the big Fed replied. "First off, they've only got a dead man's word, with no corroboration. Second, if they tip their hand too early and Albano toughs it out, they lose the others. At the moment ONI and CID are opting for oblique surveillance in cooperation with the FBI. From what I hear, they're getting nowhere fast."

"Two names," the Executioner reminded Brognola.

The slide projector whispered, and Miguel Albano's likeness was supplanted by a street scene. From the people, architecture and the signs in Spanish, Bolan guessed it had been taken in San Juan, although it could as easily have been Caracas, Acapulco or Miami's Calle Ocho. This was candid work, most probably a hidden camera. The central focus was a short Hispanic man with a mustache and what appeared to be a scar across his forehead, as if someone long ago had tried to split his skull and came up short.

"Francisco Obregon," Brognola told the room at large. "According to the FBI, he runs the ANI—or else he takes his orders from a honcho they're unable to identify. When Sanchez started telling tales, he mentioned Obregon as a receiver for the arms that disappear off the base around San Juan."

"So why's he on the street instead of sitting in a cage?" McCarter asked.

"No hard evidence," Brognola answered, scowling at the screen. "Of course, the Bureau's had him in for questioning a dozen times, but Obregon takes caution to the level of an art form. This guy's absolutely paranoid about his telephone, surveillance, anything that might result in serving time. He never meets with more than one or two subordinates at any given time, and they do their talking in a car he's swept for bugs. Then they go their separate ways. If someone takes a fall—which hasn't happened often with the ANI, so far—Francisco always has an ironclad alibi with ten or fifteen witnesses. The Bureau hasn't linked him to a bullet yet, much less a violent crime."

"Could they be wrong about this guy?" Encizo asked.

"No way." Brognola shook his head emphatically. "He's thirty-five years old next week and he's been working for the independence movement one way or another since he turned sixteen. He had three brothers in the FLN, two dead, one serving life without parole in Michigan for murder one. Francisco learned from their mistakes, but he's a terrorist all right. Last year he flew to Mexico, supposedly for a vacation, but we tracked him slipping into Cuba for a huddle with the Fidelistas."

"Castro's in on this?" There was a sudden cutting edge to Rafael Encizo's voice.

"We think he's covering the ANI's expenses, at the very least. There might be more in terms of free advice on how to run guerrilla operations, this and that. In fact, it could be critical. Without the Soviets to prop him up, Fidel begins to look his age. Instead of being Moscow's outpost, now he's suddenly the only Communist of any prominence outside Red China. He could use some allies, even if he has to start with Puerto Rico. On the flip side, even if he goes down swinging, he can always say he went out fighting the United States. Remember the Moncada barracks?"

"'History will absolve me.'" Encizo quoted Castro's early speech from memory, speaking through clenched teeth.

"Or maybe not," Brognola said. "At Castro's time of life, some analysts are thinking that he might not care for absolution like he used to. Now and then old soldiers like to go out in a blaze of glory. Try to, anyway."

"Fanatics." Yakov Katzenelenbogen sounded weary, not surprising for a man who had been fighting zealots all his adult life.

"Another link with Cuba, even though it's shaky at the moment," Brognola said. "Sanchez talked about a crony of Albano's serving with a naval unit on the mainland, somewhere near Miami. They were cooking up some kind of a coordinated strike, but Sanchez never got the chance to tell us what it was, assuming that he even knew.''

"He didn't have a name for any of the stateside players?" Blancanales asked.

"Unfortunately, no.''

"But we've been hearing from the ANI around Miami Beach," McCarter said, recalling Brognola's account of the attempted bombing.

"Right. The mainland military angle could be off, but we can't take the chance. Whichever way it goes, we need to roll these jokers up before they start improving their techniques.''

Gary Manning frowned. "That might be easier said than done.''

"We've got a plan worked out," Brognola said. "It ought to cover all the bases going in.''

"It's coming out that gets a little hairy," James replied.

"Not much that we can do for you on that score," Brognola admitted ruefully.

"Let's hear the plan," Bolan said, feeling the big Fed's reluctance to commit his troops on what was clearly more than just a routine probe.

Brognola half turned in his chair to face the Executioner. "The Bureau has another operative working on the ANI in Puerto Rico, strictly undercover. You'll make contact when you get there, find out what the agent has to say and run with anything he gives you. Jack will be on tap in case you need a set of wings.''

Grimaldi cracked a smile. "We aim to please.''

"Meanwhile," Brognola continued, "Rafael goes back in uniform. You're in the the Navy now.''

"Terrific.''

"We've prepared a cover for you, Puerto Rican background, New York City, sympathetic with the independence movement. It should stand a fair amount of scrutiny. Besides, they're one man short, at least."

"I don't care much for how the last one left," Encizo said.

"He wasn't a professional survivor," Leo Turrin offered.

"Flattery will get you nowhere, Leo."

"That leaves four of us," Katz said, speaking for the other men of Phoenix Force.

"You're going in as weapons dealers," Brognola told him, "looking for a ready source of military hardware. You have no political agenda and you aren't particular about your clientele, as long as they have cash on hand."

"The ANI might not take kindly to a mercenary overture," Katz commented.

"I'll leave the fine points up to you. A judgment call. I'd guess that even with potential backing from Fidel, the ANI can always use another source of income. If it damages the U.S. military one way or another, that's just icing on the cake."

"We tap Albano?" McCarter asked.

"Negative. The Bureau has an eye on someone who can help you out. He sells primarily to shooters from the drug gangs, but he's handled bulk lots on occasion. Washington believes he has at least a nominal connection to the ANI. Put down some earnest money, play it any way it feels. I'm not about to second-guess you on the ground."

"I don't imagine you'll be needing us in Puerto Rico," Lyons said.

"Miami," Brognola replied. "We're nailing down both ends at once to make sure no one wriggles through the net. The Bureau has another contact down in Dade, a Cuban with connections. If he can't come up with anything off-hand, you'll have to dig it out yourself."

"And when we find Albano's buddies?"

"Make a firm ID across the board, make sure you have them all and roll the bastards up."

"Coordination with San Juan?" Blancanales asked.

"In the time frame we're considering, it shouldn't matter. Katz and Striker will be checking in from Puerto Rico when they can. If we have any major setbacks that require delays, you'll hear about it from the Farm."

"We're not concerned with an indictment here, I take it," Blancanales said.

"If Justice thought there was a chance of prosecution," Brognola responded, "no one would have bothered calling me."

"Okay, just so we're clear on that."

"It's open season on the ANI," Brognola answered for the record, looking grim. "It would be nice if you could wrap this up without a full-scale war, but we'll have uniforms on call in case it comes to that. The Navy angle has some people worried."

It should worry more than some, Bolan thought, but kept the observation to himself. Instead, he asked, "What kind of uniforms?"

Brognola blinked, as if he hadn't really thought the question through before it reached his ears. "Whatever you require, I guess. Considering the Navy link, we'd probably start off with ONI, their version of the CID, and Marines for muscle if you need that kind of help. It goes that far, we're looking at publicity nobody wants to see."

"It won't be quiet," Bolan said, "no matter how it goes."

"Agreed. We've already got a jump on damage control at this end."

"The Navy goes along with this?" asked Calvin James, himself a former Navy SEAL.

"They haven't got much choice," Brognola said. "One leak about a nest of traitors operating in the ranks, they're looking at all kinds of Senate hearings, miles of headlines, slashes in appropriations—hell, you name it. My impression is, they'll sanction anything that makes the problem go away without a full-blown circus in the media."

"We can't control the press," Carl Lyons said.

"The bottom line is a solution to the problem, one way or another."

"Fair enough."

Leo Turrin cleared his throat and spoke up. "We'll discuss the details of your separate assignments individually, if that's all right. Support nets, contacts, this and that."

"I'll take an extra helping of your 'this and that,'" James said.

Encizo grinned and said, "I've got your 'this and that' right here."

"I don't collect those miniatures, all right?"

"Let's take a break," Brognola offered. "We can run the independent briefings later on this afternoon, say three or four o'clock?"

There was a murmur of assent as figures rose around the conference table, drifting toward the door.

Barbara Price was waiting for Bolan as he emerged from the War Room, greeting him with a gentle smile.

"You've got a lot to think about," she said.

"I've thought about it."

"And?"

Unlike the men of Able Team and Phoenix Force, Mack Bolan had no contract with the crew at Stony Man. He was an independent operator, free to turn down any task that ran against his principles or that he deemed to be impossible.

"Somebody has to do the job," he said, and let it go at that.

"Okay."

He checked his watch. "I've got a couple hours free, before they start the briefings. Would you like to take a walk or something?"

"Or something."

"Well . . ."

"Your place or mine?"

An unaccustomed grin lit up the soldier's face.

"I thought you'd never ask."

CHAPTER THREE

San Juan, Puerto Rico
Wednesday, 1520 hours AST

The men of Phoenix Force arrived in Puerto Rico on three separate flights, departing from Norfolk, Savannah and Jacksonville respectively, with their arrivals spanning two hours. Rafael Encizo caught the military shuttle flight from Norfolk, wearing Navy blue and carrying his transfer orders in a GI duffel bag. The orders looked official, and in fact they were, arranged by pulling certain covert strings between the Oval Office and the Pentagon. For all intents and purposes, Encizo was a naval ensign for the next few days, until his mission was completed and the smoke began to clear, at which time any paperwork pertaining to his present task would disappear.

Yakov Katzenelenbogen caught the flight out of Savannah, pretending not to notice Gary Manning three rows back, along the starboard side. They would regroup once they were on the ground, but for the moment anyone watching inbound flights or checking commercial passenger lists would find no apparent connection between the two men. They traveled unarmed, with bogus passports printed at Stony Man Farm on State Department blanks. No one had a reason to suspect that they were anything but what they seemed to be—specifically, an Israeli pharmaceutical supplier and a midlevel editor employed by a Canadian publishing firm.

Calvin James and David McCarter flew out of Jacksonville an hour after Katz and Manning left Savannah. Once again the Phoenix Force warriors shunned each other at the airport and on board their flight. According to the paperwork they carried, James was a television sports announcer from Montgomery, Alabama, on vacation by himself; McCarter was a British architect residing in America, escaping from his heavy work load while employers hammered out the final details of a shopping mall in Tallahassee.

Once they hit the ground in Puerto Rico, they could let the covers slide—except for Rafael Encizo, who was living his for the duration of their mission in San Juan. None of the warriors carried weapons, but their needs would be provided for upon arrival through a link coordinated by the FBI and Stony Man. Their real work, posing as a syndicate of weapons dealers with illegal clientele, would start once they were settled in and ready to proceed.

To make things doubly difficult on any adversaries, Katz and Barbara Price had chosen flights to different airports. Katz and Manning checked their bags through Puerto Rico International, the Isla Verde Airport east of town, while James and McCarter touched down at Isla Grande, fifteen minutes from their Miramar hotel. By three o'clock the warriors had surveyed their rooms, changed clothes and started drifting toward the sixth-floor suite where Katz was waiting for them.

The gruff, one-armed Israeli had already swept his room for listening devices with a compact scanner built to mimic a transistor radio. In fact, the sweeper picked up local stations perfectly without the earphones, but insertion of the jack and slow rotation of the tuning dial enabled Katz to scan for any active bugs within a range of sixty feet. His telephones might still be tapped somewhere between the hotel switchboard and the central relay station in San Juan, but he was certain that the phone itself hadn't been fitted out with an infinity device, transforming it into a microphone. If there were any bugs beneath the carpet, tucked away inside the walls or furniture, they were the flesh-and-blood six-legged kind, and Katz would let them be unless they crossed his path.

"First up," he told the members of his team when they were all assembled in the sitting room, "we touch our Bureau contact for the personal equipment we'll be needing. I've already called ahead, the public phone, downstairs—and everything's arranged. In forty minutes we can head out and collect the merchandise."

"That's good," Calvin James said. "I feel a little naked, as it is."

"You all have rental cars?" Katz asked.

Heads bobbed around the circle, all affirmative.

"So, what about Montoya?" Manning asked.

"I have a call in to his office," Katz responded. "This phone, just in case. I was informed that he would call me back within the hour. Checking out my bona fides, no doubt."

José Montoya made his living from the sale of contraband, excluding drugs, which would have brought the Puerto Rican Feds down on his back like Judgment Day. His merchandise reportedly included weapons, ranging from the smaller pocket pistols to the kind of military hardware favored by guerrillas, terrorists and upscale members of the underworld. It was assumed that certain officers and politicians earned a kickback from Montoya's sales, allowing him to stay in business for the past twelve years. And several of his leading rivals had been jailed when they were found with drugs in their possession, having blown the social contract with their sometime partners on the flip side of the law.

It was the kind of symbiosis that existed everywhere between police and certain "friendly" criminals, allowing not-so-friendly crimes to flourish on the streets. In this case, though, a bit of localized corruption would be useful if it greased the wheels for Phoenix Force to reach its targets in the shortest time.

"What say we go pick up our hardware, then, and get this program underway?" James asked.

There was a murmur of assent from his companions, and Manning and McCarter rose to their feet.

"Let Cal and Gary make the pickup," Katz instructed. "Our supplier has the shopping list."

"And me?" McCarter asked, already sensing what his job would be.

Katz smiled. "You make sure everyone gets back here safe and sound, within the hour. When Montoya calls, I don't want anything to slow us down."

"We'll be here," James said. "No sweat."

Isla Grande Airport, San Juan
1540 hours

THE CESSNA CITATION 1 had been Grimaldi's choice for transport, with its double Pratt & Whitney T15D-1A turbofans providing a range of 1,535 miles with a maximum cruising speed of 404 miles per hour and an altitude ceiling of 41,000 feet. The aircraft also seated eight, which left them ample room for all or part of Phoenix Force, if it came down to that.

The flight between Miami International and San Juan's Isla Grande Airport took two hours and twenty-seven minutes, time enough for Bolan to consider what was waiting for him on the island below. He knew the history behind the ANI, beginning in the 1890s when America had claimed

Puerto Rico as a prize in the Spanish-American War. Resistance had been more or less a constant theme of Puerto Rican life since then, although it seemed to blossom more at certain times than others. In the 1950s Puerto Rican separatists invaded Congress, shooting up the gallery, and gunmen from the island tried to assassinate President Truman at Blair House, in Washington, D.C. Twenty years later the radical FLN had launched a series of bombings and armored-car robberies designed, as they claimed, to "educate" Americans on the plight of "captive" Puerto Rico. The FLN had faded with attrition in the early 1980s, but some of the old die-hards were obviously still around, perhaps doing business in a new form as the Army of National Independence.

In any case the politics wasn't Bolan's concern. He knew from personal experience that creeds and platforms were the window dressing used by terrorists and human predators around the world. Some of the triggermen undoubtedly believed in what they preached, to the extent that they felt justified in killing anyone at any time to put their point across. For others, Bolan knew, "the cause" was a convenient smoke screen, offering a cover of legitimacy while they murdered, raped and looted, filled their pockets and got fat on other people's pain.

Whichever way it went, sincerity made no impression on the Executioner. It might determine strategy in dealing with his enemies, but it would never undermine his personal determination to eliminate the savages before they had a chance to kill again. Regardless of ideals or ideology, the terrorists had set themselves apart, beyond the pale of civilized behavior. They were living like barbarians, and so he meant for them to die.

Grimaldi had his clearance from the tower after circling for several moments, and he lined up on the east-west runway, dropped the landing gear, decelerating into their approach. Beside him Bolan watched the earth rush up to meet them, confident in Jack's ability but wondering if this would be the time when steel or rubber failed, a bolt sheared off or a tire went flat, to leave them in a smoking, twisted pile.

It wasn't. Touchdown was as smooth and effortless as Bolan could have hoped for. In another moment they were rolling off the runway toward a row of private aircraft lined up on the south side of the strip. It was a fair hike to the terminal from there, about two hundred yards, but squat electric carts were ready on the mark for travelers who drew the line at exercise.

The private flight had let him pack a little something extra in his luggage, and Brognola's call to State had greased the wheels at customs. Passports were examined, but their baggage got a rubber stamp, with Bolan and Grimaldi moving on to claim the rental cars they had reserved twelve hours in advance. Grimaldi had a Dodge Daytona waiting; Bolan palmed the keys for a Toyota MR2. They needed separate vehicles in case their schedules fell apart and they were forced to move on separate fronts. Beyond the obvious, it also complicated enemy surveillance prospects if their cover should be blown.

"We're booked at the hotel," Grimaldi said in confirmation, moving toward his waiting Dodge.

"I'll see you there."

"Right."

They would have separate rooms, as well as cars. Another hedge in favor of security, though Bolan hoped their cover would survive a few more hours at least. Beyond that point, events would start to gather a momentum of their own, and there'd be no turning back.

Miami, Florida
1440 hours EST

THE CHARTER HOP from Richmond to Miami International solved two problems at once, avoiding any theoretical surveillance on commercial flights and giving Able Team a way to move their basic hardware past security without a major rumble, explanations and the like. The less attention they attracted going in, Carl Lyons thought, the better chance they had of coming out the other end alive.

It wasn't open-and-shut even then, but at least it gave them an edge to begin with. It was the most that Lyons could hope for in a situation like this, where they were virtually flying blind.

Two vehicles were waiting for them at the hangar where their charter flight nosed in. The four-door Volvo was a stylish workhorse, while the Porsche 928 provided flash—and a reliable top-end speed of one hundred forty-five miles per hour, if needed. Communications would be Schwarz's problem, and he never traveled far without a set of compact two-way radios, no bigger than a pack of king-sized cigarettes. With Velcro or a simple magnet, they could hide a radio inside each car and stay in touch within a radius of six or seven miles. Beyond that range it would require a larger unit, but the Ironman trusted Schwarz to come up with the goods upon demand.

In Vietnam the friendly troops had called Schwarz "Gadgets" for his skill with same, an inborn artistry that seemed to cover anything and everything from printed circuits and transistors to mechanics and explosives. If it used electric power or had moving parts, the logic went, then Schwarz could fix it, modify it, make it sing and dance upon command.

Or close enough, at any rate, to see the mission through.

Their base of operations was a two-bedroom apartment in a complex on Le Jeune, just north of Flagler Street. The place was used by agents of the DEA from time to time, on loan to Able Team through Hal Brognola's Justice contacts. It would never pass for gracious living or the upper crust, but it was a place for a weary grunt to rest, assuming he could find the time.

And time was critical, the Ironman realized. Whatever might be brewing with the ANI, it stood to reason that the latest scheme would be designed to put their early exploits in the shade. The military angle made it sticky, both in terms of access to destructive hardware and the prospect of a strike against presumably "secure" facilities or personnel. A cell of terrorists within the U.S. Navy was a time bomb waiting to explode, and from the recent action in San Juan, it looked as if the fuse was burning short.

It was a short mile from the airport to the complex on Le Jeune, and there'd been no indications of a tail along the way. The rented Porsche and Volvo seemed to fit the neighborhood, reminding Lyons that Miami was a town where wealth could spring up overnight and disappear as quickly, gambled on a horse race or a shipment of cocaine. Dade County was a land of instant millionaires and paupers, where the yo-yo action never stopped and debts were sometimes paid in blood.

No drugs this time, ironically, but if the game had shifted, Lyons knew the basic stakes remained the same. It would be life or death as always, any time the Able warriors took the field.

He didn't park beside the Volvo, leaving room for several cars between the two. It was a simple ploy, and it wouldn't deceive determined trackers, but it was the best that he could do with what they had.

The duffel bag was heavier than Lyons's suitcase, and it dragged down his left arm as he carried it upstairs. Inside were three Uzi submachine guns, extra magazines and parabellum ammunition packed in boxes, fragmentation grenades and silencers designed to fit the threaded muzzles of the SMGs. Schwarz had a matching bag, chock-full of other lethal hardware, and the men of Able Team each wore a side arm of their own selection. Lyons opted for a big Colt Python, while his comrades leaned toward semiautomatics.

It was enough to get them started, and if they needed other weapons, something extra for a special job, they could arrange delivery on half an hour's notice with a call to Stony Man.

Schwarz held the door for Lyons as he entered, scanned the parking lot below from force of habit, then finally closed and latched the door.

"No shadows?"

"None that I could see," Lyons replied.

"Okay. We've got four hours before we meet our contact from the Bureau. Time enough for showers and a bite to eat."

"No Cuban food," Blancanales said from where he sat on the couch. "It gives me gas."

"Chinese, okay? I'll order in."

"Suits me." Lyons headed toward the nearest bedroom with his suitcase and the heavy duffel bag. His stomach growled in answer to the thought of food, reminding him that he had eaten nothing since the three of them had sat down to breakfast hours earlier at Stony Man.

And hunger, Lyons knew, would be the very least of their assorted problems in the hours and days ahead.

U.S. Naval Base, San Juan
1500 hours AST

IT FELT STRANGE being back in uniform and subject to the code of military discipline. Old memories of Cuba and his

early training in the States came flooding back to Rafael
Encizo, some of them unwelcome, even painful. There were
things in life a man would rather put out of his mind.

No matter.

The Navy wouldn't have been his first choice, but at least
his background gave Encizo something of an edge. He was
adept at handling boats, expert at underwater demolition
and conversant with the terminology that he would need to
see him through a tour of duty in San Juan. He wouldn't be
required to pilot any carriers or battleships, though he could
navigate and plot a course with fair precision on demand.

In fact, the uniform he wore was merely window dressing. His assignment had no more to do with sailing or the
finer points of naval tactics than it did with breeding or-
chids for a flower show. He was an actor this time out,
playing a critical role in a drama where bad reviews could get
him killed.

Simply put, Encizo's cover was that of Geraldo Escobar,
a Bronx-born Puerto Rican whose parents had instilled in
him a reverence for his island homeland and a correspond-
ing hatred for the pale-skinned Yankees who had domi-
nated Puerto Rico for the best part of a century. He kept his
feelings to himself, didn't associate with rebels for the most
part and had joined the Navy on his own, intent on finding
some way to repay the pain and degradation Anglos had in-
flicted on his forebears. If by chance he should encounter
some like-minded individuals around San Juan, he might
not be averse to joining forces for a strike against the common enemy.

He had already seen Miguel Albano, just a glimpse, in
company with a companion named Gregorio Ruiz. Another Puerto Rican and a two-year petty officer, Ruiz wasn't
suspected of involvement in Albano's rumored criminal ac-
tivities so far, but he would still bear watching. Going in, the

Phoenix warrior would require a point of contact, some way of connecting with ANI that made it all seem natural. And he would have to force the pace, for he was working on a deadline now, with no time to spare.

The worst part of it was that he could sympathize with certain feelings that propelled his enemies toward their extreme behavior. Encizo's native Cuba had been occupied by the United States at the same time Puerto Rico was seized, and while technical independence was restored four years later, continued Yankee dominance was demonstrated by maintenance of a military base at Guantánamo Bay, periodic invasions to "restore order" and financial support for leaders like Fulgencio Batista, who lined their bulging pockets at the expense of Cuba's population. Even Castro's revolution had initially been supported by the CIA as an alternative to endemic government corruption, before Fidel captured Havana and declared himself a communist in 1959.

The Puerto Rican case was less extreme...unless you were a native of the island who regarded Yankee troops and tourists as a personal affront. Puerto Rico was governed by laws made in Washington but had no voice in Congress. Seeds of discontent could put down roots in fertile soil like that and blossom into revolution, pent-up anger and frustration giving rise to violence in the name of progress.

It wasn't Encizo's job to analyze the ANI or judge its members on the basis of their politics. Phoenix Force was on the case because philosophy had made the quantum leap to terrorist action in San Juan. Regardless of the cause, he couldn't—wouldn't—countenance the massacre of innocent civilians in the name of "liberation."

If Albano and his cronies were involved in terrorism, as the FBI's deceased informant had reported, it was time to shut them down. According to the files at Stony Man, assorted acts of violence traced directly to the ANI had claimed at least a dozen lives in nineteen months. And if the rebels were expanding, planning something bigger for the days ahead, it was Encizo's job—together with the other troops from Stony Man—to break the chain of mayhem and eliminate the danger at its source.

Beginning now.

Despite the sense of urgency he felt, Encizo knew that he could only do so much to move the game along. He had a plan of sorts in mind, but it could only work if circumstance fell into line and he paid close attention to his timing. One mistake could ruin his approach, spoil everything.

And it could also cost his life.

So be it.

He had known the risks from the beginning. Danger in and out of itself was nothing new. It was part of the job description, recognized and accepted in advance. If death was waiting for him somewhere down the line. Encizo took the fact in stride.

Failure, on the other hand, was something else.

He finished dressing and double-checked his uniform to make sure everything was squared away. The man who faced him from the mirror seemed an image of himself in younger days, before he'd recognized or understood the brooding evil in the world.

And yet for every evil there were antidotes.

The Phoenix Force warrior had a plan, but it would take raw courage and determination to succeed against the odds.

He smiled at his reflection in the mirror, let the smile become a snarl and smacked his fist into an open palm.

There could be no time like the present to proceed.

CHAPTER FOUR

Old San Juan
Wednesday, 1830 hours

The historic fortress at El Morro was a natural for meetings. The tourist traffic guaranteed to cover any reasonably cautious gathering, especially if they kept it one-on-one. As Bolan left his gray Toyota in the parking lot, he double-checked for watchers, anyone who seemed a bit too casual. As far as he could tell, he had no tail.

He bought a guidebook for a dollar, thumbing through it as he strolled around the spacious grounds. It told him that construction on the two-hundred-acre fort had begun in 1546 and wasn't finally completed until 1783, a delay that made modern government contractors look like paragons of thrift and efficiency. Towering one hundred forty-five feet above the Atlantic, this great bastion of colonial Spain had repulsed assaults by Drake and Hawkins in its day, standing fast until the bitter end in 1898. This rocky soil was consecrated with the blood of heroes, cut down over time in the defense of a regime that some of them had neither championed nor even fully understood. But they had done their duty to the end, and that was all a soldier really hoped to do.

Survival was a bonus in the hellgrounds, and there were no guarantees.

He gazed across El Morro's seawall, toward the San Juan cemetery with its elaborate circular chapel, afterward scaling the ramparts for a breathtaking view of the sea. There were labyrinthine tunnels, as well, but Bolan remained aboveground, waiting for his contact to arrive.

His would-be ally had no face or name as yet. It was a waste of time to build a mental image that might bear no physical resemblance to the stranger once they met. Better all around for him to wait and see who showed up with the proper recognition signal in due time.

The whole thing could have been a setup, but he didn't think so. There had been no bugs in his hotel room or Grimaldi's, nothing to suggest that he was followed on the drive from his hotel to Punta del Morro. Just in case, he was wearing the Beretta 93-R autoloader in a shoulder rig designed to accommodate its custom silencer. With any luck at all, the gun wouldn't be needed here, but he had stayed alive this long by covering his bets.

The warrior watched a group of Japanese approaching, every member of the tour carrying at least one camera, their guide expounding on El Morro's history. It had to seem doubly foreign to an Asian visitor, he thought, this Spanish ruin built on soil now claimed by the United States. If it had been a country club or swank resort hotel, perhaps one of the tourists would have made an offer for the property. In this case they were limited to staring, snapping photographs and pondering the enigma of a nation that had shifted from crass imperialism to a strange, debt-ridden form of global philanthropy in the past sixty years.

"You're interested in history, I see."

The voice was soft and feminine. It came from Bolan's blind side, and it took him by surprise. He turned, blinked once and came up with the answer she was waiting for.

"I've always thought that history was being made today."

She smiled and finished off the ritual. "If only we could choose the ending we prefer."

He let himself relax a little, scanning the vicinity for loiterers before he shook the hand she offered.

"Mike Belasko."

"I'm Miranda Flores. Welcome to San Juan."

The name might be an alias, but Bolan's visual inspection led him to believe that everything else about the lady was real. She wore her dark hair loose and shoulder length, went easy on the makeup and preferred the sort of casual attire that flattered her athletic build. He couldn't picture her at Quantico, competing with a class of macho would-be G-men at the FBI Academy, but that was male chauvinism talking and he let it go.

"I haven't seen much of the town so far," he said.

"You'll get your chance," she told him, and her smile began to fade. "I'm sorry that it came to this."

"How's that?"

"I worked with Tony Camarena for the past two years, and now he's dead. We thought the FLN was dying out, and now we've got the same old problem with a brand-new name."

"It happens that way sometimes."

"So I've noticed. Washington said they were sending out a troubleshooter, top priority. You don't look much like FBI to me."

"You've got good eyes."

"I guess that means you're with the Company."

"Not quite."

"I see."

Or maybe not, but she had clearly been around the Bureau long enough to recognize a case of need-to-know. Miranda Flores let it drop and shifted gears without a hitch.

"You have a car?"

He cocked a thumb in the direction of the parking lot. "Back there."

"You drive, I'll navigate. The chamber of commerce wouldn't appreciate this tour, but we'll hit all the low spots you might need to know."

"I'm in your hands."

"For the moment," she replied. "But once you know the ropes, my friend, you're on your own."

He smiled at that. The Executioner wouldn't have had it any other way.

Miami Beach
1750 hours EST

THEY TOOK THE VOLVO four-door to Flamingo Park, off Alton Road, to catch the early round of jai alai. Schwarz bought the tickets, and the Able Team warriors found three seats together in the bleachers, halfway down. The first game was in progress as they entered, four men locked in combat for the winning point.

"Who's up?" Lyons asked, watching Schwarz unfold the program he had picked up with their tickets at the cashier's cage.

"Our man goes in the second round," Schwarz said. "Enrique Dimas, playing one-on-one."

"We ought to find the locker room and catch him now."

"No rush," Blancanales said. "Let's find out what kind of nerve he's got before we have our chat."

The first game ended with a score of thirty-five to twenty-nine, with all four players sweating through their brightly colored shirts. They shook hands all around like gentlemen and cleared the courts. There was an intermission, mostly for the benefit of the officials, six or seven minutes slipping past before the next two players took the court.

"That's Dimas in the red," Schwarz said.

Their contact was a Cuban, five foot six or seven, pushing thirty, with a slender build that promised strength but lacked the bulk of an obsessive bodybuilder. He would be a lady-killer, with his classic profile, thin mustache and tapered sideburns. Schwarz could almost see him in a snow-white dinner jacket, velvet slacks and glossy patent leather shoes, flagging down the waiter in a stylish nightclub, ordering champagne.

He didn't look like someone who was walking on the razor's edge between Miami's violent underworld and federal agents pledged to cleaning up the town. Small chance of that, Schwarz thought, but every now and then the Feds got lucky with a slick informant who could be their eyes and ears beyond the pale. And if the go-between should make a handsome profit on the deal, well, that was life.

Or death, if anyone among the heavies learned that Dimas swung both ways.

Their contact won the coin toss for the serve and got things rolling with a pitch that sent his opposition racing for the back wall of the court. Schwarz was vague about the rules of jai alai, but he appreciated any sport where men were tested to their limits, striving for perfection or the next best thing. He watched the game without attempting to absorb its finer points, observing Dimas under fire, deciding that the man had brains, dexterity and nerve.

Those qualities could make him valuable as an ally, treacherous if he was playing one side off against the other for some private gain. They had no means of testing him within the time available, and it would all come down to trust—Brognola's in his Justice contacts, Schwarz's trust in Hal, and trust between the men of Able Team.

If all else failed, they had each other. It had been enough in other killing situations and it might again.

The match was done inside of fifteen minutes, Dimas punishing his young opponent, scoring twenty-one before his adversary racked up half as many points. The men of Able Team were on their feet and moving as the winner left the court, retiring to the locker room and showers. Lyons waited by the door while Schwarz and Blancanales went inside.

Enrique Dimas didn't seem surprised to see them there, although he registered displeasure with a frown. They had a bank of lockers to themselves, but he spoke softly, conscious of the fact that voices carried at the best of times.

"You are from Washington?" he asked the Politician.

"More or less. They told you we were coming?"

"Yes."

"Then you know why we're here."

"The Puerto Ricans, yes?"

"What can you tell us?"

"There is much to say, but this isn't the time or place."

"We haven't got a lot of time to spare," Schwarz said.

"I need to ask my contacts certain questions. Carefully, you understand? It is important that we finish all our business when we meet next time." The slender Cuban smiled. "I have an image to protect."

"So, when?"

"Tomorrow morning. Do you know the cemetery, Woodlawn Park?"

"We'll find it," Blancanales said.

"Be there at ten o'clock."

"It wouldn't be the best idea to stand us up."

Enrique Dimas glanced from one man to the other, still frowning. "I play jai alai, not Russian roulette."

"We understand each other, then."

"Indeed."

Emerging from the steamy locker room, Schwarz took a grateful breath of pure Miami smog. "You think he's playing straight?"

"We'll find out soon enough," the Politician said.

Carl Lyons joined them. "When and where?"

"Tomorrow morning, ten o'clock," Schwarz said. "We're going to a funeral."

Old San Juan
1900 hours AST

JOSÉ MONTOYA WAS A FENCE. He ran a pawnshop on Calle Marina, moving stolen goods from a selected clientele of thieves, but strangers who approached him on the premises were treated to a Puerto Rican version of the great stone face. Montoya frowned and shrugged, occasionally grunted if he thought an answer to some foolish question was required, but the intrusive guests got nowhere with presumptuous inquiries, propositions, hints of some outstanding profit to be made. If the intruders sounded threatening, Montoya had a loaded pistol on the shelf beneath his register. He also had three burly sons with extensive street-fighting experience, at least one of whom remained in the shop whenever it was open for business.

The serious strangers phoned ahead, as Yakov Katzenelenbogen had done on Wednesday afternoon as soon as he was finished sweeping his hotel room for electronic bugs. Names were mentioned, pleasantries exchanged, and Montoya finally agreed to a meeting. His customer would understand, of course, that such discussions never took place in his shop. These topics called for open air, some elbow room, a chance to look around and estimate how many ears were tuned in to the conversation.

Montoya chose the Parque de las Palomas, adjoining Cristo Chapel on Old San Juan's scenic Calle del Cristo. There were doves to feed, and benches with a fine view of the harbor. He could even guarantee the benches would be empty when his would-be customer arrived.

It was too much for Katz to take the team along, but no one in his putative profession traveled far without a bodyguard. He fingered Calvin James and left the others well behind, prepared to file reports and launch reprisals if the meet went wrong in any major way.

They walked together down Calle del Cristo with its blue ballast stones, past the looming cathedral and Cristo Chapel, the latter erected in memory of a young eighteenth-century horseman who had spurred his mount over the seventy-foot bluff. Neither man nor horse survived the idiotic stunt, but both had been remembered fondly for the past two hundred fifty years by locals and tourists alike.

Three of the benches in Parque de las Palomas were indeed empty. The fourth was occupied by a young hulk who glanced up at their approach and whistled sharply between clenched teeth. Katz felt Calvin James go tense beside him, expecting a trap, as their eyes drifted toward a nearby public rest room.

"Easy," Katz advised. "They're only being cautious."

"Same with me," the former Navy SEAL replied.

James had an Ingram MAC-10 submachine gun concealed beneath his light nylon windbreaker, and both Phoenix Force warriors were packing the new Beretta 96, chambered for the same 10 mm rounds that were standard issue for the FBI. The weapons were man-breakers, but Katz hoped they could avoid a confrontation in the park. Montoya and his sons weren't the target in San Juan, and it would be a waste of precious time to get bogged down with adversaries on the fringe.

A younger version of the slugger on the bench emerged from the public toilet, studied Katz and Calvin for a moment, then ducked back inside. When he reappeared, an older man was behind him, speaking softly to the young man, waving his other son off with the flick of a wrist. The brothers drifted off to stand beside the Cristo Chapel, watching closely, their jackets pointedly unbuttoned, while Calvin James sat down on the bench farthest from Katz and Montoya. It wasn't exactly privacy, but it would do.

"You mentioned old friends in Miami," Montoya said, settling on the bench so that a foot of open space remained between himself and Katz.

"The Prio brothers."

"How are the boys these days?"

"I wouldn't call them boys," Katz said. "Antonio was forty-seven when he took two bullets in the head three months ago. Arturo's on death row at Starke, and Jesus has the best part of a twelve-year sentence to finish in Atlanta on a federal drug rap."

"Some would say that makes your story difficult to verify," Montoya told him, putting on a narrow smile.

"And yet you're here."

"I am a businessman."

"So let's do business."

"What is it that you require?" Montoya asked.

"I deal in equalizers," Katz replied. "A man or group of men who feel inadequate need reassurance. Something to impress competitors, potential enemies, so they can maximize their full potential, even sleep at night."

"We have such men in Puerto Rico, too."

"I'm told that you have sources for the kind of hardware that I need."

"*Pistolas?*"

Katz smiled and shook his head. "I don't want toys. My customers are serious about their business and about their fears. They think in larger terms."

"Such merchandise is readily available in the United States, I understand."

"It has been in the past. These days, with new restrictions from the government, demand exceeds supply."

"There is a possibility that I can help you," Montoya said, "but the risks involved prohibit me from offering a discount."

Katz responded with a shrug. "My customers expect to pay top dollar. Disappointing them would spoil my day."

Montoya smiled. "I like a man who takes such pleasure in his business. We shall be amigos, I can tell."

Katz wore his own smile like a mask.

"My thoughts exactly," he replied.

Santurce, Puerto Rico
1915 hours

THE GOLDEN DRAGON occupied one corner of a side street west of Avenida Ponce de León, in the Santurce suburb of San Juan. It was a hangout popular with tourists, servicemen and whores. It did a thriving trade in American dollars. Santurce, with its shopping malls and modern office buildings, was a symbol of the modern age in Puerto Rico, cherished by the island's more ambitious businessmen, despised by those who viewed the mainland's contribution as a curse.

Picking out the bar had been no problem for Encizo. He had simply asked around the naval base and made a mental list of half a dozen clubs where military personnel were prone to congregate. He had already checked two other bars before he reached the Golden Dragon, trolling for familiar faces, pleased to recognize Gregorio Ruiz with several comrades as he let his eyes adjust to smoke and neon.

Drifting toward the bar, Encizo ordered beer and found an empty stool a few yards down from where Ruiz and his companions stood. The club seemed busy for a Wednesday night, although he had no real criteria for judging normal business in San Juan. On weekends, he decided, it would almost certainly be wall-to-wall.

Encizo nursed his beer and counted hookers, trying without much success to eavesdrop on Ruiz and company. They weren't boisterous, which made it difficult, but he picked up on the antagonism they directed toward a group of white Marines who occupied a large booth on the far side of the room. From what he heard and saw, it seemed to go beyond the normal swabble-jarhead rivalry familiar to the veterans of every foreign conflict in living memory. In theory, Marines and sailors were all part of the same Navy, but their historic quarrel went back to the halls of Montezuma and the throes of Tripoli. No one could ever cite a cause, but when their blood was up or they had managed to imbibe some alcohol, they often fought like cats and dogs.

Still, this was different.

Watching from his outpost on the sidelines, Encizo picked up a different flavor to the comments passed among Ruiz and his companions. There was racial animosity at work, beyond the simple rivalry of uniforms and units. Judging by the glances some of the Marines were casting toward the bar, they felt it, too, and they weren't inclined to let it slide.

It was a stroke of luck, Encizo later thought, that two of the Marines mistook him for a member of Ruiz's clique—or maybe they were simply frightened of accosting five Hispanic sailors when they had a chance to hassle one alone.

He saw them coming and braced himself. His right fist wrapped around the frosty handle of his beer mug while the left hand rested flat against his thigh. Ruiz and company were watching as the two Marines eased up on either side of Encizo and leaned against the bar, pretending not to see him as they flagged the barman down. An elbow struck his arm and spilled some of the amber liquid from his mug.

"You need to watch that, Pancho."

Glancing to his right, Encizo focused on an oval face with freckles, teeth like crooked Chiclets, pink scalp showing through the regulation buzz on top. The young man might be twenty-one, but that was pushing it.

"The name's not Pancho."

"Jesus, Nick, you shoulda known that." The Marine on Encizo's left flank was talking now. "This isn't Pancho. Can't you tell he's Speedy?"

"Hey, I think you're right, man. Speedy Gonzalez. I musta got him mixed up with some other spic."

"You boys appear to have an attitude," Encizo said.

"So what?" The challenge came from Nick.

"So, this."

He had the move mapped out before it ever started. Toss the beer at Nick's companion on the left to blind him while Encizo swung the heavy mug back toward those grinning Chiclet teeth and hammered several of them down Nick's throat. The mug was thick and heavy: you would need a brick to crack it, or perhaps a young man's muscle-plated skull.

Encizo swung back to his left and drove the mug into his second adversary's face. He felt a crunch of cartilage, but still no damage to the beer mug as he vaulted off his stool, prepared to face the other six or eight Marines now charging toward him, shouting racial insults with a single voice.

It might have been a massacre, except Ruiz and his companions waded in with fists and boots, as if on cue. The fighting quickly spread, some of the nearby tourists bored or drunk enough to want some of the action, others racing for the nearest exit at the sight of blood. Encizo saw Ruiz go down, a blond Marine delivering a solid one-two punch and trying for a follow-up with combat boots once he was down.

It was the chance he had been waiting for.

Encizo caught the tall blonde with a sucker punch from nowhere, maybe broke his jaw, but it was difficult to say. The mug was getting heavy, so he ditched it, ducking to lift Ruiz before another adversary tried to keep him on the floor. The barman had a telephone in one hand and a sawed-off pool cue in the other, jabbering to the authorities and waiting for the first fool who would try to come across the bar.

"SPs are coming!" someone shouted, heralding the swift arrival of the shore patrol.

"Let's go!"

Half carrying Ruiz, Encizo headed for the men's room and an exit granting access to the alley out in back. Two other uniforms were close behind him, Navy blue, no time for arguments or explanations as they ran.

They were a block away and strolling casually down the sidewalk, never mind their bruises, when Ruiz gave Encizo the eye and said, "You did all right back there."

Encizo shrugged. "Those Yankees want some shit, I'm ready for them."

"Yankees, eh? So what the hell are you?"

He bristled, stood his ground. "I'm Puerto Rican, man. You got a beef with that, let's settle it right now."

Gregorio Ruiz looked thoughtful for a moment, then finally cracked a smile.

"Relax, *hermano*. You have friends here. I believe this just might be your lucky day."

"I hope you're right," Encizo said. And smiled.

CHAPTER FIVE

Ponce, Puerto Rico
Wednesday, 1930 hours

Puerto Rico's second city lies within an easy ninety-minute drive from San Juan on Route 52, midway along the island's southern flank. Residents of Ponce call their city the "Pearl of the South," cherished dreams of wide-open commerce and tourism that have thus far failed to materialize. A city of one hundred fifty thousand residents, with a scattering of tourists, it was far enough from San Juan and the U.S. Naval base to be ideal for what Miguel Albano had in mind.

He had left his uniform behind and driven in his private car, a three-year-old Chevrolet with six payments outstanding. There was nothing to connect him to the naval base unless somebody turned his pockets out and checked his wallet, which would mean he was already dead, disabled or under arrest.

Barring disaster, then, he was clean, just another face in the crowd. Even the pistol he carried, a double-action Browning automatic chambered in 9 mm parabellum, was private stock, with no link to the arsenal on base. In fact, since it was stolen property that he had purchased secondhand, Albano could discard the weapon on a moment's notice, knowing it couldn't be traced to him as long as he took care of fingerprints.

He felt a kind of freedom on the road, without the hated uniform of the oppressor nation on his back. No matter that the very trip itself had been involuntary, springing from an urgent summons. He was pleased to meet Raul Gutierrez anywhere at anytime. The Cuban understood his needs and offered the assistance of his Fidelista comrades in their common war against the Yankee pigs.

Miguel Albano didn't call himself a Communist, per se. He was conversant with the late events in Eastern Europe, from the crumbling of the Berlin Wall to the collapse of communism in the very land where it had taken root. Albano didn't need a foreign ideology to fuel his rage at the United States. He was a Puerto Rican patriot, committed to the goal of independence for his homeland and his people. Anyone who helped him toward that end had to be a comrade; anyone who tried to stop him was the enemy and would be dealt with in a manner fit for tyrants.

If Fidel believed an independent Puerto Rico would be ripe for Cuba's rusty brand of communism, that was his mistake, and he would learn his error soon enough. Meanwhile, if he wished to help the revolution on its way, his help was welcome.

He parked downtown and locked the Chevrolet before proceeding toward the Catholic University on foot. Across the street he made a show of checking out the Ponce Museum, closed to tourists now, but still an eyecatcher with its subtle lighting out front.

Besides, no one would take him for a tourist. He belonged here.

He was home.

Albano saw Gutierrez coming from a block away. The Cuban's military bearing was the first thing that you noticed, followed swiftly by the piercing eyes, like scalpels shaving slivers from your soul. Gutierrez had the knack of looking deep inside a man and picking out his secrets, using them against him as the need arose. So far, Albano's dealings with the Cuban had been friendly, but he knew that he would have to guard against the day when things might change.

When that day came, Albano would be ready. He had secrets that Gutierrez hadn't managed to unearth yet, a trick or two held in reserve for self-defense.

"Miguel."

The Cuban's smile was like his handshake, there and gone almost before it had a chance to register. Solemnity was more his stock in trade, especially in recent months, since Cuba and the Fidelistas had been stripped of their support from Moscow. It could be a cold, cruel world without a bear to keep you warm.

"Raul." Albano's tone was neutral, offering no insight to his thoughts.

"You're making progress, I believe," Gutierrez said. "Your plan is almost ready to proceed?"

"Three days," Albano told him. "Four at the outside."

"Excellent." This time the Cuban's fleeting smile seemed genuine. "You have done well."

"So far," Albano said.

"Of course."

"There is a chance that we might fail."

"Have faith, Miguel."

It should have been a joke, those words emerging from the lips of an acknowledged Communist, but he appeared to be sincere. The Catholic roots, Albano thought, were never truly severed in Latinos, even after thirty years of purges and suppression by a godless government.

So be it.

Faith could do no harm, but it could still come down to failure, even with the preparations he had made to cover different contingencies. A single slipup anywhere along the line could be fatal.

"I have the information you requested," Gutierrez said, fishing an envelope from his pocket and passing it across. "Such data isn't easy to obtain these days, without our comrades in the east."

"And yet you manage."

"There is something to be said for perseverance."

"While I have you here, Raul—"

"Another favor?"

"If you would be so kind."

The Cuban flicked his false smile on and off. "My wish is but to serve."

Gutierrez wanted more than that, Albano knew, but he wasn't prepared to call the man a liar yet. Not while the Cubans were prepared to help the ANI survive and stage its greatest coup in three or four days' time. Once he had struck the blow for liberty and had a chance to gauge its overall effect, there would be time enough for cutting ties with the Havana regime.

But not just yet.

Miguel Albano knew he could afford to wait.

Old San Juan
1940 hours

"THEY HANG OUT HERE sometimes," Miranda Flores told Bolan, pointing toward a small cantina on the corner as she spoke.

They were proceeding west on Avenida Munoz Rivera, riding in Bolan's gray Toyota MR2. He followed her direction toward the tavern with its garish neon lighting, older compacts filling up the tiny parking lot.

"The ANI?"

"And sympathizers," she confirmed. "It isn't always easy telling which is which."

It was the fifth location she had pointed out with ANI connections in the space of ninety minutes. She had more, but they would have to leave the old-town section to complete the tour.

"You seem to have a decent handle on their operations," Bolan commented. "Are you sharing with the Puerto Rican Feds?"

"Across the board," she told him, knowing that wasn't precisely true, that her superiors inevitably made a point of holding certain information back. "They roust assorted suspects every now and then, most often in the wake of an attack. It gets them nowhere."

"You were banking on the Sanchez link," he stated rather than asked.

"Damned right. The military angle is a killer, any way you break it down. On one hand bad publicity for all concerned. A nest of traitors in the Navy for a start, and you can picture how it grows from there. The flip side could be even worse, with leaks of classified material, the theft of weapons we've already documented, maybe even cases of deliberate sabotage."

"But nothing solid yet."

"Aside from what our pigeon told us, no."

"It's good of you to get me started." He was smiling as he spoke, but she could find no trace of humor in his tone. "I don't know what your people have in mind from this point on."

"I'm handling liaison all the way," she said. "If you have questions, anything at all, you come to me."

"You might regret that offer."

"It's official."

"Were you briefed about my methods?"

"More or less. You clean things up, I understand."

"Sometimes I leave a bigger mess than what you started with. It comes from chopping up the pieces."

"Troubleshooter?"

"Right."

"I see."

"When things get rolling, you might wish we never met."

"I do my job," she told him, suddenly defensive.

"All the same, we'd better cover all we can tonight."

"The other sites are all outside San Juan," she told him. "Have you got the time?"

"It's why I'm here."

"Okay, let's go. Two blocks, a left and double back to catch the highway headed west."

In fact, her companion's words disturbed Flores more than she let on. Her training at the FBI Academy had stressed observance of the law, a view sometimes more honored in the breach than the observance once an agent hit the field. It wasn't like the Hoover days, from what she had heard, but there were still a wide variety of covert operations going down, with black-bag jobs and bugging in the absence of official sanction, shady deals with felons and informants to complete a shaky case. You started out with high ideals and honorable motives, working overtime to bring the bad guys down, but in that first year on the street, a fledgling fed discovered good and bad were strictly relative... and subject to interpretation by the Bureau brass.

Plea bargains were supposedly reserved for prosecutors, handed out before a trial, but she saw similar examples daily on the street. A thief or dealer struck a bargain with arresting officers, and his charges were minimized—perhaps dismissed entirely—if he gave them someone bigger, higher up the food chain. Local cops and Feds alike survived on their relationship to criminal informants, accent on the "crimi-

nal,'' and most arrests were only possible because some
lesser bad guy cut himself a deal.

But this was different. She could feel it in her bones.

Flores understood what Mike Belasko's warning meant.
He wasn't in San Juan to root out radical informants and
persuade them to betray the ANI. Unless she missed her
guess, he had a more direct approach in mind.

And that spelled murder.

Didn't it?

She understood the rationale for vigilante justice, wet
work, termination with extreme prejudice and all the other
doublespeak employed by cloak-and-dagger types around
the world. If you couldn't defeat a problem with the book,
you threw the book away and used a dose of cyanide, a
blade or bullet—anything at all to do the job.

Which made Belasko CIA or something similar. It was a
new one on Flores for the Bureau to recruit from outside
agencies, much less where wet work was concerned. And
that, in turn, led her to wonder what the hell was really going on.

Flores's training called for a reaction, some direct response to a potential violent felony, but her experience advised her not to rush her play. If she began to blow the
whistle, there was still a question of precisely who her audience might be. Belasko had the full approval of her local
supervisors and apparently the same held true for Washington. That limited her options from the start, unless she
felt like going public, talking to the press, and that idea left
a rancid taste in her mouth.

So she would watch and wait.

It might not be as bad as she expected. If it was that bad,
or worse, she would attempt to find a friendly ear somewhere between San Juan and Washington.

There was no rush. Not yet.

She had a tour to conduct, and it would be much easier if she did not imagine every man or address pointed out along the way as targets in a shooting gallery.

San Juan was close to an explosion as it was. The fuse was laid, and it would burn with deadly speed once it was lit.

It frightened her to think the man who rode beside her might be carrying the lethal spark.

El Convento Hotel, San Juan
2015 hours

JACK GRIMALDI HAD BECOME a pro at killing time. He had been willing to ride shotgun on the play when Bolan went to meet his contact from the FBI, but Bolan had preferred that he remain on tap for an emergency with Phoenix Force or a message from the base at Stony Man Farm. It was a gentle way of saying that the big guy wanted privacy, and that was fine with Jack. He would sit tight at the hotel and keep his fingers crossed that Bolan wasn't walking into an elaborate trap.

The problem was, you never knew exactly whom to trust in covert operations. With his time spent in the military, then a commissioned flyboy for the Mafia, and finally as part of Bolan's team, Grimaldi reckoned he had seen it all— or nearly so, at any rate. He had observed confusion and corruption in the Army on his tour in Vietnam, where non-coms made a bundle hawking merchandise they stole from the PX, and heroin went home with fallen heroes in their body bags. The Mob had almost come as a relief, a bunch of cutthroat pirates who were looking out for number one and very seldom tried to play it any other way. It was the troop of politicians, businessmen and crooked cops who made Grimaldi shake his head on that tour, selling out their country and themselves for the almighty dollar or a taste of something that would get them through the night.

And then came Bolan.

It was better working with the big guy; Grimaldi had no doubts whatsoever on that score, but it continued his exposure to the seamy side of life. Where he had formerly been treated to a glimpse of rank corruption here and there while flying mobsters back and forth across the continent, now he was rolling in it, learning all their dirty little secrets from the horse's mouth, and he discovered that the Mafia was only part of it. At every level of the government, there was a clique of power brokers bent on profiting from any circumstance, no matter how it might affect the people they were pledged to serve. At Bolan's side he saw corruption and subversion in the church, in law enforcement, the Intelligence community, in banking circles where a cocaine baron or a terrorist could flash a smile and close a million-dollar deal like any decent person off the street.

It changed a person, learning things like that about society, about your trusted friends.

About yourself.

Grimaldi had been close to selling out, he realized, when he was flying for the Mob. A soft nudge either way, and he could just as easily have turned up on the Bolan hit list rather than on Brognola's roster of the team at Stony Man.

Some mornings Jack Grimaldi still believed in luck.

But not so much today.

It troubled him to think of terrorists disguised as U.S. military personnel, although the concept hardly qualified as new. It had been commonplace in Vietnam for members of the NVA or Vietcong to masquerade as ARVN soldiers, setting up their strikes, and you could trace the concept back through history if you had time. It was the reason both sides in a war traditionally executed soldiers caught without their uniforms; it neutralized potential spies and saboteurs. The Trojan horse was nothing but a giant time bomb, ticking with the heartbeats of the warriors packed inside.

This time felt different, though. He didn't have the measure of the problem yet, but Jack Grimaldi trusted intuition, the reaction of his gut in killing situations. He couldn't put his finger on the problem yet, but there was something heavy they had missed, a section of the puzzle that was out of place, preventing them from scoping out the long view, seeing where it led.

He flashed on lives at stake, by hundreds—maybe thousands—but he couldn't pin it down. He was still working on it half an hour later, when the phone rang at his bedside. He snared it on the second ring.

"Hello?"

The big guy's voice came back at him. "Let's take a ride."

"I'm on my way."

GRIMALDI DROVE, with Bolan in the shotgun seat. The MR2 was Toyota's experiment in midengine, rear-drive sports cars, unrivaled by the competition with its fuel injection and a supercharger boosting the output of its four-cylinder engine to 145 brake horsepower at 6,400 RPM.

In other words, the little car would move.

Their destination was a combination office-and-garage that served a lower-budget trucking company, located near the docks off Avenida Fernando Juncos. According to Miranda Flores, the concern was owned and operated by a member of the ANI who kept his brother revolutionaries on the payroll, sometimes using trucks from his garage to haul suspected contraband. The firm—Primero Transport—had survived spot checks along the highway and at least two searches of the downtown premises. The man in charge was smart or lucky, maybe some of each.

"You trust the lady, Sarge?"

It was a question he had asked himself, and Bolan had no final answer at the moment. "It's provisional," he said at last. "I'm making this up as I go."

"Is that supposed to reassure me?"

"Hey, at least you've got the wheels."

They were approaching target now, Grimaldi slowing for the drive-by, checking out the office and attached garage. No sentries were visible, but light was showing through the office windows. Bolan had him drive around the block, returning from the west and parking fifty yards downrange.

"I don't mind going in," Grimaldi said.

"It doesn't have the feeling of a two-man job," the Executioner replied.

Grimaldi didn't argue; he knew better. When the big guy had his mind made up, the case was closed. They also served who only drove and waited.

"Night watchman, maybe."

"Let's find out."

As Bolan spoke, he reached behind the driver's seat to lift a small athletic bag. Inside he found a mini-Uzi submachine gun, several extra magazines, two frag grenades and a packet of incendiary sticks. The Uzi magazines and firesticks filled the outer pockets of his Army-surplus jacket, while he clipped the grenades to his belt, one on either side of the buckle.

"Five minutes," Bolan said. "If I'm late, you leave."

"I hear you."

Bolan knew Grimaldi well enough by now to doubt that the man would leave him flat in any circumstances, short of iron-clad certainty that he was dead, but there was also his responsibility to Phoenix Force and Stony Man. Whatever happened, the Stony Man pilot would do his job. That much was certain in the warrior's mind.

"I'm out of here."

He moved along the sidewalk, keeping in the shadows, thankful that the San Juan docks had low priority in terms of streetlights. In a moment he had reached the western end of the garage and slipped past it, listening for telltale sounds of movement as he made his way around the back.

He found the access door exactly where he hoped that it would be, and it was locked. A kick took care of that, and Bolan hesitated for a heartbeat on the threshold, breathing oil and diesel fumes, his Uzi cocked and ready just in case his entry was opposed.

Three trucks regarded him with absolute disinterest, headlights staring back at him like flat, blind eyes. He moved to the connecting door, where light poured through a windowpane, and listened long enough to pick up voices on the other side. He couldn't say how many, but it sounded like a minimum of three.

His left hand found the knob and tried it—open. Bolan braced himself, then stepped through the doorway, counting heads before his targets had a chance to register the presence of an interloper in their midst.

Four men in all. One was seated at a cluttered desk, the others grouped around him, two men standing, while the fourth had found himself a folding chair directly opposite the boss. Four pairs of eyes stared at him in shock, but they recovered swiftly.

The standing targets were his greatest risk to start with. Bolan saw them break in opposite directions, as if they might have practiced the maneuver, each man digging for a weapon underneath the baggy shirt he wore. The gunman on his left was closer, and a 3-round burst ripped through his chest at close to point-blank range, the impact slamming him against a nearby filing cabinet, dropping him before he had a chance to reach his gun.

The second gunner made it, hauling out a nickel-plated belly gun, but Bolan caught him with a rising burst before he had a chance to aim and fire. The parabellum manglers spun him in a sloppy pirouette and dumped him facedown on the ancient, cracked linoleum.

The boss was rummaging inside a drawer, presumably for hardware, when the Uzi swiveled into target acquisition. On the far side of the desk, his sole surviving guest had one leg hoisted at an awkward ankle, grappling with an ankle holster.

Better luck next time.

The Uzi tracked from left to right and back again, both targets jerking, sprawling from their chairs. Blood pooled beneath them where they lay, unmoving on the floor.

Bolan considered using one of his grenades, but decided against it. Instead, he dropped a firestick in the middle of the fat man's cluttered desk, retraced his steps to the garage and slipped another in the fuel tank of each truck in turn. He was outside and making for his own car when the first one popped and hungry flames began to feed inside the office. He was back at the Toyota, sliding in beside Grimaldi, when the trucks went up like giant fireworks, thunderclaps in rapid fire.

Round one.

Initially the ANI wouldn't know what to think of the attack, and that was fine. Confusion helped to even out the odds, and at the moment Bolan needed all the help that he could get.

"Next stop?" Grimaldi asked.

He thought about it, running down the mental list. There was a billiard hall where members of the ANI reportedly spent time. He rattled off the address, pointing Grimaldi in the right direction.

CHAPTER SIX

Southwest Miami
Thursday, 0950 hours EST

Woodlawn Park Cemetery lay one block east of Coral Gables and immediately south of Highway 41, the famous Tamiami Trail. Rosario Blancanales thought the cemetery made a perfect rendezvous. There was no traffic to speak of on a Thursday morning, and there was time to spare before the first scheduled funeral cortege arrived at half-past eleven. It even felt right. They had come to speak of death, and it was only fitting that they do so in the company of corpses.

Lyons parked the Volvo on Thirty-fourth Street, the western boundary of Woodlawn Park, and waited in the car, an Ingram submachine gun tucked just out of sight beneath the driver's seat. They had already dropped Schwarz on Sixteenth Street, to the south, and he was walking in with flowers, posing as a mourner, carrying a compact subgun concealed in armpit leather. There were other solitary visitors at scattered points around the cemetery, couples here and there, so the appearance of another two or three wouldn't inspire suspicion from the ground crew. As he sat waiting, Blancanales spotted one of them in denim coveralls, trimming grass around a stately monument with his battered Weed Eater.

Life goes on, and never mind the presence of the dead.

"Stay frosty," Lyons cautioned, shifting slightly in his seat.

"I heard that."

Blancanales left the Volvo, spent a moment straightening his tie and let the 12-gauge stakeout-model Ithaca lay flat against his ribs. The swivel mount would give him easy access to the shotgun at a moment's notice, and he also wore his favorite Beretta Model 92 beneath his left arm in a shoulder rig.

Between the three of them, he reckoned they were covered. If it blew up in their faces, they would have to play the rest of it by ear.

Enrique Dimas should be waiting for him at the point they had agreed on. Whether the informant would have brought some kind of backup, Blancanales couldn't say, and he didn't particularly care as long as the supporting cast stayed well away from center stage. It seemed unlikely that the Cuban would desire another witness to this meeting, but the Able Team warrior had given up on second-guessing strangers in the field.

In Vietnam he had been tagged "the Politician" for his expertise at settling quarrels without resorting to violence, negotiating terms with different tribes and factions in the hostile countryside. The recent work of Able Team didn't rely to any great degree upon diplomacy, but Blancanales kept his hand in with informants, snitches, contacts in the other cloak-and-dagger arms of government. If he could talk a problem out instead of killing, he would gladly make the extra effort. But the opposition he encountered these days seldom made negotiations easy or productive.

Which, inevitably, brought the Politician back to force of arms.

He wondered how much information Dimas had been able to collect about the ANI. It would have been a touchy subject in the Cuban quarter, overlapping interests on the wrong side of the law conflicting with a basic difference in political philosophy. Most Cuban exiles and their children were politically conservative and patriotic to a fault, though some still blamed the Kennedys for failure at the Bay of Pigs in 1961. Above all else, they hated Communists in general and the die-hard Fidelistas in particular, an everlasting hatred that rubbed off on anyone who took a dime from Castro or appeared to toe his party line.

Conversely, giving up Hispanics to the law for any cause might still be seen as ethnic treason in Little Havana, where a new generation of Marielitos had put down roots since 1980, growing fat on profits from the drug trade, murdering or terrorizing those among their countrymen who stood for law and order. It wasn't the same Miami Blancanales had experienced at age nineteen, or even twenty-five.

Times change, he thought, and seldom for the better where it counts.

Off to his left, another grounds keeper was mowing the grass, wheeling his mower around ankle-high headstones with practiced ease. Some thirty yards ahead of him, a man knelt in the shadow of a larger monument, clutching flowers in one hand, making the sign of the cross with the other.

Dimas had arranged to meet him at the park's memorial chapel. Open from nine to six, the chapel was available for prayers by mourners of any denomination, as long as worshipers of santeria left their goats and chickens outside.

Another moment brought him to the chapel. Blancanales hesitated on the threshold, glanced around himself, saw nothing to suggest that he was being tailed.

So much for the precautions; he had done his best.

He opened up the left side of the double doors and stepped inside.

ENRIQUE DIMAS KNEW the risk that he was taking when he stepped onto the manicured grounds of Woodlawn Park. He had done everything he could to keep from being followed, but you never really knew for sure. A thing like this, the only way for him to get the information he required was asking questions in the barrio, and questions were like pebbles dropped into a pond. The ripples spread, alerting schools of predatory fish and solitary parasites. Before you knew it, they could strip you to the bone.

At twenty-eight years old, Dimas knew the fine points of survival inside out. He watched his back, affected casual demeanor and attacked his subject with discretion, listening to gossip on the street or asking "harmless" questions, guiding aimless conversations into new and more rewarding channels. He considered it a minor art form, milking information from his friends and casual acquaintances without allowing them to know that they were being used. It was a lot like jai alai in certain ways, except that one was fast and furious, the other often tedious and slow.

But either game could get you killed if you let your guard down and took your eye off the ball.

He sat in a pew halfway back, pretending to meditate, waiting for the Fed to show himself. The snubby .38 revolver tucked inside his belt was stainless steel, a satin-finish Smith & Wesson. It was shit for distance work, but in the narrow confines of the chapel Dimas thought that he could do all right.

The chapel doors were heavy, and they made a shuffling sound when they were opened. Dimas twisted in his pew and saw a figure framed in silhouette, the morning sun behind him, blacking out his face. It could have been the Fed or anybody else. His right hand found the .38 and gripped it tightly, his index finger sliding through the trigger guard.

He glanced behind him again as the door swung shut. This time he recognized the Fed and let himself relax a little as his new acquaintance joined him in the pew. So far, they had the chapel to themselves.

"You're late," Dimas said.

"I was checking out the grounds."

"You like to visit graveyards?"

"No, but I've had lots of practice. Did you find out what I need to know?"

"It took a while. I went a thousand out of pocket."

That was bullshit, but they both knew how the game was played. The Fed dug in his pocket, palmed a wad of bills and counted off the right amount before he handed it over.

"So?"

"It wasn't easy, like I said. These people you've been looking at have everybody nervous, understand? They don't sell drugs—not yet, at least—but they've been moving weapons, and they like to practice in the Everglades."

"Who doesn't?"

Dimas shrugged. "It makes me think about Omega Seven in the old days. You remember those guys?"

"I remember. Some of them are still around."

"But they're retired, you know. Moved on to other things. These Puerto Ricans want to fight, I promise you. Word is they've got some Navy guy involved. Luis Camacho. I don't know about the military angle, but these guys got weapons up the ass, and that's for real."

"About these sessions in the Glades . . ."

He was prepared for that, a clincher that would give the Fed his money's worth.

"They have some kind of camp set up. It's nothing fancy, living off the land, that kind of shit, you know. From what I hear, the place is rigged up so it can't be spotted from the air."

"Location?"

"That's the hard part," Dimas told him. "On a thing like this, not many people know, and those who do aren't big on talk."

"You didn't go a grand out of pocket for nothing," the Fed replied.

"Hell, no, I got you something, man. I'm talking reliability here. It's not like I can double-check this thing with half a dozen guys."

"I'm listening."

"I never did so good when I was studying geography, okay? This guy I was talking to, I had him sketch it out."

He drew the piece of typing paper from his pocket, folded into quarters, passed it over and waited while the other man examined it. The map was crude, of course, but major landmarks were included. It should be no problem if they found a guide who had his shit together. Airboats, maybe, or canoes.

And if the *federales* blew it, they were gator bait.

It wouldn't be Dimas's problem, either way.

He heard the chapel door swing open and saw a wedge of sunlight on the wall. Dimas turned back to glance across his shoulder, freezing at the sight of two men pushing through the open doorway with a third bringing up the rear.

The two in front were holding guns.

"Get down!" he blurted, groping for his own revolver as he suited words to action, dropping to his knees and hoping that the pew would cover him at least from the initial rounds.

The Fed was quick, professional. One moment he was staring at the hand-drawn map, and a heartbeat later he was huddled on the floor, a stubby shotgun in his hands. Some kind of harness held the weapon underneath his jacket, out of sight until he needed it for self-defense.

The gunmen opened fire from fifty feet away, the bullets from their automatic weapons ripping wood and plaster as they sprayed the left side of the chapel. Dimas wriggled toward the far end of his pew on knees and elbows, muttering a prayer from force of habit. When the shooters took a break, he popped up out of cover, steadying his Smith & Wesson in a firm two-handed grip, and pegged a round in the direction of the nearest gunner.

They were waiting for him, swiveling to bring him under fire, a swarm of bullets chewing up the hand-carved pew and slamming Dimas backward to the floor. He couldn't feel his legs or anything below chest level, but he heard the shotgun blasting back at their assailants, solid crashing sounds like thunder in the confines of the chapel.

Dimas tried to ask God what had happened to his life.

And with the question on his lips, he died.

SCHWARZ HAD THE GUNNERS spotted from a range of fifty yards, but there was no way he could cut them off before they reached the chapel. They had barely crossed the threshold, passing from his line of vision, when all hell broke loose inside. The muffled sounds of rapid small-arms fire reached Schwarz in spite of heavy doors and thick stone walls, and he began to run. The Uzi that he wore beneath his jacket slapped against his ribs with every step.

Too late, goddammit! They had come from nowhere, on his blind side, closing from the north and covered by the little church itself until they had to step around and face the entrance.

Schwarz was halfway to the chapel when a bullet whispered past his face, the sharp report an instant later, like the sonic boom that trailed a speeding jet. Instinct and training took control as Gadgets dodged, went prone and rolled, the Uzi scanning for a target as he came to temporary rest.

One of the Woodlawn janitors was firing at him with an automatic, crouching in an effort to correct his aim. The shooter's lawnmower had taken off without him, forgotten, cutting an erratic path until it slammed into a headstone and the motor stalled.

By that time, Schwarz had stitched the gunman with a burst across his chest, a flush of crimson soaking through his denim coveralls. The guy went over backward in a sprawl, his pistol bouncing on the grass.

Someone else was firing now, the bullets churning sod a few yards off to Schwarz's left. He rolled and twisted, getting up on one knee, the Uzi braced against his hip and facing in the opposite direction.

Jogging toward him through the sunlight were a man and woman, each with pistols in their hands. A second glance told Gadgets there was something odd about the female, maybe in her stride, but he was caught up in the raw mechanics of survival at the moment, laying down a screen of cover fire.

His parabellum manglers caught the man and spun him through a jerky little dance. The woman kept on coming, firing for effect, until Schwarz hit her with a rising burst that knocked "her" wig off and revealed a crew cut.

Three down, and three inside the chapel. Were there more to deal with, lurking somewhere on the grounds?

Schwarz lurched erect and turned back toward the church, where gunfire cracked behind its stained-glass windows.

Come what may, he still had work to do.

INSIDE THE CHAPEL Blancanales dropped the nearest gunner with his first blast from the 12-gauge, crimson spraying into the air as the buckshot ripped through flesh and fabric, hammering his target to the floor. The other two reacted swiftly, ducking out of sight to left and right among the pews.

He glanced at Dimas, stretched out on the floor, and had no time to wonder if the snitch was breathing. There was blood all over, probably a lung shot, maybe multiples. If he was still alive and paramedics showed up in the next ten seconds, maybe he would have a chance.

Dream on.

Survival was the Politician's top priority, with odds of two-to-one, a possibility of other hostile guns outside. At first he thought the distant gunshots were an echo in his ringing ears, but he distinguished pistol fire from what he guessed would be an Uzi submachine gun.

Gadgets?

There was no time to contemplate his comrade's problems as the two surviving gunners sprang up simultaneously, pinning Blancanales with triangulated fire. He ducked and crawled across the carpet, digging with his knees and elbows, ready with the Ithaca in case they tried a rush.

The far aisle was a narrow passageway between the pews and wall. The Politician risked a peek around the pew in front of him, drew back like a retreating turtle, then braced himself to make his move. Instead of jumping up, he pushed his head and shoulders clear, the Ithaca in front of him, and crawled into the aisle.

So far, so good.

As if on cue, the gunners opened fire again, but they were aiming at the point where he had dropped from sight before. He wormed his way along the carpet, edging closer to the source of automatic fire. Blancanales started counting pews, afraid his adversaries would come in search of him before he reached the necessary vantage point. Three pews, and two more left to go.

The gunners took a break, perhaps reloading from the sounds they made, and Blancanales hesitated, fearing they might hear him crawling closer. When they came up firing, he was ready with the 12-gauge.

He didn't even have to aim, he was so close, squeezing off a blast that hit the gunman like a hammer stroke and slammed him over sideways in a cloud of scarlet mist.

Blancanales worked the shotgun's slide, sat up and found the third man facing him from twenty feet away. They fired together, but automatic weapons called for greater discipline and fire control. They tended to climb or wander from the recoil, and that law of physics saved the Politician's life. His buckshot charge was dead on target, and the gunner vaulted backward, landing draped across the pew like a forgotten suit of clothes with something soft and wet inside.

All done inside the church.

As Blancanales rose, he checked his pocket, felt the map and doubled back to check Enrique Dimas. He was dead, his time and luck run out as surely as the blood that spilled from ragged wounds.

But from the sound of things, there was some killing left to do outside.

The Politician ran to join his comrades on the firing line.

CARL LYONS FELT the trouble coming, but it took a blast of gunfire from the cemetery to put him in motion. He twisted the Volvo's ignition key, brought the engine to life and scooped his Ingram SMG from underneath the driver's seat as he put the car in motion.

Fifteen yards remained before he'd reach the open gate. It granted access to a blacktop drive that wandered through the cemetery, sparing visitors and funeral processions the need to walk from the main parking lot on Thirty-second

Street. Lyons knew where he was going, concentrated on the chapel as he pushed the Volvo up to forty-five and started cutting corners on the curves.

How far? He had the layout fixed in mind from their preliminary rundown. It should be something like a hundred yards from street to chapel. Any second now—

A blur of movement drew Lyons's attention to his left. A human figure raced over open grass, as if to intercept the car. A second glance confirmed the runner had a sawed-off shotgun in his hands. The shooter wore a mourning suit, his jacket open, flapping like a cape behind him as he ran.

Instead of swerving to avoid his adversary, Lyons cranked the Volvo's steering wheel to meet him, driving one-handed with his Ingram braced on the windowsill. The gunman recognized his danger, skidded to a halt and fired a hasty blast that somehow missed the Volvo clean. He pumped the shotgun's slide and was trying for a second chance when Lyons stroked the Ingram's trigger, squeezing off a 6-round burst.

The parabellum shredders cut a fist-sized pattern in the gunner's shirt, the explosive impacts sweeping him completely off his feet. His shoulders hit the grass before his buttocks landed, and the second shotgun blast was wasted on a line of fleecy clouds.

Lyons kept the Volvo moving toward the chapel, noting other bodies on the turf, a mower wedged against a headstone on his right. A quick check told him Schwarz wasn't among the dead that he could see, but that still left the chapel, both doors standing open on a dark interior as Lyons set the parking brake and left the Volvo's engine running.

He was EVA and tracking with the Ingram when a human figure filled the doorway, still in shadow. He hit a crouch, the Ingram cocked and locked, his index finger taking up what little slack the trigger had, when he was frozen by the sound of a familiar voice.

"It's over, Ironman."

Blancanales stepped across the threshold, Gadgets on his heels. Their suits were rumpled, but he saw no blood or other evidence of wounds.

"Are you two all right?"

"We're getting there."

Lyons stood and approached his comrades, carrying the Ingram loosely at his side.

"Your contact?"

"Finished," Blancanales said.

"Well, shit."

"We had a little chat before the party crashers did their thing. Let's talk about it on the road."

A wise idea. No sirens yet, but they would soon be on their way. Their recent firefight wouldn't literally wake the dead, but there were other living bodies somewhere on the Woodlawn grounds, and one of them was bound to find a telephone.

"You want to check out these jokers before we go?" Lyons asked, nodding toward the figures of a man and what appeared to be a woman stretched out on the grass nearby.

"The three inside are clean," Schwarz said. "We're talking pros."

"Well, shit," the Ironman repeated.

"You're starting to repeat yourself," Blancanales said.

"Yeah. Must be old age."

"Let's hit the street before your arteries start to harden, okay?"

"Your wish is my command."

But Lyons didn't like it. Even after they were safe and miles away from Woodlawn Park, debating what had happened at the cemetery, he was troubled by the fact that someone—anybody—could have set them up and fielded half a dozen contract killers overnight, complete with credible disguises. Lyons knew there was a chance the trap was meant for Dimas, based upon some existing grudge, but if it went the other way it meant their cover had been blown with barely one day on the job.

And that was bad.

Especially since they still had no idea who might be stalking them.

Or why.

CHAPTER SEVEN

Old San Juan
Thursday, 0530 hours AST

It was early for Francisco Obregon to be awake and doing business, but the night just past had been a waking nightmare, bloody chaos. Not that Obregon had anything against a bit of bloodshed; he regarded violence as a useful tool in the promotion of a social revolution that had been delayed too long, but that perspective only covered violence he was dishing out.

Receiving was an altogether different proposition.

The beach near Fort San Cristobel was perfectly deserted at this hour of the morning. Obregon could strip his clothes off if he liked, do naked cartwheels on the sand, but he wasn't in any mood for acrobatics.

What he needed at the moment were some answers.

What he craved was sweet revenge.

He saw Miguel Albano's car before it pulled into the parking lot. Albano wore civilian clothes, a lightweight nylon jacket covering his plain blue shirt...or was it meant to hide the pistol tucked inside his belt? Albano never left the base without a weapon now that their offensive had begun.

For his part Obregon preferred the compact Heckler & Koch MP-5 K submachine gun that he wore beneath his left arm in a custom shoulder sling. Lifted from the naval armory with Albano's help, the little stuttergun provided all the firepower Obregon would ever need—at least, until the great day came.

And it was coming soon.

He waited for Albano on the sand. It would have saved some time to meet the other man halfway, but Obregon had fallen into an uncompromising mood. The night's events had soured him, raised specters of potential failure he couldn't afford.

For a determined revolutionary, failure was the same as death, and Obregon had always been a most determined man.

"You're late," he muttered as Albano closed the gap, facilitating normal conversation.

"It's a wonder I got off the base at all. My shift begins at seven, so we'll have to make it quick. What's the emergency?"

"You haven't heard?"

"Heard *what*, Francisco?"

"The attacks last night."

Albano frowned. "I'm listening. Why don't you start at the beginning."

"Very well, Primero Transport."

"What about it?"

"Someone burned it down last night. Four men were killed, all ours, including Pepe Ramos."

Obregon was pleased by the expression on Albano's face. The Navy man was clearly shocked, and he required a moment to collect his thoughts. "An accident, perhaps?"

"No accident. The trucks and office were deliberately set on fire. Our friend with Channel Three says Pepe and the rest were shot before the office burned."

Albano's frown had deepened to a full-fledged scowl. "But who?" he asked. His tone said he was talking to himself.

"There's more," Obregon told him, feeling the peculiar morbid satisfaction that was part and parcel of delivering bad news. "Some thirty minutes later Sancho's billiard parlor was attacked. One man, as far as anyone can say for sure. He came in tossing smoke grenades to rout the customers. One of our soldiers tried to stop him."

"And?"

"That's number five we lost."

"I told that goddamned Sancho to forget about the drugs," Albano said.

"It wasn't the Colombians, Miguel. A gringo, tall, no clear description from the witnesses."

"They sent for a mechanic."

"Escobar would rather kiss a donkey's ass in public than do business with a gringo. You know that as well as I do."

"So? What are you telling me, Francisco?"

"We have trouble at a time when we can least afford it. Someone is attacking us, Miguel. They want to snatch our victory away before we have a chance to taste it."

"Who, then?"

Obregon considered the question, but finally shook his head in frustration. "I don't know, Miguel."

"So find out! In two days we proceed, regardless of the risk. There might not be another chance."

"Perhaps we should delay the exercise until—"

"There *is* no exercise, Francisco. This is war. We have been waiting for this moment all our lives. A major blow against the Yankee mainland, one that will demand attention from the world. The plan proceeds on schedule. Do you understand?"

Obregon nodded grudgingly. He understood, all right, and one day soon that condescending tone would land Albano in a world of trouble. When the time came, he would

teach Miguel that even sons of lowly peasants had their
pride . . . and their revenge.

"I have begun inquiries. We will learn the names, Miguel.
They will be punished for their insolence."

"Then we have nothing more to say."

Albano turned and started back across the beach, in the
direction of the parking lot. Francisco Obregon was glad to
be alone once more, to organize his thoughts.

He meant to keep his word, but not from any sense of
loyalty to Miguel Albano. Obregon had invested his life in
the struggle for Puerto Rican independence, and he
wouldn't watch his dreams go up in smoke without a fight.

But first, before he sought revenge, it was required that
he identify his enemies. And that, he knew, could be a
problem.

As it happened, he had no idea of where to start, but he
would think of something. Soon.

Their time was running short, and he had none at all to
waste.

Rio Piedras, Puerto Rico
0750 hours

THE PAST NIGHT'S RAIDS were merely warm-up exercises for
the Executioner. It was enough to make his presence felt,
alert the leaders of the ANI to opposition in the neighborhood. It would be going overboard to launch an all-out blitz
and try to bring the private army down before he could
identify their ultimate objective.

Urgency was one thing; reckless haste was something else.

Until they knew exactly what the ANI was planning for
their masterstroke. It would be hazardous to drive the rebels too far underground. Instead, he hoped to keep them
guessing, maybe even draw them out a bit in self-defense. If

the diversion worked, it would disrupt their plans while simultaneously granting Rafael Encizo time to uncover the plan that Jaime Sanchez had been hoping to expose the night he died.

He drove the Porsche 928 this morning, south from San Juan proper to nearby Rio Piedras. The sports car's Bosch K-Jetronic fuel-injected V-8 engine could manage one hundred forty-five miles per hour at need, but Bolan held it to a sedate sixty-five on the short trip south. The last thing on his mind was playing tag with Puerto Rican traffic cops, especially with the hardware resting in a military duffel bag behind his seat.

The Walther WA-2000 sniper rifle was a unique weapon, thirty-six inches overall, weighing in at fifteen pounds without its telescopic sight or six rounds of 300 Winchester Magnum ammunition. The rifle's bullpup design reduced length, and the twenty-six-inch barrel was clamped at each end in a state-of-the-art frame, fluted longitudinally to provide more cooling area in combat. The Walther technicians had gone with a gas-operated firing mechanism to minimize recoil and eliminate the time wasted on bolt manipulation between shots. Bolan had replaced the standard Schmidt & Bender 10-power sight with his favorite Leupold 20-power to complete the package, sighting the Walther in at Stony Man before he'd left with Jack Grimaldi for San Juan.

It was a lethal package, and he would be needing it today.

His target was a rural safehouse operated by the ANI for members on the run. According to Miranda Flores, there were six or seven guns in residence at any given time, including two who hung around the place full-time, combining maintenance and physical security.

He would require an on-site visual reconnaissance to nail it down, and he was drawing closer by the moment, veering off the southbound highway on a narrow access road that wound into the wooded hills outside Rio Piedras. Navigating on his information from Flores, Bolan knew when it was time to pull off in a roadside picnic area and change into his camouflage fatigues. He took the Walther in its duffel bag and locked the Porsche. A few moments later the forest had enveloped him. He was invisible.

The warrior felt at home.

In six minutes he reached his destination. Trees were thick along the steep crest of a hill that overlooked the safe-house, giving him a panoramic view of both the house and its surrounding property. One of the residents was packing off a chain-link fence that circled the perimeter, a shotgun tucked beneath his arm.

The house was small, perhaps three bedrooms. He imagined trigger-happy radicals penned up inside, cramped for space, afraid to step outside while the police were searching for them high and low. It would be claustrophobic with a dozen gunmen, tense but tolerable if the number was reduced by half. In any case, the comfort of the occupants wasn't his personal concern.

He knelt beside the duffel bag, unzipped it and lifted out the Walther sniping piece. Its magazine was locked and loaded, with several spares inside the bag. He worked the bolt to chamber a live one, raised the weapon to his shoulder and scanned through the Leupold's lens.

A 20-power scope works miracles at ranges of a thousand yards and up. Inside a hundred, where the Executioner was stationed now, he could have counted hairs inside the walking sentry's nose. Instead, he gave the man a quick once-over, shifting to the house and checking out each window in its turn.

Two had the draperies pulled tight, a washout in the sniper's view, unless he tried a shot at night, with lights inside the house to cast a silhouette against the blinds. No luck in daylight, and he concentrated on the last two windows he could see. The curtains were open, giving him a glimpse inside the house.

The living room was sparsely furnished, with a sofa, low-slung coffee table and some mismatched chairs. Whoever did the shopping had apparently been drawn to flea markets or garage sales, opting for economy in lieu of style. The plaster walls were bare as far as he could see, except for the obligatory crucifix above the sagging couch.

The other window let him peer inside a kitchen that would never pass for clean. He couldn't see the sink, but something brown and crusty occupied a skillet on the ancient, grease-stained stove. The small refrigerator had been white at one time, but a layer of caked-on grime had turned it beige, with handprints marked by smudges up and down its length.

One gunner was in the kitchen, his head and shoulders moving past the window, out of sight, in the direction of the living room. A small correction let the Executioner track the human target on to where a second man had settled on the couch.

And that made three.

If there were more around the property somewhere, he would remain alert to signs of movement, try to smoke them out if there was time. Right now Bolan was ready to proceed with what he had.

It was a toss-up between taking the outside sentry first or saving him for later. His first shot would alert all comers, giving those inside the house a chance to dive for cover if he dropped the yard man first. Conversely, if he left the sentry on his feet while scoping targets in the living room, there was a chance of accurate return fire.

But the yard man had a twenty-inch shotgun, no threat at all beyond a hundred yards, and barely accurate at half that range.

The house was it, then, while he had the chance.

He lined up on the couch, his Leupold 20-power's eyepiece filled with a pair of beady eyes, a flattened nose, mustache and lips that rippled when their owner spoke. It might have helped his cause to eavesdrop, but he didn't have the time or necessary hardware for the job. Besides, the Executioner had come to make a point.

His index finger curled around the Walther's trigger, taking up the slack. A gentle squeeze, and the rifle kicked against his shoulder, sending 220 grains of death downrange at a speed of 2,680 feet per second. Impact was explosive with the Silvertip Super-X projectile, a shower of glass followed by implosion of the porcine features.

There was no time to waste as Bolan pivoted to bring his secondary target under fire. The second gunner in the living room was gaping at his comrade, trying to decipher what had happened to the dead man's face. He turned and seemed to stare at Bolan through the shattered window, opening his mouth as if to shout a warning to the dead.

Round two bored in between those open lips and mushroomed on impact, unleashing some 2,900 foot-pounds of destructive energy. The gunner's skull was vaporized above the jawline, but his almost-headless body managed to remain erect for several heartbeats, pumping crimson, finally slumping backward to the floor.

It was the sentry's turn, and he was on the move as Bolan swung around to track him. It was doubtful that he could have seen the Walther's muzzle-flash by daylight, but he still squeezed off a blast in the direction of the trees, his buckshot scattering far and wide before it ever reached the target zone.

A running target made things dicey with a 20-power scope, but it wasn't the first time the warrior had been forced to press his luck. His third round drilled between the runner's shoulder blades and punched him over on his face, an awkward somersault that ended with his body lying twisted on the grass. A tremor shook his limbs, but it was death intruding on the flesh and not a sign of stubborn life.

He waited for a full two minutes after that, alert for any sign or sound of movement from the house. If there were other troops inside, they had decided that discretion was the better part of valor, lying low and waiting for their enemy to slip away. He finally obliged them, knowing it would be a risky waste of time to search the house.

San Juan was waiting for him, and the Executioner had work to do.

MIRANDA FLORES WONDERED what she might be getting into with the tall American who called himself Belasko. He was definitely not an orthodox investigator—didn't seem like any cop whom she had ever known, in fact—but there was more to it than that. Flores's own work called for sacrifices, compromises to complete distasteful jobs. She was involved in such a situation now, but she had never killed a man herself or helped to take a life.

Until last night.

Her guided tour with Belasko had been spotting targets, plain and simple. She had known that when the radio alarm went off on Thursday morning, offering breathless news accounts of violence in the city overnight. A trucking company had burned with four men trapped inside, and unknown gunmen had attacked a pool hall on the other side of

Old San Juan, igniting smoke bombs, shooting one man dead when he resisted the attack.

Both target sites had been included on Flores's list of places owned or frequented by members of the ANI. That blood was on her hands, as if she had gone out and pulled the trigger herself.

And what had she expected, after all? Before she'd left Belasko Wednesday night, she understood that he wasn't a law-enforcement "troubleshooter" in the ordinary sense. He wouldn't solve a mystery so much as blow the case wide open, let the chips fall where they may.

A part of her reaction to the morning's news was guilt. She hadn't been entirely honest with Belasko, spooning out the information when he asked but never hinting that her source might be more intimate than paid informants on the street. He wouldn't know about her personal involvement with the ANI unless her supervisor let it slip. And even *he* wasn't yet privy to the full extent of where Flores's search for evidence had led her.

Within the past six weeks, Miranda Flores had been intimate on eight or nine occasions with Francisco Obregon. She eavesdropped on his conversations when she got the chance and tailed him to his meetings when the opportunity arose. Thus far Obregon was content to treat her like a piece of pretty furniture—the Latin lover's patented approach to females—and he didn't seem to doubt her slavish loyalty.

When he began to doubt, her days as an effective undercover agent would be numbered. So, too, would the days remaining in her life.

She could have tried to clue Belasko in, a hint perhaps, but there was something in the man's demeanor that restrained her. Was she frightened he might judge her conduct, view her with a jaundiced eye? Or was it the embarrassment and shame within herself, reflected in his own uncompromising view of life?

Whatever, she had kept the nuggets to herself, for what it might be worth. From all appearances, there was an element of risk involved in hanging out with Obregon if he was wearing Mike Belasko's bull's-eye on his back. Grenades and automatic weapons seldom managed to discriminate between potential targets in a crowd, and while her training prepared Miranda Flores for a line-of-duty death, she didn't relish the idea of dying with Francisco Obregon.

How would the Bureau brass react if they knew she was bedding Obregon to pick his brain and filing pillow talk in her reports? Informants were encouraged to do everything within their power to collect substantial evidence, but they were usually criminals themselves. Credentialed agents were expected to maintain a different standard in the field, regardless of their circumstances. On the record, narcs didn't use drugs, and Bureau agents always watched a contract killing from the sidelines, taking mental notes for future reference in court. No one in Washington would ever publicly admit the dirt rubbed off.

Reality was something else.

Flores thought she just might tip Belasko off to her reality next time they met . . . if he survived that long. Meanwhile, she would be living with the fact that everything he did—and anything he suffered in the process—was to some degree her personal responsibility.

For holding back.

For taking it this far.

She kept her fingers crossed and said a silent prayer that she would never have to face Francisco Obregon in court.

Perhaps a little troubleshooting was the best way, after all.

U.S. Naval Base, San Juan
0830 hours

"YOU DID ALL RIGHT last night."

Gregorio Ruiz was smiling, chewing bacon as he spoke, and Rafael Encizo found the combination something less than appetizing over breakfast.

"Fucking Yankee jarheads," he replied. "They need a lesson."

Encizo and his companion sat together in a corner of the mess hall by themselves. The breakfast crowd was sparse, the early shift already at their duty stations. There were times when the Cuban could only wonder how the modern military functioned with the changes it had undergone in recent years.

Ruiz, still smiling, said, "I had a look inside your file at personnel, *compadre.*"

It had been expected, but he had to play the part, and Encizo stared back at him with feigned suspicion. "Why?"

"I got my reasons. Just because a guy can fight and *habla Espanol,* it doesn't mean he's one of us, *comprende?*"

"That depends, who's 'us'?"

Ruiz leaned closer, elbows on the table, staring deep into Encizo's eyes. "A group of Puerto Rican patriots who feel the Yankees must be driven from our shores at any cost. Perhaps you feel the same?"

Encizo frowned. "I never really thought about it that way. Growing up in Brooklyn, there were always Anglos looking for a fight, you know? Somebody wants to teach the spic a lesson, see how much he'll take before he runs home crying to his mama. Me, I never ran home crying, but I never thought that much about the politics or anything."

"It's time you started then, amigo. You're in Puerto Rico now. Screw Brooklyn, eh? You're *home.* In San Juan the

Yankees are the strangers, outside looking in. They like to throw their weight around, but one day soon we're going to surprise them. Wait and see."

Encizo paused just long enough to make Ruiz believe that he was weighing options, making up his mind. "I'd like to help," Encizo said at last.

"We just might have a place for you, at that. I'll have to ask, of course. It's not like I'm in charge, you understand, but we just lost one of our people not so long ago. Do you believe in fate, amigo?"

"I'm starting to," Encizo told him, putting on a smile.

And that much was the truth, at least.

Believing didn't cost a thing until you had to put your body on the line.

Washington, D.C.
0745 hours EST

IT WAS EARLY TO BEGIN his working day, but Hal Brognola shunned established hours. If he beat his secretary to the office four days out of five, so be it. He could always dictate correspondence to his tape recorder, scan the files of current cases and reach out by telephone for contacts on the far side of the globe.

And there was always Stony Man, its crew available around the clock in case he wanted updates or advisories on any given problem, day or night.

This morning the big Fed was pondering reports from Florida and Puerto Rico. He had barely slept the previous night, perhaps three hours total, interrupted frequently by dreams that brought him wide awake, mind racing, trying to manipulate the pieces of a puzzle he couldn't yet solve.

There was still so much they didn't know about the Army of National Independence, even with FBI surveillance teams and infiltrators on the job. It seemed to be an outgrowth of the FLN, perhaps a bit more radical, and clearly better situated when it came to penetrating U.S. military installations. When the story broke on that, there would be hell to pay in Washington, but that wasn't Brognola's primary concern. His job was to eliminate the threat before it turned into a national disaster.

Fine.

Except so far he didn't have a clue as to what the heavies had in mind.

The men of Able Team were onto something in Miami; there seemed little doubt of that. The ambush and elimination of their prime informant had the FBI pissed off, but Brognola's connection to the White House had contained the Bureau's natural desire to flood Miami with suits and kick some radical ass. Able seemed to have a lead, as slender as it was, and they would follow it as far as possible before they wrote the whole thing off as hopeless.

Meanwhile, in San Juan the Phoenix Force warriors had established contact and were on their way, from all appearances. God only knew where it would take them, what Encizo might be doing with his new companions at the local Navy post, but the big Fed refrained from second-guessing soldiers on the ground whenever possible. Their reading of the situation would be more immediate, more accurate than his, and he had learned to trust their judgment when the chips were down.

And there was Bolan.

His approach to rattling the ANI was vintage Executioner, a razzle-dazzle that would leave the enemy off balance, wondering exactly where the next punch might be coming from and why. It was a risky business, skating on the thinnest ice you could imagine, but high-stakes gambling was the big guy's stock in trade. If there was anything to learn from rumbling on the streets and breathing down the necks of his assorted enemies, Mack Bolan was the man to find it out.

And having gained that information, he would act.

Oh, yes. Brognola had no doubt of that.

San Juan was in for one hellacious weekend. A part of him was wishing he could be there, while the rest was perfectly content to sit in Washington and watch the storm clouds massing from a distance. Standing next to Bolan on the firing line was one rough way to go, and Brognola would never quite forget the times when he had been there, seen it all and smelled the heady scent of combat for himself.

Next time, perhaps, if he was feeling restless, tired of hanging out among the diplomats and hacks in Wonderland. In case he felt like cutting loose and risking everything on one roll of the dice.

"God keep," he told the silent office, wondering if anybody up there really gave a damn.

His secretary knocked and stuck her head in. "Morning, Chief. Need anything?"

"No, thanks. I'll let you know when I do."

Brognola almost wished he was a praying man with the capacity for shifting ultimate responsibility to God or anyone at all to give himself some breathing room.

Fat chance.

He would be sweating this one out alone, and that was what they paid him for.

Brognola had a hunch that this week he would earn his keep.

CHAPTER EIGHT

The Everglades
Thursday, 1320 hours

Most visitors are startled by their first view of the Everglades. Conditioned by years of exposure to Hollywood
images, they expect a place of brooding shadows, where the
sun never shines, and prehistoric reptiles squirming in the
stagnant muck with fungus sprouting on their scaly hides.

In fact, the fourteen-hundred-square-mile swamp is
mostly open to the sky, so flat that a man mounting a
twelve-foot ladder near Cape Sable might theoretically gaze
for a hundred miles in any direction without sighting a natural point of land higher than his head. One early explorer
called the Everglades a "river of grass," and it remains the
single largest expanse of saw grass on earth. In its autumn
rainy season, the swamp's average depth is a mere nine
inches, sluggish rivers winding in and out among the ham-
mocks—clumps of trees and undergrowth—where the sun
beats down from dawn to dusk.

There *is* another version of the Everglades, however,
closer in appearance to the Gothic version spawned by
Hollywood. Along the swamp coast, including the Ten
Thousand Islands, mangrove thickets grow so dense that
sunlight rarely warms the lower branches or the twisted, in-
terlocking roots. The mangroves trap debris in shallow,
brackish water. Blue-green algae forms a slimy carpet,
topped by layers of silt deposited by storms. Mosquitoes

swarm in spring and summer, breeding in the stagnant pools where parasitic eels and leeches lie in wait for prey. In the past twenty years the alligators have begun to make a comeback.

It is along the coast, among the mangrove swamps, that outlaw paramilitary groups have pitched their tents and practiced making war for more than thirty years. At one point, in the early 1960s, Cuban exiles gathered there with blessings from the CIA and Washington. In later years the troops included "freedom fighters" from Honduras, Guatemala, Chile, Nicaragua—some of them convened with government assistance, some in bald defiance of authority. Along the way there were persistent rumors of communities established by Colombians, rebellious Seminoles, satanic cults and outlaw motorcycle gangs. The ANI had tapped into a long tradition of concealment in the Everglades . . . if they were there at all.

The airboat carried three men easily, with Lyons at the helm. He left the navigation to Blancanales, comparing the crude map prepared by Enrique Dimas with a large-scale survey chart. It wasn't much to go on, even so, but at the moment it was all they had.

Outstanding.

The attack at Woodlawn Park said something for the credibility of their informant—or at least the risk that others saw in Dimas while he was alive—but they still hadn't managed to identify the shooters, checking back at frequent intervals with Metro-Dade for autopsy results and such. Of seven gunners, five had clearly been Hispanic, with the other two uncertain in the absence of ID. Smart money had them down as Cubans, but they couldn't rule out Mexicans, Colombians or Puerto Ricans. In his time Enrique Dimas had been known to drop inform on half the ethnic groups in southern Florida, and that meant enemies enough to go around.

Still, Lyons had no great faith in coincidence. If someone had eliminated Dimas on the day before their meeting, or the day after, he might have shrugged it off as bad luck, chickens coming home to roost. In this case, though, he had a hunch that something—maybe the specific questions Dimas had been asking in the barrio the night before he died—had generated more antagonism than the guy was counting on.

Tough luck and then some if the men who pulled the pin on Dimas were the same ones Able Team had been dispatched to hunt. It would mean wasted time and effort if the ANI had pulled up stakes and moved their secret base camp in the Everglades. They might come up with nothing but a name to chase around Miami while the other leads grew cold.

Luis Camacho.

It had taken all of half an hour to run the name through Stony Man, confirming one such on the roll of Navy personnel assigned to Key West Naval Air Station. Ensign Camacho was in fact a native Puerto Rican, three years in the uniform, expected to re-up and make it a career. He was a helicopter pilot, rated excellent by his superiors, with no apparent politics or attitude that contravened performance on the Navy's terms.

In short, his name could just as easily have been selected on a whim to smear an honest, patriotic fly-boy, as for any solid link to revolutionary actions by the ANI.

And yet . . .

They were loaded for bear, three M-16 A-1s with numbers that would lead the Bureau of Alcohol, Tobacco and Firearms around in circles if they lost one and a snoopy agent ran a trace. Grenades and side arms, fighting knives and camouflage fatigues—the whole nine yards. With a little warpaint on his face, Lyons might have thought that he was back in the Louisiana bayou, playing tag on a survival exercise, instead of skimming toward a real-life, real-death confrontation with his enemies.

"I'd estimate another mile," the Politician warned him, checking out each map in turn.

Lyons drew the airboat's throttle back, decelerating, steering toward a nearby hammock that appeared to offer cover. When he killed the engine, they began to drift a little. Schwarz and Blancanales piled into knee-deep water, helping him negotiate the narrow inlet that would bring them to a tiny cypress cover and keep the airboat safely out of sight. They tied it off, ran down a final check on their equipment and prepared to do the rest on foot.

"I hope we're not just jerking off," the Ironman said.

"If we come up empty," Schwarz answered, "all we've got is wet fatigues and maybe some mosquito bites."

"That's what I mean."

If they were right, of course, the Able Team warriors would be risking much more, but at the moment any risk seemed preferable to marking time and watching as their only lead went up in smoke.

"So keep your fingers crossed," the Politician said.

It couldn't hurt, Lyons thought as he eased into the tepid water, checking out the darker mangrove swamps ahead.

It was a strange sensation, hoping for a contact with your enemy on one hand, knowing that the odds were all against you if a confrontation did go down. How many personnel could they expect to find around a temporary camp, assuming that there was a camp?

He focused on the men in front of him and on the tree line, taking each step as a separate event. At once he wished they were inside the brooding tree line, cloaked in shadow, rather than advancing through the open saw grass with the sun almost directly overhead. A sniper in the trees could mow them down and never break a sweat.

Stop that!

For all intents and purposes, the next mile was the most important of his life.

Lyons only hoped it wouldn't be his last.

THEY HUNG TOGETHER for the first part of their trek, moving in single file, separated by an average thirty feet to make things difficult for snipers. Blancanales had the point, with Schwarz behind him, Lyons bringing up the rear. In fact, it made no difference who went first, but Pol had been the navigator since they left the airboat rental station at Monroe, and he continued in that role once they had left the boat behind.

The sunlit marshes were behind them now, and the brackish water was somewhat deeper, coming almost to his waist. Each step raised swirling clouds of mud, combined with moss and algae to obscure the bottom from Blancanales's view. He tried to concentrate on compass points while watching out for quicksand, faltering each time a hidden object brushed against his legs. Was it a root this time? An eel? A gliding water moccasin? Could he expect the stab of lethal fangs if he took another step?

Blancanales's mind coughed up the stories he had heard of alligators mauling swimmers, drowning some and ripping giant chunks of flesh from others, leaving them for dead. A tabloid nightmare? Was it true that hungry sharks sometimes invaded coastal marshes in their search for prey?

The ancient cypress trees around him stood on roots that arched above the water. They looked like sturdy legs, as if a giant squid had somehow learned to walk on tiptoe. The roots and arching limbs were thick with hanging moss, no brilliant colors in this world of green, gray and brown. The military-style repellent covering his face and hands kept most of the mosquitoes at a distance, but a few were stubborn and refused to be put off. Pol clenched his teeth and let them feed, aware that slapping at insects could produce a sound like pistol shots and warn his enemies of their approach.

If there were any enemies to warn.

The worst scenario, aside from ambush and annihilation, would be simply wasting all this time in the pursuit of nonexistent foes. There was a possibility, however slight, that Dimas had been lying, selling bogus information on the ANI, with his assassination unrelated to the case at hand. Before he wrote the matter off, though, Blancanales meant to have a look and find out for himself.

The trip wire told him they were onto something. It was strung across the narrow creek between two cypress trees, an inch or so above the water's surface. Blancanales might have missed it, but a drifting leaf had snagged against the wire and lodged there, bobbing as the sluggish current tried to pull it free. He gestured for a halt and traced the wire back to its source, a Claymore mine wedged between the fat roots on his left.

Five minutes later, after Gadgets had defused the mine, they cut the trip wire and continued on their way. If nothing else, at least they knew that someone cared enough to booby-trap the channel as a warning or a means of self-defense against surprise attacks. Whatever lay ahead, guerrilla camp or moonshine still, the operators were prepared to kill for privacy.

Ten minutes farther on, they left the major stream and crept into the cypress forest, merging with the shadows there. It cost them time, but they were close enough to smell their adversaries now, a stew pot on the fire and tobacco smoke. Another moment and their ears picked up the sound of voices speaking Spanish.

Contact!

Still, they had to verify that they weren't about to meet a group of Cuban fishermen or smugglers. The Claymore could have been a wild coincidence, though Blancanales didn't buy it for a moment. He was certain when his eyes picked out the sentry in his camou uniform, relaxing on a cypress root and paying less attention to his duties than he should have if he wanted to survive.

"He's mine," Schwarz whispered, gliding out past Blancanales like a swamp wraith with his rifle slung across his back.

The Politician gripped his rifle tighter, finger on the trigger, waiting for the slipup that would cost them their advantage of surprise and praying it would never come.

CLOSING ON THE SENTRY from his blind side, Gadgets drew the Ka-bar fighting knife and held it ready for a killing thrust. He had to take the lookout silently or they were finished. Other troops were close enough for him to hear their voices, though he couldn't see their campsite yet. One shout, much less a gunshot, would bring everybody on the run with weapons blazing.

Schwarz allowed himself a moment to observe the man he meant to kill. The sentry's weapon was a Smith & Wesson M-76 submachine gun, technically obsolete but still deadly in capable hands at any moderate range. It rested in the gunner's lap, his knees drawn up, heels braced against a sturdy cypress root in front of him, his buttocks planted on another while he smoked a cigarette.

So much for discipline.

Schwarz concentrated on his footsteps, careful not to lift his boots for fear of sucking noises, gliding them along the bottom like a skater. The sentry had his eyes fixed on the major channel, fifty yards due north, where boats would come from if they managed to avoid the Claymore farther out. It never crossed his mind that anyone would try a different route, approaching through the cypress grove, and that's what got him killed.

Schwarz slipped a hand across the sentry's nose and mouth, dislodged his cigarette and jerked his head back sharply, throat bared to the combat knife's blade. One slash was all it took, and Gadgets dragged him from his perch, the Smith & Wesson lost, legs thrashing for another moment while the sentry's life bled out into the swamp.

He wedged the body underneath a nearby cypress root and sheathed his knife, unslung the M-16 and flicked off its safety. Lyons and Blancanales were approaching through the swamp, speed and caution running neck and neck.

"I'd say another twenty, thirty yards," he told them, nodding toward the sound of voices and the fragrant smell of wood smoke on the breeze.

"Fan out," Blancanales said. "Say five minutes to position. Wait for me to start the fireworks. When you pick your targets, make it count."

They separated, slogging through the hip-deep water on divergent courses, closing on the enemy. Five minutes later Schwarz was huddled in a mangrove thicket, staring through a screen of hanging vines and Spanish moss across a clearing where two dozen men in paramilitary dress were eating out of Army-surplus mess kits, several of them grouped around the fire. Schwarz brought the rifle to his shoulder, choosing a preliminary target.

Waiting for the signal to begin.

LUIS CAMACHO WAS SICK of the Everglades and bored with the company of his fellow revolutionaries. They were mostly simple men or peasant stock, unlike himself. Their conversation was restricted to the basics: sex and politics, or politics and sex. The politics was limited to slogans he had heard a thousand times before, and he suspected that the sex was mostly fantasy or outright lies.

Unfortunately, mingling with the simple folk was part of working with the ANI. Their revolution was presented to the media and public as a grass-roots movement, meaning that they needed peasants in the ranks as cannon fodder. Once the victory had been achieved—soon now, Camacho told himself—there would be certain changes made. The native government of Puerto Rico wouldn't emulate its Yankee puppet predecessor, but neither would it be a radical democracy by any means.

Elite control was necessary at the top to guarantee that things ran smoothly, with appropriate rewards for those who risked the most for victory.

He didn't mind the Fidelistas thinking they were in control. It was a matter of convenience at the moment, beneficial to the ANI without involving any iron-clad promises. If the Havana bureaucrats imagined Puerto Rico would be theirs to play with when the smoke cleared from the coming fight, so be it. History would quickly prove them wrong.

Camacho took another bite of stew, resisting the urge to spit it out on the ground. He refused to consider the ingredients, something one of his compatriots had snared around the camp, no doubt. Another hour, ninety minutes at the most, and he would manufacture some excuse to leave. He would be needed at the base, of course. That always did the trick.

He was about to try another spoonful when something strange and terrifying happened. Twenty feet in front of him a soldier named Arranza pitched face forward from a crouch, his head colliding with the stew pot, ending with his cap and forehead actually resting in the fire. The man didn't move except for spastic twitching in his legs, and the explosive sound of rifle fire explained his leap a heartbeat later.

Instant chaos gripped the camp as automatic weapons opened up along the shaded tree line, firing short precision bursts. Camacho saw another man go down, immediately followed by a third. He tried to spot the snipers, quickly gave it up as fruitless, breaking from his place on the perimeter and sprinting for the stand of cypress where their skiffs and airboats were concealed.

It was unthinkable, a raid against the camp, but he couldn't waste time imagining who might have been responsible. Camacho had to save himself, preserve the secrecy of his affiliation with the Navy. Even if the FBI or CIA had found their hiding place, it didn't mean that all their secrets were revealed. His own position in the master plan, for instance, was unknown to most of those around the campfire. Only two or three among two dozen had the basic information they would need to guess at what he had in mind for D-Day.

Felix Quintana was ten feet in front of him, running back toward the firefight, when a bullet whispered past Camacho's ear and struck the slender man between his eyes. Quintana staggered, sprawling, and Camacho started running in a zigzag pattern, hoping he could throw the snipers off. A few more yards...

He made it, thrashing through a wall of saw grass, losing flesh along the way, not caring as he reached the nearest airboat, fired it up, cast the lines off and started backing clear. He could have waited for another moment, tried to pick up stragglers, but Camacho's urge to save himself was paramount. He brought the helm around and jammed the throttle forward, leaning forward as the giant fan behind him caught the air and he began to skim across the water, echoes of the firefight fading rapidly.

IN THE END they lost at least three gunners to the swamp. Two slipped away on foot, and Lyons knew they might not make it back to where they came from, miles from nowhere, with the ammunition stores depleted and night coming on. The third escapee had been lucky. He'd latched on to an airboat and was miles away before they finished mopping up around the camp.

"I make it twenty-one," Blancanales announced, finishing the body count.

"That's with the sentry?" Schwarz inquired.

"He makes it twenty-two."

The search for ID was a wasted thirty minutes, turning pockets inside out and ripping shirts to check for dog tags, coming up with zip. Whatever else they knew or didn't know about the conduct of guerrilla war, these ANI commandos clearly cherished anonymity.

The lone survivor, while he lasted, was a young man in his twenties, gut shot, dying in considerable pain. When Blancanales tried to question him, he sneered and spit up bloody mucus, answering with curses when they asked for names. Carl Lyons was about to let him have a mercy round between the eyes when fate stepped in and pulled the plug.

"You think Camacho's here?" Schwarz asked.

"One way to check," Lyons said, "is to call the naval air base and have somebody check it out. If he's away, we'll need to check back now and then in the next few hours to find out when he makes it home."

"Assessment." Blancanales sounded tired, a trifle bitter.

"Mixed results," Lyons replied. "We've confirmed the accuracy of our source, but he's no longer with us. None of these guys are about to tell us anything. Camacho is our only chance to find the military link, if he's alive."

"It almost makes me hope he got away," the Politician said.

"Almost?"

"It cuts both ways. If he's alive, this kind of bash might trigger a reaction that we can't anticipate—or maybe drive him underground. And if he's here somewhere—" the Politician scanned the littered killing ground "—how many comrades does he have in uniform?"

"One thing," Schwarz said. "If he was counting on this crew for any kind of major play, they've been rained out."

"That's something," Blancanales granted.

"Damn, we should have thought about their transportation," Lyons muttered. He had finished off the skiffs and airboats that remained, but he resented letting any of the enemy slip through.

"Next time," Blancanales said.

"If there is a next time."

"Right. That's what I meant to say."

"We'd better split," Lyons said, "before somebody rings the dinner bell."

And so they did, a wet hike to the airboat, winging on from there to race the smell of death that merged inseparably with the overall aroma of the swamp.

But Lyons was wondering about the ANI and what they did for reinforcements. It was preying on his mind the whole way back, until they stowed their battle gear and dropped the airboat at its dock.

The worst part was he had a feeling they would soon find out.

CHAPTER NINE

Bayamon, Puerto Rico
Thursday, 1520 hours AST

The meeting site lay eight miles west of San Juan proper, on the outskirts of Bayamon. Montoya had selected a warehouse where some of his hardware was stored prior to sale. Police protection was more economical in outlying towns, and Montoya was able to mount a guard of his own without arousing undue suspicion.

In fact, it was the very meeting site that set a worm of doubt to wriggling in the back of Yakov Katzenelenbogen's mind.

The waiting had been bad enough. Presumably Montoya would have tried to check on his connections in Miami, where selected state and federal files had been revised to coincide with Katzenelenbogen's cover story. Barring leaks in Hal Brognola's office, it should hold, but that was still no guarantee of smooth sailing with Montoya or the ANI. A hundred different things could still go wrong at any point in the negotiations, and he had to be prepared for trouble all the way.

McCarter drove the rented Chevrolet sedan, with Katzenelenbogen riding in the shotgun seat. Behind him Calvin James and Gary Manning sat with automatic weapons in their laps, alert to any sign of a surveillance team. It had been clear between San Juan and Bayamon, as far as they could tell, but that was only part of getting through the meet alive.

The worst was yet to come.

They had discussed the different possibilities ahead of time, smoothing out fine points of strategy on the drive from San Juan to Bayamon. The Phoenix Force warriors were prepared to play the cards as they were dealt, however it went down.

Ideally Katz was hoping for a lead from the Montoya camp to his suppliers, something in the nature of an introduction if he promised larger purchases in weeks to come. Conversely, if the set began to fall apart, they might be able to coerce some names or basic information from Montoya in the worst scenario.

If he survived.

The final plan was relatively simple. They had rolled out early for the meet, with time to spare on a reconnaissance of the surrounding area. The warehouse had been situated on a dead-end gravel road, surrounded by trees. Ostensibly its placement kept the operation from becoming a public eyesore, but the layout also served to shield Montoya's business from prying eyes.

And in this case, the security precautions could also work to Katzenelenbogen's advantage.

He was taking out insurance, dropping Calvin James and Gary Manning at a point before they reached the warehouse, leaving them to circle through the woods and come up on the meeting unobserved. That way, if anything went wrong, Katz had a pair of aces up his sleeve.

They made the drop two hundred yards before they reached the warehouse, with McCarter braking to a halt, the Chevy's engine idling. James and Manning took off through the woods in opposite directions, disappearing from view

before they turned and started to run parallel to the unpaved access road.

"Okay," Katz said, "let's do it."

On the floor between his feet, Katz had a metal attaché
case stuffed with hundred-dollar bills. One thousand of
them, on the nose. It was his earnest money, drug loot con-
fiscated from Colombians in southern Florida and cycled
through Justice channels to the treasury at Stony Man.
Montoya was a canny businessman and he demanded cash
up front. With any luck, a hundred large would whet his
appetite and keep him coming back for more.

A vintage Lincoln Continental stood outside the warehouse, polish gleaming underneath a brand-new layer of
dust. A lookout stood nearby, taking advantage of some
shade, and he raised two fingers to his mouth as they approached, emitting a shrill whistle of warning.

On cue a side door of the warehouse opened, and another man emerged. Katz recognized him as one of Montoya's sons from their previous meeting. The young man's
suit was tailored linen. The weapon slung across his shoulder was an H&K MP-5 SD-3 submachine gun, complete
with telescoping butt and factory-installed suppressor on the
muzzle.

"Montoya's loaded for bear," McCarter said.

"As expected," Katz replied. "Remember, nice and easy
does it."

"Did you tell that to the other side?"

"We're all one happy family now."

"You hope."

McCarter parked beside the Lincoln, and they stepped out
into tropic sunshine. Even with the Chevy's air-con-
ditioning, Katz felt the perspiration trickling underneath his
arms. His shirt would be soaked in minutes, and the thought
reminded him of those TV commercials for a leading anti-

perspirant: No matter what, don't ever let them see you sweat.

Too bad.

He took the lead, McCarter on his heels, and waited on the loading dock while each of them in turn was frisked by Montoya's son. In fact, they were clean, a refinement Katz had insisted upon over McCarter's strenuous objections.

If it hit the fan, they would have to do some fancy footwork to survive.

When he was satisfied, Montoya's son stood back and nodded toward the open door. Katz led the way inside and found another of the dealer's children standing in a clutch with three men Katz had never seen before. All four of them were armed, the hardware on display.

Montoya occupied a folding chair behind a table someone had positioned in the center of the warehouse. Despite the curious surroundings, he resembled royalty awaiting the petition of a lowly supplicant.

"My friends," Montoya said, not rising, "please come in and join us. Make yourselves at home."

DESPITE THE OPPRESSIVE humidity, it was dry and dusty in among the trees. Calvin James wiped a sleeve across his forehead, blotting perspiration, and continued on his way. His Uzi submachine gun, weighted by its silencer, was warm and heavy at his side.

James didn't rush, although he felt a driving sense of urgency. He knew that Katzenelenbogen and McCarter would be near the warehouse now, but he couldn't afford to go crashing through the trees like the proverbial bull in a china shop. There might be lookouts posted in the forest, even booby traps, and any premature disclosure of his presence in the area could doom his comrades on the spot.

Still, he was making decent time and hoped that Manning would be keeping pace on his side of the road. Ideally they would reach the warehouse more or less together, coming in from different angles, cutting off retreat in case Montoya's people tried to break and run.

But that would be the worst scenario, he realized. A sudden flight would mean there had been trouble at the meeting, with Katz and McCarter on the spot without a gun between them. James dismissed the haunting image from his mind and concentrated on the game trail he was following, one foot behind the other, taking care.

He spied the warehouse moments later as he came through the trees and drew closer to the clearing where the gravel access road became a kind of giant cul-de-sac. He saw that there was room enough for trucks to turn around and back up to the loading dock. There were no eighteen-wheelers on the scene today, however, just a Lincoln and the Chevy driven by McCarter to the meet.

One sentry lounged on the loading dock; none other was visible from where James stood. He couldn't catch a glimpse of Manning through the trees, but it wasn't required. Their tasks, although coordinated, were completely independent. Each of them would have to watch out for himself.

James circled to his left along the tree line, staying under cover, watching out for other sentries as the first one disappeared from view. There were windows on the west side of the warehouse, and no one on the roof that he could see. Two jeeps were parked around in back, and he had time to speculate on that and what it meant before he made his move.

Three vehicles for the Montoya team meant—what? How many men? Between the jeeps and Lincoln he would estimate a minimum of eight, perhaps a dozen. Were they all inside the warehouse now? If not, were some positioned in the trees?

James frowned. It was a risk that he would have to take, since he didn't have time to make a thorough recon of the woods.

He squared his shoulders, took a firm grip on the Uzi and emerged from cover, stepping into sunlight from the shadow of the trees. If someone opened fire, assuming that the first rounds didn't take him down, he was prepared to scramble back and go to ground. A shot right now would ruin everything, of course, but he could see no other way to go.

In fact, the woods were silent. No one challenged James as he began to jog in the direction of the warehouse, homing in on a metal ladder fastened to a corner of the eastward-facing wall. Perhaps the jeeps were always parked there, a convenience for the regular warehouse crew. They might have no relation to the meet.

He took one more glance around before he nimbly scaled the ladder, leading with the Uzi as he reached the broad, flat roof. He was alone, no snipers crouching under cover of the bulky air conditioner, a row of skylights beaming sunshine to the massive storage space below his feet.

He moved on tiptoe, taking care to make no sound that would betray his presence to the men inside. The nearest skylight was positioned twenty feet from where he stood, and James crept in that direction, hoping for a glimpse of Katz, McCarter and the rest.

No luck.

On hands and knees, he moved in the direction of the second skylight. This one gave a bird's-eye view of several men, Katz and McCarter among them. Four of the others held weapons in attitudes of casual readiness. The center of attention was a portly, balding man who sat behind a folding card table, meaty hands clasped in front of him.

Montoya.

James stretched out prone and kept his eyes fixed on the grim tableaux.

For now, the only thing that he could do was watch and wait.

JOSÉ MONTOYA WAS a businessman. His primary consideration was the profit he could earn on any given deal. Distractions cost him time and money, two things he could definitely not afford to lose. Unfortunately for his profit margin, though, Montoya had his orders, and they couldn't be ignored.

It had been necessary for him to discuss the meeting with his contacts in the ANI. How else could he obtain the military hardware that his newest customers desired? It was a simple matter, normally—a phone call or a meeting to arrange the shipment, maybe a delay if certain items were not readily available. This time, however . . .

They were getting paranoid, these revolutionaries. He had seen it all before, the way religion, politics or sex corrupted men and turned their minds around. When anyone became obsessive on a given subject, he was lost. It clouded logic, killed the appetite and interrupted sleep.

Worse yet, it interfered with business.

He had done his best to put the young men off, explaining that he had no talent for interrogation. Never mind, they told him, they would send an expert to conduct the questioning. Montoya's job was simply to arrange the time and place, as if he were a hunter laying out a snare.

Where were the "experts" when he needed them? Somewhere outside, where they wouldn't be seen. Montoya had to set things up before they could commence their dirty work.

"You brought the money." He was staring at the metal attaché case carried by the older, one-armed man. At least there was a profit to be made from this day's work.

"Right here." His would-be customer set the case in front of Montoya, its weight settling on the card table with a solid thump. "The merchandise?"

"Of course." Montoya offered a limp-wristed wave toward some crates stacked behind him. The arms and munitions were here, for all the good it would do his visitors. "But first..."

The one-armed man appeared to understand, as if he were accustomed to this kind of deal. He opened up the case, his good hand clearing one latch, then the other, throwing back the lid. Montoya saw the hundred-dollar bills in tidy stacks and rows. It was a sight to warm the heart.

"If you don't mind..."

The one-armed man was moving toward the stack of crates that held his merchandise. Montoya felt a tightening around his heart and knew that it was time to cut things short. He flicked a glance in the direction of his son and saw four automatic weapons rise as one.

"Unfortunately that will not be possible," Montoya said. "There are some questions you must answer for my peace of mind."

OUTSIDE THE WAREHOUSE Gary Manning held his position and waited, covering the sentry on the loading dock. The Uzi was a deadweight in his hands, his face and torso bathed in perspiration from the cloying tropic heat. A fly had found him and was buzzing stubbornly around his head, but Manning let it go, intent on covering the warehouse.

They hadn't been able to arrange a signal in advance, since Katzenelenbogen and McCarter would be out of sight and they had traveled to the meet unarmed. Likewise, it would have been too hazardous for either one of them to wear a wire, so Manning couldn't eavesdrop on the conversation to pick up on verbal threats or warnings from the enemy. He had to play it by ear and hope that any choice he made wouldn't react against his comrades on the firing line.

He heard the new arrivals coming well before he saw them. They were careless, plodding through the trees some twenty yards to Manning's right as if they were expected and discretion was a waste of time. He counted four as they emerged from cover, and moved toward the warehouse. Each of them was casually dressed, the emphasis on denim, rumpled khaki, well-worn hiking shoes.

And each of them was armed.

One man toted an automatic rifle, while the other three wore pistols on their belts. The sentry saw them coming, raised a hand in greeting and smiled. If they were late, it didn't seem to bother anyone.

Or was their tardy entrance prearranged?

The Phoenix Force warrior had to make a choice. He could allow the four to go inside or stop them. There was a risk involved in either case, since he couldn't surmise the new arrivals' motives. If he took them out, would he be saving Katzenelenbogen and McCarter from a deadly ambush or disrupting a productive meet?

In fact, the choice was taken out of Manning's hands a heartbeat later when the sound of automatic fire erupted from the warehouse roof. That made it Calvin James, and there was nothing he could do but join the party now.

The sentry and his four companions froze, all staring up at the warehouse roof, hands clenched around their weapons. Manning recognized an opportunity when it was handed to him, and he wasted no more time.

The sentry on the loading dock was closest to the door, and Manning hit him with a burst across the chest. His target slumped back against the wall and dropped to a seated posture, leaving crimson tracks behind him all the way to the floor.

At once the new arrivals scattered, seeking cover, two of them behind the Lincoln Continental, one behind the Chevy. The fourth kept going, sprinting for a corner of the warehouse that would leave him safe from Manning's line of fire.

He almost made it.

The big Canadian swung the Uzi to his left and triggered a burst that drilled his moving target in the back. Momentum kept the runner going for a few more paces, gravity asserting its command as dying muscles failed. The dead man fell facedown and lay unmoving on the gravel, like a cast-off mannequin.

The gunner with the autorifle had a fix on Manning now. He popped up from behind the Lincoln, laying down a burst of fire that missed by several feet. But it was close enough to make the Phoenix Force warrior shift as the rifleman ducked out of sight, anticipating movement, ready when the shooter popped up in a new position, near the Continental's trunk.

The Uzi shuddered in his hands, a short burst reaching out to close the gap between a marksman and his target. Forty feet away the rifleman lurched backward and sprawled against the Chevrolet, a last burst from his rifle winging off at treetop height. His denim shirt was stained deep violet from the fresh blood soaking through, and then he dropped from sight.

Three down, and two remaining in the contest.

Manning's adversaries did their best to pin him down, but it was difficult from their position, trapped behind the cars with only handguns to return his fire. The second man behind the Lincoln went for his companion's rifle, but it cost him dearly. Rising to his feet, the weapon in his hands, he never got the chance to fire before a burst of parabellum manglers knocked him off his feet.

And that left one.

The gunner must have understood that he was all alone. Who knew what images flashed through his mind—exploding cars and lakes of burning gasoline, perhaps—but something made him break from cover, dodging toward the trees. He squeezed off two quick shots, then his luck ran out as Manning overtook him with a rising zigzag burst that cut across his legs, whipped back to drill his chest and throat before he fell.

Manning stepped from cover, reloading on the move, homing in on the muffled sounds of combat from inside the warehouse.

The others needed him, and he was on his way.

CALVIN JAMES HADN'T BEEN certain what was happening. He saw Katz freeze before he reached the crates—presumably their stash of stolen hardware—and a strange look crossed McCarter's face. The four men to his left had raised their weapons, threatening, but no one had fired yet. The fat man at the table spread his hands and spoke, as if explaining some unpleasant fact of life to children.

Was he looking at a rip-off in the making? Were they haggling about the price? If Katz intended to debate the matter, it would ruin everything and place their lives in deadly jeopardy.

He cursed the distance and the pane of glass that kept their words from reaching him. If he had some idea of what was going on . . .

McCarter saved it for him, waiting for the nearest gunner on his right to step in close, as if to prod the former SAS commando with his Ingram subgun. The Briton wouldn't stand for not having any of it. James saw him drive an elbow hard into the gunman's face, his free hand locked around the Ingram, claiming it for himself with simple leverage. A backhand with the little submachine gun left his adversary short of teeth, and then the Briton swung around to face the others, who were suddenly aware of danger in their midst.

James squeezed the trigger on his Uzi, blasting out three-quarters of the skylight with a burst that took the gunners by surprise. At once a blast of gunfire from the parking lot below him reached James like an echo—Gary Manning jumping in with everything he had.

But where was all the other gunfire coming from? At last count there had only been one shooter on the warehouse loading dock.

James concentrated on the task at hand, saw Katzenelenbogen leaping for the cover of some wooden crates as bullets winged in his direction, gouging divots in the concrete floor. The fat man struggled to his feet, a shiny pistol filling one hand. James had a choice to make. He knew that Katz would want to grill Montoya, but he couldn't let the man cut loose and nail McCarter from his blind side.

Compromising in a heartbeat, James hit Montoya with a short burst from the Uzi, bullets ripping through his arm and shoulder, forcing him to drop his weapon as he toppled over on his side. The wound might yet prove fatal, but he wouldn't die immediately.

Meanwhile, James had other fish to fry.

MCCARTER SAW HIS CHANCE as the nearest gunner stepped close, a cruel grin on his swarthy face. The Ingram MAC-10 in his fist stretched out to prod McCarter's ribs, and that was all it took.

He went inside the move and grabbed the Ingram with his left hand, swung the right around and snapped his elbow square into his adversary's face. The gunner's nose produced a satisfying crack as it collapsed, limp fingers giving up their purchase on the Ingram for a crucial instant. Now he had it, pivoting, the stubby weapon an extension of his fist. Teeth shattered as he put his weight behind the blow and watched his target drop.

The giant skylight overhead exploded with a burst of automatic fire, glass raining down and shattering on contact with the floor. McCarter caught a glimpse of Calvin James, saw Katz as he leaped headlong toward the nearest stack of crates for cover, bullets chipping concrete at his heels.

McCarter knew the Ingram's rate of fire. Its thirty rounds of ammunition could be wasted in a second and a half unless he kept his wits about him, exercising discipline, and he had no spare magazines at hand. Three gunners were on their feet, one firing after Katz. And Montoya had some kind of nickel-plated weapon in his hand, prepared to fire.

James solved the latter problem with a bird's-eye burst that dropped Montoya on his side, a wounded walrus thrashing in his own fresh blood. McCarter used a 6-round burst to nail the gunner moving after Katz, his parabellum shockers ripping through the target's rib cage, spinning him before he fell.

The other two were blasting at the Briton now with more enthusiasm than precision. Leaping to his left, McCarter hit the concrete floor with force enough to empty his lungs, but he didn't release the Ingram. Both hands locked around the weapon, he fired three measured bursts.

One of his adversaries, brandishing a riot shotgun, staggered as the parabellum rounds punched through his chest. Already dying on his feet, the gunner managed one more blast, but it was well off target, riddling José Montoya with a dozen buckshot pellets as he wallowed on the floor.

The second gunner also went down firing, hot rounds from his submachine gun streaming toward the open skylight as he fell. James responded with an angry burst that made the dying gunner dance before his legs gave out and dropped him sprawling on his back.

And that left one.

The soldier whom McCarter had disarmed was on his hands and knees. He shook himself, blood spraying from his shattered face. He struggled to his feet, required a moment to correct his balance, finally reaching back to drag a pistol out from underneath his shirt.

McCarter had him covered with the Ingram, and he knew that James was also watching from the skylight. If they had any hope of questioning survivors, it resided with the man who stood before him, fresh blood streaming down his face and soaking through his shirt.

"Don't do it!"

If he heard or understood, the gunner didn't care. He raised the pistol, sighting on McCarter from a range of twenty feet, and it was over. The converging streams of automatic fire ripped through him, slammed him backward to the floor. This time there would be no getting up, no second chance.

McCarter glanced around the killing field, saw Katzenelenbogen on his feet and turned to face the door as Gary Manning burst across the threshold.

"Five outside," the Canadian said. "Montoya had four of them waiting in the trees."

McCarter lowered his Ingram. "Bloody hell."

"We won't learn anything from this crowd," Katz declared. "One thing, at least."

"What's that?" McCarter asked.

"We've got the money and the guns," Katz said. "There's no such thing as too much hardware. Let's sort through it and decide what we can use."

So it became a shopping trip, McCarter thought, and it had only cost ten lives.

Before the game was finished, he suspected that would only be a small down payment on the total price.

CHAPTER TEN

Key West Naval Air Station
Thursday, 1720 hours EST

Luis Camacho finished dressing in the hated uniform of the oppressor, staring back at his reflection in the full-length mirror. His hands had stopped trembling, and that was a blessing. It was bad enough that he had run to save himself, but there had been no choice. A necessary sacrifice was one thing; pointless suicide was something else.

He turned back toward the dresser, found the glass of vodka and drained it in one swallow. There'd be nothing for the duty officer to smell, and it would help to steady his nerves. The last thing that he needed at the moment was a careless fuckup on the base to call attention to himself.

Thus far the radio had carried no reports of what had happened in the Everglades that afternoon. It could be days or weeks, Camacho knew, before the dead were found, and in the meantime predators would be at work, erasing any clues to their identity. The skiffs and airboats might be traced, of course, but even so...

Camacho wondered if he was the sole survivor of the raid. It was entirely possible that there were others, maybe somewhere in the swamp, but he assumed the worst. In any case, it was essential that he touch base with Albano first, explaining what had happened, how he'd managed to survive.

But what *had* happened in the Glades beyond the obvious? Perhaps two dozen soldiers had been lost, and he had no idea of whom to blame. The FBI wasn't above eradicating enemies, but Yankee G-men made a fetish of observing the proprieties. They came with legal paperwork and made a point of waiting for their suspects to resist arrest before they opened fire.

The CIA had different rules, of course, but Camacho still had his doubts. Even in the days when Langley waged its secret wars without direct approval from the White House, it had never staged a full-scale massacre on U.S. soil. There was no reason to believe the Company would take such risks today, and that left . . . what?

Camacho thought about the right-wing paramilitary forces active in his homeland, little more than death squads serving the political regime in power and its Yankee puppet masters on the mainland. They had tried to ambush members of the FLN and ANI from time to time, inflicting casualties, but never anything on such a scale as he had witnessed in the Glades that afternoon. Moreover, he was virtually certain that the fascist lackeys weren't organized enough to mount a raid in the United States.

Who, then?

Common sense prevented Camacho from pouring another shot of vodka for himself. He had to think about Albano, find a way to get in touch before it was too late.

Calling from the base would be unthinkable, of course. It might be paranoia, but Camacho knew that phone calls between military installations were registered, and he feared that they might be recorded, as well. He checked his watch, compared it to the digital clock beside his bed to verify the time.

He still had half an hour, give or take, before he was required to be on duty. Slipping off the base again today would be a risk, but it was one that he would have to take. Each moment wasted raised potential problems for the master plan.

Suppose the bodies in the swamp had been found but not reported yet? He had returned the rented airboat to its dock without incident, and the vehicle left no tracks in the swamp. A false name had him covered at the rental agency, and he had paid in cash. There was nothing to link him with the massacre unless he had been seen.

And if he had, what of it? Strangers had run through the murky swampland, automatic weapons hammering, their airboats throwing up mighty wakes of spray. If anyone could pick Luis Camacho from a lineup under those conditions, they deserved to win.

But he wouldn't concede defeat. Not yet.

He had a duty to Miguel Albano and the cause they served. If he was called upon to sacrifice his life another time, so be it. At the moment he was still alive and running, with a job to do.

In preparation for the Day.

Their enemies were confident, and that was good. When men grew overconfident, they made mistakes. The Yankees who controlled his island homeland had already made their share of grievous errors, but the worst was yet to come.

The soldiers who had died that afternoon were best forgotten. Most of them were peasants anyway. Camacho didn't question their devotion to the cause, but they were frequently misguided and naive, believing that the new regime would cast itself in terms of radical democracy, where everyone was equal, every man a king.

Of course, they were mistaken. Government required a dominant elite, men like Albano and himself who had the brains and strength to organize a ruling party. Peasant troops were good for the front line, but they weren't competent to make decisions.

They would learn that lesson soon enough.

But first the Yankees needed a decisive lesson, one that would encourage them to set his homeland free.

That day was coming soon.

But first he had to make that phone call.

And he had to make it now.

San Juan, Puerto Rico
1830 hours AST

THE PICKUP WAS ARRANGED by telephone. Miranda Flores was waiting at the curb outside a small bodega in Condado when Bolan pulled up in his Toyota MR2. She closed the door behind her, looking grim, and they traveled for two blocks before she found her voice.

"You've been a busy boy."

"I've got a job to do," the Executioner replied.

"Same here. I didn't think it was supposed to play like this."

"You're in the middle of a war zone," Bolan said. "There's worse to come."

She forced a bitter smile. "You mean we're not in Kansas anymore?"

"Not even close. Is that a problem?"

"Maybe. Back at the academy they never taught us this guerrilla stuff, you know? It was the Federal Bureau of Investigation, not annihilation."

"Maybe you should take a breather," he suggested. "I can go the distance with your number two."

"There is no number two," Flores answered. "Anyway, I can't drop out. I'm too connected with the case."

"Connected how?"

They covered two more blocks, approaching Avenida Ponce de León, before the woman spoke again. "I'm not just covering the ANI. I've cultivated a relationship with Francisco Obregon, if you can call it that."

The pieces started falling into place for Bolan then—Flores's detailed knowledge of the ANI, the hangouts favored by his adversaries. More to the point, he heard the woman's feelings coming through, a mix of guilt, embarrassment and shame.

"You understand my problem now," she continued. "My supervisor doesn't even know how far it's gone. He doesn't want to know, I promise you. If we were shooting for indictments, I'd be compromised before they finished drawing up the paperwork. Defense attorneys might not make entrapment stick, but they'd play hell with reasonable doubt."

"I don't foresee a trial," Bolan told her.

"That's supposed to make me feel good? If I'd kept my distance, maybe we could make a case in court. We might not need a troubleshooter on the streets."

Mack Bolan knew the old refrain by heart. "If only..." You could chase that ghost in circles until your life ran out, and it would make no difference in the end.

He knew exactly how Flores felt. Nobody had to spell it out for Bolan after all that he had seen and done since he'd begun to wage his private war against the savages. In mortal combat there were times when sex became a weapon, every bit as potent as a rifle or a grenade. The difference lay in preconceived ideas about morality, the sexist double standard that endured from Plymouth Rock to modern-day America. The classic view was crystal clear: a man who used his sex to win advantage in the cloak-and-dagger game was a macho stud, James Bond incarnate; women who pursued a similar approach were sluts, tramps, whores.

So much for logic in the killing grounds.

"You've got a job to do," Bolan said, "and you're doing it. Sometimes the rule book doesn't fit your circumstances, and you let it slide. I'm not about to judge your choices."

"No?" She half turned in her seat to face him. Flores was still frowning, but the expression had altered somewhat, revealing less self-deprecation.

"Judgment's not my purview," Bolan told her. "I'm in the disposal business."

"Are you telling me ends justify the means?"

"Sometimes," he said, "means justify themselves."

"That makes it easy."

"Not at all. We live with our decisions every day."

"So what's the answer?"

"Get on with your life. Do what you have to do and keep your focus. Nobody can make those choices for you. Any second-guessing by the Monday-morning quarterbacks is all beside the point."

"I'd like to cut it loose sometimes."

"That's natural. The point is that you stick it out regardless. That says something in itself."

She was almost smiling now. "Are you a troubleshooter or a counselor?"

"Let's say I've been there, more or less."

"This feeling dirty, does it ever go away?"

"I'll let you know."

"It sounds like both of us could use a break."

He thought about that. It would be easy, right. A little respite from the blood and the brutality.

As if on cue, the pager on his belt began a muted chirping sound, demanding his attention. Bolan switched it off, already scanning the sidewalk for a public telephone.

It would be Katzenelenbogen or Grimaldi. No one else possessed the coded number, and he knew that neither one would try to get in touch on anything but urgent business.

"Saved by the bell," Flores quipped as he pulled into a filling station and parked near the phone booth.

"No," the Executioner replied. "Not even close."

SITTING IN HIS CAR outside a nightclub south of Fortaleza Street, Miguel Albano brooded over the disasters of the past twelve hours. First the raids against his people in San Juan and the surrounding towns. Then came the call from Florida, Luis Camacho on the line, reporting the fiasco in the Everglades. Two dozen of their soldiers were dead, and he had no idea of whom to blame. Now it was Obregon and the Montoya business, one more in a series of defeats that he could never have predicted.

What the hell was happening?

Albano didn't wish to meet with Obregon tonight, but there had been no choice. Their great day was approaching swiftly, and Obregon had a central role. Miguel could spare the time to placate him, if necessary, and he also hoped to find out more about the incident in Bayamon. Their conversation on the telephone had necessarily been cryptic, both men conscious of the risks involved. Perhaps when they were face-to-face...

Albano had been cautious driving from the naval base, allowing extra time to make sure there was no one on his tail. The nightclub was Obregon's choice, but he had checked it out, three times around the block before he pulled into the lot and parked his car against the fence where he could watch the driveway and the street beyond. The pistol in his belt was a civilian automatic, as cold as ice, and he could ditch it on the sidewalk if he had to without fear of having it traced back to him.

Five minutes. Obregon was always prompt. He never showed up late or early for a meeting, though Albano knew he had to be taking some sort of precaution to protect himself. A born survivor, that one. He would never let his guard down for an instant, most especially now.

He recognized the man's car before it pulled into the parking lot. Albano was positioned with an empty space on either side of him, and Obregon parked on his right, a short walk to the passenger door, which had been unlocked in advance. Nobody watched them as far as he could tell.

"You weren't followed?"

Miguel didn't answer the question, and Obregon accepted his silent rebuke with a frown. "Explain what happened with Montoya."

"I'm not sure." Obregon scowled and shook his head. "We had the meeting covered, but it fell apart. Ten dead, including fat José and those he brought along."

"The weapons?"

"Some of them were left. A few."

"So now we arm our enemies."

"It should have been a simple thing."

"Should have." The contempt was palpable in Albano's voice. "And who do we suspect?"

"The men who struck at us last night perhaps?"

"That's not an answer, Francisco."

"No. I wonder...."

"What?"

"If we should delay the main event perhaps."

Albano clenched his fists to keep from lashing out at Obregon. He knew the man wasn't a coward. They had joined in raids together that would break a coward's nerve, but he was shaken now. A part of it, Albano realized, was the uncertainty, not knowing where the next assault might come from, who their enemies might be.

"There will be no delays," Albano said at last, when he could trust himself to speak. "We have our chance, and it might never come again. To throw it all away is a betrayal of our homeland and ourselves."

Obregon's face was solemn in the semidarkness of the car. His eyes were pools of shadow as he turned away, scanning the lot and the sidewalk in search of answers, an argument that might persuade Albano to change his mind.

"So many soldiers gone."

"More than you know."

Albano briefed him on the news from Florida. He watched his companion's face go blank with shock, a trace of sadness creeping in before the anger blanked out everything.

"And still—"

"No damned delays! We go on Saturday or not at all."

"If you're mistaken . . ."

"No mistakes. Arrival is confirmed. The signals pass across my desk. It would require a special order from the Pentagon to stop us now."

"All right, Miguel."

"You'll have our people ready?"

"Yes."

"No matter what."

"You have my word, Miguel."

"And find out who these bastards are."

"I'm working on it."

"Work harder. I want them to pay for what they've done." He turned away from Obregon, as if speaking to himself. "I want everyone to pay."

The dome light flared briefly as Obregon let himself out of the car. After another moment, he pulled away, leaving Albano alone in the nightclub's parking lot.

Delay. Postpone. Put off.

It was the same old litany of failure that had dogged Albano from his childhood. Every time he felt some triumph was within his grasp, there was a nagging voice of "reason" in his ear, explaining why he ought to let the moment pass him by. Failure was built into the equation for a Puerto Rican in an Anglo-dominated world. The military had a different way of beating down "minorities"—no matter that Albano was a member of the born-and-bred majority in Puerto Rico—but it all came out the same.

Albano knew the rules and he pretended to observe them when it served his purpose, but a day was coming when the old rules would be swept away. When that day came—on Saturday, in fact—the Yankees would be in for a surprise.

And it would be Albano's pleasure to deliver that surprise in person.

Even if it wound up costing him his life.

BOLAN DROPPED Miranda Flores on a narrow residential street in Miramar, apartment houses stacked on either side. She didn't give him the exact address, and Bolan didn't ask. He left her standing on the sidewalk in the middle of the block, and she hadn't moved by the time he turned the corner, rolling out of sight.

The call had been from Jack Grimaldi, speaking on behalf of Katz and Phoenix Force. There had been problems at the meeting with Montoya, but they didn't talk about the details on the telephone. Instead, he drove from Miramar to the hotel where Katz and his commandos had their separate rooms.

And thought about Miranda all the way.

Grimaldi waited for him in the lobby, poring over something in a Spanish-language magazine as if he were a native. Catching Bolan's eye, he winked, put down the magazine and fell in step beside him, moving toward the elevator.

"Clear?"

"So far," Grimaldi said.

"What was the magazine about?"

"Some kind of travelogue, I think. I like the shots of women at the seashore. *Muy bonita.*"

"So you're broadening your mind."

"No pun intended, right."

They stood and waited for the elevator, both of them with jackets open just in case. The car arrived and Bolan stepped inside, Grimaldi on his heels. If anyone was watching them, it didn't show.

Grimaldi punched a button for the fourth floor, and they made the trip in silence. Anything could happen when the doors slid open, though it seemed unlikely that their adversaries could have tracked them here, much less set up an ambush while Grimaldi staked the lobby out.

In fact, they had the hallway to themselves. Grimaldi pointed to the left and led the way to number 413. McCarter answered to Grimaldi's knock and ushered them inside.

Relief washed over Bolan as he saw all four of them alive and well. Encizo was conspicuous by his absence, but the other Phoenix Force warriors seemed fit enough despite their recent brush with sudden death. Katz came to greet him, shaking hands left-handed.

"What went down?"

"They saw us coming," the Israeli reported. "Four guns inside, and others waiting in the trees. We'd still be out there if it hadn't been for Cal and Gary."

"Any notion on what might have tipped them off?"

"It wasn't just Montoya," McCarter said. "I'm convinced of that. He didn't have the look."

"He damned sure doesn't have it now," James added.

"We need to double-check with Stony Man," Grimaldi said, "and see if anybody ran your cover through the network."

"I've already been in touch," Katz told him. "They're looking at it now. And if the cover's firm?"

"Let's say it satisfied Montoya," Manning offered, "but it wasn't good enough for his suppliers."

"Meaning someone in the ANI?"

"Yeah, if that's where he's been getting hardware."

"We've checked the merchandise," McCarter said. "It's GI all the way."

"And you retrieved it?" Bolan asked.

"The stuff that we could use," James told him. "Fixed the rest. Whoever tries to use it will be in for a surprise."

"At least you made some waves," Grimaldi pointed out.

"You've made a few yourself," Katz answered, including Bolan in the remark. "Any word on whatever it is they've been planning?"

"No dice. I think we need to turn the heat up while we've got the chance, before they get their act together. You were lucky with Montoya. If they'd sent a few more guns or handled it a little differently, I might not have the pleasure of your company right now."

"You won't get rid of us that easy," James replied, all smiles.

"What did you have in mind for turning up the heat?" Katz asked.

"The target's less important than its impact on the ANI. I want them rattled, nervous. Nervous men make more mistakes."

"We don't know what they're planning for the big punch yet," McCarter said. "If we get too close, they might call it off."

"I'm betting on the opposite effect," Bolan said. "If they're really that gung ho for revolution, they won't call it off. We might even get lucky, see them move it up."

"Some luck," Manning put in, "if we don't know what it is or where and when they mean to pull it off."

"I'm open to suggestions if you've got another plan."

"Let's stick with what we've got," Katz suggested. "If we were turning up the heat, where would you start?"

Bolan thought about it for a moment, scanning the faces around him, running the list of potential targets in his mind. It made no difference, really, from the standpoint of strategic value. Agitation was the key.

"Albano?" James suggested.

Bolan shook his head. "Not yet. Whatever's going down he's in the middle of it. If we drop him now, it might just drive them underground. We need to wrap this up."

"What, then?" Grimaldi asked.

The warrior frowned, deep in thought, then he smiled.

"I just might have a spot in mind."

CHAPTER ELEVEN

Catano, Puerto Rico
Thursday, 2330 hours

The Tiburon Hotel had been abandoned by its owners in September 1978, a casualty of rampant inflation and the stubborn refusal of Yankee tourists to stay overnight in a coastal town seven miles west of San Juan. Condemned in 1983, the seven-story hulk had sold to native buyers eight months later, changing hands at least a dozen times before it was acquired by front men for the ANI. The revolutionaries had no plans to open up the Tiburon again, but it wasn't deserted, either.

From his early tour with Miranda Flores, Bolan knew the Tiburon Hotel was used by Puerto Rican nationalists as a combination arms dump, safehouse, meeting place and home away from home. Its drab facade was overgrown by weeds and creepers, and the windows were painted black or boarded over to conceal what passed within. The neighborhood was sparsely populated, and the Tiburon's few neighbors had been bribed, persuaded or intimidated to refrain from speaking with police.

The plan, as Bolan spelled it out, was relatively simple. He would take the roof while Grimaldi and the men of Phoenix Force assaulted different floors or cut off retreat at ground level. Any gun bearers were the enemy, and Bolan's commandos were taking no prisoners.

Scorched earth.

If they couldn't precipitate a hasty move by leaders of the ANI, perhaps they could depopulate the ranks and make it harder for the revolutionary band to carry out its aims.

They split the team in two and parked their cars a quarter mile away, to east and west. Grimaldi and McCarter went with Bolan, and James and Manning stayed in the other car with Katz. The Phoenix Force warriors had no shortage of equipment after sorting through Montoya's stash, and they were dressed to kill.

The last two hundred yards were risky, the warriors keeping a sharp lookout for traps, stray dogs and sentries. Bolan left McCarter on the ground floor, then he and Grimaldi scaled the rusted fire escape hand over hand, taking care to keep it quiet on the torturous ascent. Grimaldi stayed behind on the fourth floor while Bolan moved on to the roof, surprised when he arrived and found no guards on duty.

The Executioner was dressed in midnight black, an Uzi submachine gun slung across his shoulder. The Beretta 93-R nestled in its shoulder rig, with the heavy Desert Eagle automatic riding on his hip. The military harness held spare magazines, grenades and a trench knife.

He was ready.

Bolan moved across the broad, flat roof, each step a challenge. In the building's present state, he knew that any careless move might send an echo through the rooms below. Indeed, there was an outside chance the roof itself might buckle underneath his weight, though it appeared secure.

He reached the entrance to the stairwell, built beside an air conditioner long since disabled by exposure, rust and rats. The door was locked, but Bolan didn't bother with a pick. He used his trench knife, gouging at the flimsy wooden frame until the latch came free. A screech of rusty hinges told the world that he was coming . . . but was anybody listening?

There was one way to answer that.

He sheathed the knife, took a firm grip on his Uzi and started down the stairs.

THERE WERE FIRE ESCAPES on two sides of the Tiburon, east and west. Calvin James mounted the rickety ladder facing westward, half expecting the whole contraption to break away at any moment and plunge to the ground. He held the CAR-15 assault rifle in one hand, the stock braced against his hip, while his free hand hovered near the rough, corroded handrail.

Just in case.

Rock-throwing vandals had shattered most of the windows on the Tiburon's first three floors, and they were boarded over now. Beginning on the fourth floor, someone with a can of spray paint had blacked out the remaining panes of glass, working from the inside. Even with the cover and the outer darkness, James watched his step, aware that he was vulnerable to attack each time he passed a window. Anyone could lie in wait behind those blacked-out panes, prepared to fire at any unexpected sound.

He stopped on the fifth floor, one floor below what would have been the penthouse suite in better days. Those days were long behind the Tiburon at this point, though. It had begun life as a tourist trap, then became a hiding place for rebels. Now, within the next few moments, it would be transformed again—into a slaughterhouse.

James checked his watch. Another twenty seconds remained before the numbers clicked and he went into action. Crouching on the fire escape, he glanced down through the rusty latticework and caught a glimpse of Gary Manning two floors down. With Katz and McCarter on the ground floor working upward, they should have the hotel covered.

Unless they ran into an army, found themselves outgunned and got their asses kicked. In which case it would hardly matter what the ANI was planning for the next few days or weeks.

One thing about the dead: they have no burning interest in the daily news.

His waiting time ran out, and James swung the muzzle of his CAR-15 against the nearest blacked-out window. Diving through, he held the carbine ready, cocked and locked, to handle any opposition waiting for him on the other side.

In fact, the musty corridor was empty... for about two seconds flat.

A drowsy-looking gunner stepped into the hallway from a bedroom on the left and three doors down. He had a pistol in his hand, no shirt on, khaki trousers hanging low around his hips and bare feet. He blinked at James for an instant, tried to raise his gun and went down in a heap as half a dozen 5.56 mm tumblers opened up his chest.

The gunfire roused another gunman who had managed to ignore the breaking window. This one had his clothes on when he stepped into the hall, immediately dropping to a combat crouch and leveling a riot shotgun at the stranger who confronted him.

James hit the threadbare carpet as a swarm of buckshot rattled overhead. His adversary pumped the shotgun's action, lining up another shot, but the Phoenix Force warrior got there first, a short burst from his carbine stitching holes in plaster and ripping flesh. The young guerrilla slumped in a lifeless, twitching heap.

Somewhere in front of him, an unseen woman had begun to scream. He hoped she was a noncombatant and resolved to face that problem as it came. In any case, he had to check it out. This was a scorched-earth mission, and he couldn't leave potential enemies alive.

Cursing under his breath, James edged along the hall-way, following the sound of screams.

GRIMALDI FIRED a short burst from his Uzi submachine gun at the doorway where a pair of gunmen crouched. One of them ducked backward while the other stopped a bullet, slammed against the doorframe and clutched at his side. The guy kept firing with a heavy automatic even so, and he was accurate enough to pin Grimaldi down.

At least the first two rooms had been unoccupied, their doors long since lifted off the hinges and removed. Without a place to duck and hide, Grimaldi would have been trapped in the cross fire outside, cut down and riddled in the open corridor.

There were three gunmen that he knew of, two positioned in the next room on his right, while number three was farther down and on Grimaldi's side. Two automatic weapons and a pistol spit rounds into the plaster wall and chewed up the doorframe, winging ricochets around the musty room.

There could be more defenders waiting for him, holding back until they had a decent shot, but numbers were irrelevant as long as one or two could keep Grimaldi down. Unable to retaliate, he was effectively eliminated from the fight.

As Grimaldi stepped into the adjacent bathroom, he watched the open door in case they rushed him. There were no surprise in the Tiburon, with mirror-image rooms, the bathrooms back-to-back. Which meant there just might be another way to flank his enemies.

He chose a point midway between the shower and the toilet and fired a short burst from his Uzi that gouged a fist-size pocket in the plaster. It was deep enough to hold a frag grenade, and Grimaldi removed one from his web belt, slung his SMG and pulled the pin.

Four seconds, five at the outside. No problem, if he got it right the first time out.

He opened his fingers and dropped the safety spoon. One second was gone, and counting, he stuffed the frag grenade inside the plaster pocket. Two down as he swiveled on his heels and bolted for the bathroom door. On three he found a neutral corner and hunched himself into a fetal curl.

The shock wave brought a rain of dust down from the ceiling. Grimaldi was on his feet before the echoes died away, returning to the bathroom, ducking through a six-foot hole the blast had opened up between one bathroom and another.

In the corridor outside, his enemies were shouting back and forth, uncertain what had happened. They were smart enough to recognize a hand-grenade explosion, but they couldn't figure why the Yankee bastard would have set one off inside the room where he was hiding. Had he killed himself by accident? One voice insisted someone check it out; another told him he could do the job himself if he was in a rush.

Grimaldi had the next move charted in his mind before he made it. Striding toward the bedroom door, he palmed another frag grenade and dropped the pin. The Uzi slapped against his right hip as he reached out for the doorknob, numbers running in his mind.

Precision was the key.

He threw the door wide open and saw startled faces just across the hall, one twisted in a mask of pain. He pitched the frag grenade, then brought the Uzi up and raked the doorway with a zigzag burst. He took a quick step backward, out of range, before the second blast sent shrapnel ripping through the walls.

The gunner two doors down was standing in the open when Grimaldi burst into the corridor and caught him with a rising burst. The parabellum firestorm punched his target through a jerky little dance and dropped him facedown on the carpet, leaking crimson into moldy shag.

Grimaldi backtracked to the smoking bedroom on his right, where two bodies lay crumpled on the floor. The gunner he had wounded earlier was dead now, jagged wounds from shrapnel draining blood from his chest and abdomen. The other body had absorbed its share of red-hot metal, and Grimaldi didn't need a second glance to know that the man was dead.

The Stony Man pilot went in search of other prey. He heard the sounds of combat echoing above him and below, reminding him the battle wasn't over yet.

McCarter HAD EXPECTED trouble going in. It stood to reason that the ANI would have at least one sentry posted on the ground floor, stationed to repel intruders.

In fact, there had been three.

They had the entrance covered, two men slouched in ratty chairs, a third positioned on the staircase leading to the second floor. It was a hot night, typical of Puerto Rico in the summer, and the front doors of the Tiburon were standing open to admit a fitful breeze. A welcome cross draft was provided by a window on the far side of the foyer, where the plywood cover had been cast aside.

McCarter took the window and had his targets covered with his M-16 as Katz maneuvered to approach the door. If it was clear, they had decided that the Briton would go first, climb through the window and secure the entryway before Katz made his move. If there was any opposition on the scene, like now, McCarter would begin the process of elimination while Katz provided backup for his play.

He set the M-16 for semiauto fire and sighted on the staircase gunner, judging him most likely to escape and block their path if anything went wrong. The first round had to count, or he might never have a second chance.

He took a shallow breath and held it, stroked the rifle's trigger lightly and held his fix on the target as a 5.56 mm bullet drilled the Puerto Rican gunner's face. The explosive impact hurled the dead man sideways, his shotgun slithering through the sudden gap between his knees. The corpse slid down four steps and landed at the bottom like a limp sack of laundry.

The survivors were immediately on their feet and pivoting to face McCarter, weapons tracking, when an egg-shaped object sailed in through the open double doors and landed at the nearer gunner's feet. The man glanced downward, and McCarter shot him in the chest, the assault rifle's report lost in the sudden flash and thunder of the frag grenade.

One moment he was standing there, a blank look on his face, and then the gunner seemed to come apart. The shock wave threw his sidekick back against the staircase, bleeding from a dozen wounds, but he was still alive and moving when McCarter fired a rapid double punch into his face.

Katz came in through the double doors, McCarter through the window. Gunfire echoed on the floors above them as the others made their entry to the Tiburon Hotel.

They were advancing on the stairs when someone on the floor above unleashed a subgun burst. The shooter couldn't see them yet, but he had gauged the situation well enough to have a fix on what was happening below. One man could hold the stairs indefinitely if he wasn't rooted out, and every wasted moment meant more danger for their comrades on the floors above.

"I've got a stun grenade," McCarter said. "You want to cover me?"

"You're covered."

"Right."

The flash-bang stun grenade was only lethal if it burst directly in the target's face, or if the target had a heart attack from shock. Concussion did the rest, blinding and deafening those on the receiving end of the blast. While McCarter would have preferred a clean kill, at least this way the grenade wouldn't kill him or Katz if he missed his pitch.

"On three!"

McCarter started counting and braced himself, the M-16 tucked underneath his arm. Katz opened up beside him, raking the second-floor landing. The Briton broke out of a standing start, taking the stairs two at a time, his legs driving like pistons. He triggered a burst from his assault rifle, glimpsing movement on the stairs above, a scuttling manshape, running for cover.

The pitch was an overhand lob. McCarter saw the canister loop out of sight, then he was dodging backward, a burst of submachine-gun fire raking the wall near his face.

"Look out!"

He made the last four steps in a desperate leap, the flash and echo pushing him along like a giant hand between his shoulder blades. He hit the floor on hands and knees, sliding several feet before he came to rest.

Above him, in the stairwell, someone had begun to howl in pain. It was a desolate, unearthly sound.

McCarter picked his rifle up and started back to still that wailing voice.

WHEN GARY MANNING BURST in through the blacked-out window on the third floor, he surprised a gunner just emerging from a room immediately on his left. The Puerto

Rican gaped at the Phoenix Force warrior for an instant, then recoiled and darted back into the bedroom, lunging for the weapon he had left behind.

Manning was with him all the way, triggering a blast from his SPAS-12 assault shotgun that punched his target forward, airborne, toes barely skimming the carpet before he collapsed on a filthy, unmade bed.

A naked woman poked her head out of the nearby bathroom, shrieked at what she saw and ducked back out of sight. The big Canadian made a judgment call and let her go, retreating to the corridor where voices rose in a hubbub of fear and confusion.

Manning stepped out to meet them, leveling his shotgun from the waist, confronting four gunners in various stages of undress. Another woman spoke up from the doorway of a bedroom halfway down, but her companion rasped a terse command and she fell silent.

Time to rock.

He cut loose with the SPAS, three blasts in rapid fire, from left to right. The 12-gauge Magnum buckshot rounds unleashed blind havoc in the murky hallway, spraying blood and mutilated tissue wall to wall. Manning surveyed the damage, four assailants down and out, before he put his feet in gear and started pacing off the corridor.

The stairs were twenty yards in front of him, reverberating with the sounds of battle from above and below. Manning drew replacement rounds from the bandolier crossing his chest, thumbing them into the shotgun's loading gate as he moved toward the stairwell. Passing each door on the way, he glanced inside—the frightened woman gaping back at him from one—then kept going. Once he cleared the floor, he would be free to join the others mopping up.

A shot exploded from the doorway on his right, and Manning felt the bullet whisper past his face. He spun in that direction, dropping to a crouch, the SPAS thrust out in front of him to meet his enemy.

The gunner had been hasty with his first shot, jerking it instead of taking time to aim. A second chance would probably have saved him, but the SPAS was blasting at him now, double-aught pellets ripping through flesh, fabric and plaster in a hail of sudden death. The tattered straw man vaulted backward, blown completely off his feet and out of his shoes. He hit the floor flat on his back and remained there, unmoving.

The Phoenix Force warrior turned and checked the hall behind him. No one moved now, but he could hear one of the women sobbing somewhere out of sight.

All done for this floor.

Manning turned again and started down the stairs.

BOLAN CAUGHT the final sixth-floor gunner with a burst that rolled him up and left him stretched out on his side, the shiny automatic pistol inches from his lifeless fingertips. That made four down, and from the racket on the floors below, his fellow teammates were meeting opposition all the way.

He went to join them, breaking for the stairs, reloading his Uzi on the run. The fifth-floor landing reeked of cordite, but Calvin James had already cleared the scene, leaving scattered bodies behind.

The Executioner kept going, feeling an explosion rock the stairs beneath his feet. Grimaldi and James saw him coming, hesitating for a moment on the stairs while Bolan caught up.

"I thought you stopped to make a sandwich," Grimaldi said, putting on a crooked grin.

"They didn't have pastrami," Bolan answered, brushing past the pilot and proceeding down the stairs.

They met a gunner in the stairwell, coming up to greet them with an Ingram submachine gun in his fist. Three guns went off together in the narrow space, converging streams of fire hurling the guerrilla backward in a kind of awkward somersault, head over heels. Even so, a wild burst from his Ingram nearly tagged Grimaldi, a dozen parabellum rounds etching abstract patterns on the wall.

"Too goddamned close," Grimaldi muttered.

They stepped across the fallen gunner's body on the third-floor landing. To their right a shape was coming toward them down the hallway, moving with determined strides. The Executioner was lining up a shot when something familiar tugged at the back of his mind.

"I guess I missed one," Manning said.

"He didn't get too far," Grimaldi replied. "You clear?"

"Two women back there. Neither one is armed."

"I passed one up on five," James said. "Let's book."

"The last two members of their team were mopping up the second floor when they arrived, Bolan leading the way. He came up on the blind side of a shirtless gunner with an M-16, about to fire at Yakov Katzenelenbogen at the far end of the hall. A burst from Bolan's Uzi dropped him where he stood, the rifle trapped beneath him.

Katz turned back to face the sound of gunfire, nodding as he recognized his comrades stepping from the shadows. McCarter emerged from one of the nearby bedrooms a moment later, snapping a fresh magazine into his assault rifle.

"Done?" the tough Israeli asked.

"Looks like."

"Eight gunners on the first two floors," McCarter reported.

They went around the circle then, a hasty tabulation of the dead. A curl of smoke was drifting down the stairs from somewhere overhead. One of the frag grenades had struck a spark somewhere. The Tiburon was burning.

"Time to go."

They trooped outside, stood together a moment in the clean night air before they separated, double-timing toward their cars. The sparsely settled neighborhood was wide awake by now, lights coming on in clapboard houses here and there. There might not be a telephone in every house, but someone would be calling the police before much longer if the call hadn't been made already.

The ANI wouldn't be crippled by the strike tonight, but that wasn't the plan. The Executioner hoped to prod the terrorists enough that they would rush their scheduled operation, start to make mistakes.

And it would take some time to see if they had been successful. It was coming up on midnight now, with hours yet to go before the dawn.

How many men had Bolan killed since his arrival in San Juan? Not half enough.

Tomorrow he knew would be another killing day.

CHAPTER TWELVE

The summons from Francisco Obregon was no surprise. He often called Miranda Flores at peculiar hours, and his male ego demanded that she come to him on command, regardless of the time or what she might be doing when he called. In normal circumstances, off the job, it was the kind of macho idiot's approach that would have chilled her interest in a man the first time out, but this was strictly business.

She had replayed the conversation with Belasko in her mind at least a dozen times since they had parted, drawing comfort from his words and from the fact that he had seemed sincere. In retrospect she understood that sleeping with the enemy would seem like small potatoes to a man whose daily job included wholesale murder. Even so, she knew Belasko had been speaking from the heart, and something in his words had touched her own.

But she was working now, and it was back to Obregon again.

Flores knew exactly what he wanted—what the bastard always wanted when he called her in the middle of the night. Obregon didn't call her up to pass the time of day. In fact, he thought that having conversations with a woman was a monumental waste of time, since—in his view—they were incapable of formulating an intelligent opinion. Pretty women were designed for sex, the rest for coping with domestic drudgery.

It was a twisted kind of man's world in the ANI, and that was one more reason why Flores longed to shut their operation down.

Tonight, though, she would have to be the same submissive baby doll that Obregon had come to know and . . . well, not love exactly, but depend on in his macho way. He needed an audience for his performances, one that wouldn't judge or criticize, but rather validate his dreams and fantasies.

Flores didn't deceive herself into thinking that Obregon respected her or that he would hesitate to throw her over in an instant for another woman. Loyalty between the sexes meant no more to this man than respect for human life, but at the moment he appeared to need her, and she meant to take advantage of that fluke while it lasted.

With any luck it would be enough to put Obregon and his comrades away. . . if not by legal means, perhaps on Mike Belasko's terms.

She dressed quickly after hanging up the telephone. No bra, because Obregon liked her that way, and older panties, because he often ripped them from her body in a tedious display of "manliness." The dress she chose was short, low cut and snug. A whore's dress, she decided, checking her reflection in the mirror.

Looking at herself that way, she nearly lost the feeling of self-worth Belasko had attempted to restore. Almost. But thinking of Obregon and the job she had to do, it came back to her in a rush. No G-man sent from Washington could penetrate the ANI as she had done, albeit imperfectly. Her sacrifice would bring the revolutionary killers down one way or another, and that thought in itself gave her strength to walk out the door.

It was a fifteen-minute drive to Obregon's apartment in Old San Juan. There was no traffic to speak of on the streets at this hour, with working men and women safely home in bed. She passed police cars on the way, some of the officers regarding her with thinly veiled suspicion, and she felt a sudden urge to laugh at them. Such macho men, imagining they knew what happened in the city they had signed on to protect. While they were rousting drunks and petty thieves, Miranda Flores was en route to meet one of the most dangerous gunmen in Puerto Rico, working overtime to bring about his destruction.

In the past she had nurtured mixed feelings about working alone. It pleased her in a way, making her feel strong and competent, trusted by her superiors, important for the contribution she could make to public safety. At another level running solo had the saving grace of allowing Flores to cover her tracks, hide her secret shame from colleagues—mostly male—who would never understand what she had done, her motives, the driving force behind her approach to this case. The guilt and shame were part of that, but less so since her conversation with Belasko.

Still, sometimes she wondered, even when the case was done—assuming she survived—how many months of scalding showers it would take before she started feeling clean again.

And if she never did, then what?

Miranda reckoned she would face that problem when it came.

She pulled into the parking lot of Obregon's apartment house and killed the engine, locked the car and left it, her high heels clicking on the pavement as she followed the familiar route through darkness to his door. He had been waiting for her, dressed in nothing but a towel around his waist. His greedy hands were on her breasts before the door swung shut behind her.

"Ah, my little one."

Flores put her sensibilities on hold and went to work.

Havana, Cuba
2250 hours EST

RAUL GUTIERREZ HAD WORKED for G-2, the Cuban secret police, for the past fifteen years. In that time his contacts and assignments had ranged from Chile, Nicaragua and the Dominican Republic to the dark continent of Africa, where he helped organize revolutionary forces in Angola. Of all the different parties, groups and races he had worked with, though, the Puerto Ricans rated near the bottom of his list.

Gutierrez didn't trust them, for a start. In any case where Cuban cash and agents were invested in another country, he assumed that the recipients had personal agendas of their own, in spite of their professed allegiance to the people's revolution. It was nothing to Gutierrez if they hated him behind his back as long as he was also feared. His clients had to realize from the beginning that the hand that doled out cash and arms one day could form a fist of steel the next and crush them where they stood.

Exporting revolution from Havana was a sacred duty for the die-hard Fidelistas, and they labored on despite the collapse of Communist regimes in Eastern Europe and the USSR. They might not have a prayer of planting any red flags in the Western Hemisphere, but there was something to be said for chaos in itself, especially when the United States could be embarrassed at a minimal expense to Cuba.

With the Puerto Ricans, it had seemed like easy pickings at the start. The FLN had nurtured a tradition of revolt that predated Fidel's triumph in Cuba, and deep resentment outlasted the organization's apparent suppression in the late 1980s. With the successor ANI, things were even simpler: military infiltration allowed the new crop of rebels to arm themselves for the most part, sparing Havana the risk and expense of running weapons into U.S. territory. It was easy to provide advice, occasional shipments of cash or drugs for resale on the black market.

Still, the old truism remained: if something seemed too good to be true, it probably was. Gutierrez couldn't shake his feelings that the ANI—specifically Miguel Albano and his cronies in the U.S. Navy—had contrived some secret plan to use the Fidelistas to their own advantage. Not the covert aid per se; that much was taken for granted. Rather, he suspected some malignant plot to smear Havana, let the Cubans stand as scapegoats when the final act was staged. His warnings to the G-2 brass had fallen on deaf ears so far, and so Gutierrez was resigned to do his job.

But he would keep his eyes wide open all the way.

The latest troubles, for example, were discouraging in the extreme. Last night and through the morning, someone had been sniping at the ANI around San Juan, his contacts claiming ignorance of who would try to take them out and why. His last call from Albano, moments earlier, brought more bad news. There had been yet another skirmish with their unknown adversaries on the island, plus a massacre in Florida, with more than twenty revolutionaries dead. Again the names and motive of their enemies remained a blank, but it was fair to say that someone had a clear fix on the ANI and was attempting to destroy the group.

Which meant that "someone"—possibly the CIA or a related agency—might also know about the Puerto Rican contacts with Havana.

Short of phoning up the FBI himself and risking execution for his efforts, there was nothing Gutierrez could do to halt the relentless chain reaction already in progress. Albano and company had their masterstroke planned for Saturday, the wheels already in motion, and Raul's superiors were looking forward to the headlines that would follow. Such embarrassment to the United States would take a generation to erase, if they could ever wipe the stain away.

But it was one thing to humiliate a clumsy giant, something else entirely to live with him after the fact…especially when the giant was still armed and nursing a ravenous hunger for vengeance.

If Gutierrez was correct in his suspicion that Albano and the ANI were looking for a way to blame G-2 for their approaching masterstroke, it meant retaliation from the States would be directed toward Havana rather than San Juan.

It all made sense when he considered it from the viewpoint of professional paranoia, ingrained by years of dwelling in the shadow world of subversion and counterintelligence. If the Americans blamed Puerto Rico and the ANI for what was coming, it would mean acknowledging the decades of oppression that produced such hatred in the first place. Worse, the country's ranking military leaders would be made to look like fools for placing revolutionary ingrates in positions of responsibility, allowing them to execute their strike in rank defiance of the flag they claimed to serve.

Conversely, if the Cubans were to blame, then it became a Communist conspiracy directed at a blameless nation by the enemy outside. Puerto Rican nationalists weren't at fault, for they had only been seduced by cunning plotters from Havana, ethnic pride perverted into something savage and malignant.

Such an act cried out for harsh reprisals, but the U.S. government would never nuke San Juan. It could and might unleash a firestorm over Cuba, though, and never mind if certain puzzle pieces failed to mesh. There would be time enough to sift the rubble with a white-haired government commission when the smoke cleared, mocking up reports to justify the razing of Havana as an act of self-defense.

Gutierrez told himself that he was letting his imagination run away with him, but he wasn't convinced. He had already done his best with what he had to make G-2 withdraw support from the Albano faction, but his strenuous objections had been overruled. Given the circumstances, he could only make the best of a bad situation and cover his own ass.

To that end, Raul Gutierrez had been making plans. For the past three months he had begun to transfer cash from various accounts outside Cuba to a bank in Zurich, his insurance policy against the day when storm clouds over Cuba assumed the shape of a nuclear mushroom.

Gutierrez would be long gone by then, winging his way to a new life abroad. But first he had more work to do.

There still might be a way of satisfying his superiors without allowing the Albano faction of the ANI to jeopardize—indeed, destroy—his already tenuous world. It would require some thought, but Gutierrez was good at thinking, spinning plots and moving other men around the map like pawns in a chess game.

It was his specialty, and he had never played for higher stakes.

Key West Naval Air Station
2250 hours

LUIS CAMACHO HAD the graveyard shift all month, but Gadgets Schwarz had double-checked to make sure he was at his duty station just in case. The afternoon had been traumatic for all concerned, and the last thing Schwarz wanted to do was walk in and find Camacho waiting for him, maybe with a pistol in his hand.

A visit to the Key West station, with Blancanales posing as a CID investigator, had confirmed Camacho's movements for the day. They couldn't prove he had gone near the Everglades—not yet—but signing in and out established time parameters that fit the action. Pol had even formed a guard on duty at the gate that afternoon who spoke about Camacho looking "kind of rattled, nervous-like, you know" on his return.

It was enough for the men of Able Team to run with, since they weren't bound by legal rules of evidence in any case. Camacho wasn't headed for a trial, regardless of his crimes. In his case, justice would be more direct . . . and terminal.

They couldn't simply drop him now, however, since the Puerto Rican team still had no fix on what the ANI was planning as their "something big." The Able Team warriors didn't know what role, if any, Camacho would have in the grand design, but they had fairly narrowed down the range of possible accomplices on the base.

Aside from Camacho himself, there were only two Puerto Ricans assigned to Key West Naval Air Station. One of those was on furlough for the next eight days, a long-distance collect call verifying his presence with relatives in the South Bronx. The other was a twenty-year veteran assigned to maintenance and repair of jet engines. He seemed apolitical, with no apparent link to Camacho, and he raised no objections when he was temporarily reassigned—at Able Team's suggestion—to Chase Field Naval Air Station at Beeville, Texas. In a few days, if all went well, the lifer would be back at his old duty post, regaling his pals with embroidered versions of another government snafu.

Meanwhile Schwarz had Camacho's quarters to himself. The Navy uniform felt strange, but he was used to playing different roles on his assignments out of Stony Man. Somewhere along the line, Brognola's clout had filtered down from the Pentagon to Key West, where the station's CO was physically aware—but technically ignorant—of Schwarz's presence on the base. His mission hadn't been described to the CO, nor would it ever be.

Schwarz stood outside Camacho's door for most of a minute, listening to the pulse throb in his ears, checking the grounds to make sure he wasn't being watched. The door was simple, even with the separate dead bolt. Once across the threshold, Gadgets took a penlight from his pocket, switched it on and made a quick scan of the darkened room.

There was no kitchen in the flat, per se, although Camacho had a hot plate and refrigerator. The furnishings were Spartan throughout, and it was apparent that Camacho had no interest in redecorating. He was only passing through.

The bedroom next. A mix of uniforms and civvies hung in the closet, shoes below, a lonely dress-parade cap on the shelf above. The dresser drawers revealed Camacho as a man who rolled his socks but didn't bother folding his underwear. Beneath the tangled Jockey shorts, Schwarz found a switchblade knife, a ring of keys, two hundred fifty dollars in twenties, rolled up and secured with a red rubber band.

Big deal.

His last stop was the nightstand by Camacho's bed. It had a single drawer containing several condoms and a highway map of Florida. Schwarz took a chance and spread it open on the bed, scanning quickly with the penlight. The only mark he could discover was a small red circle, drawn in ink, around the site of Cape Canaveral, two hundred seventy-five miles to the northeast in Brevard County.

Frowning, Schwarz folded the map and replaced it in the nightstand drawer. His final task before he left involved the placement of a tiny bug in each room of Camacho's flat. The nightstand was ideal for one, a self-adhesive microphone secreted underneath the sliding drawer to monitor Camacho's pillow talk. A coffee table in the living room provided Schwarz with what he needed for the other bug, a little wafer that would be invisible unless a searcher got down on his hands and knees to search the table's underside.

It might all be a waste of time, Schwarz realized. Assuming that Camacho had no allies on the base and was wise enough to keep himself from babbling on the telephone, the bugs would be a wash-out. Still, you never knew until you tried.

Schwarz checked the walk outside before he left the flat and took time to lock the door behind him. Barring ESP, Camacho would be unaware of the intrusion when he came off shift. By that time Able Team would have him covered, listening in shifts for any careless comment that could give them some idea of what the ANI was planning for its masterstroke.

And if they came up empty, then what?

There was always the direct approach, abduction and interrogation. Schwarz hoped Camacho had loose lips, but he wasn't about to hold his breath for any miracles.

And he couldn't escape the nagging sense that they were running out of time.

Stony Man Farm
2400 hours

THE SECOND DAY ENDED with a whimper for Aaron Kurtzman, seated at his console in the Stony Man computer room.

The late reports were in from Florida and Puerto Rico, more dead all around, but it was still too early to say if the good guys were winning.

Some days the Bear had problems sorting out exactly who the good guys were, but when the mood came over him, it quickly passed. You only had to look around and assess the damage done by human predators around the world to know which side you should be on.

Kurtzman thought he would have made a decent pacifist if he was living in a pacific world. Unfortunately that wasn't the case. The savages were still intent on raping, pillaging, devouring whatever they could reach. Under those circumstances, there was no such thing as an effective nonviolent response.

So be it.

At the moment Kurtzman had more concrete and specific problems on his mind than the philosophy of pacifism versus armed resistance to aggression. He had friends out there prepared to sacrifice their lives if need be to prevent some grim, as yet unspecified event from coming down, and he was worried that they might not be in time. Regardless of their sacrifice—and so far, thankfully, they seemed to be unscathed—it all might be a waste if they couldn't locate the proper targets and coordinate their strike in time.

He sometimes thought that mankind's greatest blessing—and its most debilitating curse—was the gift of imagination. "Lower" animals moved through the days of their existence bent on feeding, reproducing, resting when they felt the need, but man was built to worry, hope, anticipate. In many situations, Kurtzman realized, the fears a person built up in his mind before the fact were worse than any trauma he would suffer if the worst scenario should come to pass.

Like now.

His mind had run the gamut from political assassination to chaotic rioting and hostage situations, skyjacks, sabotage of health facilities and food supplies. What were the Puerto Rican revolutionaries plotting as their ultimate expression of contempt for the United States? Considering their infiltration of the military, both in Puerto Rico and in Florida, was there a chance for them to threaten national security?

Enough.

He had to let it go, or Kurtzman knew that he would never get to sleep at all. Tomorrow was another day, and in a few more hours he would doubtless have a whole new body count to survey, running up the score. God willing, he wouldn't find the names of any friends among the dead.

He heard the door open and close behind him and turned in his chair to find Carmen Delahunt watching him from a distance. The fiery redhead, an FBI computer analyst recruited by Kurtzman for the Stony Man team, was frowning at him thoughtfully.

"What's new?"

"Not much," he told her wearily.

"You ought to catch some sack time."

"I was on my way."

"I see that." Moving closer to him, she drew one hand from the pocket of her white lab coat and ran a manicured finger around the lip of Kurtzman's coffee mug. "My guess would be you've got enough caffeine inside you to keep the Eighth Army marching for two or three days."

"I've built up an immunity," he told her, trying for a smile.

"So prove it."

"Hey, Mom, I'm a big boy now."

"Big boys need care, the same as anybody else."

"Is that an offer?" Delahunt glanced away, and Kurtzman was amazed to see her blushing. He could feel the color rising in his own cheeks now. "Hey, wait, I didn't mean... I'm sorry, Carmen. Friends?"

"I'll let you know."

"You have to think about it?"

"No." The blush was fading as she smiled. "You're finished here?"

"Seems like."

"I was about to crash. You want to walk me home?"

"I wouldn't mind."

"Okay, let's go."

Kurtzman switched off his monitor and left the rest as it was. The Stony Man computers were on twenty-four-hour alert, year-round, monitoring Intelligence sources that ranged in sophistication from media wire service reports to high-flying surveillance satellites that circled the globe from thousands of miles away. The electronic brain would keep running without him, a fact that sometimes made Kurtzman feel like one more cog in an elaborate machine.

But not tonight.

Right now he felt extremely human, and the feeling wasn't all that bad.

"Unless you're really tired," he said, "I might suggest we stop off for a nightcap."

"Mess hall's closed," she reminded him.

"Right."

"I've got some brandy back at my place if you don't mind water glasses."

"Not at all."

"Okay."

The blush again, but he was ready for it this time, and it didn't wipe away her smile.

Okay.

It couldn't hurt, he thought, to stand down for a little while. It just might do him good.

And that would definitely be okay.

CHAPTER THIRTEEN

San Juan Naval Base
Friday, 0430 hours AST

Gregorio Ruiz was still rubbing sleep from his eyes when he answered Miguel Albano's summons, straightening his uniform from force of habit while he waited for Albano to answer the doorbell. It had to be bad news, this early in the morning, and Ruiz was trying to prepare himself for anything.

But he wasn't prepared for the appearance of his friend. Albano looked old and haggard, like a man who hadn't slept for days. He stepped out on the narrow porch in darkness, glancing here and there as if he thought Ruiz might have an escort hiding in the shrubbery.

"I'm clean," Ruiz informed him, irritated that Albano would question his ability to spot a tail.

"Inside."

Ruiz obeyed, but warily. They didn't stand on ceremony or on military courtesy when they were by themselves. Albano held a slightly higher rank than Ruiz in the U.S. Navy, but his real authority came with his position as group leader of the ANI. Ruiz felt no more allegiance to the star-spangled flag or the uniform he wore than he would for a piece of used toilet tissue.

"What is it?" he demanded once the door was closed and safely locked behind him.

"Trouble."

"More?" Ruiz groaned inwardly. They had already lost a number of their troops in the past twenty-four hours, and he was aware of the trouble in Florida, as well.

"Somebody hit the Tiburon," Albano informed him, settling on the couch.

Ruiz was trembling now. He found a chair and sat. "How bad?"

"Police are picking up the pieces. No survivors that we know of. There were twenty, maybe twenty-five of our men in the place when it went down."

"They must have done some damage to the other side."

Albano shook his head. "No trace of anyone else. If they killed or wounded anyone, the bastards had a chance to carry out their casualties."

Ruiz was stunned. A part of him was ready to deny the awful news, but he couldn't avoid reality. If Albano's body count was accurate, including Florida, it meant that roughly half their soldiers had been wiped out in little more than a single day.

"What can we do?" he asked, feeling the first tendrils of panic creep into his soul.

"Stand firm!" Albano snapped. "Tomorrow is our day of triumph. Nothing else can take priority."

"Without soldiers—"

"No! The special team is still intact. No one has touched them yet, and no one will. It is our destiny."

There was no reasoning with Albano when he got that way, his adrenaline pumping, flying high on the dream of independence and his own role in the new regime. If things went wrong, though, there would be no revolutionary government. The best they could look forward to was life inside some federal prison on the mainland.

"Your call, Miguel." Ruiz could think of nothing else to say. He was committed to the struggle, too, and there could be no turning back. "Just tell me what to do."

"We have to watch our backs." Albano appeared to think about it for another moment, finally raising his eyes to meet Ruiz's. "The new man you were telling me about, what was his name?"

"Geraldo Escobar. His family lives in New York City."

"Does it seem like a coincidence to you, the way he showed up out of nowhere just when everything began to fall apart?"

"I checked his papers out, Miguel. He transferred in from Oceana NAS, Virginia Beach."

"Get rid of him!"

"You think he's mixed up in the trouble we've been having? Listen to yourself. It makes no sense."

"So if I'm wrong, at least we take the side of caution."

"It's too damned soon. The FBI and CID are still investigating Sanchez."

"Let Francisco handle it."

"Like last time?"

"Jaime took us by surprise. You know that. Tell Francisco what we need and watch him so he does it right."

Ruiz was startled by the order. "Me? You're asking *me* to give Francisco the word?"

"Not asking you, Gregorio. We need this taken care of. I'm not letting anything or anyone postpone our victory. We've come too far this time. No turning back."

"Francisco won't—"

"He will," Albano interrupted, "if you make him understand I sent you. He has just as much to lose on this as we do. More, if they connect him with the hit on Sanchez. He's our brother, after all. We live or die together, no?"

"Of course, but—"

"Nothing. If I'm wrong about this Escobar, so be it. One life, more or less, means nothing in a revolution. Everyone's expendable, you understand? Someday you show me I was wrong, we'll raise a monument on Fortaleza Street and make him martyr of the year. Right now he's a potential danger and he has to go."

"All right, Miguel. I'll handle it."

"I knew you would. And watch yourself, Gregorio. Outside the brotherhood, we don't know who to trust these days. The Yankee bastards have eyes everywhere."

"I'm covered."

"Good. Get in touch with Obregon as soon as possible. We don't have any time to spare."

"Okay."

He was dismissed, no longer needed, and Ruiz let himself out of the apartment, listening as Albano double locked the door behind him. His mind was already shifting gears toward the conversation he would have with Obregon, the death sentence he would pass on his newest friend.

Or was the man, in fact, a mortal enemy?

Whatever, he was marked for death, and that was all that mattered. Ruiz had lost many friends in the past twenty-four hours, some of them known to him for years, one or two from his childhood.

Geraldo Escobar meant nothing when he thought about tomorrow and the triumph they were looking forward to. His life was a grain of sand in the desert, a drop of water in the sea.

Less than nothing.

But Ruiz would have to look out for himself if he intended to survive and share the coming victory.

A revolution made no difference to the dead.

Old San Juan
0515

MIRANDA FLORES HATED staying overnight with Obregon, but this time she had decided to make the best of a bad situation. Up before dawn, while Obregon lay snoring in the twisted, sweaty sheets, she pulled her clothes on silently, resisting the urge for a steaming-hot shower that would doubtless wake him up.

She always felt so filthy after one of their encounters, but she thought of Mike Belasko, heard his words again and concentrated on the task at hand. Obregon might be paranoid, obsessed with secrecy, but he was also something of a pack rat. His apartment was a sty, in fact, because he kept old books and magazines forever, stacked in heaps with older clothes he seldom wore, appliances that needed fixing, tapes and records she had never heard him play.

And notes.

The man didn't keep a diary in the sense that anyone would recognize, but he made hasty, scribbled notes of conversations, random thoughts, his future plans. They weren't organized or filed away, much less contained within a single volume, but were scattered here and there throughout the flat. On one occasion she remembered sitting on the sway-backed couch and feeling paper brush against her legs. Extracting it from underneath the cushion, she had found an ancient, crumpled shopping list with more notes in the margin: "Call Miguel, 9:30."

It was nothing in itself, but cause for hope that she might stumble over something more substantial if she searched Obregon's pigpen.

There was no time to waste.

Flores set about her task with dedication, pulling the bedroom door shut before she started scouring the parlor.

Drawers were first, then the coffee table and adjacent kitchen, yielding recipes and self-reminders, one sheet that appeared to be ballistics tables . . . and a list of names.

She counted thirty-five, all male, Hispanic to a man. None of them were familiar at a glance, though some were fairly common names, and she assumed that all or most of them were members of the ANI. The list went in the pocket of her slacks, and she continued searching, turning over snapshots to examine them for names or dates, recalling faces now and then.

She noted that Obregon managed to avoid the camera, but he still kept photographs of others. Two or three she recognized from bars and nightclubs they had visited together, when Obregon was showing off his latest conquest. One, a dark man with a scar along his jaw, had dropped by the apartment two weeks ago. Obregon had turned grim at the sight of his visitor, shooing Miranda into the bedroom where she had tried without success to eavesdrop on their muted conversation.

Plotters.

She couldn't remove the photographs without alerting Obregon, but she took time to memorize the faces, determined to double-check them against police and FBI mug books at her first opportunity. If nothing else, at least she would have further evidence that Obregon was consorting with known terrorists and revolutionaries, salving her conscience against the moment when Belasko took him down.

That day was coming, Flores realized, and it wouldn't be long. She had mixed feelings as she pictured Obregon stretched out on the floor, blood leaking from fresh bullet wounds.

She hated the man, of course, for what he was and all that he had put her through, and yet—

"I missed you."

Flores jumped at the sound of Obregon's voice, unable to prevent a squeak of fright from slipping through her teeth. She spun to face him, bumping the drawer shut with her buttocks as she turned.

Too late.

The pistol in his hand was leveled at her heaving chest.

"I'm waiting for the lie, darling." He was smiling at her now. "Or should I guess? You're looking for coffee? Aspirin? Maybe my grandmother's recipe for flan?"

She knew that it was useless, staring at the pistol and his mocking, almost lifeless eyes. He had to kill her now, the only question being whether he would try to question her before the moment. Certainly he couldn't shoot her here without a risk of waking up the neighbors, having one or more of them report the sound of gunshots to police.

"You're busted, Francisco."

"Ah?"

"I'm FBI." She frowned and nodded toward the automatic in his fist. "You hand that over, come along with me, and there might be something I can do to shave your time."

She couldn't tell if it was rage or shock that brought the color rushing to his cheeks until Obregon burst out laughing at her, loud and long, the automatic jiggling in his hand. It took long moments for him to regain composure, stifling his mirth.

"Perhaps you ought to whistle for your SWAT team, little one. They must be waiting in the flower beds outside to save you."

"I've filed reports on everything," she told him, mad enough for both of them by now. "And I mean everything. They read about your bedside manner back in Washington, you know? The FBI director knows about your problem with the premature eja—"

His fist came out of nowhere, looping toward her face, a hurtling comet trailing curses in its wake. Flores had no time to raise her hands before it struck her cheek and set off fireworks in her skull. The floor rushed up to meet her, and she kept on falling, plunging through linoleum and plywood, through the earth itself, into a vast abyss of darkness.

Screaming all the way.

San Juan Naval Base
0530 hours

RAFAEL ENCIZO ROSE with the sun, limbering up with some brisk calisthenics in his quarters, rolling out for a jog around the base when he was finished with the warm-up. He'd do two miles before breakfast, then take a shower that would sluice the perspiration from his body.

Encizo's mind was elsewhere as he ran, evaluating progress since he'd set foot on the base. Matters weren't progressing with Ruiz as swiftly as he would have liked, and he had thus far only glimpsed Miguel Albano from a distance. But he couldn't force the pace too much without focusing attention—and suspicion—on himself.

And that, he realized, could be the last mistake he ever made.

Snatches of news from the radio had enabled him to keep up with his comrades tackling the ANI around San Juan. Police appeared confused by the sudden outbreak of violence, but they were blaming a clash between right-wing and leftist guerrillas at the moment, condemning both sides with fair equanimity. If anyone had a clue that something else was actually going on, they were keeping the news to themselves.

Encizo felt sidelined at the moment, almost like a slacker who failed to pull his weight. The barroom brawl that had introduced him to Ruiz had been a stroke of luck, but after their initial introduction, Ruiz had turned cautious, taking his time about introducing Encizo to the on-base organization.

Ruiz's caution was understandable, of course. Encizo had appeared at the worst possible time in terms of infiltrating a covert organization. The ANI was just recovering from the fiasco of one traitor's execution, and was suddenly under attack by unknown enemies on the streets of San Juan. At one level Encizo realized he was lucky Ruiz would speak to him at all, but the sluggish pace of his progress was still maddening to a man of action.

His comrades were out there on the firing line, risking their lives on an hourly basis, scoring goals against the common enemy, while he killed time in relative comfort at the naval base, contributing nothing of any consequence so far. For all he knew, the game could fold that very afternoon, and he would have missed the whole thing, aside from trading punches with some drunken, bigoted Marines.

By the same token, he might be on the verge of an important breakthrough. He was supposed to join Ruiz for lunch that day somewhere off the base, and the change of scene led Encizo to hope they would be discussing something more than routine service duties. Encizo's induction to the ANI, for instance, replacing the man they had recently lost.

There was an outside chance the luncheon date could be a trap, although Encizo was convinced he had done nothing to alert Ruiz or put his enemies on guard. Of course, when you were dealing with an outfit like the ANI, its members lived in a state of perpetual suspicion and distrust, surviving day to day on a diet of paranoia and rage.

The rage kept them going, focused on their objectives, however bizarre; the paranoia made them jump at shadows, but it also gave some guerrilla fighters a kind of sixth sense when it came to spotting danger from a distance.

Either way Encizo knew he had to take the chance. There was a job remaining to be done, and no consideration of personal risk would prevent him from completing that job. For him the jeopardy wasn't an aphrodisiac, as described by some professional warriors, but neither did it dominate his thoughts. Risk came with the territory, and he would deal with any challenge that arose, relying on his training and experience to see him through.

Back at his quarters, Encizo showered off and dried himself, slipping into the uniform of the day. He would change into civvies before keeping his lunch date with Ruiz, but that was hours away yet. In the meantime he would work his morning shift, shuffling papers in personnel, taking the opportunity to scrutinize files on Albano, Ruiz and several friends of theirs whom he suspected of belonging to the ANI.

When the smoke cleared on this one, there would be hell to pay among the Navy brass, recruiting die-hard subversives for military duty and placing them together at a base where they could do the most potential harm. It might not be enough to call for a congressional investigation, but the press and television would be merciless.

Too bad.

If someone got the ax for this mistake, it would prevent similar snafus in the future. Or would it?

As long as human beings made the rules and supervised their application, there would be mistakes—some trivial, some catastrophic. And as long as human beings were imperfect, someone else would be employed to clean up those mistakes. Encizo hated thinking of himself as a garbage man, but that was what it boiled down to sometimes. He and the other Phoenix Force warriors were involved in toxic-waste management, but the waste they dealt with was human.

And less deadly for that.

He spent a moment checking his Beretta Model 96, chambered for the powerful 10 mm round, and left it in the bedroom dresser, hidden underneath his neatly folded Jockey shorts. The weapon would be going with him when he went to lunch, but he couldn't report for morning duty with a pistol on his hip.

Appearances were everything.

Encizo only hoped they would not get him killed before he had a chance to do some good against his enemies.

Ocean Park, San Juan
0620 hours

FRANCISCO OBREGON LOOKED nervous in the early-morning light. There were dark shadows underneath his eyes, and his face was lined with wrinkles that Gregorio Ruiz had never noticed in the past. He didn't know Obregon's age—perhaps midthirties—but he could have passed for ten years older in his present state.

"We're in the shit, Gregorio." No greetings or amenities. Obregon jumped straight into his story of betrayal by a woman, cutting off Ruiz before he had a chance to speak.

And not just any woman, mind you. Obregon had found himself a piece of ass direct from Washington, a member of the FBI, no less. It sounded like dumb luck that he had caught her poking through his things that morning when she thought he was asleep. Ruiz could only grit his teeth and ask himself how much the bitch already knew, how many secrets she had passed on to her Yankee masters during several weeks of bedroom dalliances with Obregon.

The idiot! Ruiz was sorely tempted to unleash his rage, produce the pistol tucked inside his waistband and eliminate the man whose rampant sex drive had endangered all of them. Francisco had been thinking with his cock again, and it wasn't the first mistake that he had made in recent days. With Jaime Sanchez, he had botched the ambush only yards from where they stood right now, a simple execution turned into a running battle that involved police, the FBI and CID.

Albano would be livid when he heard the news, but would it change his mind about tomorrow? Standing in the pale gray light of dawn, Ruiz was doubtful. He had seen Miguel's determination in the flesh that morning, ready to proceed in spite of any risk. Francisco might have spoiled their chances for success, perhaps condemned their shock troops to defeat and death, but he would not postpone the Day.

So be it.

"Is the woman dead?"

Obregon shook his head. "No. I have her safely under lock and key."

Too late, Ruiz thought to himself. "I will inform Miguel of what has happened. He will not be happy with your indiscretion, Francisco."

"Please, I—"

"In the meantime do not kill the woman. She must be interrogated, thoroughly debriefed. We must know how much information she has passed to her superiors, you understand?"

"It will be done, of course."

"And no mistakes."

Obregon bristled but made no reply. His position was already tenuous enough, and he knew it.

"There is something else that you must do," Ruiz continued. "It is urgent."

"Tell me."

He explained about Geraldo Escobar in short, clipped sentences, describing Obregon's target, relating the details of their scheduled luncheon meeting. Obregon absorbed the information, nodding as he listened.

"He is a traitor, this one?" Obregon asked, when Ruiz had finished.

"So Miguel suspects."

"But you are not convinced?"

Ruiz dismissed the question with a shrug. "It doesn't matter what I think. Miguel is still in charge, and he is right to take no chances on the eve of what we've all been waiting so long for."

"A spy, perhaps." Obregon's voice had lowered almost to a whisper.

"Yes, perhaps."

"I'll bring my best men. Have no fear."

"I'm not afraid, Francisco." Ruiz held back from stating the obvious, that *he* hadn't been sleeping with an agent from the FBI.

"Miguel will not be disappointed."

"I sincerely hope not."

In the past his dealings with Obregon had often been unpleasant. The older man lorded it over Ruiz, flaunting his real or imagined rank in the ANI like a badge of honor and authority. The shoe was on the other foot today, since his blunder with the woman placed Obregon in mortal jeopardy. He needed all the friends that he could find, and so he treated Ruiz with a newfound respect.

It felt good for a change, as if Ruiz was finally making progress. If only it weren't too little and too late.

He would report Francisco's blunder to Miguel at once, but it would make no difference in the end. Ruiz knew that as surely as he knew the time of day. But he was bound to try.

And when they made their move on Saturday, whatever happened, he would know that he had done his best to smooth the way.

The road lay straight ahead to victory or death.

And it could still go either way.

CHAPTER FOURTEEN

Old San Juan
Friday, 0715 hours

Miranda Flores was late for their follow-up meeting, scheduled before he'd dropped her off the previous night, and Bolan was growing concerned. He sat in the small coffee shop at the window table and watched pedestrians clog the sidewalk in their rush to various downtown jobs. Flores knew the city, understood its ebb and flow. She would have allowed herself time to reach her destination.

Late was bad news, any way you sliced it, but the problem might be something simple, like an automotive breakdown. Bolan gave her five more minutes, tried her number from the café's public phone and got no answer.

Dammit!

He wasn't especially concerned about new information from Flores or his personal desire to see her again. It was the simple fact that dropping out of sight meant trouble. A professional would either keep the date or get in touch somehow, reschedule and explain the reason for her change of plans.

Miranda Flores was a trained professional, but there was still no sign of her, no word of explanation.

Bad.

He dropped some money on the table, left the coffee shop and moved along the crowded sidewalk, past his parked Toyota, to another public telephone. He chose a booth this time, where he could shut himself inside and have some privacy, still covering the coffee shop from twenty yards away in case Miranda finally showed up.

There was no point in hassling with the local FBI. Flores's job was undercover, and the Bureau would protect her with denials all the way. If Bolan called their office, he would only jeopardize himself, perhaps wind up with unmarked squad cars closing off the block while he stood waiting in the booth.

He knew a better way.

The bilingual operator handled his collect call to Stony Man Farm, patching Bolan through to the outside line reserved for emergency calls from the field. He didn't recognize the male voice on the other end, but there was no reason why he should have. The young man accepted charges for the call, noted Bolan's code name—Striker—and had Aaron Kurtzman on the line in record time.

"What's shaking, Striker?"

"Trouble." Mindful of the open line that anyone could monitor, he kept it cryptic. "I was scheduled for a meeting with the field rep from our sister company, but something held her up. She doesn't answer on her private line, and I don't have an address for her. Can you run it down from your end?"

"Shouldn't be a problem," Kurtzman told him, "but it's bound to take some time. Let's say an hour, give or take. Where can I reach you?"

Bolan thought about it, knowing he couldn't monopolize the phone booth for an hour. Even if his luck held out and no one tried to make a call, he would be noticed loitering around the booth, perhaps reported to the police.

"We'd better make it the hotel," he said at last, reluctantly.

"Okay. I'm on it. Bye."

The line went dead, and Bolan cradled the receiver and walked back to his car. Depending on the circumstance, an hour could be forever. People died in seconds from a killing wound; they bled to death or died of shock in minutes flat. An hour with a skilled interrogator could become eternity.

He stopped the morbid train of thought before it traveled any further. Just because Miranda missed a breakfast meet, it didn't mean that she was dead or being tortured by their common enemy...and yet his instinct told the Executioner that something had gone badly, desperately wrong.

The only thing that he could do was wait.

In fact, it took the Bear just forty minutes to obtain Flores's address from the FBI. The call came through at 8:09 a.m., and Bolan memorized the street, the address and apartment number, all of it. At half-past eight he stood outside her door, tried knocking twice and picked the double locks when there was no response.

The good news was he didn't find Flores lying dead in her apartment. On the flip side, there was nothing to explain where she had gone until he checked a tiny notepad that she kept beside the telephone. A single word—a name, in fact—was written on the pad in tidy script.

The name was "Obregon."

He saw the whole scenario played out in front of him as if projected on a movie screen. Flores went back to her apartment after he had dropped her off. The phone rang, Obregon requested—no, demanded—that she join him. Where? It made no difference. She hadn't come home, hadn't touched base to cancel their appointment, and the latter fact, if nothing else, confirmed his darkest fears that something had gone wrong.

It took only one minor glitch to blow a cover, and he had no time to waste on second-guessing what had happened to

Miranda Flores overnight. If she was still alive, she needed help.

If she wasn't, God help the men responsible.

They could expect no mercy from the Executioner.

MIRANDA FLORES'S HEAD throbbed painfully, a brutal headache roosting in the space behind her eyes. It felt as if a large balloon had been inserted through one nostril, then inflated to the point where it began to stretch her very skull. Miranda felt each heartbeat in her aching head, accompanied by a high-pitched whining in her ears. She couldn't touch her face, since her hands were tightly bound behind her back, but she suspected Obregon had broken something—possibly her nose, perhaps her cheekbone—when he knocked her down.

It had been foolish, taunting him about his sexuality when she was conscious of his moods, the temper he could barely hold in check on better days. He might have killed her on the spot instead of merely knocking her around, and she was grateful for the second chance at life.

For all the good that it would do her.

She was seated in a straight-backed wooden chair, wrists secured with what felt like stout loops of wire. Her ankles were likewise bound to the chair's front legs. It felt like wire again, but she couldn't lean forward far enough to see for sure.

As if it mattered.

She was trapped and beaten, fresh out of hope. Time was difficult to estimate in a windowless room without knowing how long she had lain unconscious, but logic told her that she must have missed her scheduled rendezvous with Belasko by now. He would be worried, perhaps even trying to find her, but how much could he really do to help?

Miranda regretted playing it close to the vest with her address. If Belasko found her apartment, he might also find the note beside her telephone, naming Obregon. And what then? Exactly what was she expecting him to do on her behalf?

Obregon's apartment was on the list of targets she had given to Belasko, but Miranda was no longer there. In fact, she didn't have a clue as to where she was. A house, presumably, although her cell could just as easily have been a spare room in a shop or office building.

No.

Obregon would need privacy for what he had in mind. When he began to question her, as he inevitably must, it was predictable that she would balk, resist with everything she had. As he employed more forceful measures, she was bound to scream, and that could prove embarrassing if there were customers or pedestrians around.

A house, then, definitely. Still, the certainty didn't identify a given town, much less a neighborhood or a specific street. And if she knew precisely where she was confined, what earthly benefit would that provide? She couldn't beam the address to Belasko telepathically, and calling out for help was clearly hopeless.

Trapped.

The grim reality came back to her full force. It overrode the thirst and hunger that were only minor irritants compared to her oppressive fear of agonizing death. Obregon liked to inflict pain; she knew that much from personal experience, and there were others like him in the ANI. They would be motivated now to find out what she knew and who else might possess the information she had gleaned from pillow talk or snooping in the dusty corners of Obregon's flat. Beyond interrogation, they would want to punish her for making them look foolish, injuring their macho pride.

A sound of footsteps brought her head up, muscles tightening across her shoulders. She had been positioned in the chair so that her back was to the door, with a blank wall several feet in front of her. Still, she could pick up noises from behind her, emanating from the corridor outside her cell. Miranda knew they would be coming for her sooner or later, and it was almost a relief when she heard a key turn in the lock, immediately followed by the sound of boot heels on the wooden floor.

Francisco Obregon stood in front of her, waiting for Miranda to meet his gaze. She didn't flinch from what she saw there, even though she knew it spelled her death.

"You have betrayed me."

"No. I did my job."

"A Judas. What would your director have to say about one of his agents fucking the enemy?"

"Why don't you ask him for yourself?"

A cryptic smile turned up the corners of Obregon's mouth. "I might not have the chance," he said. "But there are questions you must answer now."

"I don't feel much like talking," she replied.

That made Obregon laugh out loud. "You will, my dear, I assure you."

Stepping close, he hooked the fingers of his right hand in the neckline of her cotton blouse and ripped it sharply downward, popping buttons, shredding fabric, leaving her exposed. Before she could react, the hand came back, a vicious one-two-three that rocked her head from side to side and left it throbbing with new spasms of pain. Blood drooled from her torn lower lip and spattered the curve of her breasts.

"The truth, now, if you please," Obregon said. "From the beginning."

"Go to hell!"

"I've been there," he informed her. "Maybe I should take you on a guided tour."

OBREGON'S APARTMENT was deserted when Bolan got there, and he refrained from torching it in deference to the neighbors. As it was, he left a short note on the door, pinned there with a stiletto. Printed out in bold block capitals, it read "The woman, safe and sound. No substitutes. No deals."

It was a weak beginning, but you ran with what you had. Mack Bolan's second stop was a cantina near Fortaleza Street, known as a watering hole for militant nationalists, including members of the ANI. The place was closed that early, but he found the back door open, with an old man sweeping up inside. The sweeper took one look at Bolan, the Beretta in his hand and made a snap decision to comply with any reasonable orders.

"You speak English?"

"Sí, señor."

"How's that?"

"Yes, sir."

"You're all alone here?"

He nodded. "No one else comes in before ten, ten-thirty."

"But you have a number for the manager?"

"El numero?"

"The telephone. For an emergency?"

"Oh, *sí.* One time the toilet overflowed and—"

"Right, that's fine. You run along and find a phone booth, will you? Tell the man his tavern just burned down."

"Burned down?"

"You're catching on. One other thing."

"Señor?"

"You tell him that I have a message for the ANI. Can you remember that?"

"Yes, sir."

"It's short and sweet. I want the woman back unharmed. They don't want to consider the options. *Comprende?*"

"Bring the woman back. No harm."

"That's close enough. Take off now."

The old man gestured vaguely toward a storeroom in the back. "My lunch."

A twenty-dollar bill changed hands. "On me," the warrior said. "Now hit the road."

Alone, he palmed a handful of incendiary sticks, dropped one behind the bar, another in the storeroom, two more in the tavern proper. He was well outside and moving briskly toward the parked Toyota when the firesticks popped, and by the time smoke started pouring from the open service door, the Executioner was several blocks away.

The word would spread, but he wasn't prepared to let it go at that. Until he saw Miranda Flores safe and sound, he meant to keep up unrelenting pressure on his enemies.

The Executioner was blitzing on.

Key West Naval Air Station
0915 hours EST

"HE'S ROLLING," Carl Lyons told the microphone attached to his lapel. "I'm on it."

"Roger that," the voice of Gadgets Schwarz acknowledged from the plastic earpiece Lyons wore.

They had been waiting half an hour for Camacho to appear. The target's phone call, placed at 8:30 a.m., hadn't been a toll call to Miami. He had spoken to a Cuban by the name of Hector, with the Able Team warriors taping every word. It was a cryptic call, little more than an exchange of greetings, closing with an agreement to meet "at the usual time and place."

It was all as vague as hell, and Lyons had drawn the assignment of tailing Camacho, while Schwarz and Blancanales stood by in Dade County. It was one hundred sixty-four miles from Key West to Miami on U.S. Highway 1, traversing the Florida Keys and a corner of the Everglades before civilization reared its chrome-and-concrete head at Cutler Ridge, Perrine and South Miami. That was close to two and a half hours, even if Camacho managed seventy miles per hour all the way through tiny towns and speed traps.

Lyons had a sense of wasted time as he fell in behind the Puerto Rican's car, but there was nothing he could do about it. Tracing Hector was a washout, since his number belonged to the pay phone in a Cuban social club on Calle Ocho. Camacho was their only lead, and they would have to run with it for good or ill.

It was significant, perhaps, that he should call a Cuban rather than a fellow Puerto Rican. It suggested that Camacho might be running short of comrades from the ANI in Florida, a hopeful sign for Able Team if it came down to any further head-on confrontations with their chosen enemies. Conversely ringing in a Cuban also made the game more complicated, with suggestions of a broader operating base, unknown accomplices, even foreign support from Havana.

They would simply have to wait and see.

Lyons kept a respectful distance from Camacho's vehicle on Highway 1, letting other traffic come between them when he could, falling back to the limits of sight when they had the road to themselves. There was no way for Camacho to shake him in the Keys short of swerving down a side street in the tiny towns they passed through on their journey north and east. Stock Island. Summerland Key. Big Pine Key. Marathon. Key Colony Beach. Duck Key. Layton. Islamorada. Most were simply wide places in the road, featuring gas stations and convenience stores, the kind of mom-and-pop fast-food restaurants that were either hidden treasures or lurking ptomaine traps.

Camacho motored through each town in turn without attempting to dislodge his tail. In one respect the isolation of this highway through the Keys worked to Lyons's advantage. Traffic bound for the mainland had only one route to follow, and so it was less suspicious to find the same car behind you for miles on end than it might be, for instance, between Coral Gables and Miami.

Time enough to sweat that out if they drove into the city, Lyons thought. In any case, there would be traffic all through Metro-Dade to cover him, unlike the lonely stretches here with sky blue water pressing close on either flank and no place to hide.

Lyons was feeling the pressure, drumming nervous fingers on the steering wheel, when Camacho slowed as they approached the town of Plantation, braking for a right-hand turn on the access road leading to a tourist attraction called McKee's Museum. Lyons drove on past the cutoff to be safe, then doubled back and pulled in cautiously, riding his brakes, ready to draw the Colt Python on a moment's notice if Camacho had some kind of trap waiting for him.

"We've got a stop," he said into the tiny microphone. "Plantation Key. Could be the meeting."

"Watch yourself," Schwarz warned.

"I didn't know you cared."

In fact, there was no trap. His target had parked at one end of a gravel lot fronting the museum, next to a year-old Chevrolet sedan. Lyons found himself a strategic parking slot with a clear line of sight to the subject vehicles. He reached underneath the passenger's seat of his Porsche 928 to retrieve a directional microphone and compact tape recorder.

Just in case.

His turnaround and backtrack had consumed perhaps two minutes, and in that time Camacho had found himself a companion, presumably waiting in the Chevy. Both men were seated in Camacho's vehicle now, and Lyons had his first glimpse of Hector through field glasses, memorizing the craggy profile and receding hairline on sight. It was warm out, typically, and Camacho had his windows down—not that a thin pane of safety glass would have defeated Lyons's particular earphone. The model he carried was designed for penetration, and it was fitted with a voice-activated recorder plus filters to screen out useless background noise.

He switched earpieces, listening in as he taped the conversation going on some fifty feet away. Both men were speaking Spanish, and his knowledge of the language was unequal to high-speed translation. He would have to play the tape for Blancanales, which meant further delays, but it was the best he could do in the circumstances. There was no way to rush the action without risking a major snafu, and he ruled out the "easy" solution of a stroll to Camacho's vehicle, the rapid solution that two trigger-pulls of his Magnum would bring.

There was simply too much at stake. Until they knew what the San Juan contingent of the ANI was planning, how Luis Camacho fit into those plans, a move to take him out risked jeopardizing Bolan and the men of Phoenix Force together with their mission as a whole.

So it remained a waiting game.

His subjects talked for twenty minutes on the nose, most of it wasted on Lyons as he picked out names or scattered phrases, leaving the bulk for Blancanales to translate at his leisure. Lyons jotted down the make and license number of Hector's Chevrolet, just in case the car turned out to be his own rather than a loaner or the subject of tomorrow's grand-theft-auto bulletin. He watched the Cuban leave Camacho's car and get in the Chevy, backing out as Lyons slid down in his seat to hide.

Camacho followed moments later, turning left on Highway 1 in the direction he had come from. "Looks like our subject's headed home," the Ironman told his distant audience. "I'd like to follow Hector, find out where he goes."

"Feel free," the word came back from Schwarz. "Our pigeon has a duty shift this afternoon. He isn't going anywhere."

"Affirmative. I'm headed your way."

Lyons made a right-hand turn and kissed Camacho off, pursuing Hector.

He was running with the hounds.

San Juan
1140 hours AST

BOLAN'S STRING of lightning raids around San Juan had rocked the city, prompting special newscasts on the local radio and television channels. Reporters counted seven dead, all gunmen known for prior affiliations with the FLN or ANI, but no one seemed to have a clue as to their enemy's ID. The word was circulating on Miranda Flores, street-wise, but it hadn't made the news.

Still, Bolan estimated it had reached the proper ears by now, transmitted on the terms of need-to-know. There was no answer from his adversaries, which could only mean that they were standing fast, prepared to weather out the storm or carry the battle to Bolan, given half a chance.

He meant to let them have that chance almost immediately, but it wouldn't be precisely what the revolutionaries had in mind.

One of the places Puerto Rican nationalists gathered to discuss their grievances and vent their rage against the Yankees was a tavern in Condado, west of Calle Labra. Bolan knew that a fair share of patrons on any given day were noncombatant sympathizers with the cause, if that, but this was a special day. If he read his enemies correctly, they would be closing ranks, prepared to do or die in the final extreme.

How many of them were privy to operational details of the "something big" planned by ANI leaders? In all likelihood, few members of the rank and file would be briefed in advance, and fewer still would know enough to jeopardize the operation if they were picked up for interrogation. On the other hand, he thought there was a fairly good chance of discovering where Obregon took "special" prisoners he wanted to interrogate at length.

You only had to ask the proper questions, choose the proper subject.

He nosed the MR2 into an alley, eastbound, coming up behind the tavern, parking two doors down. He left the car and took his H&K MP-5 SD-3 submachine gun with him, fire selector set for 3-round bursts to start. He held the silenced weapon against his leg, as inconspicuous as possible, and picked his way around the garbage scattered at his feet.

A lanky gunner was emerging from the back door of the club as Bolan got there, gaping in a double take that would have been hysterical if it was anything but life-and-death. The choice was his, and when he made it, groping underneath his baggy shirt to reach a weapon, Bolan raised his subgun and fired into his sunken chest. The impact slammed him back against a wall of cinder blocks, from which he slithered down into a boneless fetal curl.

Inside, the place was dark and smoky, not quite cool enough for comfort. Bolan checked the men's room, left it to the flies and moved on to the tavern proper. He counted seven heads: six drinking, one behind the bar to serve. Nobody seemed to notice him for several seconds, then it clicked with the two men seated at the bar. There was a cry of warning, sudden desperate moves for hardware, and all hell broke loose.

He shot the gunners closest to him first, three rounds apiece to lift them off their stools and slam them over backward on the polished wooden floor. His thumb was on the fire-selector switch, shifting the subgun into full-automatic mode as he spun toward a table where three men sat hunched over glasses of beer.

Again the choice was theirs. He was prepared to let the noncombatants walk, if there were any in the tavern, but the three men at the table came out shooting. Tried to, anyway, but only one of them was quick enough to clear the holster with his weapon as a stream of parabellum shockers drilled the hardmen from left to right.

Already turning as they fell, he caught the final patron with a shiny automatic in his hand, just turning from the jukebox, lining up his shot. The submachine gun stuttered, and Bolan saw his target crumple in a heartbeat, going down to stay.

The bartender was still undecided, frozen in a half crouch with his right hand stretching toward a shelf beneath the bar, when Bolan turned to face him with the subgun.

"Your choice," he said.

The barkeep straightened, kept his empty hands where they were clearly visible. "Okay."

"You want to live?"

The man jerked his head in a nod, sweat glistening across his brow.

"Francisco Obregon. You know him?"

The answer was obvious from the bartender's expression, but he hesitated for an instant, finally nodding, eyes locked on the bore of Bolan's weapon.

"He's with a friend of mine right now," the warrior said. "Thing is, she doesn't like his company. I want to pick her up, but I don't have the address. Can you help me out?"

"*Señor,* I don't know—"

Bolan leaned across the bar and held his subgun inches from the man's face. "You see these people every day," he said. "They like to talk. You hear things. One more chance."

This time the barkeep managed an address, repeating it upon command. "Francisco goes there sometimes when he wants his privacy. If he's not there, I don't know where to find him. On my mother's life."

"On yours," the Executioner corrected him, already turning toward the exit that would take him back outside.

He felt the move before he saw it coming and swiveled back to catch the barkeep lunging for his pistol. Four rounds from the H&K improved on his velocity, his face colliding with the beer tap, spewing foam and amber brew.

"My treat," Bolan said, and he took himself away from there.

He had a rendezvous to keep, but first he had to get in touch with Phoenix Force.

"YOU'LL LIKE THIS PLACE," Ruiz said as he parked the car. "Great food, and we can talk without all kinds of interruptions."

"Fine."

Encizo wore his civvies, and the Beretta was tucked into his belt beneath the loose tail of his floral-patterned shirt. The restaurant on Avenida Ponce de León was almost empty. Two men dined at a table near the tinted windows, two more in a small booth on the left. Ruiz kept walking past the counter to a table in the back.

"They know me here," Ruiz explained, a broad smile to the waiter hovering around them as they took their seats. "The meal's on me. Pick anything you like. There's nothing on the menu that I wouldn't recommend."

"That's good to know." He ordered black bean soup and *asopao,* a wet rice stew with fish, and waited while Ruiz decided on a steak, well-done.

"We have a lot to talk about," Ruiz informed him when the waiter had retreated with their orders.

"I'm listening."

"You want to help our cause?"

"I told you that already."

"Understand, Geraldo, that I can't leave anything to chance. One slip could ruin everything, you know?"

"Is there some kind of test I have to take?"

Ruiz looked thoughtful for a moment. "Maybe that's exactly what we need," he said at last. "A test. I know you've got the nerve, but we need something that will bind you to the movement, make you one of us forever."

"Like what?"

Ruiz was mulling that one over when a pained expression crossed his face. He glanced across the table at Encizo, frowned and said, "Excuse me for a minute, will you? Nature calls."

Encizo watched the Puerto Rican rise and walk back toward the men's room, disappearing from his view. Some thirty seconds had elapsed when movement in the corner of his eye caused the Phoenix Force warrior to glance around the almost-empty dining room.

Up front the two men by the window both had risen from their table and turned to face him, their right hands disappearing underneath their baggy shirts. In the booth on his right, two more gunners were on the move, taking positions to bring their target under fire.

A trap!

Encizo ducked below his table, tipping it for cover as he drew the sleek Beretta automatic from his waistband. A pistol cracked, the bullet whining overhead, and Encizo found his target, squeezing off two quick shots that dropped the nearest gunman on his backside, blood spurting from rents in his bright-patterned shirt.

The others broke for cover, one of them slow off the mark, Encizo's third parabellum round punching through the shooter's cheek, pitching him sideways through the restaurant's front window and into the street. The two survivors were blasting away at him now, peppering the corner where he was compelled to make his stand, their bullets knocking chips of wood and plastic from the table that became Encizo's shield.

He glanced back toward the men's room, saw their waiter stretched out on the floor, hands clasped above his head and babbling a prayer. There was no sign of Gregorio Ruiz dashing to the rescue, and alarm bells started going off inside Encizo's mind.

First things first.

He had to move and soon, before the two remaining gunners had a chance to blast him out from under cover. Seizing the initiative, he fired two shots to pin them down, then vaulted clear, careering toward a nearby booth that offered better sanctuary from incoming fire.

One of the shooters saw his move coming and rose from a fighting crouch, bracing his pistol in both hands to sight on the now-moving target. Encizo got there first, triggering a double punch that spun his mark around and dumped him on the floor, a twitching corpse.

And that left one.

The sole survivor had no trouble calculating odds, and he was ready to withdraw, but getting out intact was something altogether different. Squeezing off a hasty burst of fire, he struck off for the door, but Encizo was ready for him, lining up his shot and putting two rounds through the floral fabric covering his adversary's spine. The dying man had two strides left before his legs gave out and pitched him headlong toward the door, his skull impacting on the glass with a resounding crack.

Encizo scanned the battlefield for any other threats, already moving toward the men's room with his pistol cocked and ready. It was fifty-fifty that Ruiz would be there, waiting for him, maybe with a weapon in his hand.

Encizo lost the bet. An open window near the urinals revealed all he had to know about his companion's retreat. He turned and sprinted for the sidewalk, hurdling the body of his final kill, and made it just in time to see the brake lights of Ruiz's car wink brightly on the turn before he vanished into traffic.

Gone.

Pedestrians were gaping at him, dodging to escape this wild-eyed gunman in their midst. He backtracked through the restaurant to find another exit, counting on an alley at the rear to take him out of there before police arrived.

And where exactly could he go?

To find a telephone and get in touch with Phoenix Force.

The shit was coming down, his cover well and truly blown. If that meant danger for the others, they deserved to know.

CHAPTER FIFTEEN

Loiza Aldea, Puerto Rico
Friday, 1345 hours

Waiting was the hardest part for Bolan, but he had to get it right the first time. That meant gathering his forces, briefing them on what had happened to Miranda Flores and preparing them for what he hoped would be a relatively simple rescue operation.

Simple, right.

How many times had that description failed to match the circumstances on a strike that was precisely laid out in advance? He understood the way things happened in the real world, as opposed to being plotted on an antiseptic drawing board at Stony Man Farm. Once living, breathing people got involved, the game could go to hell in any one of several thousand ways, and you would never see it coming until the action blew up in your face.

Still, they would have to cover all their bets beforehand, try to get it right and hope for luck along the way. As for Miranda, if they came too late...

The warrior closed his mind to that eventuality. If she was dead or worse, there would be time to cope with that discovery when it arose. Until then there was nothing wrong with hope, as long as you retained a firm grip on reality and did your part to make things work.

Loiza Aldea is a coastal town, roughly eighteen miles due east of San Juan. Small enough to rank as "quaint" by

Yankee standards, it absorbs sufficient tourist overflow that Anglo strangers on the street don't strike many of the local residents as odd or threatening. A daylight raid had special risks, of course, but waiting for the dark would be too much, an act of negligence and needless cruelty for Miranda.

And there was Rafael Encizo's late report to be considered, too. His cover had been blown, coincidentally or otherwise, and while Miranda didn't know of his existence, the attack on Encizo had come so close to her abduction that it strained the very definition of "coincidence."

Something was breaking on the island; Bolan felt it in his gut and in his bones. He still had no idea exactly what his enemies were planning, but his instinct told him they were getting close.

Another warrior might have left Flores to her fate and concentrated on the central task, but Bolan couldn't work that way. In all his life, regardless of the risks involved, no friend in need had ever been denied a helping hand. There were occasions when his efforts had been futile, true, but never once from lack of trying on his part.

Grimaldi drove the MR2, with Bolan in the shotgun seat, a duffel bag of hardware planted on the floor between his feet. Behind them Phoenix Force packed a dark sedan with guns and muscle, Gary Manning at the wheel. Encizo's premature return had come as something of a shock, but he was anxious to rejoin the battle and square off against his enemies.

Their target was a rural ranch-style house that occupied four wooded acres on the western edge of town. With cultivated fields on either side, it offered privacy ideal for rest and relaxation—or for grilling traitors, if you found one hiding in the ranks. It might turn out to be a bust, the late bartender's desperate bid for life, but Bolan had another of his hunches going in.

Pay dirt.

They used a handy grove of trees to hide the cars, no special effort, but enough to make them inconspicuous on any kind of careless drive-by. All of them were dressed for hiking, with high-topped boots and denim or fatigues, the kind of clothes that pass for Army-surplus casual throughout America and its protectorates. The weapons coming out of trunks and duffel bags would pass for Army-surplus, too, but they were all in perfect working order.

Bolan and his troops were literally dressed to kill.

He sketched a crude map in the dirt and made assignments, watching while the soldiers synchronized their watches. It took ten more minutes for the last of them to get in place and mark his angle of attack.

Ten minutes, added onto all Miranda must have suffered since she disappeared that morning—if, in fact, the lady Fed was still alive.

The warrior concentrated on his work, running a quick check on his M-16 before he put the cars behind him, merging with the dappled shadows of the forest, drifting to the east.

LYING IN THE WEEDS McCarter checked his watch again and scanned the south flank of the house. A swarthy man had glanced out through the nearest window moments earlier, but he was gone now, lost to sight, and it was still impossible to tell how many occupants were holed up in the house.

They had discussed the risks of failure, since they were running with a lead they had no time or opportunity to verify through trusted sources. On the plus side they had found the house exactly as described by Bolan's pigeon, from its geographical location to the faded coral paint job and surrounding trees. That didn't place their hostage in the house, however, and it told them nothing in the way of information on the hostile force they would be facing when they made their move.

With seven guns McCarter reckoned they should have a decent chance of pulling off the strike, but it could still go sour. If they got pinned down outside the house, tied up while anxious neighbors called for the police, it would be all for nothing. Worse, they might be forced to make a choice between surrender and resisting local officers in what could only be a killing situation. Either way police would spell disaster for their mission and perhaps an unintended triumph for their enemies.

McCarter's thoughts were interrupted as a side door opened and two men stepped out into the yard. The shorter one closed the door behind him, and the pair started to walk toward a garage twenty yards beyond the house. One of them scratched himself beneath the baggy shirt he wore, and sunlight glinted from the chrome butt of an automatic in his belt.

The Briton knew that it was time before he checked his watch again. He brought the CAR-15 assault rifle to his shoulder, sighted on the moving targets while his index finger found the carbine's trigger. McCarter squeezed slowly, delicately, as he held his breath.

His first round dropped the short man, boring in behind one ear and tumbling on impact, hydrostatic shock an instant killer with a head shot. Number two turned, startled by the sound of his companion slumping to the ground.

McCarter watched him try to draw and run for cover all at once. The target's body twisted, pivoting and breaking for the house, his shirttail flying as he wrestled with the handgun in its clip-on belly holster.

Too damned slow and awkward to survive.

The next round from McCarter's carbine punched in just below the gunner's raised left arm and knocked him sideways, sprawling on the grass and spewing crimson from a ruptured lung. The shot had pierced his heart, as well, or close enough, and he was clearly dying now, the final tremors of his body fading as the Phoenix Force warrior rose from cover and headed toward the house. He heard reports of other weapons firing on selected targets, tightening the ring.

McCarter had no time to dawdle.

He was running when the first of the defenders opened up with automatic weapons, firing from the house. Bullets raised spurts of sod around him, ripping up the lawn.

MIRANDA FLORES, naked as the day she was born, her flesh mottled with the evidence of Obregon's assault, was drifting in and out of fuzzy consciousness when sudden gunfire brought her back to life. It sounded close, despite the muffling walls, and something told her help was on the way.

She could be wrong, of course. The left- and right-wing zealots in San Juan were fond of battling one another in the streets and in the countryside, wherever they could find a target for their mutual hatred. Miranda had no cause to welcome an attack by neofascists who would turn their guns on her as readily as any other target, even burn the house if they could find a way.

But, no. Her grim survivor's instinct told her this was something else. Belasko, coming to her rescue? There was so much shooting now, guns blasting from the house and on the grounds outside. Could one man be the cause of so much violence? Could he survive, much less arrange for her escape?

Hurried footsteps pounded down the corridor behind her, and Miranda stiffened in her chair. The first thought in her mind was that Obregon or a member of his crew was coming back to silence her for good, but then she heard the clomping noises suddenly recede. Apparently her captors had more pressing matters to contend with at the moment than a naked, hog-tied woman locked inside a cell.

She strained against the wire that held her wrists, but it was knotted tightly enough to cut her as she tried to free her hands. Fresh blood provided lubrication, but it wasn't good enough, and in another moment she gave up, frustration gnawing at her like a hungry rodent trapped inside her rib cage.

Dammit!

If her wrists were tightly bound, Flores's legs were even worse. She had no leverage there at all, and her attempts to free one ankle or the other only cramped the muscles in her thighs. The pain was trivial, but she was getting nowhere and she knew instinctively that time was running out.

How long before a burst of automatic fire ripped through the walls and knocked her sprawling, dead before she even hit the floor? The woman's frustration flared into rage, renewing her struggle against the unrelenting bonds. Blood pattered on the wooden floor beneath her chair as wire bit into heaving flesh, releasing crimson rivulets.

And still, her struggle seemed to have no positive effect.

A submachine gun stuttered in the corridor outside, perhaps ten paces from her cell. Flores cringed but kept on straining at her bonds until the door burst open, its locking mechanism shattered by a solid kick.

It would be over quickly now. She offered up a silent prayer for mercy, just a bullet in the head. She didn't care to see it coming or behold the face of her executioner.

A black man wearing faded denim stepped around in front of her, an Uzi submachine gun looking almost toylike in his hands.

"Miranda Flores?"

Sudden hope was tempered with caution. "That's right."

"We need to haul ass out of here."

"Suits me."

The man stepped around behind her, spent a moment with the wire that bound her wrists, and suddenly her aching hands were free. Flores brought her arms around in front to hide herself as best she could, but her anonymous savior kept his eyes averted as he knelt to free her legs. When that was done, he sorted through the pile of clothing Obregon had shredded when he stripped her hours earlier.

"These things won't do you any good," he said. "Sit tight a minute, okay?"

"All right."

The warrior stepped outside the cell, beyond her line of sight, returning moments later with a baggy shirt and a pair of slacks. The shirt was torn and bloodstained, sickeningly moist against her body when Flores put it on, but she was grateful for it all the same. The slacks were easily two sizes too large around her waist, but when she cinched the belt up to its final notch they stayed in place.

"All set?"

"I'm decent, anyway."

"We'd better go, then."

"Thank you."

When he looked at her, his eyes were warm. "No sweat."

Outside she saw the dead man he had stripped to clothe her, recognizing one of Obregon's ANI comrades, a gunner named Pepe. Miranda stooped beside him, took the automatic pistol from his flaccid hand and checked its load. Six rounds remained.

"Now I'm set."

The man smiled.

"Okay," he said, "let's do it."

A BURST OF AUTOMATIC FIRE sent Yakov Katzenelenbogen diving for the cover of some shrubbery, the last two bullets coming close enough that he could feel them whisper overhead. He had the shooter spotted, second window on the left, but getting in position for a shot was something else. The bushes that concealed him might obscure the gunner's view, but they wouldn't stop probing rounds from finding Katzenelenbogen where he lay.

He had to move, and quickly, before his adversary made corrections and found his range.

Katz rolled out to his left ten feet or so and came up on his elbows, sighting with his M-16 as bullets ripped the screen of shrubbery where he had lain a heartbeat earlier. The sniper's outline was a murky silhouette above the windowsill, but it was good enough. Katz stroked the rifle's trigger, sent four lethal tumblers off to close the gap and watched his target fall back out of sight.

In combat you hoped for the best and assumed the worst, trusting no kill until it was positively confirmed. For all he knew, the gunner might be grazed or merely startled, but his absence from the window bought Katz precious time.

The tough Israeli scrambled to his feet and rushed the house at a diagonal, the windows covered as he ran. Around him sounds of combat echoed from the woods and three sides of the house, as his comrades weighed in with everything they had except grenades. Explosives would have jeopardized the woman Bolan hoped to rescue, and while bullets also put her life at risk, there had been no way to approach the house without a running fight.

Katz neared the sliding doors that opened on a patio of sorts and cleared them with a long burst of fire. Plunging through as shattered glass rained down around him, the Phoenix Force leader went down behind a sofa, groping for another magazine as shotgun pellets rocked the couch. Tattered fabric and stuffing floated down over the Israeli as he lay on his back, snapping the fresh mag into place.

He couldn't see the gunner from his present hiding place, but there was still a chance to bring him down with guile and guts if he could make the timing work. It was a risk, of course, but sitting still and waiting for his enemy to blast the couch apart was certain death.

Sliding on his back and pushing with his heels, Katz made his way as quietly as possible to the far end of the couch. A few more inches would expose his head and shoulders, but he required a suitable diversion first. He took the empty rifle magazine and tossed it so it clattered against the wall some fifteen feet away.

The shotgun blast that followed was directed toward the wall instead of Katz's hiding place. He seized the moment, shoving with his feet and leveling his assault rifle from floor level, catching the shooter in profile. By that time the guy had recognized his fatal mistake, but it was too late to wind back the clock and start over. He swung to face Katz, pumping desperately at the shotgun's slide action. But the grim expression on his face told Katzenelenbogen that he knew it was a waste of time.

A burst of 5.56 mm shockers stitched their crimson tracks across the gunner's chest and punched him over backward in a lifeless sprawl. Katz crossed the room in three long strides and verified the kill.

How many left?

There seemed to be less firing from the house and grounds, but that could simply mean that the defenders had begun to play it cagey, depriving the raiders of viable targets. For all he knew, Katz might have been the first to penetrate the house. His choices were to forge ahead or fall back on the patio and wait for reinforcements.

When you spelled it out that way, he thought, it really was no choice at all.

Katz moved out from the dying room, continuing the hunt.

THE TUNNEL HAD BEEN Obregon's idea. The first time that he saw the safehouse with its separate garage and woods on every side, he recognized strategic weakness in the site. An enemy could creep up on their blind side, ring the house with guns and trap them, cut off from their vehicles in the garage. A man who tried to run the gauntlet would be riddled in his tracks before he covered even half the twenty yards of open ground.

The tunnel was Obregon's answer, granting access from the house to the garage and back again without exposing friendly troops to hostile fire. It had taken the best part of three months, a dozen soldiers working night and day to get it done, but now Obregon had his secret exit from the house.

Just when he needed it.

Given half a chance, he would have liked to take the woman with him, or at least go back and finish her, but he had given that job to Pepe Ramos, thereby shaving crucial moments from his own escape. The eight men who were still alive would buy some precious time for Obregon and draw their nameless enemies directly to the house. With any luck nobody would be waiting for him when he got to the garage and made his break on wheels.

The tunnel started from his private quarters, with a trapdoor hidden in the bedroom closet. It came out underneath a workbench in the large, three-car garage, a refinement that would cover Obregon's arrival even if the enemy had stationed men inside the garage itself.

Inside his bedroom, listening to sounds of combat raging just outside, Obregon double-checked his Taurus PT-100,

.40-caliber automatic, jacking a round into the chamber before he lowered the hammer softly with his thumb. He would have liked to take more weapons with him, but the other guns were all beyond his reach now, and the raid had caught him by surprise.

He would make do with what he had this time.

He opened up the closet, pushed his meager stock of clothes aside and threw the trapdoor back. The tunnel smelled of moist, cool earth, and it was as black as pitch. Obregon took a penlight from the closet shelf and flicked it on, illuminating crude steps gouged into the earthen wall and reinforced with bits of lumber.

With a final glance around his quarters, Obregon shut the closet door behind him, tucked the Taurus pistol in his waistband, gripped the penlight in his teeth and started his descent. Before he reached the tunnel's floor, he reached back up and shut the trapdoor, trusting its layer of carpeting to retard discovery if and when the enemy got that far.

By that time, if his luck held out, he would be well away, beyond their reach.

The tunnel was a simple earthen tube with reinforcing slats of lumber hammered into walls and roof. He had to scramble on his hands and knees, but there was room enough on either side and overhead to make the narrow passage bearable to anyone but claustrophobes. His hands and slacks were grimy by the time he reached his destination, pausing underneath the separate garage, but he was safe.

So far.

Another set of hand- and footholds led him to a second trapdoor, this one underneath the workbench. He took care to make no noise as he emerged in darkness, working without the penlight until he established that he was alone. Spi-

derwebs trailed across his face, but Obregon ignored them.
He had more to fear than scrabbling insects now.

He stuffed the penlight in a pocket of his shirt and drew
his pistol, easing one of the workbench cabinets open a
fraction of an inch. Pale sunlight entered the garage through
several windows on the opposite wall, the nearest vehicle
casting a shadow over his hiding place as he carefully
scanned the garage.

All clear.

Obregon wriggled free and shut the cabinet door behind
him, moving to the middle car in line. It was a vintage Pontiac sedan with power underneath its hood and bodywork
that might with luck protect him from at least the first few
rounds of hostile fire. Beyond that he was on his own.

The cars were always ready for immediate departure, with
keys in the ignition and noses toward the swing-out doors
that Obregon refused to lock unless the site was unat-
tended. Minor details made the difference between survival
and extinction in emergencies, and while he obviously
couldn't help himself from being taken by surprise, Obregon always tried to keep a few tricks up his sleeve.

He slid into the driver's seat, the Taurus locked and
loaded in his lap. He turned the key and smiled with satisfaction as the engine caught first time around. He reached
down to release the brake, remembering his seat belt at the
final instant.

Now!

Obregon braced himself and stood on the accelerator,
both hands locked around the steering wheel. The Pontiac
shot forward, struck the wooden door and slammed it open,
shattering a portion of the plywood frame. Another heartbeat and he was outside, tires finding traction on the gravel
drive, a glimpse of startled figures near the house, one of
them turning back to intercept him.

Gunfire.

Obregon hunched down and kept the pedal to the metal, praying for the first time that he could remember as an adult, running for the open road.

THE GUNNER HAD BEEN waiting for a shot at Bolan, crouching in the shadows of the pantry, but he blew it with a hasty shot before he found his mark. The bullet whistled inches over the Executioner's head, and he answered with a short burst from his M-16 that spun the dead man on his heels and slammed him back against the wall, face first. From there he crumpled to the floor, but Bolan had already put him out of his mind, in search of other targets.

It was winding down from all appearances, a sputtering of gunfire now and then with longer silences in between. The Executioner had dropped three enemies, his latest kill included, and he reckoned the defenders had to be near extinction now.

As if in answer to his thoughts, a pair of gunners surfaced in the corridor on Bolan's left, unloading pistol rounds in rapid fire. He hit the floor, returned fire in a knee-high spiral as he rolled behind a padded easy chair for cover. Even on the move, he saw one of his targets stagger, losing balance as the 5.56 mm tumblers drilled his legs.

The guy was down but far from out, still firing as he hit the floor. His partner, frightened but unscathed, reloaded on the move, kept pumping bullets into Bolan's tattered shield. A few more inches to the left...

The warrior was braced for his move, a heartbeat away from do-or-die commitment, when a sudden storm of subgun and pistol fire ripped through the corridor, eclipsing the reports of his adversaries' weapons. Bolan recognized the sound of dying screams, more rapid fire, then silence.

It was time to take a chance.

He risked a glance around the corner of his hiding place and saw Calvin James bending over the prostrate gunners, inspecting his handiwork. Behind James, Miranda Flores stood with an automatic braced in a firm two-handed grip. She was dressed in a baggy, bloodstained shirt and ill-fitting trousers, but the blood wasn't hers, and she seemed reasonably fit.

Bolan scrambled to his feet and went to join them. On closer inspection, he noted the bruising on Flores's face, the pain reflected in her eyes, but she was still alive and walking on her own. The rest of it would heal with time, and perhaps some distance from the killing grounds.

"You showed up just in time," he told them, glancing at the prostrate bodies of his enemies.

"We aim to please," James said.

"Who's pleasing who?" The question came from Jack Grimaldi, just emerging from the parlor with McCarter on his heels.

"Is everyone accounted for?" Bolan asked.

"Getting there," McCarter replied. "I caught a glimpse of Manning in the yard. Katz must be in here someplace."

"Here!" The sound of Katzenelenbogen's voice was muffled by an intervening wall before he poked his head in through the kitchen door. "All clear?"

"Looks like."

"You want a head count?" James inquired.

"Forget it," Bolan told him. "Time to go."

The tall Canadian was waiting for them just outside, watching dust settle on the narrow access road, a grim expression on his face.

"What's wrong?" Grimaldi asked.

"I missed one," Manning answered. "Coming out of the garage, he took me by surprise. I know I hit the car, but he kept going."

"Only one?"

"As far as I could tell. The trouble is, it looked like Obregon."

"No sweat," Bolan said, clapping Manning on the shoulder. "We can bag him next time."

"Next time, right." The Phoenix Force warrior didn't sound convinced.

But there was bound to be a next time, Bolan knew. The raiders had accomplished their objective in recovering Miranda Flores, safe and fairly sound. It would have pleased him to include Francisco Obregon in the body count, but there was a plus side to letting him go. That way the word of one more failure would be sure to reach Albano and the other ANI commandos, prodding them to either cut their losses and abandon their idea for "something big" or else perhaps accelerate their timetable, running under pressure, making them prone to careless mistakes.

Whichever way it went, he knew the end was coming soon. The terrorists were running short of time and able-bodied soldiers. They would have to make a move and make it soon, before attrition rendered them helpless.

Soon, the hellfire warrior told himself.

And for the moment winning back Miranda Flores would be victory enough.

CHAPTER SIXTEEN

San Juan
Friday, 1427 hours

By now Miguel Albano had decided he could judge good news or bad by simply listening to his telephone ring.

The phone was ringing now, its shrill tone grating on his nerves.

Bad news.

What other kind was there these days?

Albano lifted the receiver gingerly, as if he feared it might explode. "Hello?"

"Miguel? It's me." Obregon's voice was strained and breathless, like a runner's near the climax of a marathon. "We have a problem."

"Stop! Where are you?"

Obregon was smart enough to answer with the number of the public phone booth he was calling from. "It's clean," he said.

"Wait there. Ten minutes."

Hanging up the telephone, Albano left his quarters instantly and walked the hundred yards to reach a pay phone mounted on the wall outside the naval station's PX building. It was open to the elements and anyone who happened by, but he was less concerned about pedestrians than federal bugs. With everything he had endured the past two days, it wouldn't have surprised him to discover his connection to the ANI was known from San Juan back to

Washington. It hardly mattered now, when they were so close to the payoff.

All he needed was a few more hours. He could stall the Yankee pigs that long by covering his tracks and taking various security precautions while they searched for evidence to validate their paperwork. Meanwhile his troops were standing by to make the long-awaited day of judgment a reality for those who tried to beat his people down.

He dropped a quarter in the pay phone's slot and punched the number out from memory. Obregon picked up instantly, his voice still breathless.

"Yes?"

"What happened?"

"They were everywhere, Miguel. I don't know how they traced us. Coming from the woods, we were surrounded."

"At the safehouse?"

"Yes. I barely made it out alive and had to ditch the car at that. Too many bullet holes."

"The woman?"

"Dead, I think."

"You think?"

"I sent a man to do it—"

"While you saved yourself."

Obregon sounded peevish now. "Somebody had to warn you, eh, Miguel? If everyone was dead, you'd never know in time."

"How many men?"

"Eleven."

Make that fifteen, with the men Ruiz had lost that afternoon in his abortive effort to eliminate the man who called himself Geraldo Escobar. Another seven in the morning's latest raids by enemies unknown. He saw disaster heaped upon catastrophe these days, but nothing could defeat Albano while his special team was still intact and waiting for his order to proceed.

"You weren't followed from the safehouse?" he demanded.

"No, Miguel, I'm certain of it."

He had learned to view Obregon's certainties with skepticism in the past two days. Still, in the heat of combat it seemed doubtful that their enemies would manage a successful tail unnoticed. Even with his recent failings, Obregon was still a savvy warrior, skilled in covering his tracks. The safehouse at Loiza Aldea was most likely betrayed by someone on the street, perhaps already dead.

"Do you have a place to stay?" he asked.

"Of course."

"Then listen carefully. You are to have no contact with the special team until I tell you otherwise. No contact with our troops at all. You understand?"

"It shall be as you say, Miguel."

"You have a number at your hiding place?"

Obregon gave it to him, and Albano wrote the number on a scrap of paper from his wallet, then put the scribbled note away for future reference.

"I'll be in touch when it is time for you to move," Albano said. "Until then you do nothing, speak to no one. Understand?"

"Yes."

Obregon might feel put-upon, but he wasn't in a position to object. His string of failures would be grounds enough for execution if he came to trial before the ANI, and Obregon was wise enough to know that. He would grasp at any opportunity to save himself from judgment now, no matter what the cost to pride.

"Be careful. Stay available."

"Miguel—"

Albano cradled the receiver, cutting off what sounded like a plea for sympathy. He made a mental note to deal with Obregon when there was time—if there was time—tomorrow, once the master plan was underway.

Tomorrow.

Even with the weight of recent losses on his shoulders preying on Albano's mind, he couldn't shake the almost childlike feeling of anticipation as he counted down the hours until his final triumph. There were times, remembered dimly now, when he had thought the Day would never come.

But it was on its way.

Tomorrow, bright and early.

Smiling to himself, Miguel Albano turned and walked back to his quarters, whistling on the way.

Havana, Cuba
1330 hours EST

RAUL GUTIERREZ LIT a fresh cigar, then reconsidered and snuffed it out with angry, stabbing motions in the ashtray on his desk. He wished the ashtray could have been a human face, perhaps Miguel Albano's. At the moment any member of the worthless ANI would do.

But there was no one in the office for Gutierrez to attack. He clenched his teeth and kept the anger bottled up inside. It could be used constructively against his enemies once he was able to control and channel his initial fury.

Hector had called from Miami with the latest news of turmoil and disaster from his contact in the Puerto Rican camp. Someone had laid an ambush in the Everglades and terminated most of the ANI's mainland contingent. Gutierrez didn't know how many men were dead, and he didn't care. He had no sympathy for bunglers, and his priorities had to be security, his personal protection and the interests of Havana in the Puerto Rican enterprise.

At last report, the plan was still in motion for tomorrow. He would have another eighteen hours, give or take, to watch events developing, make plans to cut his losses if it fell apart. He wondered what else could go wrong and knew the answer in advance.

Anything and everything.

For all his confidence, Miguel Albano had proved himself to be a careless revolutionary, ignorant of the basic precepts for guerrilla warfare. He held himself out to his troops as an inspirational leader, fueling their zeal with his own, but the end result more closely resembled a cult of personality than a bona fide army of national liberation.

Over two decades Gutierrez had dabbled in revolutionary politics throughout the Western Hemisphere, and he was constantly dismayed at the political ineptitude displayed by his Latino brethren. Governments were toppled regularly in Latin America, juntas variously banished or established, but the end result was seldom any kind of basic change. Machismo and venality combined to sabotage the revolutionary spirit, one strongman stepping in to take the place of another when the smoke cleared and the casualties had all been counted. Since World War II, only Cuba and Nicaragua had established revolutionary governments by force of arms, and Nicaragua's Sandinista regime had endured for barely a decade before its collapse under pressure from U.S.-backed Contra commandos.

All things considered, it was a sorry performance record, and Gutierrez had his doubts about the viability of Cuban communism once Fidel had gone the way of all flesh.

Or when the Yankee government in Washington began to look for scapegoats for Miguel Albano's "master plan."

Raul Gutierrez had served the people's revolution for all of his adult life, but he felt no urge to witness its destruction, especially when the disaster could so easily become his own. Self-sacrifice was more appealing to a youthful warrior than to seasoned bureaucrats in middle age. Gutierrez meant to savor his declining years, and he could only do that if he managed to survive.

His plans were made, the exit route established—from Havana to Kingston on a bogus passport reserved for "special" occasions. Back from Jamaica to Miami, where he would await departure for Switzerland on American soil. It was the last place any of his friends or enemies would look for him, Gutierrez knew, and he already had the Intelligence apparatus in place to assist with his escape.

Hector, at least, was dependable to a fault. Loyal subordinates were a blessing in crisis situations.

They were also expendable.

When Gutierrez made his move, he didn't plan on leaving a trail for his enemies to follow. Thieves and traitors might spend their lives jumping at shadows, living in fear of pursuit, but Gutierrez had better things to do with his time.

Like living.

In that respect, Albano's grand design might yet turn out to be a blessing in disguise. It offered freedom at a time when he was more than ready for a change.

And all he had to do was stay alive for one or two more days.

Beyond that, as the Yankees said, he would be home and dry.

Miami, Florida
1400 hours

"BINGO!"

Coming through the door to the hotel room, Blancanales fanned the air with a manila envelope.

"It took you long enough," Lyons said.

"That's the Bureau for you. Hal got onto Washington and shook it loose or else we never would have gotten anything."

"So give," Schwarz prompted from the sidelines, standing at a window with a view of freeways down below.

The Politician took a seat and drew a sheaf of papers from the envelope. Each page was headed with the standard Bureau filing codes for classified material, and Blancanales was obliged to burn those documents once he had shared the information with his comrades.

SOP.

"Okay. The license plate is registered to Hector Aguilar. We've got his address here, a place off North Miami Avenue. Twelve years in the United States. He came in with the boat lift out of Mariel in 1980. Claimed political asylum, and the immigration people couldn't turn up any record of convictions on the island, nothing they could hold him on. He was naturalized in '86, outstanding in his civics class."

Carl Lyons scowled. "A patriot. Be still, my heart."

"If this guy's clean," Schwarz said, "I'm Whoopi Goldberg."

"Never mind the sex change, Gadgets. He's a plant, all right. The Bureau thinks G-2, out of Havana. More than likely there were several hundred sleeper agents mixed in with the dregs Fidel unloaded while he had the chance. It's perfect when you think about it. So far no one's managed to unravel any of them, but the FBI keeps watching."

"Watching with their eyes closed, from the way it sounds," Lyons said. "We're in town two days and catch him dirty, but the Feds spend twelve years on this guy's case and they've got nothing?"

"Not exactly. He's been in and out of Mexico a couple dozen times, presumably for meetings with a contact who's afraid to hang around Miami. Every time the Bureau pins a tail on Hector, he gets cute and throws it off, but nothing obvious. It could all be coincidence."

"Or someone running interference," Gadgets said.

"Or that."

"So, if he's G-2, what's the Puerto Rican angle?" Lyons asked.

The Politician shrugged. "Nobody knew there *was* a Puerto Rican angle till we brought it up. Offhand I'd say Havana might enjoy provoking trouble on the island. They've been taking lots of flak since Moscow pulled the rug out. Call it a diversion or a show of force, whatever. Maybe Fidel just wants to go out with a bang."

"You want to squeeze this guy and see what tune he sings?" Lyons asked.

Blancanales shook his head. "Not yet. We've got him covered, but I'm more concerned about Camacho. He'll be carrying the ball if anything goes down. I only wish we had a handle on his orders going in."

"Suppose we do?" Schwarz asked.

"How's that?"

"The map I spotted in his quarters."

It had been preying on the Politician's mind, a clue that might mean everything or nothing. Cape Canaveral.

"He'd have to get there first," Blancanales said.

"So, the guy's a helicopter pilot, right?"

"They've got Sikorskys on the base, I would imagine," Lyons said.

"Well, shit."

"We ought to tell somebody," Gadgets muttered.

"Tell them what?" Blancanales asked. "That a Navy pilot has a road map with a circle on it? What's the charge, defacing Rand McNally?"

"If we're right, though—"

"If we're right, the bastard's covered. We can handle it."

"You hope," Lyons said.

"On the flip side, if we're wrong, it won't do any good to start a flap for nothing."

"I wouldn't mind some extra spotters," Lyons said.

"We'll split the difference. Let me make a call," Blancanales replied. "I'll request some special hardware, just in case."

San Juan
1500 hours AST

MIRANDA FLORES SPENT a quarter of an hour in the tub at Bolan's hotel suite, soaking the worst of her aches and pains away before she slipped into a blouse and slacks retrieved from her apartment and joined him in the sitting room for an in-depth debriefing. They had discussed her captivity nonstop on the drive back from Loiza Aldea to San Juan, but there were still unsettling blank spots in the picture, details Bolan wanted to resolve.

"We've covered Obregon's apartment," the warrior told her. "Can you think of anyplace else he might go to ground?"

The FBI agent considered it, tossing her head in a negative. "I didn't even know about the place where I was taken. Damn, I feel so stupid, getting caught that way."

"It happens," Bolan said. "You can't watch all the angles by yourself."

"I've never screwed things up like this before."

"We're still ahead, as far as I can tell." Or maybe not. In any case, he didn't need to add that any slim advantage could be wiped out in an instant if their adversaries caught a break. "About that list of names..."

"I can remember half a dozen of them," she replied, "but none of them were what I'd call distinctive. Picture the Miami phone book, and you're looking for a Charley Smith or William Jones."

"That's not much help."

"You're telling me!"

"You think it was some kind of roster for the ANI?"

"What else?" She hesitated, frowning. "Even so..."

"What is it?"

"Well, it struck me as peculiar that Francisco would have written down the names at all. Security, you know?"

The same thing had occurred to Bolan when she first described the list, but the peculiarity led nowhere. Even if the thirty-odd men on the roster formed some kind of special unit in the ANI, he had no way of learning what that unit was supposed to do... unless he got his hands on Obregon.

"He didn't tell you anything at all?"

Flores shook her head again. "He wanted me to do the talking. As it was, I tried to snow him with the things he should have known already. Tony Camarena. Jaime Sanchez. Throw a little bluff in just to keep him guessing."

"Oh?"

She forced a smile. "I told him we—that is, the Bureau—had him covered on his big surprise. I think it shook him up a bit at first, the fact I mentioned it at all, but by the time you tracked us down, he had to know that I was bluffing."

"You were taking quite a chance."

Flores shrugged. "I didn't have a lot to lose, you know? No matter what I did or said, Francisco had to bury me when he was finished asking questions. Off the top I figured that my only shot would be to try and drag it out."

"It cost you, though."

"I'll mend."

"You show a lot of nerve."

"Is that a compliment?"

The warrior smiled. "I guess it is."

"My, my."

"The best thing you can do is take it easy for a while, lie low until we wrap this up. We have to figure Obregon has blown your cover off with everybody he could reach before we hit the farm. However many guns the ANI has left, they'll all be aimed at you next time you show your face."

"You can't believe I'd sit this out!"

"I don't see any options."

"We can nail it down together. I don't want to run the show, but I won't let you cut me out like it was last week's news."

"We're running out of time," he said, "and you've run out of angles. We got lucky with the safehouse, or you'd be a memory by now. I don't have any room for sideshows at the moment."

"Damn you!"

"Bottom line, Miranda. You can volunteer for R and R, or I can talk to someone at the Bureau. Either way you've done your part. You're out of it."

Fury smoldered in her eyes, but she had nothing more to say. Without another word she rose and stormed off toward the bedroom, slammed the door behind her with sufficient force to rattle pictures on the nearby walls.

So much for personal diplomacy.

It would have been a relatively simple thing to keep her on, create some kind of busywork for her to do around the suite, but she had done enough already—risked enough—and Bolan had no time reserved for coddling the sensitive just now. Miranda Flores on the streets would mean Miranda on his mind, distracting him from life-or-death decisions, dulling his reactions when they counted most.

She had survived interrogation by the enemy, and she wouldn't succumb to wounded feelings. There were others in San Juan, however, who were moving toward a date with death. The Executioner intended to be present when they kept that rendezvous.

And he would carry in his mind a partial list of names.

Stony Man Farm
1520 hours EST

"HE ASKED FOR WHAT?"

"You heard me right," Aaron Kurtzman said, leaning backward in his chair to stretch his burly arms.

"A Stinger? What on earth—"

"He didn't say. Some kind of backup. 'Just in case,' he tells me."

The call from Blancanales in Miami was the latest in a string of messages received at Stony Man Farm within the past few hours. Most of them described new bloodshed, raised the body count, but they avoided any reference to an ultimate solution. Leaders of the ANI were still at large, their "something big" still unidentified, a phantom that haunted Barbara Price.

"You think we're losing it?" she asked.

The Bear considered that a moment, then finally shook his head. "Not yet. We've got the opposition playing duck and cover in San Juan, with all the losses on their side so far."

"They blew Encizo's cover," she reminded him. "And the woman from the Bureau."

"Even so. On top of Sanchez, now they have to sweat out two more infiltrators that they know of. Maybe paranoia makes them careless."

"Want to bet?"

"I'm not a betting man."

There had been much killing in the past two days, but from the periodic field reports it was impossible to point out any concrete progress. Members of the ANI were dying left and right, but Bolan and his troops hadn't set out to wage a war of pure attrition. They were angling for a line on "something big." For all they knew, that plan could be executed by a hard-core team of two or three—perhaps a single man.

And at that moment they had no idea of what that something was.

Frustration nagged at Price and put her nerves on edge. She felt like snapping at her friend across the table but knew that it was pointless and restrained herself. The mission was consuming time, but it was still on track, no major setbacks for the Blue Ridge team as yet. If it required another day, she knew that Striker and the rest were equal to the task.

But each successive hour of front-line duty bumped the odds that something would go wrong, that Striker or a member of his hunting party would be listed as a casualty. In modern brushfire wars, the golden rule of limited exposure still prevailed. The more time special agents spent in contact with their enemies, the greater were their risks of injury or death.

She pushed the morbid thoughts away and concentrated on the up side. Each and every foray by their enemies had been repulsed so far. By any estimate the ANI was running dangerously low on personnel. If they had any kind of masterstroke in mind, the revolutionaries would be forced to launch it soon or kiss the whole damned game goodbye.

And somehow, knowing that did nothing to relieve her mind.

She had a vision of herself inside a house of mirrors, hostile faces all around her, knowing only one of them was real. She could defend herself against an enemy of flesh and blood, but not against the phantom images surrounding her. It was impossible to guess which one would suddenly spring forward, reaching for her throat.

She needed sleep, but there was time enough for catching up when they were finished with the mission, everybody safe and sound at Stony Man. Except, she realized, it might not be that way. So far, not counting the raid that had killed several persons and placed Aaron Kurtzman in his wheelchair, the Stony warriors had a nearly perfect record. Only one man—Keio Ohara, from Phoenix Force—had been lost in the course of an assignment. And every time they took the field, a small, malicious voice reminded her that they were overdue.

This time perhaps. Or next time.

"Are you okay?" The question came from Kurtzman, facing her across the table.

"Fine," she lied. "I guess I need some downtime."

"Be my guest. If anything starts happening, you'll be among the first to know."

She thought about it, shook her head and swept her eyes across a line of blank computer screens. "I'll stick it out awhile. We need to get that package organized for Pol first thing."

"Okay. Don't say I didn't offer."

"No." She rose and left him with a worried smile. "I won't."

The head of Able Team was asking for a missile in Miami, and she didn't have a clue what it was needed for. One more unanswered question, riddles piling up around her till she felt cut off and trapped.

At least she had a job to do, and its details would distract her for a while. She hoped.

San Juan Naval Base
1650 hours AST

"IF THEY WERE COMING, they'd have been here, dammit!"

"Even so..."

Ruiz was almost trembling, and Miguel Albano felt like lashing out at him, a slap across the face to steel his nerves. It was the least that he deserved, considering his latest failure to perform a relatively simple task. In other circumstances, if they had the luxury of time, Albano might have convened a formal court-martial, but they were coming down to the wire now, and he needed every man he had left.

So close.

Perhaps when they were finished, if Ruiz was still alive...

"They won't attack a military base, correct? We have the perfect short-term sanctuary here. It doesn't even matter if they know us, since they have no evidence of what we've planned."

"Miguel—"

"Enough!" Ruiz had ways of making any plan sound hopeless, and Albano's patience was exhausted. "It is bad enough you let this spy escape and kill four of our soldiers in the process. Don't compound your own mistake by trying to subvert our one great chance for victory."

Ruiz considered a retort but thought better of it, simply nodding to himself. He wisely kept his eyes averted from Albano's face, afraid of what he might discover there.

"Francisco has the team prepared," Albano said at last, the anger ebbing now. "By nine o'clock tomorrow morning, they will be in place."

"I still wish I was going with you," Ruiz said.

"But you have work to do right here."

Albano's tone was softer now, almost forgiving. It disturbed him, placing more trust in Ruiz when he had failed so recently, but there was no alternative. The others were required to execute the main phase of his master plan. Ruiz would stay behind to do his job, and even if he failed—again—the loss would be a relatively minor one.

In fact, it might resolve the question of his penalty for failing to eliminate the spy.

"It shall be done, Miguel." The earnest tone was freighted with a nagging premonition of disaster waiting in the wings.

"And afterward," Albano said, "we will discuss your new role in the revolutionary government of Puerto Rico."

If that prospect encouraged Ruiz, he concealed his reaction well. The expression on his angular face was grim, resolved. Albano had seen the look before, on the faces of men who knew—or at least suspected—they were going to die.

"You have all the equipment you require?" Albano asked.

"Don't worry. I won't let you down again."

"Not me, Gregorio. The movement. We are servants of a cause much greater than ourselves."

"I meant to say."

Albano sipped his glass of whiskey, savoring the taste. He felt like toasting something, anything, but his excitement made a jumble of his thoughts. So much to organize, remember, execute. One failure in the next few hours, anywhere along the line, could bring his dreamworld crashing down.

But once the plan was underway—

"To freedom!" he declared, and drained his whiskey in a single gulp.

Gregorio Ruiz, who had no drink in front of him, could only nod and parrot his superior. "To freedom."

Albano's eyes were shining.

"To the greatest moment of our lives."

CHAPTER SEVENTEEN

San Juan, Puerto Rico
Saturday, 0815 hours

The special troops had started gathering unobtrusively near midnight, each man arriving on a schedule of his own. Francisco Obregon had greeted each in turn with a solemn handshake and brief words of encouragement to this or that one.

For the most part they appeared at ease. These soldiers had been chosen from the rank and file for their intelligence and nerve, a process of selection that Miguel Albano shared in part with Obregon. Beyond the choice of personnel, their training had been specialized, and they had been protected—shielded, really—from the daily operations of the ANI. When raids were organized, lives risked on this or that short-term campaign, the special troops were left at home. In fact, they had no duties whatsoever but to master their appointed skills and hold themselves in readiness against the Day.

This day.

Sometimes it felt to Obregon as if he had been waiting all his life. The various indignities his father and the other members of his family had suffered through the years came down to this, a moment that would live forever in the history of Puerto Rico. When he looked back, the murder of his first policeman was a trivial diversion, the attacks on government facilities and Yankee businesses mere stepping-stones.

This was the day Obregon had been waiting for since he was born, unknowing until Albano conceived the plan and put it into action. Finally the years of anger and frustration, poverty and fear, were culminating in an opportunity to turn his life around. Before the day was out, his enemies would learn a lesson in humility, find out what it was like to have their noses rubbed in the dirt, compelled to bow before a master they despised. If he could only see their faces in the White House and the Yankee Congress when the word came down...

But no.

Francisco Obregon had work to do this day. He had been chosen—honored—to accompany the special team on its historic mission. He was going with Albano and the others, off to strike a blow for freedom that the Yankees and the world at large would certainly remember for a hundred years to come.

If their descendants lived that long.

In fact, the risk of a counterproductive apocalypse had declined in the past twelve months. The collapse of the Soviet empire made everything simpler, ruling out the sort of deliberate misunderstanding that could have sparked World War III. If the Yankees went hunting for a scapegoat, they would almost certainly direct their wrath at Cuba, a risk Albano and his ANI compatriots were more than willing to accept.

Castro has served his purpose, but he was a political dinosaur. The world was changing, and old men were required to step aside to make room for the young, the revolutionary innovators.

Obregon buttoned the collar of his U.S. Navy uniform and studied himself in the mirror. His new haircut felt strange, leaving his ears and the back of his neck exposed, but it was part of the total package. Each of the others had shaved and had his hair trimmed prior to suiting up. Their brass might not be polished to the nth degree, but they would pass inspection where it counted. By the time discrepancies were correlated, recognized by anyone in power, it would be too late.

The bus was also regulation, purchased with an eye on uniformity and painted to resemble any other standard Navy vehicle. Some minor details on the inside had been overlooked, but they weren't important. All that mattered was the first impression, a facade to get them past the gate without a hassle.

And it helped, of course, to have their own man on the gate this morning, standing watch. The sentry's orders were specific and they didn't come from Washington.

Obregon felt the urge to laugh out loud, but this was much too serious. He had been waiting for this moment all his life, and now that it had finally arrived, he dared not jeopardize it with frivolity.

Besides, his time was running out.

"The bus!" he told his men. "Prepare to board. It's time."

The members of his special team lined up, each carrying a compact duffel bag with gear and weapons packed inside. Whatever happened in the next half hour, they had made their preparations in accordance with the plan.

No word was spoken as they trooped outside and took their seats on board the bus. Obregon waited with the driver, standing to the side and counting heads from force of habit, more to occupy his mind than for any other reason. Everyone was present and accounted for, no pieces missing from the puzzle.

Ready.

In another moment they were all aboard, the driver in his seat, Obregon perched behind him with a heavy duffel bag between his feet. His heart was pounding savagely, but he wasn't afraid. It was exhilaration coursing through his veins.

The bus began to move, and Obregon sat back, his face turned toward the window. Six or seven minutes to the base, with traffic. Once inside . . .

He smiled at his reflection in the glass.

It had the makings of a grand, historic day.

San Juan Naval Base
0840 hours

COMMANDER RUPERT Woodhouse pushed his empty breakfast plate aside and lit a cigarette, glancing across the mess table at his first officer, Captain Albert Trask. Around them muted conversation from the other officers created a kind of murmuring background music to his private thoughts.

Woodhouse felt relaxed, but he was never perfectly at ease in port. Unlike some officers and men in the submarine service, he relished sea duty, living for the times away from land, submerged or otherwise, when he could test himself against the greatest single force on earth.

At present, though, the *Thresher* was in port, docked at the San Juan Naval Base after completing its circumnavigation of Cape Horn twelve hours early. They had put in near midnight, well ahead of schedule, and he had granted shore leave to dispensable members of the crew. Eight of his eleven officers and ninety of his one hundred fifteen enlisted men were now ashore, unwinding as sailors had from time immemorial, risking hangovers and worse in pursuit of momentary pleasure.

Commander Woodhouse had seen his share of ports, his share of bars and easy women. As a lifelong pragmatist and bachelor, he wasn't constrained by marriage vows or puritanical conceits, but this time—at the age of forty-seven—he was simply tired. If they were in San Juan another day or two, he might get out and test his land legs, but for now he was content to stay on board and see the *Thresher* pampered in her berth.

They would be shipping stores that afternoon, including rations, medical supplies and sundry other items needed for the next leg of their journey. From San Juan they were expected in Australia two months down the road, and there were exercises to be carried out along the way. Not war games in the sense of joining up with any fleet, but solo exercises of the hunter-killer sort that kept commandos and their men in fighting trim.

So many things had changed the past two years, including cutbacks in defense, but Woodhouse had no fear of suddenly becoming obsolete. America would always have her share of enemies abroad, whatever label or philosophy they chose to hide behind. His father had seen action on a cruiser in the North Atlantic during World War II. It had been Nazis then, a right-wing menace to the peace of all mankind, with Stalin's left-wing storm troopers waiting in the wings. Today the Russians might be down and out, but there were avaricious Arabs, Red Chinese, Vietnamese and North Koreans, plus a brand-new Germany to think about. Tomorrow, for all he knew, there would be other bogeymen to guard against.

In essence Woodhouse was a kind of watchman at large, equipped with some of the most magnificent—and potentially destructive—home-security devices ever conceived by man. His submarine was one of the sleek Los Angeles Class, the only U.S. Navy nuclear attack submarines capable of matching speeds with a carrier task group. Its armament included six horizontal firing tubes for conventional torpedoes, UUM-44A-2 Subroc, or Mk 48 A/S torpedoes, plus fifteen vertical launching tubes for Tomahawk tactical nuclear missiles. The 360-foot hull was coated with anechoic tiles to frustrate enemy sonar, no mean feat with a craft the length of a football field, which displaced some 6,900 tons when submerged.

Woodhouse was proud of his ship and what she could do, but like most committed lifers in the push-button age, he hoped he would never have to put the *Thresher* through her paces in a real killing situation.

The sound of his own name distracted Commander Woodhouse as the disembodied voice of a communications officer requested his presence on the bridge. Woodhouse rose, crossed to the bulkhead intercom and acknowledged the message, leaving his plate and silverware for one of the mess hands to stow.

There had been something in the voice of his communications officer. Not fear, exactly, but something close to it.

He found three strangers waiting for him on the bridge, covering part of his skeleton crew with side arms. Bulky silencers made the pistols look fat and awkward, but no less lethally efficient.

As Woodhouse drew near, one of the gunmen—clad in a spotless ensign's uniform—stepped forward and addressed him without the customary salute. Woodhouse let it go, since the young man obviously had his hand full.

"Good morning, sir." The ensign's elocution was as textbook perfect as his message was bizarre. "You're being relieved of command at the moment. We'll be putting to sea as soon as my men are on board."

Aboard the Thresher
0845 hours

IT HAD ALL GONE like clockwork so far. Albano and Ruiz were waiting when the bus arrived, their third companion on the base standing watch at the gate, a volunteer for morning sentry duty. Obregon and the special team were even a half minute early, rolling through the gate unopposed after a cursory inspection of their forged papers.

Perfect.

It was risky business on the base itself, where any challenge might have touched off a free-for-all firefight, but the military mind-set worked to their advantage. The bus and its passengers had been cleared at the gate; hence they must be legitimate. Unfamiliar faces meant nothing on a Navy base, where different ships were constantly arriving, changing personnel and putting back to sea. The nuclear attack sub *Thresher,* for example, had recently unloaded most of its crew for shore leave, new faces all.

And some of them were about to be replaced.

The plan had been simplicity itself, so basic that Miguel Albano was amazed no one had thought of it or something like it in the past. Who had the weapons and the means of transportation to effect a major strike against the target of your choice anywhere on earth? Which armed institution recruited its personnel from the streets, more or less at random, with few—if any—security precautions?

The U.S. military was an ideal Trojan horse, the perfect vehicle for retribution on a massive scale. If you could tolerate the weeks of boot camp, bide your time through special training and manipulate the placement system to your own advantage, call upon selected comrades from outside, there were no limits to the damage a committed zealot might inflict—a loaded rifle carried by a member of the presidential color guard; two soldiers squatting in a missile silo, somewhere on the open plains of South Dakota; a strategic long-range bomber crew; or—

There had been no way for him to manage twenty-five or thirty members of the ANI on the base, but that was where the Cuban angle worked to his advantage. Once Albano had struck his paper bargain with Havana, he found out that his suspicions were correct. The Cubans had a Russian submarine they used for training purposes, one of the Victor Class, and while its various controls were different from those on an American submersible attack craft, there were certain basic similarities, enhanced by stolen blueprints, U.S. training manuals and the like. Small groups of Puerto Ricans had been trained, no more than five or six men at a time, until he had the thirty men he needed, in addition to himself and Obregon.

It seemed so easy, looking back, that he was moved to pause and wonder where the past two years had gone. The Day had been a long time coming, even longer for the patriots who sat in prison cells and families who grieved for nationalist heroes rotting in their graves.

Gregorio Ruiz was with Albano when they met the bus, but he wouldn't be coming on their grand adventure. There was work for him to do around the base, some mopping up and preparations for a minor secondary strike if anything went wrong on board the submarine.

But nothing would go wrong. Albano felt it in his bones.

There was a sentry on the dock beside the submarine. The young man was bored with standing watch, confused when he beheld the double file of uniforms approaching, the spit-shined regulation shoes in perfect step. The sentry wore a pistol on his hip, but he made no attempt to draw it as the new arrivals stood in front of him. His curious expression turned into shock when Obregon produced a weapon of his own.

The sentry was disarmed and marched back aboard the *Thresher*. Obregon, Albano and a half-dozen members of their special team went below with pistols drawn, rushing the bridge and demanding an audience with the commander before their new hostages could sound an alarm.

Now here he was.

Commander Woodhouse was a stocky man with close-cropped, graying hair, broad chest and shoulders underneath his tailored uniform, strong hands that flexed unconsciously with their desire to wrap around Albano's neck.

But he was cool. Albano gave him that.

"Who are you people? Let me see your orders."

Smiling as he raised the automatic pistol with its silencer attached, Albano said, "You're looking at them."

Woodhouse scowled. "And you expect to waltz a nuclear attack sub out of here without a crew, without supplies, a day ahead of schedule? No one bats an eye, is that the plan?"

"I have my own crew, as you see," Albano told him, nodding back toward the companionway, where members of his special team were boarding now. "With luck our journey shouldn't be a long one. We won't be serving any banquets on the way."

The sub commander glared back at Albano. "And suppose we don't cooperate?" he challenged.

Smiling with the pleasure of a dream come true, Albano turned and drilled the nearest sailor with a point-blank round between his eyes, blood spattering the bulkhead as he fell.

"In that case," he responded, "each and every one of you will die."

San Juan Naval Base
0900 hours

IF ANYONE HAD ASKED Gregorio Ruiz how he felt about being left behind when the *Thresher* sailed with her new team on board, he would have mouthed some appropriate line about duty and sacrifice, a patriot's responsibility to see his mission through.

The honest truth was that in a way he felt relieved.

So much had happened in the past two days, most of it bad, that he was having second thoughts about the master plan. Indeed, he had been having second thoughts about his whole involvement with the ANI, but there was nothing he could do to turn the clock back now. Albano would see him dead before he let a trusted comrade walk away.

But Albano was out of touch just now. He had his hands full with the submarine, his plan to force concessions out of Washington at any cost. Ruiz could cut and run if he was so inclined, before the hijacking was noted and the base was closed. Who was there left to stop him?

No one but himself.

Because he *was* a patriot, regardless of the fear that gripped him now, when they were standing on the brink of an apocalypse, so many of his friends already killed, a nameless enemy intent on finishing the sweep around San Juan. Ruiz had work to do, if he was able, and he knew that he could never call himself a man if he refused to try.

It was a relatively simple task, compared to what Albano had in mind. Ruiz had weapons and explosives hidden in his quarters on the base, with timers for the plastic charges. One way or another, win or lose the crucial play, he was supposed to plant those charges at strategic points around the naval reservation, primed to detonate around the time Albano delivered his personal ultimatum to Washington.

Whatever became of Albano and his men aboard the *Thresher,* one Yankee outpost in Puerto Rico would be crippled, with communications severed, fuel and ammo dumps destroyed. If possible, he was supposed to catch the ranking officers at mess or at their duty stations, kill as many of them as he could before his time ran out.

It wasn't necessarily a suicide mission, but Ruiz accepted the fact that he would probably die. The prospect briefly depressed him, but he countered the black mood by considering his options. Life in prison for his terrorist crimes if he was captured by the CID or FBI. An eight-by-ten-foot cell where he would watch the seasons change through cold steel bars, his body wasting through the years.

Assuming he was able to escape, what would his life be like without Albano and the excitement of their revolutionary quest? Ruiz's widowed mother lived in Altosano, barely scraping by on what he sent her from his weekly paycheck. One of his sisters was married to a drunken idiot, with three kids of her own; the other was a low-rent hooker in New York. The family name would die with him, in glory or disgrace.

The choice was his.

Ruiz chose glory, even if it meant that he could number the remaining hours of his life on his fingers with some left over.

So be it.

A man was shown his duty, sometimes only once in life, and if he did his best, at least his memory would be preserved by future generations. If he had to die, perhaps Ruiz could be an inspiration to the freedom fighters of tomorrow.

And, he told himself, there was an outside chance—however tiny—that Albano might succeed. The Yankee pigs in Washington were experts in survival, at the polls and otherwise. Perhaps they could be made to understand that the time had come for Puerto Rico to be free at any cost. Once they absorbed that fact and weighed their own self-interest in the balance, they would have a choice to make.

And if Albano won the day, it meant Ruiz had hope. Assuming he was still alive when Washington caved in.

But he would deal with first things first.

Inside his quarters, he removed the duffel bags concealed beneath his bed, extracted fifteen plastic charges and began to set the timers, leaving intervals that would allow for placement, making detonation simultaneous. When he was finished there, he took the Ingram MAC-10 submachine gun, loaded it and double-checked his dozen extra magazines.

And there was nothing more for him to do but wait.

He still had time before he had to plant the charges, longer yet before his move against the officers on the base. Once he began depositing his parcels at selected sites, Ruiz knew there could be no turning back. If he was going to desert and save himself . . .

Too late.

Gregorio Ruiz was out of choices.

He had passed the point of no return.

Aboard the Thresher
0927 hours

IN THE PAST eighteen months, Miguel Albano had become a self-taught expert on the subject of nuclear attack submarines in general, and the Los Angeles class submarine in particular. He knew, for instance, that the *Thresher* was powered by a one-shaft S6G pressurized-water-cooled nuclear reactor, with two geared turbines generating 35,000 horsepower on the shaft, for a top speed in excess of thirty knots, submerged. The electronics included hydrophones, the BQQ-5(A) multipurpose spherical sonar array, BQS-15 short-range sonar, BPS-15 surface detection radar, and the sophisticated BQR-21 DIMUS—Digital MUltibeam Steering—sonar conformal array. All of which meant that the sub would be impossible to take by surprise.

And with the anechoic tiles that lined her hull, Albano knew the *Thresher* should be able to elude pursuers well beyond the time he needed to select his firing position and broadcast his ultimatum to Washington.

And if they were intercepted by surface or submarine craft en route, well, it was the firepower that truly pleased Albano. The Mk 48 A/S torpedoes were electrically powered, fired from the same 21-inch horizontal tubes that handled the larger UUM-44A Subroc missiles. Each Subroc was a two-stage solid-fuel rocket, carrying a nuclear depth charge for deployment against strategic-missile submarines. After launching, the rocket motor ignited underwater, and the missile surfaced, homing on a preset point at which the depth charge separated, reentered the sea and detonated at a predetermined depth.

But the submarine's kicker, without a doubt, had to be the fifteen BGM-109 Tomahawk Sea-Launched Cruise Missiles—SLCMs—carried in vertical-launch tubes along the *Thresher*'s spine. Twenty-one feet in length and 20.9 inches in diameter, the Tomahawk was launched with the 7,000-pound thrust of a tandem rocket boost motor, propelling the SLCM clear of the ocean's surface. Once airborne, the Tomahawk's wings and tail fins deployed, air inlets opened, and the Williams F107 turbofan sustainer engine kicked in with 600 pounds of thrust after a zero-G pushover, while the booster engine burned out and dropped away. A Tomahawk could cruise for some 1,550 miles at a speed of 550 miles per hour, using inertial guidance until it reached the target coastline. From that point onward, the Tomahawk exploited terrain contour matching—TERCOM—using contours of enemy terrain stored in its guidance library. On the final approach to its target, terminal guidance was switched on, using digital scene-matching area correlation—DSMAC—as one of the most precise guidance methods in military service. Bull's-eye accuracy was guaranteed, with targets refined to the point that a Tomahawk could be directed to a particular window, doorway or vehicle on command.

In a pinch it could even find the Oval Office of the White House...and the *Thresher* would have fourteen Tomahawks to spare. That made allowances for Congress and the Pentagon, State and Justice, the FBI Building and U.S. Supreme Court, Dulles Airport and CIA headquarters in Langley, Virginia. At that, pinpoint accuracy was almost superfluous, since each Tomahawk carried a nuclear warhead of 250 kilotons, guaranteeing a hundred percent kill factor inside a one-and-a-half-mile radius.

If he got tired of battering Washington and its suburbs, Albano could always drop a Tomahawk on Wall Street, maybe Constitution Hall in Philadelphia, or Boston's Old North Church, perhaps the Norfolk shipyards. Cruising south, he could soon be within range of Charleston, Savannah, Miami—even New Orleans and Houston.

The possibilities were limitless.

Standing on the bridge as they steered north toward the mid-Atlantic, Albano felt truly powerful for the first time in his life. It was a new, unique feeling for a child of peasants, used to living as an insignificant cog in the master's machine, and Albano meant to cherish it as long as it lasted.

He had set his face toward victory, and there could be no turning back. If this was to be the last day of his life, at least he wouldn't live it as a slave.

CHAPTER EIGHTEEN

Old San Juan
Saturday, 1005 hours

The news flash came by way of Stony Man Farm, to Phoenix Force in Puerto Rico. Yakov Katzenelenbogen touched base with Grimaldi, who in turn got Bolan on the line. By 10:00 a.m. the seven warriors and Miranda Flores had convened in Bolan's hotel suite to plot their strategy to see if they could salvage something from a situation that was rapidly disintegrating while they watched.

"It never would have crossed my mind," Flores told the room at large from her position on the couch at Bolan's side. "A submarine?"

"That's what Albano counted on," James said.

"What kind of hardware is she carrying?" McCarter asked.

Katz grimaced as he answered. "With the fifteen Tomahawks on board, enough to make the Eastern Seaboard look like Judgment Day plus one."

"Two hundred fifty kilotons times fifteen. Jesus." There was weary resignation in Grimaldi's voice.

"So, that's the bad news," Bolan said. "We need solutions."

"Make that miracles," McCarter interjected.

"At the moment I'll be satisfied with strategy."

"The Navy's after him by now," James stated.

"With everything they have," Katz said, "for all the good that it will do."

"They must have ways of tracking ships," Flores interjected, "for a circumstance like this."

"Each vessel has communications gear, of course," Grimaldi said. "There are homing devices in case of emergency, but most of them have to be activated on purpose. The *Thresher*'s crew might not have the option."

"Navstar?" Manning prompted.

Jack Grimaldi frowned and shook his head. "If the sub's running on the surface, sure. Make target acquisition, and the Navstar link will bring your missiles home like shooting fish in a bucket. If they run submerged, though—like they ought to, if Albano wants to live past lunch—the satellites won't do us any good at all without an activated homer."

"Dammit!"

"It would help if we could get a fix on where they're headed," James remarked.

"The Tomahawks can travel just a fraction over fifteen hundred miles," Katz said. "If we assume a target stateside, that leaves—what, about a third of the Atlantic Ocean?"

"If he's sitting still, at that," Flores added glumly, staring at her shoes.

"That's right," Grimaldi said. "With fifteen Tomahawks on board, he could run from Miami to Maine, lighting fires all the way, before anyone zeroes him in. Maybe go deep for a while and head east, take a shot at London or Paris for the hell of it."

"He'll want American targets," Bolan said with confidence. "That's the name of the game."

"What's more American than Washington, D.C.?" Katz asked.

"L.A.," James said.

"Too far."

"Manhattan. Philly. Newark." James was on a roll.

"His major beef is with the government," Bolan said, cutting in before the ex-Navy SEAL had a chance to recite the names of every East Coast city from Portland to Fort Lauderdale. "He might not stop with Washington, but I'm betting he'll start there."

"Okay," Grimaldi said, "that leaves us with potential offshore launch sites anywhere within a radius of fifteen hundred miles. Somebody got a map?"

They found one, measured out the distances and sketched their killing zone. If the *Thresher* lay well offshore, near the limits of its effective firing range for SLCM contact, it could still drop Tomahawks on targets within roughly two hundred miles of the nation's capital, ranging north as far as New York City and southward to the neighborhood of Portsmouth, Virginia. Conversely the closer Albano brought the sub toward shore, the farther his firing range extended north and south for secondary launches, with targets ranging well into Newfoundland and the Caribbean.

"You don't just grab a submarine and sail away," Grimaldi said. "They needed training, and they didn't get it from the U.S. Navy. Even Albano's never worked in the submarine corps."

"That narrows down the field," McCarter said.

"But Able Team marked a Cuban contact in Miami," Bolan added. "Possible G-2, according to the Bureau. That way they'd have hands-on practice."

"The easy way to clear this up," Encizo said, "is why don't we ask them where they're going?"

"Call them up, you mean?" McCarter asked.

Encizo shook his head. "My guess would be they only trained a special crew. That means somebody had to stay behind. We haven't wiped them out. So find whoever's left behind and squeeze 'em till they sing."

"It's worth a shot," Bolan said.

"What about the *Thresher?*" Jack Grimaldi asked.

"You get along with Navy brass all right." Grimaldi blinked. "I guess."

The Executioner looked thoughtful now. "How would you feel about a cruise?"

Old San Juan
1015 hours

WATCHING THE SUBMARINE depart without him was the hardest thing Francisco Obregon had ever done. Disappointment was part of it, he knew. He wanted to be involved in the great climactic moment, even though he hadn't been a part of the specialized training in Cuba, and he knew he would only be deadweight on the final voyage. He had brought the crew to their destination, an authority figure they feared and respected, but there was still a vestige of hope for the payoff, until...

He knew it was over when Albano began to speak about security precautions on the island, reminding Obregon of what he had to do, shaking his hand in farewell before it was time to cast off the submarine's mooring lines and clamp down the hatches. Illogical disappointment welled up in Obregon's chest, no less bitter for the fact that he had been expecting nothing less.

He drove the bus off the base and ditched it in an alley, leaving his uniform jacket and tie behind, deliberately scuffing the spit-polished shoes to detract from their shine.

Wiping down the steering wheel and other surfaces for fingerprints was a fine point, but he took no chances, just in case. No one looked twice at his white shirt and Navy trousers as he put the scene behind him, sticking to side streets for most of the hike back to his hideout.

It would be comforting to linger there and wait, tune in the television news and watch the world go crazy when Albano started giving orders to the Yankee pigs in Washington. A treat, but Obregon wasn't allowed the luxury of freedom. He had work to do, assembling the remnants of their army in San Juan, preparing for the hour when Washington would crumble—one way or another—and the ANI would march triumphantly into the governor's mansion, seizing the reins of power in the name of the Puerto Rican people.

They were running desperately short of men by now, which was a problem. But he had already summoned twenty from surrounding provinces, and they were standing by. Who would have led them if Obregon had been granted permission to remain aboard the *Thresher* as it sailed? No matter. Fantasy was one thing, and reality another. He was living in reality today, and that was all that counted.

Changing into his civilian clothes, a budget suit and tie, Obregon stared at his reflection in the full-length mirror, Obregon stared at his reflection in the full-length mirror. It wasn't as dashing as a uniform, but it would do when he confronted Puerto Rico's governor. There would be newsmen on the scene, inevitably, snapping pictures, shouldering their video cameras and jostling for a decent angle on the shot.

It suddenly occurred to Obregon that *he* would be the man on every television screen from Moscow to Manhattan in the days ahead. Albano might be in command, calling the shots from his seaborne command post, but the submarine was hopelessly out of touch with media contacts. At best, Albano could open his radio channels, beam his comments to the world at large without a face to match the words. Someone in Navy personnel could maybe find a snapshot for the cameras, smiling in his uniform, the way they did for people who were dead or missing.

Perfect.

While Albano made history, Francisco Obregon would *become* history, playing to the cameras, granting interviews to all comers once the smoke cleared. By the time Albano set foot on dry land again—assuming he ever made it back— there would have been some changes in the starting lineup. Obregon would be the man to see, with troops around him, millions of his grateful countrymen chanting his name in the streets as if he were the pope or a visiting movie star.

And maybe things would work out after all. Perhaps his disappointment on the dock was meant to be, a stepping-stone before his final triumph, taking everybody—himself included—by surprise.

Stranger things had happened in the course of history. A river changed course and drowned the sleeping population of a rural town, creating a new lake where their homes once stood. Sudden death propelled a virtual nonentity into the White House, paving the way for nuclear holocaust or sweeping social reforms.

Plans were meant to be followed, but they were also subject to change without notice. Obregon meant to follow Albano's schedule as written...up to a point. He would make all the moves, connect all the dots, but at the final moment it would be Obregon in control, for all the world to see.

A twist of fate, perhaps, but he was glad to help fate out if necessary.

Starting now.

Kingston, Jamaica
0950 hours EST

RAUL GUTIERREZ DEPLANED without incident at Palisadoes International Airport, wondering if anyone around the office complex in Havana would have missed him yet. His departure had been hasty, true, but he was in and out on any given day. It would require some time for anyone to really think of him as missing, putting two and two together. By the time they checked his home and started looking for his car, he should be safely in Miami.

Waiting.

There had been some doubts within the final hours that Albano and his people would have nerve enough to pull it off. The bulletin from San Juan, broadcast to the Guantánamo naval base and picked up by G-2's electronic ears at the same time, confirmed the *Thresher*'s removal from port by unauthorized persons unknown.

Gutierrez had to give the Puerto Ricans credit. They had carried off their coup so far, but they had far to go. The journey wasn't long in miles, but every hand was turned against them now. If things went wrong—*when* things went wrong—Albano wouldn't even have the Russians to make sympathetic noises on the floor of the United Nations in New York.

Too bad.

It was a miracle, Gutierrez thought, that they had even come this far. Especially considering the past three days, with so much killing and disruption, all of it directed at the ANI. He still had no idea of who was out to bust Albano's operation, and he didn't care. It was enough for Raul Gutierrez to be off and running toward his new life, free and clear.

In that respect, at least, the episode would be an epic milestone in his own career. It was ironic, he decided, that the one man truly liberated by the ANI should be a Cuban officer with more than twenty years of service in the cloak-and-dagger trade.

Would wonders never cease?

He hoped not.

In Miami, Hector would be waiting for him with another set of airline tickets. There had been no opportunity to double-check his flight time, but it didn't matter if he spent the night in Florida. One Cuban more or less would pass unnoticed in the crowd. Besides, the government was busy hunting Puerto Ricans now and waiting for a voice of thunder from the sea to speak its words of doom.

Gutierrez gave the rebels credit for audacity. Their plan was doomed to fail, of course, but it was still a bold endeavor. Best of all, it covered his departure from Havana, via the United States, with all the chaos he could hope for.

His new passport named him as a citizen of Venezuela. Any major background check would prove the story false, but that would only happen if authorities in Switzerland had cause to question his veracity. In fact, Gutierrez planned to be a model immigrant, avoiding conflict with his wealthy neighbors, shunning contact with police. There was no reason anyone should ever doubt him, no way for his former comrades in G-2 to track him down.

It would have been a different story in the old days, when Havana cultivated close relations with the KGB. In cases of defection to the Continent, Raul Gutierrez and his colleagues simply made a phone call to their Russian counterparts and deadly wheels began to turn. The end results might be abduction or assassination, but it seldom failed.

Today there was no active KGB, no Russian interest in pursuing fugitives from Cuba. If and when G-2 went looking for him, they would doubtless trace him to Jamaica, given time...but then?

Where would a Cuban officer with over twenty years of service to the state seek refuge in the world at large? America was close at hand, but that meant grappling with the FBI and CIA for starters, running into one brick wall after another. It would soon be evident that he hadn't defected in the classic sense, bartering secrets for a farmhouse in Idaho or Minnesota. Once that was established, the usual motive stripped away, his trackers—if they cared enough to carry on the hunt—would have to think again. It was conceivable that they would think of Switzerland, but seeing through his plan and bringing Raul Gutierrez back for trial were very different things.

The Swiss had built their very culture on neutrality, a passion for the right of privacy and self-determination. If and when the bloodhounds ran him down, Gutierrez could stand and fight within the law, claiming political asylum from the Communists...or he could disappear once more.

But he would think about those options when the time came. At the moment he was free and clear, about to start a brand-new life. The money in his numbered Swiss account was waiting for him, and he had enough packed in his bags to get him by in the meanwhile.

It was a bright new day, and life was good.

The secret agent's faith in starting over made him smile...but he didn't forget to watch his back.

Hutchinson Island, Florida
1005 hours

THE MEETING SITE had been selected with a view toward privacy. Pol Blancanales lounged against his rented car, arms crossed, his shirtsleeves rolled up past his elbows, a safari Stetson casting shade across his somber face. Beside him, on the fender of the car, a walkie-talkie was tuned to receive any message from Carl Lyons, who was watching the narrow access road that led across a causeway to the mainland.

Hutchinson Island was mostly swamp at its southern tip, boasting a few historical landmarks from the era of Spanish exploration, offering refuge to campers and hikers, underage dopers and skinny-dippers of every description. Seldom patrolled except on demand, in the case of emergencies, its humid forests were a welcome respite from the neon-chrome bustle of Florida's Gold Coast.

The last time Hutchinson Island made headlines had been twenty years ago, when a renegade cop used the swampland as a dumping ground for young women he raped and murdered—more than twenty in all. The cop was doing life at Starke, still denouncing his conviction as a Byzantine frame-up, and Hutchinson Island had retreated into pleasant obscurity, well-known to locals, terra incognita to the world at large.

It was a perfect place to make the pickup, halfway from Miami to their target zone.

Except that the delivery boy was running late.

Blancanales checked his watch again, the corners of his mouth turning downward to a scowl. A Spanish curse was forming on his tongue when the walkie-talkie suddenly hissed static, the Ironman's voice coming through.

"Contact."

The Politician raised the handset and keyed the button for transmission. "Roger that."

He wore his pistol openly, no jacket to conceal it or impede his draw. Lyons would have told him if the new arrival drove a squad car. This would either be their man or some third party who would benefit from being warned away in no uncertain terms.

In either case, it was a break in the monotony.

He heard the jeep before he saw it, rolling over gravel, bouncing in the ruts carved out by frequent rain squalls. Coming into view, the vehicle slowed, its driver checking out the clearing, ready to reverse direction if he smelled a trap.

The contact would be federal, Blancanales assumed, but he wasn't concerned about affiliations at the moment. All he wanted was the hardware he had ordered via Stony Man, and soon, before their time ran out.

The driver satisfied himself they were alone—no glimpse of Gadgets showing through the trees where he had taken up his post an hour earlier—and pulled the jeep up close beside Pol's car.

"Nice day for hiking."

"If you don't get lost," Blancanales replied, finishing the recognition signal to his contact's satisfaction.

"Right. Let's get this done. You wanna check the merchandise?"

"I do."

"So lookee here."

The young man left his engine running, scrambled from the driver's seat and walked around behind the jeep as Blancanales stepped from his sedan. Pol's shirt was plastered to his back from the humidity, despite the hour.

"Step right up."

His contact drew a tarp aside to reveal a high-impact plastic case some six feet in length, two feet wide and one foot deep. As Blancanales watched, he snapped the latches open, threw the lid back and revealed what lay within.

"You checked out on this little toy?" the stranger asked.

"No sweat."

"If you say so, fine by me."

It was the latest model FIM-92B Stinger Post—for passive optical scanning technique. Unlike the early tail-chaser models, the new Stinger Post was guided by an all-image infrared seeker, vastly enhancing its capabilities for picking a chosen target out of the sky. The IR-guided missile measured five feet overall, with a 70 mm diameter and folding wings with a 5.5-inch span. Its maximum effective range was 5,500 yards, reduced by 250 yards in vertical flight for altitude limitations. The Stinger weighed thirty-five pounds, close to seven of that residing in the HE-fragmentation warhead with its automatic proximity fuse. Its sophisticated guidance mechanism was detachable for use with subsequent throwaway launch tubes.

In Afghanistan, Stingers had made life hazardous for pilots and crews of the Russian Hind gunships, and their pinpoint accuracy made the weapons a hot item among terrorists from Belfast to Palestine and Sri Lanka. Commercial airlines lived in fear of the day some psycho with a private ax to grind would park his car outside a major airport, remove a black-market Stinger from the trunk, aim and blow an aircraft out of the sky.

Blancanales took the weapon from its carrying case, shouldered it to remind himself of the feel and checked the sighting mechanism to be sure that it was fully operational. The Stinger Post would be a one-shot deal in terms of stopping Luis Camacho, but one shot was enough if you placed it correctly.

"It'll do," he told the stranger, placing the Stinger back in its case and making the transfer to his own vehicle. The stranger—CIA, whatever—nodded once and put his jeep in reverse, cutting a tight one-eighty before he powered out of sight along the unpaved access road.

"All clear," Pol said into the walkie-talkie, wishing that was true.

He had his weapon, and his target was identified, but the ultimate firing zone was still a calculated risk. If Blancanales blew that part of it, the Stinger would be useless.

Stony Man Farm
1025 hours

TRACKING GEAR HAD TAILED the *Thresher* along its northbound course when those in command ignored radio demands for an explanation of the unscheduled departure. San Juan had the submarine on-screen for the best part of half an hour . . . until it reached the Puerto Rico Trench.

More than five miles deep in places, the trench includes the greatest known depth of the Atlantic Ocean, recorded in 1961 by the USS *Archerfish*. There may in fact be greater depths unknown to surface-dwelling man, where giant squids and creatures new to science dwell in the eternal darkness, but five miles give or take was adequate to take a nuclear attack sub off the San Juan radar screens for good. Once hidden by the great abyss, the *Thresher* could run east or west at will, emerging at any one of a thousand different points, remaining submerged for days or weeks on end.

Striking whenever, wherever she chose.

And that, of course, was the rub.

It shouldn't be supposed, however, that the *Thresher* had vanished without a trace. Five life rafts, with six men in each, had been recovered twenty miles due north of Arecibo. Commander Rupert Woodhouse and his men were all accounted for, except one ensign shot and dumped at sea by the men who had captured the sub. The *Thresher*'s commander even had a message for the world, delivered in the tight-lipped tones of one who blamed himself for failure, watching his career go down in flames.

The message was simple and direct. The subjacking had been accomplished by Puerto Rico's Army of National Independence, acting on behalf of "the people." Total freedom for the island nation was their goal, and they would be in touch with terms before the day was out. If Washington agreed without delay and set the wheels in motion for releasing Puerto Rico from the yoke of Yankee slavery, everyone involved could celebrate a happy ending. On the other hand, if macho Yankee politicians tried to flex their muscles for the media, the *Thresher*'s Tomahawks would fly.

So far, the media was ignorant of what was happening. The Pentagon and White House meant for it to stay that way as long as possible. The First Amendment notwithstanding, certain stories had such grim potential for destroying public confidence—and wiping out political support—that Washington was loath for them to see the light of day.

Which left it to the Navy and, to some extent, the team from Stony Man.

"I don't know what they want from us," Price said. "The Navy can't find its own ship, and what are we supposed to do?"

"It cost about five hundred million dollars coming off of the assembly line," Kurtzman said. "The theft alone would raise a major flap without the Tomahawks and the extortion angle."

"So?"

"Hal's been in contact with the Man, reminding him that we've got people covering the ANI. I guarantee you, the reminder wasn't necessary. Anything that Striker's team can do to squeeze the remnants, help the fleet be ready when the

Thresher makes her move, we're on the hot seat. Stateside, Able Team still thinks they've got a fix on this Camacho character. Could be a sideshow to the main event."

"Why not just pick him up?"

"For what? Unless the FBI or CID can build a solid case and take him down, we just postpone his play. Then, even if they tag the *Thresher* first time out, you've got Camacho waiting for a chance to do his thing, get even if he can."

"Put him to sleep," she said.

"We thought about it, but Pol isn't one hundred percent convinced that Camacho's alone. Ninety-nine point something, okay, but he wants to be sure."

"Suppose he's wrong about the target?"

"Something tells me we'll find out."

"Terrific."

"Anyway, Grimaldi's shipped out on the *Exeter*, leading a carrier battle group. They don't have any kind of fix on *Thresher*, but they're working hypotheticals from firing ranges, trying to be ready when she blows."

"It's not exactly fish in a barrel, is it?"

"More like hunting a minnow in Lake Michigan. The sub has all kinds of evasion gear, but the Navy still has countermeasures up its sleeve. Viking subhunters and the Sea King chopper for a start. We're not done yet."

"I hope that's right," she said, clearly not convinced.

"You can't do any more than what you've done already," he reminded her.

"That's the problem. Famous last words—'I did my best.'"

"There's worse that could be said."

"It won't much matter if we blow it."

Kurtzman frowned. "Not every defeat is your personal responsibility," he said.

"Tell that to Striker and the others."

"They already know it, Barb."

"I wish I could be sure of that."

"Could be you need a break when we wrap this up."

"I'll think about it after."

"Sure, okay."

She sipped her coffee, needing the caffeine like she needed a kick in the head. Correction. Another kick in the head. Her temples were already throbbing with tension, and she knew the fledgling headache would be a screamer by noon if she didn't relax.

Fat chance.

The enemy had slipped their net somehow, pulled off that "something big" in spades. The hijacked submarine was beyond Bolan's reach now, a whole different game, but the Stony warriors might still be able to salvage something on land.

She kept her fingers crossed, a superstitious trait from childhood she had never quite let go. It wouldn't help, but what the hell.

It couldn't hurt.

CHAPTER NINETEEN

Key West Naval Air Station
Saturday, 1105 hours

Now that it was almost time, Luis Camacho harbored thoughts of personal mortality. He wasn't frightened of the end, per se, but it had never seemed real to him before the massacre in the Everglades. He'd watched men die on every side, all of them known to him, a few of them counted as friends.

He had escaped that trap, but there was worse in store. He had a million to perform, and it could easily cost Camacho his life. Even a successful strike would leave him in grave jeopardy, hunted by the Yankee FBI and by the Navy's own investigators. With most of the stateside ANI dead or missing in action, he had no one but Hector Aguilar to count on after the deed was done—and who could really trust a Cuban when it came to that?

No matter. He would do his duty and hope for the best, expect the worst and exert every effort to destroy his enemies.

The helicopter would help. It was a Sikorsky SH-60B, designed as a multirole shipboard chopper, currently land-locked at Key West in a combined defensive-rescue mode. With a maximum cruising speed of one hundred forty-five miles per hour, the Sikorsky could reach his chosen target in something under two hours, less than half the air time granted by the hundred-gallon long-range fuel tank. A round-trip was no problem for the aircraft, but Camacho didn't plan on coming back.

One way or another, his days with the U.S. Navy were finished.

At present the Sikorsky's range and ultimate destination were less important to Luis Camacho than the chopper's armament. In its various configurations, the bird could carry weapons ranging from M-60 machine guns and 70 mm FFAR rockets to wire-guided TOW missiles and the lethal AGM-84 Harpoon cruise missile. Sadly, from Camacho's point of view, the Navy didn't stock antipersonnel or anti-armor munitions for its seagoing choppers. Torpedoes were the standard fare, but he had found a way to improvise.

At that, he was well satisfied with his choice of the Penguin Mk 2 Mod 7 antiship missile his chopper would carry this day. A Norwegian design, the Penguin weighed in at 727 pounds with a 250-pound warhead, operating with a combination of inertial guidance and a passive infrared homing system. At sea it was designed for surface or air launches against enemy ships, the IR guidance system homing in on heat sources such as a target ship's funnel from any range up to 12.4 miles. In practice, adapting the Penguin for use on land, Camacho meant to be considerably closer when he took his shot.

Close enough, that was, to send his missile in where it would do the maximum amount of harm.

Simply loading the Penguin had required no small amount of ingenuity. Forged orders for a special "training exercise" had done the job, assisted by the military frame of mind that didn't question edicts from above. As long as there was paperwork to justify an action, it was taken as legitimate and someone else's problem if anything went wrong.

In normal circumstances, the Sikorsky would have shipped a three- or four-man crew, but Camacho was going up alone this morning. Prepared for anything, he packed his flight bag with emergency items, including a Beretta automatic pistol, four extra magazines, civilian clothing and two thousand dollars in cash. There would be no time to waste if he survived the mission, fleeing for his life with nothing but the slim advantage of manufactured chaos behind him to delay pursuit.

An optimist of sorts, he had already picked the chopper's final resting place, an isolated section of the Tosohatchee State Preserve in Orange County. From there it was a short hike to Highway 520, where he would pick up a car—at gunpoint, if necessary—and make his way back to Miami on I-95. Hector Aguilar would be waiting for him, everything prepared, and in a few more hours he would be out of the country, presumably bound for Nassau until the charter boat veered off course when the time was right and headed for Cuba.

Sanctuary.

He would be safe in Havana for the duration, until the fallout began to settle and Washington fell into line with Albano's demands. Conversely, if the masterstroke should somehow fail, Camacho would remain in Cuba, pampered in his new life as a revolutionary freedom fighter.

It was perfect.

But he had to carry out his mission first.

The Sikorsky was ready and waiting when he arrived, the maintenance chief inquiring after his copilot, frowning when Camacho explained he would be taking the chopper up alone. It was against procedure, but Camacho flashed another set of bogus orders, putting on an attitude and challenging the maintenance officer to double-check by telephone if he doubted the paperwork's authenticity. It was a high-stakes gamble, but it worked; his adversary backed down, grumbling that it wouldn't be *his* responsibility if anything went wrong.

Not much.

When word of the Camacho mission got back to Key West, there would be enough blame and accusations to go around for all concerned. Heads would roll at the naval air base, brass hats included, and the thought of so many punitive actions, transfers and reductions in rank—even courts-martial—made Camacho smile as he buckled himself into the pilot's seat.

He ran his checklist, fired the dual 1,900 shp General Electric T700-401C turboshaft engines and let the fifty-three-foot rotors come up to speed. Moments later the Sikorsky was airborne, passing over the Mud Keys and skimming blue water on its way to the Florida mainland, homing in on Cape Sable and the Everglades beyond. Far to the northeast, in Brevard County, he felt the target drawing him like a gigantic magnet, its pull irresistible.

Camacho settled back in his seat, switched off the chopper's radio and listened to the siren song of destiny.

Aboard the USS Exeter
1215 hours AST

AN F-14 TOMCAT DELIVERED Jack Grimaldi to the USS *Exeter's* flight deck, touching down at one hundred sixty miles per hour, the pilot pushing his engines to full power in case he missed the four arresting wires and had to lift off for another pass.

No sweat.

He got it right the first time, bringing the twin-engine jet fighter to an abrupt halt within three hundred fifty feet of touchdown. A team of blue-shirted handlers brought their tractor out, connected towlines to the F-14 and hauled the fighter back toward elevator number four. When it was safely chocked and chained, Grimaldi's pilot cleared the canopy and they were free to deplane.

All around Grimaldi carrier personnel were busy with their appointed tasks, distinguished at a glance by their brightly colored shirts. Aside from the blue-clad handlers, there were yellow shirts to direct the movement of aircraft on deck, white shirts to handle safety-related tasks, green to handle the carrier's four catapults and arresting wires, purple to fuel the various aircraft, brown shirts designating plane captains who supervised individual planes and red for handling weapons and ammunition.

The ensign who approached him now wore khaki, starched and pressed with creases that looked sharp enough to slit a throat. His face was young, made grim by the requirements of his job and present circumstances.

"Sir." The ensign snapped a crisp salute in honor of Grimaldi's borrowed uniform. "The captain requests your presence on the bridge."

Which meant he wanted to find out who Grimaldi was and why the Pentagon had dropped him in his lap.

Fair enough.

"Lead the way, Ensign."

Captain Thomas Londergan was a tall, thin man with chiseled features and a pair of piercing, sky blue eyes. Laugh lines marked the sunbaked leather of his face, but he wasn't laughing today as Jack Grimaldi joined him on the bridge. The men exchanged salutes and sized each other up for several seconds before Londergan pointed to a nearby door and said, "In there."

A hasty briefing had told Grimaldi that Londergan had twenty-three years in service, including the *Exeter*'s combat role in Operation Desert Storm. He had also served, at less exalted rank, in the American invasion of Grenada. His father had sailed against the Japanese under Admiral Bull Halsey, and pride of service ran deep in the Londergan family. This wasn't a man to suffer fools gladly or welcome presumptuous strangers on board his flagship.

Alone with Grimaldi inside a tiny office, Captain Londergan turned to face him, a frown etching furrows in his cheeks. "I have my orders, Mr. Grant. I'm sure you know their contents as well as I do."

"I caught a briefing, yes, sir."

Londergan forged ahead as if Grimaldi hadn't spoken, still using the pseudonym that came attached to Grimaldi's orders and military gear. "I'm to cooperate and offer you the full assistance of my task force, Mr. Grant, no questions asked. I have to tell you that doesn't set well with me."

"I understand."

"You do? I wonder." The captain sat behind his desk, leaving Grimaldi to stand in the center of the room. "It's bad enough we're hunting one of our own today, with orders to kill on sight. Now I've got a total stranger dropping in from nowhere, pulling weight enough to make me second fiddle on my own damned ship!"

"Nobody's superseding you, Captain. I'm not qualified to lead a naval task force if I wanted to. Fact is I've got one job right now, and that's to stop the *Thresher* if we catch a break and run her down."

"Twelve ships I've got here, Mr. Grant," the captain said, "and eighty aircraft. Who decides I need a stranger dropping in from out of nowhere on a one-shot deal?"

"You'd have to pass that question on to your superiors, I guess."

Londergan let that pass without comment, clenching each fist in turn with strength enough to make the knuckles pop. "You're checked out on the Sea King helicopter?"

"And the Seahawk," Grimaldi replied. "I've also flown the Viking, if it comes to that."

"Is there anything you can't do?" Londergan inquired.

"Right now," Grimaldi told him somberly, "I can't quite put my finger on the *Thresher*."

San Juan
1220 hours

TRACING REMNANTS of the ANI required some careful thought. The private army had been whittled by attrition over three grim days before Albano's main event went down, and while the ANI had troops enough on tap to crew a submarine, Mack Bolan had no way of knowing whether there were any members left around San Juan or where they might be found.

It all came down to covering the bases, checking every possibility. To that end, Rafael Encizo—alias Geraldo Escobar—had gone back to the San Juan naval base to nose around and see what he could find without involving agents of the CID. If there were any traces of the enemy remaining, he would root them out, report back to the team and follow where they led.

Meanwhile, it would be Bolan's task, combined with Phoenix Force, to work the streets and beat the bushes, looking for a trail that they could follow, anything at all to put them on the track of a surviving ANI commando. They needed someone they could squeeze for details of Albano's master plan before it was too late.

The worst part, Bolan knew, was that the critical initiative had passed from his hands to the enemy's. A key to his success in other battles had been speed, audacity, the knack for keeping foes off balance, forcing them into defensive postures, reacting to Bolan's rapid-fire assaults. He had proceeded on the same lines this time, rolling up a body count and staggering the enemy with coordinated offensives, but Albano had foxed them, holding a team in reserve and grabbing the *Thresher* from under their noses.

Now, Bolan feared, recovering the crucial edge might be impossible. The hijacked submarine was certainly beyond his reach, but there were still loose ends to tidy up around San Juan . . . if he could only scope out where to start.

They picked up with another run past Obregon's apartment, came up empty there and started working through the short list of targets remaining in San Juan. Another bar, a restaurant, a brothel in Condado where ANI triggermen sometimes hid out from police in the wake of drive-by shootings. The tavern and brothel were closed, no sign of life on the premises when Bolan and his Phoenix Force warriors crashed the party looking for a live one to interrogate. As for the restaurant, its clientele seemed strictly average this afternoon, no members of the ANI in sight. It would have served no purpose to destroy the place or terrorize its customers, and Bolan let them dine in peace.

Still hunting.

With every passing moment, Bolan's frustration mounted. He could hear the doomsday numbers falling, feel precious time slipping through his fingers while he waited for the enemy to surface, show himself and give the Executioner a target. Somewhere in the middle of the vast Atlantic Ocean, fifteen deadly Tomahawks were cruising toward their launching point; perhaps their guidance systems had already been "corrected" to direct their lethal warheads into downtown Washington, New York, Miami, Boston, Philadelphia.

Bolan tried to recall the last time he had felt so helpless, thinking back to the earliest days of his one-man war against the Mafia. It seemed to him the stakes had never been so high before, the odds so stacked against him in the final stretch.

"We haven't tried Antonio," Flores said when they had traveled several blocks beyond the restaurant.

"Who's that?"

"Antonio Rivera," she replied. "He's more or less Francisco's contact with the media around San Juan. He writes a column for the *Vigil*—that's a left-wing weekly on the island—and he has good contacts with the mainstream press and television. If the ANI was looking for a way to break a story—"

Bolan cut her explanation short. "Where do we find this guy?"

Flores checked her watch. "He's probably at lunch right now," she said. "I'll take you to his office. We can start from there."

It might be stretching, Bolan knew, but at the moment it was all he had. Long shots had paid off for the Executioner in other campaigns, and he was willing to gamble on this one.

As if he had a choice.

"Let's do it," he declared, and raised his walkie-talkie, reaching out for Phoenix Force.

Washington, D.C.
1135 hours EST

"THE WAY IT LOOKS," Brognola said, "we're screwed unless the search team finds that sub damned quickly."

Facing him across the cluttered desktop, Leo Turrin glowered, wishing he could disagree. "Location's only part of it," he said. "If anyone on board knows what they're doing with the guidance systems, we could see those Tomahawks show up on Pennsylvania Avenue or Wall Street anytime."

"I'd bet my pension someone on the *Thresher* knows exactly what he's doing," the big Fed replied. "They didn't get this far by guesswork, as it is."

And that was true, of course. No matter how he tried to minimize the danger, Turrin knew they were in major trouble now. The *Thresher*'s hijacking would be a grave embarrassment to Washington, but once the missiles started flying...

Even if they blew it with the pinpoint accuracy, Turrin realized, there would be hell to play along the coast. Suppose a Tomahawk was aimed at downtown Washington and missed by miles, detonating in Alexandria or Baltimore. The seat of government might well survive, but hundreds of elected officeholders would still see their careers go up in smoke. Political fallout from such a disaster would be as far-reaching as the radioactive variety, its effects taking longer to fade.

"We'll make it," Turrin thought to himself, only realizing he had spoken aloud when Brognola answered.

"I hope so. In the meantime we've got Able Team sitting on Camacho, ready if he tries some kind of end run on his own. At least I *hope* they're ready."

"Bureau sources estimate eighty percent of the ANI membership neutralized within the past three days. Stateside the estimate says two, three surviving members tops, including Camacho. We're making headway."

"Right," Brognola said. "And they forgot to count the bunch who went to submarine school, I suppose." He shook his head. "Somebody dropped the ball on this one going in. They caught us with our pants down, and we didn't have a goddamned clue."

"This has to be what Sanchez was about to spill when he got wasted in San Juan."

"Sounds right to me," Brognola groused. "For all the good it does us now."

"This kind of thing takes time and cash to organize. A splinter group like the ANI, they can't have much on tap in terms of backup plans."

"They don't need much if they can pull this off."

In one sense, Turrin thought, they had already pulled it off. Hijacking a nuclear submarine from a U.S. Navy base would be the propaganda coup of the decade for any terrorist group, regardless of whether the Tomahawks flew. Miguel Albano's profile showed a different sort of mind at work, however. This one wasn't satisfied with halfway measures, compromises, cutting losses.

He would want the whole nine yards, regardless of the risks involved.

"You've spoken to the Man?"

"Damned right," Brognola said. "He won't capitulate on hostages, much less secession of a U.S. territory. If anything goes wrong beyond the present point, whichever heads survive are bound to roll."

"It could be worse," Turrin said, putting on a mirthless grin.

"How's that?"

"It could be an election year."

"Is that supposed to ease my mind?"

"Not really. What's the latest read from Able Team on Camacho?"

"We had some trouble getting Pol to spell it out at first. He didn't want to sound a false alarm on top of everything that's happening."

"Seems fair."

"They found a map of Florida among Camacho's things when Gadgets checked his quarters. Someone drew a ring around the Air Force base and NASA launching site at Cape Canaveral."

For just an instant Turrin could have sworn that he was sitting in an elevator, hurtling toward the basement at a hundred miles an hour, nothing in the way of brakes. The moment passed, and he unclasped his knotted fingers with a conscious effort.

"Well."

"My thought exactly," Brognola replied. "We've tipped the base commander off, for what it's worth, but Pol still wants to stop Camacho on his own if he can pull it off."

And if he couldn't, Leo thought, there would be one more flash point for disaster on the Eastern Seaboard. One more time bomb ticking off the heartbeats until detonation, when the world would begin to come apart.

"Camacho is a pilot?"

"Right. He took off from Key West a while ago in a Sikorsky packing heavy hardware. We've been tracking him with radar to see which way he goes. For all we know, he could be homing in on Disney World."

But Turrin didn't think so. When Miguel Albano beamed his final ultimatum to the White House and the world, it would be helpful if he had a fresh example ready to exploit, hot footage to run along with his demand that Puerto Rico be released from any ties to the United States.

What better than the smoking ruins of a landmark that had been a household word among Americans for over thirty years?

"I'm sending Angelina and the kids to see her mother," Turrin said, as if the life-and-death discussion boiled down to vacation plans. "They're gone, in fact."

"Good move," Brognola said. "I talked to Helen, but she wouldn't go. You see who wears the pants."

"We're not done yet. They haven't even laid the deadline down."

"I ever compliment you on your optimism, Leo?"

"Not that I recall."

"Well, there you go."

Behind him on the wall, the big institutional clock ticked off another minute, reminding Turrin of the story told about Voltaire and the clock he kept beside his bed. Each time it struck the hour, a somber voice intoned, "One hour nearer the grave."

And Turrin knew exactly how it felt.

Brevard County, Florida
1145 hours

THE VERY CHOICE of lookout points had been a gamble in itself. It stood to reason that Luis Camacho would approach from the southwest—if he was bound for Cape Canaveral at all—but there was still a chance that Pol would miss him on the pass in spite of everything. They had the radar operators at the cape and nearby Patrick Air Force Base on full alert, for all the good it would do. Between commercial airlines, charter flights, private pilots and incoming drug planes, Florida had enough air traffic to keep the screens crowded, but Blancanales had stopped short of scrambling military aircraft to help in the search.

Above all else, he knew they must not scare off their pigeon.

If Camacho was forced to seek alternate targets, veering west toward Orlando or Tampa, maybe buzzing north toward Jacksonville, they were lost. Pol's one and only chance to stop him with his payload still on board would be Camacho homing in on Cape Canaveral, as marked out on his map.

When Blancanales spelled it out like that, he realized how great the gamble was. A circle on a common highway map, drawn weeks or months ago by God-knows-who, and he was risking any hope they had of heading off disaster on a private hunch.

Terrific.

They had confirmation from the Key West naval station that Camacho had departed from the base in a Sikorsky, flying solo with a Penguin missile armed and ready to perform on cue. A cautious duty officer had double-checked Camacho's orders—too damned late—and found he had no clearance for the flight, much less removal of a Penguin from the base. Once more the Politician had pulled every string at his disposal to abort a hot pursuit by Navy fighters.

Waiting now, he hoped that he wouldn't regret that move.

Assuming he lived long enough.

Blancanales sat in the open bed of a four-wheel-drive Toyota pickup, with Carl Lyons at the wheel. The sliding window to the driver's cab was open for communication with the Ironman, and a long-range two-way radio was fit-

ted underneath the dash. Beside Pol, in the truck bed, lay
the Stinger missile in its case, a pair of spotting glasses and
an M-16 assault rifle loosely covered with a beach towel.
Blancanales and Lyons each had federal paperwork to justify the hardware if they were stopped by police. Gadgets
was burning up the highway from Key West, racing against
time, with no real prospect for making the rendezvous.

As for Blancanales and Lyons, their chosen beat was a
stretch of Highway 520 from Rockledge, across Merritt Island to Cocoa Beach. The odds against success with any
kind of stationary post were too extreme, and even with the
mobile unit, Blancanales knew they still might miss their
quarry altogether. If he circled eastward, for example,
coming in across the water, they were screwed. It would be
too late to scramble fighters in defense by that time, though
Pol had the satisfaction of knowing Camacho would soon
be shot down as he tried to escape.

And if the rocket-launching site wasn't his target, after
all ...

Pol concentrated on the positive. It made a twisted kind
of sense, as such things went, Camacho striking at a symbol of the Yankee military-industrial complex, thereby reinforcing Albano's ultimatum when the word came down.
If nothing else, the fact that he was still airborne, still moving on a northeast course, encouraged Blancanales to believe that he was right.

A radar contact in the last ten miles or so would let him
calculate the Sikorsky's course with fair reliability. Meanwhile, mobility was their edge, a marginal advantage in
comparison to the helicopter's range, but something Pol
could stake his slender hopes on.

If he blew it, if Camacho managed to slip past them with the Penguin, it would all come down to Able Team. It had been Pol's request to leave the interceptors grounded, blanketing Camacho's mission with a cloak of secrecy. In fact, jet fighters could have nailed him at a hundred different points above the gulf, perhaps the Everglades, no risk at all to innocent civilians on the ground, but Pol had wanted to confirm his judgment of the target, make the tag himself.

It wasn't ego, even if it subsequently looked that way to a review board, when the smoke cleared. Blancanales needed to be sure, confirm that this would really be the end of ANI subversion on the mainland. There was nothing he could do about a missing submarine or the guerrillas still at large in Puerto Rico, but Camacho was his baby all the way. Surrendering his mission to another agency was worse than demonstrated weakness; it would leave the job unfinished, open-ended, Blancanales wondering forever if the work was truly done.

From inside the cab he caught a burst of static from the radio, words lost amid the rush of wind. He waited, knowing Lyons would pass the message on.

"Still coming," Lyons told him through the open window. "Dead on course."

Which meant the chopper would be passing over water when it crossed the highway east of Merritt Island, flying low, he guessed, in an attempt to beat the radar on its final run.

Too late.

Camacho would be dead on course, all right, if Pol had anything to say about it. He had one chance to do it right, the M-16 an afterthought, in case he had to do some mopping up. But if he missed Camacho with the Stinger, it would be all over.

Dead on course.

He sat back in his low-slung lawn chair, staring at the empty sky through mirrored shades.

"Come on, you bastard, let's get it done."

CHAPTER TWENTY

Aboard the Thresher
Saturday, 1245 hours AST

Traveling submerged, listening to the sounds of a submarine vessel approaching its maximum depth, was a new experience. The hull creaked and groaned like an old house settling, and Miguel Albano noted the uneasiness displayed by certain members of his crew. Their training runs aboard a Russian sub seemed incredibly distant now, and they had never practiced under combat conditions, hunted by aircraft and warships that meant to destroy them on sight.

This was reality, and fear was part of the rush.

Albano held his position on the bridge, feeling the boat around him like a living thing, watching his men perform their various duties. In a way he felt like Jonah from the Bible lessons he had studied as a child, swallowed by a giant whale and carried far from home. Unlike the hard-luck sailor, though, Albano felt no terror at his plight. The boundless sea was camouflage, this whale his transportation to a better life.

Or death.

He couldn't rule out failure as a possibility, but he wasn't dismayed by the forces ranged against him. If this was his last day on earth, it would still be a day for future generations of his countrymen to remember with pride, the day when revolutionary warriors made their stand and taught the Yankee "masters" that control of subject peoples has a price.

He had been tempted to retain some members of the Anglo crew, as hostages if nothing else, but they couldn't be trusted to perform their duties at gunpoint. One or more of them was bound to play the hero, doing anything within his power to sabotage Albano's mission at a critical moment. Better to kill them all—or, as Albano had decided on the spur of the moment, to use them as preliminary spokesmen for his message to Washington.

His time was coming, and the men he had selected for this special thrust against the enemy would get him there with grim determination and a little luck.

The working blueprints that Raul Gutierrez had obtained for the Los Angeles Class nuclear attack submarine were wholly accurate as far as Albano could tell. Navigation underwater had required the most intensive study for his special team, but they were handling the pressure well. He would be interested to see how they performed under fire, but Albano wasn't overly concerned. The members of his special team had been selected both for their intelligence and their commitment to the cause of Puerto Rican freedom. Each and every one of them had vowed to sacrifice his life in lieu of capture or defeat... and if their courage failed them, where was there to run?

Albano checked his watch, turned his attention back to the nautical chart spread before him and saw that they were more or less on schedule. At least another hour remained before he planned to beam his ultimatum off to Washington. Releasing Captain Woodhouse and his men had simply been a preview, with Albano saving the main pleasure for himself. The Yankee bureaucrats would know exactly what was coming, granted, but Albano's voice might also reach the media and spread panic in the streets.

He hoped so.

It would serve the bastards right, prevent them from delivering some vague excuse when they were forced to grant his various demands. With any luck the world would know exactly who was in control, and if the White House managed to suppress the news of his demands somehow, the truth would still be publicized once he was safely back in Puerto Rico.

Safe.

The possibility of failure cropped up in Albano's mind once more. He knew that they were being hunted by the fleet, and as a Navy man he recognized the capabilities of ships and weapons built specifically to track down hostile submarines. The *Thresher* was designed to slip through Russian sonar, but the Yankee engineers wouldn't devise a system without countermeasures of their own.

He had a decent chance, all things considered, but the ultimate result came down to speed and nerve. If he could reach the firing zone before the hunters caught him, then Albano reckoned he had won. It didn't matter if they sank the *Thresher* once he launched his liberated Tomahawks against the U.S. mainland.

For most of his life, Miguel Albano had felt powerless, a tiny cog in the Yankee master's machine, going through the motions of his life without hope of significant reward. The ANI had changed that, giving back his pride, permitting Albano to feel like a man.

Today he felt invincible.

If death was waiting for him in the next few hours, he would greet it like a cherished friend.

And he wasn't about to die alone.

Old San Juan
1250 hours

ANTONIO RIVERA LIT a cigarette, shook out the match and blew a plume of smoke in the direction of the ceiling. On the wall above his desk, a clock reminded him that it was still another hour at least before he was permitted to announce the headlines of a lifetime. If he broke the story now, ahead of time, there would be penalties involved, and he wasn't prepared to pay so great a price for fame.

Rivera's "office" at the *Vigil* was a corner cubicle some four feet square, reminiscent of the cramped library carrels where he used to pull all-nighters at the university before a big exam. He saw it as beneath his dignity, but it was more than any other paper on the island would have offered him, and left-wing weeklies were notorious for operating on a shoestring budget. As it was, Rivera's free-lance articles for other magazines and papers helped him stay afloat financially while he was waiting for the one big break he needed to succeed.

The ANI would get him there, but playing ball with revolutionaries meant you had to play by their rules all the way. In other circumstances, dealing with a labor representative perhaps, Rivera might have fudged a bit and leaked the story early to clinch his jump on the competition. In this case, however, he had been promised extreme reprisals for any deviation from the plan, and his personal knowledge of the ANI led Rivera to respect that threat.

He tried to picture the submarine in his mind as it cruised submerged toward its target zone with a crew of modern pirates on board, perhaps executing evasive maneuvers as warships and aircraft took up the chase. Albano might not pull it off, but he still deserved credit for nerve.

And however it ended, whoever came out on top, Rivera would still have his scoop.

It wouldn't be a wasted effort, then, at least on his behalf.

Rivera's nerves were getting the better of him. He needed a drink to calm himself down, and there was still plenty of time to spare. He stubbed out his cigarette, pushed back his chair and snatched his jacket from a wall hook as he rose.

If anybody in the office marked Rivera's passing, they refrained from speaking to him. He attributed their silence to the kind of jealousy that tormented mediocre talents in the presence of their obvious superiors. It didn't bother him when he was snubbed by such as these; if anything, it reinforced Rivera's sense that he was a success.

How jealous they would be if they could only peer inside his head and see the story waiting to unfold! They would come crawling to him for a break when he was rich and famous, hoping that Rivera would remember them and help their trifling careers.

Like hell.

He reached the outer hallway, moving toward the elevator. Someone was there ahead of him, a black man with a thin mustache. The button was illuminated, but Rivera punched it once again for emphasis. Superior talents had no time to waste.

A moment later, when the doors hissed open, he was first to step inside the waiting car. The black man smiled, as if amused by the display of rudeness, and Rivera should have heard the first alarms go off inside his head just then. Unfortunately he was caught up in the moment, relishing his own sensation of invincibility. He never saw the pistol in the black man's fist until its muzzle came to rest between his eyes.

"I'd keep my mouth shut if I was you."

For once Rivera did as he was told.

The elevator passed the office building's ground floor and kept on going to the basement level. When the doors slid open, there were more men waiting for him, three tough-looking Anglos. One of them produced a roll of silver duct tape and wrapped it around Rivera's head to seal his lips. Another wrenched his hands behind him and fastened handcuffs on his wrists before they led him to a waiting car. A fifth man sat behind the wheel, and it was crowded in the car before they picked up number six, another Anglo standing watch at the entrance to the basement garage.

Rivera's mind was working furiously, on the verge of panic, trying to decipher what was happening. It couldn't be the ANI, five Anglos and a black man. In his present state of panic, that could only mean a right-wing death squad, possibly police or federal agents. In his personal conceit, Rivera knew the neofascists had been stalking him for years, infuriated by his editorials that showed them up for what they truly were: imperialist lackeys of the Yankee government and brutal gangsters who oppressed their own without a second thought for common decency.

It was a wonder they had let him live so long, a bitter irony that they should come for him today of all days, when his destiny was just unfolding. He swallowed a sob of outrage, determined not to give his captors the satisfaction.

They drove him south on the expressway, past the Isla Grande Airport, to a lonely access road where woods grew close on either side. It was a dreary execution site, and not at all the sort of place Rivera would have chosen for his death.

Of course, he had no choice.

Manhandled from the car, he waited for the beating to begin and hoped it would be swift. Some of the death squads brutalized their chosen prey for hours before a close-range bullet to the brain brought merciful release. It all depended on their temperament and timing, whether they were drunk or had a list of other calls to make.

Rivera smelled no alcohol on his abductors and wondered if that was good or bad. A sober sadist might prefer to take his time and make the session last.

He was surprised when someone slit the duct tape just behind the ear. A strong hand yanked it free, uprooting some of Rivera's hair in the process, but he managed to suppress a cry of pain. Not yet. If he showed weakness, he would only make things that much worse.

But why would they remove the gag, unless—

Rivera braced himself for death, convinced they meant to shoot him instantly, without preliminary entertainment for themselves. Which one would pull the trigger? Would he see it coming? Could he stand to face the executioner with open eyes?

One of the Anglos stood in front of him, inches from his face.

"You've been working with the ANI," he said. It didn't come out sounding like a question, so Rivera gave no answer, waiting. "You were picked to break the story on their master plan."

Rivera felt himself begin to tremble, tried to stop it, but found the tremors uncontrollable.

"We need a rundown on your sources," said the grim-faced stranger, showing him a pistol, "and we need it now."

Aboard the Exeter
1250 hours

THE STANDARD CARRIER battle group consists of eleven ships besides the aircraft carrier itself. The three heavyweights in the *Exeter*'s battle group were Ticonderoga Class nuclear-powered guided-missile cruisers, weighing in at 9,600 tons with a full load, including two 5-inch guns, two octuple container-launchers for sixteen RGM-84A Harpoon surface-to-surface missiles, two triple Mk 32 mountings for 324 mm Mk 46 antisubmarine torpedoes and two Sikorsky SH-60B Seahawk helicopters on board.

Next in bulk were the two Kidd Class guided-missile destroyers, each displacing some 9,200 tons with a full combat load. Destroyer armament virtually duplicated that of the cruisers, with the exception of smaller quadruple container-launchers for eight Harpoon SLCMs and the substitution of two Kaman SH-2F Seasprite helicopters on board. Three FFG-7 Class guided-missile frigates completed the battle contingent, each shipping 3,600 tons with a full load including one 3-inch gun, one Mk 13 single launcher for forty harpoon SLCMs, two triple Mk 32 tube mountings for the Mk 46 A/S torpedoes and two Kaman Seasprites on board.

The remainder of the battle group included one ammo ship, one fuel ship and one supply ship, all screened—as was the *Exeter* itself—by warships traveling in protective screen. Three of the *Exeter*'s ten S-3A Viking subsonic jets were airborne at all times, scanning for the *Thresher* with electronic gear that had so far failed to produce a hit.

Grimaldi moved across the flight deck with a cup of coffee in his hand, feeling the wind in his face. There was nothing he could do to speed the hunt along at this point, and his silent presence on the bridge would only be an irritant to Captain Londergan. They were following the *Thresher*'s logical course, northbound, but so far they had failed to raise the sub on sonar.

So far.

There was still a chance, of course, between the S-3A Viking jets and Navstar GPS satellite coverage, but Grimaldi stopped short of optimism. Battlefield experience had taught him that whatever could go wrong in a given situation generally would go wrong. In spite of everything, there was a decent chance that Albano might reach his firing point, and the missiles might fly when—not if—Washington rejected the ANI's demands.

Giving in wasn't an option. Even if the present administration was inclined to surrender Puerto Rico without a fight, thereby committing political suicide, the timing was impossible. It would take weeks at least to shift the reins of power in San Juan if everyone cooperated in a spirit of harmony. Albano couldn't wait that long on board the submarine with his dwindling supplies of food, odds stacking up against him on the surface and a skeleton crew working around the clock.

Terrorists weren't renowned for their patience in crisis situations. They preferred to set deadlines and watch the authorities scurry around like frightened lab rats, collecting cash or commandeering vehicles upon demand. It was a power trip, in many ways a petty exercise, but no less deadly for the childish pique that motivated rash demands.

Grimaldi turned to watch another Viking take the air. The four-man Lockheed jet was lined up on the forward catapult for takeoff, poised on the track with its blunt nose toward the sea, connected to the hidden pistons by a towing strop. After a moment high-pressure steam rammed the pistons forward, hurtling toward below-decks water brakes that stopped their progress cold within a space of five feet. The Viking, meanwhile, was airborne, climbing at an initial rate of more than 4,200 feet per minute, its dual General Electric TF34-GE-2 turbofans taking over and keeping the sub-hunter aloft.

The Viking had no fixed armament, but its weapons bay could accommodate four Mk 46 torpedoes or an equal number of thousand-pound depth charges. Neither had been loaded for this flight, since the jets were only supposed to locate the *Thresher* and report its position.

Killing the sub, if and when they found it, would be Grimaldi's job.

He understood the captain's anger at being effectively preempted, cut out of the loop, as it were, and Grimaldi didn't relish his own role in the lethal game. Still, it would have to be done.

The alternatives were unthinkable.

Grimaldi lowered his eyes to the glistening surface of the ocean, staring as if he could penetrate the depths and pick out the submarine by sheer force of will alone.

No luck.

At last he reluctantly turned away and walked back toward his quarters. The wind off the water was no longer refreshing. Instead, it left Grimaldi with a grim chill in his soul.

Stony Man Farm
1215 hours EST

AARON KURTZMAN WAS manning the War Room's command console, a steaming cup of coffee at his elbow, when the hunters caught a break. It was a combination of technology and pure dumb luck that did the trick.

As far as the technology went, Kurtzman said a silent prayer of thanks for the Navstar GPS, a network of eighteen orbiting satellites that surrounded the earth, pinpointing targets with surgical accuracy and relaying their precise locations to earthbound receivers on various warships and aircraft. The system had proved its worth in Operation Desert Storm, guiding allied planes on bombing and rescue missions, while friendly naval forces utilized Navstar to decimate the Iranian navy.

In fact, Navstar was damned near foolproof—as long as the target was visible.

And that was the rub.

As long as the *Thresher* traveled submerged, it was effectively hidden from Navstar's eyes in the sky. Pinpoint precision aside, the satellites couldn't penetrate earth or water to pick out submerged or subterranean targets. In effect, locating the hijacked submarine depended on her new commander making one critical mistake.

Miguel Albano made that error at 12:15 p.m. on Saturday, bringing the *Thresher* up for an estimated two minutes and twenty-eight seconds. For all Kurtzman knew, it could have been an accident, some sort of miscalculation, or an act of pure arrogance. Whatever, Navstar had its target in a flash, recording the submarine's location at 72 degrees 4 minutes west longitude and 25 degrees eight minutes north latitude. In the elapsed time of visibility, the submarine was moving on a northwesterly course, three hundred fifty miles due east of Great Abaco island in the Bahamas.

Navstar lost the submarine at 12:17 and thirty seconds, but Kurtzman was already burning up the air, a telephone receiver cradled on his shoulder while his nimble fingers flew over the keys of his computer terminal. Within the next eight minutes, he had touched base and confirmed the Navstar sighting with the Pentagon and Hal Brognola, who was at his desk in Washington. The Bear's last call was to San

Juan, a cutout number where he left the latest news for Striker and Phoenix Force.

Grimaldi, waiting on the *Exeter*, would find out soon enough.

When Kurtzman cradled the receiver, he didn't relax. They knew the submarine's approximate location now, a decent starting point, but if the very act of surfacing had been in error, then Miguel Albano would be scrambling to save his ass, calling for evasive maneuvers, perhaps veering widely off course. Was the *Exeter*'s attack group near enough to close the gap before the *Thresher* slipped away once more? Would the chaotic moment prompt Albano to unleash his deadly Tomahawks ahead of time, before he even beamed a final ultimatum to the mainland?

Anything could happen, Kurtzman realized, and if the missiles flew within the next few moments, it would hardly matter when or where they found the submarine. Albano would have done his worst, and you could only sink the bastard once.

Against how many thousands lost?

Kurtzman stopped short of visualizing the wreckage, counting the nameless dead. The submarine was already well within striking range of Miami, New Orleans, Atlanta, even Washington itself. Kurtzman caught himself multiplying fifteen Tomahawks times two hundred fifty megatons and derailed that morbid train of thought before it left the station.

Enough was enough.

The best that he could do now was remain alert and watchful, just in case the *Thresher* showed itself again, for whatever reason. Another glimpse would be as helpful as it was unlikely, and he didn't bother with the superstitious ritual of fingercrossing.

They would either catch the hijacked submarine in time or they wouldn't. If the worst-case scenario came to pass, Navstar and other systems would record the launches, when the Tomahawks broke water, and the rest would be a matter of mounting—or attempting—some last-ditch defense. From the *Thresher*'s last confirmed position, it was eighty minutes to Miami as the Tomahawk flies, some two hours and forty-nine minutes for touchdown on Pennsylvania Avenue. There was a chance that one or two missiles could be diverted somehow, perhaps shot down, but if Albano let go with everything he had...

Kurtzman sipped his coffee, knowing it was time for him to pass the word along to Barbara Price. A few more moments, and the War Room would be crowded, everyone manning his or her post, for all the good it would do.

Not much, in fact, without another lucky break.

The hunt was on in earnest, but the fox might well have given them the slip. Again.

Next time the *Thresher* showed herself, it just might be the crack of doom. The end of life as Kurtzman knew it, now and for evermore.

CHAPTER TWENTY-ONE

Aboard the Thresher
Saturday, 1319 hours AST

Miguel Albano paced the bridge, attempting to control the anger boiling up inside him and threatening to burst his heart with rage. He felt his master plan slipping through his fingers, but he caught himself before the feeling cycled downward into black despair.

After all, he had no one to blame but himself.

It had been risky, rising to periscope depth, but he had felt the need to look around after hours of running submerged and to find out if the submarine's instruments could be trusted. Albano wanted to know if there were warships bearing down upon him, and the plain truth was that he had begun to feel a little cocky with the lethal boat at his command. Taking a peek at the surface had seemed only right, the least of his problems, all things considered.

Until it went terribly wrong.

From that point, once he issued the order, Albano could have laid the fault on someone else, but he was still in command and so blamed himself. It was a matter of releasing too much ballast, someone in the engine room explained, and by the time Albano understood exactly what was happening, the submarine had already surfaced, streaming white foam from her hull, her conning tower and long, dark spine exposed.

He had recovered swiftly, once he understood the problem, shouting orders for a crash dive. By his shaky calculations, they had been exposed for barely two minutes in actual time, and no missiles or depth charges had rained down upon them since they submerged. There was a chance his luck would hold, and they would go unnoticed in the vast Atlantic.

They were running deep now, wasting precious time on evasive maneuvers that might all be in vain. He knew the warships would be hunting him, and every moment counted now, but if they didn't have a fix on his location, then Albano might be doing them a favor, adding nautical miles to his zigzag course and giving them time to catch up.

It was a judgment call, and he wasn't prepared to gamble on the Yankee government's various spy satellites going blind at a critical moment. Stranger things had happened, certainly, but any time you started counting on a miracle, Albano found that disappointment inevitably followed.

So they would stay submerged and run their zigzag course as if the very hounds of hell were on their track—which was, in fact, a fairly apt description of the ships and aircraft he expected to be chasing them. Albano knew what the destroyers, frigates and cruisers could do to a submarine with their Mk 46 torpedoes, RUR-5A Asroc missiles and various depth charges. Throw in the Viking jets and Sea King helicopters, both designed specifically as sub-killers, and the U.S. Navy was justly proud of its ability to pursue and destroy undersea craft.

Of course, for the past four decades, the targets had always been pictured as Russian or perhaps Chinese. The Yankee ships and aircraft had never been called upon to hunt one of their own.

Until today.

Albano frowned, wondering if it would make a difference. Would some squeamish sailor hesitate before he began unloading deadly munitions on a boat that was essentially one of the family? Again Albano thought he should have kept some members from the Yankee crew as hostages, but he dismissed the notion with an angry shrug. The White House still maintained that it would never hold a dialogue with terrorists, and sailors were expendable. They signed their lives away when they enlisted in the service of their country, promising to sacrifice themselves if need be.

It would have done no good, he told himself, returning full attention to the narrow world of here and now. Survival was the top priority, at least until he had a chance to speak with someone in authority, deliver his demands to Washington. The White House knew exactly what was coming, but Albano wanted them to hear it from his own lips, recognize the years of pent-up anger and humiliation that had brought him to his present state.

And when the missiles flew, if it was necessary for him to unleash the righteous fire, no one could say that he had failed to warn his enemies, give them a chance to save themselves.

The fault was theirs, a trail of guilt that spanned the best part of a century, specific cases of oppression standing out like milestones on the long, hard road. If he was forced to use the missiles—and, Albano told himself, the odds against a peaceful settlement were grim—the world would see and understand that it had never really been his fault.

Miguel Albano had been driven to extremes, but this time he was at the wheel, and there would be no turning back. His goal was victory or death, and if the price of one should be the other, he was ready for the sacrifice.

Albano wondered if his enemies could say the same.

Lake Okeechobee, Florida
1220 hours EST

SKIMMING LOW over dark green water in his stolen Sikorsky SH-60B, Luis Camacho tried to imagine the vast Atlantic, Albano and his special team running submerged in the *Thresher*, hunted by every warship west of Bermuda and north of the equator. Despite the exposure of flying, Camacho felt better aloft, with clear visibility for miles in each direction, solid earth waiting to receive him if he fell.

The Navy would be hunting him by now, as well. He had a decent lead, and he had flown as low as possible to beat the radar nets, but they were sure to spot him on his final run, if not before, and there was no way the Sikorsky could compete with F-16A fighters in terms of speed, maneuverability or firepower.

If the hunters found him airborne, he was dead.

But there was still an outside chance to pull it off.

The launch itself would take no time at all, and in the chaos that resulted, he would have at least a slender hope of making his escape. Camacho needed time enough to put the chopper down and make a break on foot. He'd need a change of clothes, some lag time while the fighters picked up the Sikorsky and directed mobile units to the scene. It wasn't hopeless yet, but he would need precision timing all the way.

He had the Penguin missile armed and ready well before he reached the target zone. If he was overtaken prior to reaching Cape Canaveral, Camacho would unload it on the nearest target he could find. If necessary, he would fire the Penguin toward the closest city, maybe light the Gold Coast with a fireball even as he died.

But that would be a waste. His preparations had been made with a single target in mind, a devastating strike

against the Yankee pigs who had defiled his homeland for a
century. It would have been preferable to catch the NASA
people with a rocket on the pad, perhaps one of the vaunted
space shuttles lifting off when he delivered his greeting card,
but Camacho would take what he could get.

The prospect of his own impending death was almost a
physical presence in the Sikorsky's cockpit, breathing foul
drafts from the grave down his collar as he handled the
controls. It was a risk that every revolutionary soldier recognized from day one, but somehow the danger was always
postponed until tomorrow. Young men clung to their illusions of immortality with stubborn zeal until they could no
longer deny the obvious.

Camacho could die this afternoon. In fact, the odds
against survival far outweighed those favoring a successful
getaway. If he wasn't committed to the mission, he could
easily have ditched the chopper where he was, along the
north shore of the lake in Martin County, where the marsh
would hide his tracks and he could hike to Indiantown,
picking up a ride to Miami from there.

But he wouldn't allow the fear to steal his nerve away.
Camacho was a man, and if it was his fate to die this day, at
least he could display raw courage to his enemies, leave them
shaking their heads in awe of the man they had killed.

And there was still the Penguin, waiting with its warhead. Every moment in the air brought him closer to his
chosen target, hedging his bets against total defeat. If death
was all he had to fear, compared with living in a world where
Yankees ruled his homeland and his children's children
dwelt as slaves, then he had no real fears at all.

Camacho took the airship lower, nearly skimming the
lake's surface now. Away to his left, a pair of fishermen in
a skiff watched him passing, one of them raising his arm in

a kind of salute. He could imagine their sun-reddened Anglo faces breaking into smiles at sight of the Sikorsky.

How would it affect them if the fighters caught him here and opened up with their Sidewinders, blasting him out of the sky?

No matter.

Two redneck yokels were the least of Camacho's problems at the moment. He had other fish to fry, and he could smell the grill already heating up.

A short while longer, as the Yankee pigs would say, and the fat would truly be in the fire.

And the smoke from that burning would be very great.

Outside San Juan
1325 hours AST

ANTONIO RIVERA WONDERED why he was alive. By rights the Yankee gunmen should have killed him when he finished talking, but they had been satisfied to leave him in the middle of nowhere, hands cuffed behind his back, expecting them to return any moment with a change of heart and finish the job they had started.

The worst part of survival, Rivera decided, was confronting his own weakness and failure. He had spilled everything with the barest hint of rough handling and none of the anticipated torture, giving up his scoop, his contacts—anything and everything that he could think of just to save his miserable life. In fact, Rivera would have gladly fabricated details on demand, but his interrogators had been satisfied with what he gave them on the first take, huddling for a moment, one of them disappearing for ten minutes and returning with a smile on his face, nodding as if to confirm Rivera's basic information.

And Rivera had panicked then, knowing it was over. They were bound to kill him now that he had served his purpose. Whimpering, tears brimming in his soft brown eyes, Rivera knelt and waited for the bullet that would end his life. At least he hoped it was a bullet, rather than a beating or a wire garrote—God forbid the method preferred by some death squads, where the victims were doused in gasoline and burned alive!

At that point, as the seeming leader of the group approached him, Rivera felt his bladder let go, drenching the front of his designer slacks. The shame of it was nothing at that moment in comparison with his overwhelming fear. The panic didn't abate until he noticed that the Yankee's hands were empty, hanging at his sides. No weapon showing. As the man began to speak, Rivera glimpsed the possibility that he might actually survive and he was stricken by the horror of his own mistake.

"We're leaving now," the tall man said. "If I were you, I'd keep my mouth shut when I made it back to town. Your playmates might not understand."

And that was all.

They left him by the roadside, staring at the dust that trailed behind their car, his trousers plastered to his thighs. Rivera waited fifteen minutes, thinking—almost hoping— that the gunmen would return and kill him. Anything to wipe away the shame of his betrayal and the stinging knowledge of his cowardice.

It seemed a long walk back to town, his vision blurred at times by angry tears. Cars passed by on two occasions, heading for San Juan, but Rivera stumbled into the trees when he heard them coming, frightened that the gunmen might be coming back.

"If I were you, I'd keep my mouth shut when I made it back to town. Your playmates might not understand."

Indeed.

The ANI would never understand how he had broken down and spilled their secrets out for strangers—including names, addresses and other information that he wasn't supposed to know. It would be bad enough, in terms of Rivera's memory among the nationalists, if he had been tortured to death for the information, but to present himself alive and unmarked, his pants drenched with the evidence of mindless fear...

It simply wouldn't do.

He had to lose the cursed handcuffs somehow, even if it cost him flesh and blood. That done, he could begin to think about his clothing, transportation to his home—

Rivera caught himself at that. Suppose the ANI was somehow conscious of the fact that he had been abducted by the enemy? They would assume that he had spilled his guts to the interrogators over time, but his return, unharmed except for minor cuts and bruises, would be the next best thing to a death sentence.

His only hope was to slip out of town unobserved, but how was he supposed to do that with urine-soaked clothing, the minimal cash in his pocket and no car at all?

The handcuffs first.

Rivera sat in the weeds and began to twist his body like a landed fish, grunting with pain and exertion as he tried to work the manacled wrists under his feet. If he could only get his hands in front of him somehow, he could start to work on the cuffs or their connecting chain. Anything to allow himself some mobility.

As soon as he could move, it would be time to run.

And see if he could somehow save his life.

San Juan Naval Base
1330 hours

GREGORIO RUIZ WAS counting down the minutes to his great adventure. He was dressed in his civilian clothes, prepared to flee the base when he was finished...if he had the chance.

It would be hazardous, of course, but Ruiz thought he could pull it off. All it required was nerve, determination and a bottomless supply of luck. The nerve and grim determination he possessed.

He wore the Beretta automatic in a shoulder rig beneath his nylon windbreaker. Another look at the full-length mirror confirmed that the gun wasn't visible on a casual inspection. The duffel bag filled with explosive charges sat at his feet, a heavy, oblong bundle of death. Inside it the plastique charges were individually wrapped and the timers were set, waiting only for Ruiz to activate them at the final moment.

Soon.

Once more he wished that he could be on board the *Thresher* with his comrades, but his work was here. All things considered, Ruiz estimated that his chances of survival were significantly higher than Albano's. In fact, if Albano was killed, along with the members of his special team, it might actually work to Ruiz's advantage. There would be a sudden power vacuum at the top of the ANI—what was left of it, at any rate—and no one but Francisco Obregon would dare contest Ruiz's ascension to the vacant leadership.

And there were ways to deal with Obregon, oh, yes.

Ruiz felt better, slightly more relaxed, as he stooped down to lift the heavy duffel bag. It would be getting lighter as he went along, each stop around the base reducing his burden while it tightened his schedule.

Once the first charge had been planted and the timer activated, there could be no turning back. He thought once more about reneging on his promise, ditching the explosives while he waited for the outcome of Albano's challenge to the Yankee overlords in Washington. If the *Thresher* went down with all hands, there would be no one to accuse him of cowardice on the firing line.

Ruiz determined to proceed. The way he had it planned, he should be through the outer gates and well away before the charges started detonating, wreaking havoc on the vase. Whatever happened with Albano from that point on, Ruiz would be a hero to the people's movement in his own right— and a fugitive from military justice. If the daring coup didn't succeed, he would be driven underground, but there were worse things than a year or two in hiding.

Living on the run had served Fidel quite handily, in fact.

Ruiz crossed the room to a small liquor cabinet in the apartment's kitchenette. He found a half-empty bottle of whiskey, poured himself three fingers in a water glass and swilled it down. The fiery liquid nearly flooded his body with warmth and a new sense of courage.

It was almost time to go. His fear was dwindling now, a fading memory. Just one more shot of whiskey ought to do the trick, while leaving him clearheaded for the mission.

One or two more shots.

His hand was steady as he filled the glass and raised it to his lips.

Aboard the Exeter
1330 hours

THE SH-3H SEA KING helicopter was designed specifically for hunting submarines. In crisis situations it could also serve a search-and-rescue function, but its purpose, straight off the assembly line, was the pursuit and ultimate destruction of submersibles. To that end the chopper was equipped with Texas Instruments APS-124 radar, with a digital scan converter to provide scan-to-scan integration on rapid sweeps, and the ASQ-81 sonar device, a towed "bird" carried on a starboard winch. Typical armament for a combat mission included two Mk 46 antisubmarine torpedoes, but Grimaldi had replaced one of those with an advanced Mk 53 depth bomb.

He felt no exhilaration on lift-off, watching the *Exeter's* flight deck fall away beneath him. There was no thrill of the chase, anticipation for the swift destruction of his target that he sometimes felt on other missions.

There was a job to be done, and that was all. Grimaldi understood the price of failure, knew that there were only enemies on board the *Thresher* now, but something in him still rebelled against the sinking of a U.S. submarine. He would complete the task assigned because he had no choice; the options were horrendous.

The Navstar fix had placed the *Thresher* fifty miles northeast of Grimaldi's present location, and he had to assume the hijacked submarine would be executing evasive maneuvers by now. When he was closer to the target zone, he would release the ASQ-81 "bird" and try for a sonar track on the sub, anything at all to give him a fix on his prey. He would have two shots at the *Thresher* before he had to land and reload, and if he failed with those, Grimaldi knew there would be no point going back for more. His sighting of the submarine, if and when he made one, would be relayed to the various ships in the *Exeter's* battle group, and they would be ready to blanket the area with RUR-5A Asroc missiles the moment Grimaldi acknowledged a miss.

And perhaps, he thought, it would be better that way for all concerned.

Captain Londergan was already steaming at Grimaldi's intrusion on the carrier, incensed at having a stranger rammed down his throat by the brass. No matter how the orders from Washington were phrased, they still implied a certain lack of confidence, and that was bound to raise the captain's hackles. Londergan knew nothing of the Stony Man initiative and he never would. It was a critical but necessary gap in communications that left a fine officer stung by inferred criticism, anxious for the new kid on the block to blow his shot.

At one level the captain might be relieved if Grimaldi failed, but the Stony man pilot suspected that Londergan was also dreading the moment when he would have to order an all-out assault on the *Thresher*. Grimaldi had noted the solemn attitude of pilots and handlers on deck as he moved toward the Sea King, grim eyes following his progress with a mixture of resentment and respect.

The call hadn't been his, but he was ready to perform upon command.

He left the *Exeter* behind, then outran the frigate and destroyer riding point for the battle group. There was open water in front of him as far as the eye could see, with only his compass to tell him where the *Thresher* had been sighted fifteen minutes earlier. He set the course according to his compass, watching for a radar print and waiting for the proper moment to release the sonar "bird."

Would the *Thresher*'s anechoic tiles defeat the sonar buoy and all the other sensory devices carried by the trailing battle group? It seemed improbable, but he couldn't dismiss the possibility that they might fail to stop the boat in time. Failure was a risk in any human exercise, beginning with the lax security that had allowed Albano and the ANI to grab a submarine in the first place.

Finding himself at the point of so vast an operation made Grimaldi feel small, a gnat in the eye of a hurricane. No, he corrected himself: make that a wasp, with a deadly sting in his tail.

The sting would hardly matter, though, if he couldn't locate his target and deliver the killing payload. Without a new fix on the submarine, he could fly in circles until his fuel ran out and still accomplish nothing.

Above all else, it was that realization that grated on Grimaldi's nerves. To counteract the tension that he felt, Grimaldi concentrated on his instruments, gauging distance in nautical miles, drawing closer to the last known target zone with every passing moment.

Soon his own part in the hunt would start in earnest. He would have an opportunity to bring the curtain down or watch it all go up in smoke.

And at the moment he could easily have flipped a coin to find out which way it would go.

Not good enough by half.

Grimaldi focused on the sea in front of him and waited for his instruments to put him on the track of those he was supposed to kill.

CHAPTER TWENTY-TWO

Brevard County, Florida
Saturday, 1240 hours EST

"We've got him," Lyons said, and Blancanales stiffened in his folding chair. The pickup truck decelerated sharply, rocking Blancanales in his seat before he caught himself.

"Which way?" he asked Lyons through the open window to the cab.

"We have to turn around. Hang on."

Pol braced himself while Lyons put the pickup through a tight U-turn, tires squealing on the asphalt. There was no oncoming traffic to worry about at the moment, and Blancanales hoped it would stay that way for the next few minutes while he went about the dirty business of blasting a Navy helicopter out of the sky.

Assuming that his plan worked out, that is.

Beyond the initial rush of knowing he had judged the target correctly, there was still more to stopping Camacho than simply being in the right place at the right time, armed with the right weapon. The Stinger's 5,250-yard range was impressive, but still limited. Any last-minute deviation from his present course could put Camacho out of Pol's effective range, leaving the high-tech Stinger about as useful as a pygmy blowgun and darts.

Blancanales felt another urge to scramble the fighters, but he suppressed it with an effort of will. The clock was running now, and they were barely fifteen miles from Cape Canaveral. If Blancanales changed his mind and had Lyons call the jets from Patrick Air Force Base right now, Camacho would have time to make his run before the F-16s arrived to shoot him down.

Too late.

Pol knelt down in the truck bed as they drove and opened up the Stinger's plastic carrying case. He didn't hoist the mobile launcher to his shoulder yet, in case they met another car, but it was ready at his fingertips. He wouldn't stand to aim and fire, in case they needed to pursue the target, fearing that acceleration and an accidental fall might cause an accident from which there could be no recovery.

He had one shot, and Pol would have to get it right.

Another moment, and he saw the SH-60B... or was it an illusion, nothing but a trick of light reflected off the water?

No, he had it!

Blancanales raised the Stinger from its padded case and swiftly armed the electronic sighting mechanism. At thirty-five pounds, the stinger was no tremendous burden on his shoulder, yet it seemed to weigh him down, grinding his knees into the hard metal bed of the pickup. Lyons was braking as smoothly as possible, but the movement still rocked Blancanales on his knees, delaying target acquisition. Guessing, he placed the Sikorsky some six thousand yards out and closing, lined up to cross in front of them in—what, ninety seconds?

He followed the Sikorsky with the Stinger's sighting mechanism, watching it come into range. He wondered if the pilot noticed them, a toy truck on the highway with a humpbacked stranger riding in the back. It would be too far out for any kind of recognition with the naked eye, and yet...

If Camacho noticed the pickup at all, he chose to ignore it, continuing along his chosen course toward Cape Canaveral. He was into the final run now, hurtling toward the Penguin's maximum effective firing range. Was he prepared to trust the missile from a range of twelve miles out when just a few more seconds would put him on top of the target?

Everything was ruined if Camacho fired his shot before the Able Team warrior had a chance to bring him down. Mere seconds now, and Pol could feel the beads of perspiration on his forehead, rivers streaming down his chest and back beneath his shirt.

"Hold it!"

Lyons hit the brakes, and Blancanales almost toppled forward, saving it at the last instant with an open palm against the hot roof of the pickup's cab.

He let the chopper cross the highway, skimming over water to his right, before he took a breath and held it, tightening his grip around the Stinger's trigger. Everything seemed to happen at once—a flare of heat behind him, blistering the pickup's paint job, and a flash before him as the Stinger left its launching tube. Four thousand yards, give or take, and the missile's infrared tracking system locked on to the Sikorsky with unerring accuracy.

Did Camacho see it coming? Blancanales hoped so. There was satisfaction and poetic justice in the thought of his intended target straining at the SH-60B's controls.

Too late.

The Stinger found its mark, and the Sikorsky was transformed into an airborne fireball, shedding bits and pieces of itself that struck the water hissing, raising clouds of steam on impact. One of the main rotor blades broke free and spun through the air like a wicked scythe, chopping down saplings at the water's edge before it came to rest in several feet of muck.

The flaming, twisted hulk nosed over and met the water with a giant splash as the secondary detonation of its fuel tanks spewed lines of burning gasoline in all directions. Blancanales watched the water burn and held his breath for just a moment, waiting for the Penguin to explode. When it didn't, he let himself relax.

All done, at least for Pol's part of the game.

But something told him it was far from over. There could still be hell to pay and then some.

Blancanales set the empty launching tube beside him and leaned toward the open window to the cab.

"Let's go. We're all done here."

Aboard the Thresher
1340 hours AST

THE SONAR HAD BEEN tracking them for some time now, recorded on the *Thresher*'s instruments. Albano wondered if the anechoic tiles that lined her hull were working, and if so, how well they did their job.

A submarine's advantage was invisibility, the chance to move in three dimensions—up and down, as well as lateral, forward and back. Only aircraft were more versatile, and submarines were still the only seagoing vessels capable of approaching their targets from below. To combat that invisibility, military experts had devised a wide assortment of electronic tracking gear, everything from microphones that monitored engine noise and rotor wash to sonar printouts that could accurately sketch a moving object from several thousand yards away.

Sub-builders, in the meantime, were forever seeking ways to beat the system and improve their own ability to hide. The *Thresher*'s anechoic tiles were one example, meant to absorb sonar pulses instead of reflecting them back to their course, thus giving the illusion of empty space. The so-called caterpillar drive was another method, whereby water passed through shafts in a submarine's hull, fore to aft, as a means of reducing engine noise, but the *Thresher* possessed no such feature.

If the hunters got close enough, with or without sonar prints, they would hear her engines ... unless she stopped dead in the water and waited for the hunt to pass her by.

Albano thought about it, knowing that his only problem then would be the sonar. If the *Thresher* showed up on a hostile screen, he was a sitting duck.

It was Albano's decision, and he had to make the choice soon. The hunters were drawing closer by the moment, cruisers and destroyers capable of beating his best submerged speed by four or five knots per hour. Ultimately they would overtake him, and the submarine's engine noise would draw them like a homing beacon, jackals closing for the kill.

Albano considered firing the Tomahawks at once, even blindly, to prevent the enemy from cutting him off entirely, but he decided to wait. It was important to deliver his demands, confront Washington with the ANI's ultimatum from his own lips before he let the missiles fly. Otherwise, he feared the exercise would all have been in vain.

And there was pride involved, Albano grudgingly admitted to himself. Beyond the obvious success or failure of his mission, he was pledged to prove himself a man. If that demonstration cost him his life, and the lives of his comrades, so be it.

He would wait, at least a little while.

They still had time, although he couldn't guess how much.

If necessary, he could give the hunters cause to fear him, fire a few torpedoes to slow them.

The game wasn't done yet by any means.

Albano paced the bridge and tried to keep his nerves in check. Whatever happened next was destiny. He might not have the power to change its course, but he would do his best.

And he would be remembered, either way.

Gurabo, Puerto Rico
1340 hours

ANTONIO RIVERA HAD BEEN useful in a way that he would never comprehend. When he was spilling out his desperate story, naming names, he had described a visit to an ANI encampment fifteen miles outside San Juan, due south, on the outskirts of Gurabo. The site hadn't been on Miranda Flores's hit parade, nor did it ring a bell when Bolan briefed her on Rivera's revelation. Tucked away from prying eyes, the camp—almost a village, really—was described as a secure base where the revolutionaries sometimes went to hide and lick their wounds.

As described by Rivera, he had been shown around the encampment as a reward for services rendered in print, cautioned at the time of his visit that any mention of the hardsite's existence would carry the ultimate penalty. Bolan had studied the propagandist's eyes as he spoke, and he had come away convinced that Rivera was telling the truth. Whether the landlocked remnants of the ANI would run to Gurabo in their moment of crisis was another question.

And there was only one way to find out.

"It's worth a gamble," Yakov Katzenelenbogen had suggested, and the other Phoenix Force warriors readily agreed.

In any case, they had no options to pursue. Francisco Obregon had never gone back to his flat, and several other revolutionary hangouts on Flores's list were equally deserted in the wake of Albano's submarine hijacking. The secret army, what was left of it, had clearly gone to ground, awaiting the outcome of their leader's masterstroke before they made another move.

Bolan knew it would be best for all concerned if he could catch them in their hidey-hole and keep them there instead of waiting for some new act of aggression on the streets.

They took two cars for the drive south, Bolan and Calvin James riding in the MR2, Katz trailing with McCarter and Manning in a Volvo sedan that also carried the bulk of their hardware. Rivera's directions were explicit, but Bolan stopped short of driving up to the encampment itself. Instead, he continued on past the unmarked access road until he reached another, the last turn short of town, and traveled east through a tunnel of overhanging trees. He watched the odometer, gauging distance until he had covered two and three-quarter miles. A turnout showed up on the left. Bolan took it, parked the Toyota and waited for Katz to pull in behind him.

"We're on foot from here," he said. "Two klicks due north, if Rivera was telling it straight."

"And if he wasn't?" McCarter asked.

They all knew the answer to that, but Bolan had stared into the man's terrified eyes and seen the truth there. He had no doubt they would find an encampment of some sort at the end of their hike through the forest. As for who or what would be waiting there, that remained anybody's guess.

They might find a regiment, armed to the teeth, or no one at all.

It was a gamble, as Katz had said, but it was also the only game in town.

They changed into fatigues by the side of the road, keeping alert for the sound of approaching vehicles. None came, and they were ready in minutes, choosing their weapons from the stockpile divided between the two cars. Bolan wore his Beretta 93-R in armpit leather and chose an M-16 as his head weapon for the strike, a chunky M-203 grenade launcher mounted under the assault weapon's barrel. Extra magazines for the rifle and 40 mm grenades for the launcher criss-crossed his chest in heavy bandoliers. A dab of camou war paint on his face and hands completed the transformation, and he was ready to rock.

"Two klicks," Manning stated, checking the direction with his compass.

"Give or take."

"I hope we're not just chasing leprechauns," James said.

"Let's check it out," the Executioner replied, already moving through the trees and undergrowth. The others fell in line behind him, staying close enough for visibility, with room enough between them that a sniper couldn't take them all done with a lucky burst.

It was a gamble, all right, but Bolan had a feeling in his gut that they were moving toward a payoff. It would be a toss-up until the smoke cleared, but they couldn't afford to pass. Too much was riding on the line for Bolan and the men of Phoenix Force to simply watch and wait.

They couldn't reach the hijacked submarine, but they could still mop up on land. Beginning now.

The forest felt like home, and Bolan let himself fall into rhythm with the birds and animals around him, scuttling noises in the brush on either side, shrill music in the branches overhead.

Whatever lay in front of him, at least the waiting would be over soon.

He tucked the rifle underneath his arm and concentrated on following the game trail.

One step at a time.

Over the Atlantic
1344 hours

AT FIRST Grimaldi almost missed the sonar signal coming back to him from something well below the surface. It was muffled, fuzzy as with distance, but when he double-checked the reading from his ASQ-81 bird, it came back the same: twelve hundred feet. He checked the hydrophones again and this time thought he picked up on the sounds of a propeller blade.

The *Thresher?*

From his preflight briefing, Grimaldi knew there were no other American submarines in the area. One had been en route from Norfolk to Bermuda when the shit hit the fan, and it had been diverted to prevent false readings and perhaps a ghastly accident. The Russians, meanwhile, had reportedly eliminated submarine patrols so close to the United States, and friendly European nations had been warned—admittedly in guarded terms—to keep their U-boats out of the vicinity for the duration.

Theoretically that narrowed down the field, and while Grimaldi would have preferred an ironclad certainty, he had no choice in the present circumstances. He had to act and

swiftly, or the warships steaming up behind him would catch
the quarry's scent and unload with everything they had.
Grimaldi's hunting license from Washington was strictly
limited, and Captain Londergan was already operating at
the limits of his tolerance for meddlers. Any hesitation on
Grimaldi's part would give the captain a perfect excuse to
intervene, taking matters into his own hands.

So be it.

Grimaldi navigated on his sonar, circling wide around the
target once, twice, to get his bearings, pacing the submarine as it moved steadily northward. The Mk 53 depth bomb
was armed and ready, but successful application meant
more than simply lobbing it into the ocean and hoping for
a kill. In their simplest form, depth bombs rely on a pressure fuse to detonate their explosive charges at a designated
depth below the surface. Direct hits are not required, as the
explosion generates a destructive underwater shock wave,
with effective killing radius determined by the size of the
explosive charge.

In the case of the Mk 53, with its one-kiloton nuclear
warhead, pinpoint accuracy was strictly optional, but Grimaldi still needed a ballpark proximity. It was rather like
dropping water balloons from a freeway overpass, he
thought, except that here the liquid medium retarded impact and could physically divert the projectile.

He led the *Thresher* by an estimated hundred yards, allowing for speed and direction, cutting the Mk 53 loose on
his chosen target. That done, Grimaldi was up and away in
an instant, circling higher, looking for a vantage point from
which to watch the show. He started counting from the
splash of impact on the surface. Ten seconds. Fifteen.
Twenty.

The ocean seemed to heave below him, swelling for a heartbeat, then subsiding, white froth churning to the surface in a ring twice the diameter of a football field.

Were those traces of oil mixed in with the churning foam below him? Grimaldi couldn't say with any certitude. Above all else, he had to be sure, and that meant using the Mk 46 torpedo to finish what he had started.

The Mk 46 was designed specifically for killing submarines, electronically powered, with an active acoustic guidance system to eliminate the risk of near-misses and provide for reattack capabilities. The payload of one torpedo was sufficient to finish off any submarine in current service, and it would have to do the trick.

It was all Grimaldi had left.

He pictured the enemy crew in their state-of-the-art steel coffin, wondered if any of them were still alive and imagined the terror survivors had to be feeling at that moment.

Enough.

His hand found the firing control for the Mk 46, hesitated for perhaps a heartbeat and released the torpedo into free-fall.

There was nothing more for him to do but watch and wait.

Aboard the Thresher
1346 hours

THE WORST PART OF DYING, Miguel Albano decided, was the knowledge that he had gambled and lost, waited too long to fire his salvo at the Yankee mainland. The depth bomb had taken them all by surprise, and its crippling shock wave was strong enough to crumple the submarine's hull in places, flood several forward compartments and drown his men in the torpedo room.

But there was more.

At first it felt like having giant hands clapped over his ears with ferocious momentum. Albano felt warm blood coursing down his cheeks and into his collar, but that was the least of his problems. Around him large bolts exploded from the bulkhead like machine-gun bullets, dropping one man in his tracks with a shattered skull, leaving another to wail at the pain of a perforated abdomen. Showers of sparks erupted from the nearby computer console, accompanied by clouds of pungent smoke that smelled like burning rubber. Someone else was screaming, aft, and Albano wished he could find the man, strangle him into silence with his own two hands.

He had to think!

It took another moment, clinging to the housing of the *Thresher*'s periscope to keep from falling as the submarine nosed over in a lazy dive, for him to realize that all was lost. He couldn't return fire with torpedoes now if he wanted to, not with the nose flooded and the electric power flickering, about to go entirely. Red emergency lights transformed the bridge into a glimpse of hell on earth, turning smears of blood almost black on the floor, bulkhead, even on the low-slung ceiling. It even smelled like hell, with insulation frying in the consoles, crucial wiring fused together in a snarl electricians would need weeks or months to untangle.

Too late.

Albano knew that he was finished when he lurched across the tilting deck and found the radioman slumped dead at his set, earphones still in place, his forehead caved in like the front of a foam wig stand. Static whined when Albano put on the earphones and madly jabbed at buttons and twisted dials on the console, searching for a channel—any channel—that would give him access to the world outside, above the waves.

He couldn't even curse his enemies before he died, and that, Albano thought, had to be the worst indignity of all. To die was one thing, but to be denied your voice—the condemned man's traditional last word—was unspeakably cruel.

A kind of frenzy gripped him, and he tore the headphones off, discarding them. Albano started for the weapons room, aft, cursing under his breath as the deck began to tilt more sharply, forcing him to grip the bulkhead with both hands and drag himself along.

There might still be a chance to fire the Tomahawks, drawing on emergency reserve power, a last, aimless salvo of destruction, perhaps one of the fifteen missiles finding a target on the mainland.

As it was, he had nothing to lose by the attempt.

It was impossible to say if Albano actually heard the Mk 46 torpedo approaching. Technically hydrophones should have been required to pick up the sound of its propeller, but submarines collect and amplify an almost infinite variety of sounds—anything from turtles scraping their shells on the hull to the siren sound of amorous whales in the distance, performing their ancient courtship rituals.

On second thought, perhaps he merely felt the close proximity of death.

In either case, he hesitated, still some twenty paces from the room where he would find the launching tubes and their controls, his bloodied head cocked to one side, eyes squinted almost shut.

Trembling.

And in the instant before impact, when his world dissolved into the dark abyss of nothingness, Albano tried to find his voice. He might have heard the blast that killed him; no one who survived that afternoon at sea could ever say. But if he spoke at all, his words were lost to history.

In retrospect, it was a small loss, after all.

CHAPTER TWENTY-THREE

Gurabo, Puerto Rico
Saturday, 1420 hours

The sentry was a young man, in his early twenties, slender in the OD uniform that fit him like a sack. His Thompson submachine gun was technically obsolete, but no less deadly for all that. Beyond the sheer damage that .45-caliber manglers could inflict on human flesh, the weapon's very noise would alert his comrades in the nearby camp.

If he wasn't eliminated silently, there would be hell to pay.

Mack Bolan chose the Ka-bar fighting knife, seven inches of anodized, razor-edged steel. He wore the M-16 across his back like a street troubador carrying his guitar as he crept through the undergrowth, keeping to the sentry's blind side, placing each step with the care of a surgeon invading critical tissue.

At fifteen feet he saw the blemishes that marked the young man's face, a problem time would never cure. At ten feet he thought that he could smell the sentry's apprehension, even fear.

When he had closed the gap to seven feet, the soldier waited, watching while his target scanned the forest, passing over Bolan's hiding place without a second glance, then turned his back. The rest was open ground, and Bolan covered it in two long strides, his left hand clamping tight across the young man's mouth, twisting his face to the side while

the Ka-bar slid across his straining throat from left to right.
A crimson geyser sprayed the clearing, and the sentry
struggled in his grasp for a brief moment before his brain
and body started to shut down. A moment later he was
deadweight in the warrior's arms, and Bolan tucked him out
of sight among some waist-high ferns.

One down.

The Phoenix Force warriors should be in position by now,
roughly surrounding the camp. There was no fixed perimeter, per se, in terms of walls or fences, but the forest had
been cleared in an oblong some eighty yards long and fifty
yards across at its widest point. The buildings were pre-fab,
painted olive drab to keep the military spirit alive, and
camouflage netting was strung in the trees overhead to defeat an aerial recon. Access to the compound was an unpaved one-lane track, so narrow that any vehicle larger than
a standard jeep must have scraped hanging branches on either side.

The road didn't concern him now, in any case. Nobody
would be going in or out once they began their strike.

Bolan crouched on the edge of the clearing, taking advantage of the undergrowth and shadows, checking his
watch as he scanned the enemy camp.

In front of him were six buildings and an open shed that
apparently served as the mess hall in all weather. One of the
bungalows sprouted aerials, the communications hut, and
the camp's generator was housed behind it in a corrugated
metal shed. The other buildings apparently served as barracks, with no formal command post as such. He counted a
dozen fatigue-clad figures circulating around the camp or
lounging in the mess area, and he assumed there would be
others in the other buildings, out of sight.

Another glance at his watch. It was almost time.

Bolan shouldered his M-16, lining up his sights on the nearest prefab bungalow. The index finger of his left hand curled around the M-203's trigger, slowly tightening into the squeeze, holding steady on target acquisition.

The launcher made a muffled popping sound as the 40 mm high-explosive round took flight. His target was an open window, and his aim was true. A moment later Bolan watched the bungalow's east wall disintegrate, twisted scraps of aluminum sailing across the clearing and into the trees. One piece ripped the foliage several feet above his head, but Bolan didn't flinch. His full attention was focused on the camp, where startled men were racing for their weapons, preparing to defend themselves.

Around the perimeter, muzzle-flashes erupted from the shadows as streams of automatic fire converged on the camp. Men staggered, stumbled, fell, the impact of their bodies raising puffs of dust around the clearing.

Now!

The warrior rose from cover, grim death closing on his adversaries as he sprinted for the cover of the nearest bungalow.

San Juan Naval Base
1420 hours

ENCIZO'S UNIFORM and bogus orders were enough to get him past the nervous sentries on the gates, but it was touch and go for several moments as they tried to stare him down, as if expecting him to crack and blurt out his complicity in the abduction of their missing submarine. From all appearances, security was tight, but he wouldn't be satisfied until he checked the base himself, made sure no traces of Miguel Albano's taint remained.

Beginning with Gregorio Ruiz.

A simple phone call had assured Encizo that Ruiz was still on the base, and that spelled trouble with the *Thresher* out at sea. He could have spoken to the shore patrol or CID and had Ruiz arrested, but Encizo had a vested interest in the operation now and he wasn't about to let it go.

Once past the sentries, Encizo made his way directly toward Ruiz's quarters, ever conscious of the silencer-equipped Ruger .22-caliber automatic tucked in his belt at the small of his back, concealed by the cut of his uniform jacket. The lightweight weapon was a compromise, but he had loaded hollowpoints to compensate. The .22 was an assassin's weapon, when you thought about it, and Encizo's mission was the swift and sure elimination of his target on the base.

Two minutes brought him to the block of carbon-copy flats where Ruiz occupied a second-floor apartment. There was only one way to discover if the guy was home or not.

Encizo climbed the stairs and stood before the door. There was no peephole, since security around the base theoretically eliminated prowlers. There was no one to be frightened of until you left the base.

He slipped the buttons on his jacket, drew the Ruger .22 and flicked its safety off before he punched the doorbell. He waited briefly, and just as he was reaching out to give the bell another try, he heard the sound of footsteps from within. There was a moment's hesitation, and Encizo could almost feel Ruiz waiting, wondering if he should answer or ignore the bell.

Then came a snap as the deadbolt was released, and the door swung open. The first expression on Ruiz's face registered shock, bleeding into fury as he snarled and tried to slam the door.

Encizo got there first, a swift kick that bounced the door off Ruiz's chin, drawing blood from his split lower lip. The Puerto Rican staggered backward, flailing his arms for balance as Encizo lunged across the threshold, swinging the door shut behind him. He could hear the numbers falling like the ticking of a time bomb in his brain.

He raised the Ruger .22 and prepared to fire, but Ruiz leaped forward, grappling at close quarters, knocking his gun arm aside. The hollowpoint stuck a ceramic lamp and sent jagged shrapnel flying in all directions, some of it gouging divots in the nearby wall.

Encizo knew that he was fighting for his life as he blocked Ruiz's lightning attacks with knees and elbows and tried to bring the .22 around and into target acquisition. Ruiz saw the danger and struggled to keep the gun averted from his head and torso, reaching for his enemy's throat with his free hand, fingers like curved talons, raking Encizo's jawline.

The Phoenix Force warrior tried a kick to the groin, but there was no room to maneuver, and his foot glanced off Ruiz's hip, a wasted blow. Ruiz took the opportunity to hit Encizo with a straight-arm to the chest, knocking him backward, dumping him across the sofa. As he fell, Encizo saw his adversary thrust a hand beneath his jacket, reaching for the equalizer that would finish it.

Encizo fired on reflex, two quick rounds before he tumbled off the sofa to the floor. The first round missed completely, but the second drilled Ruiz's shoulder, flattening on impact, spinning the man to the left as his Beretta cleared leather. The heavier weapon pumped two rounds toward the ceiling, its report as loud as thunder in the small apartment.

The Phoenix Force warrior fired again from the floor, time enough to brace his Ruger in a firm two-handed grip for this one, lining up the shot. His third round struck Ruiz in the face, boring a tidy hole in his cheek before it mushroomed, slamming hydrostatic shock waves through his sinuses, into the brain.

Ruiz hit the carpet like a sack of laundry and lay there, motionless as Encizo scrambled to his feet. A dozen thoughts were crowding Encizo's mind all at once, competing for attention while his pulse hammered in his ears.

Had the gunfire been audible outside the flat? Was anybody home next door? Downstairs? How long before the shore patrol kicked the door in with their pistols drawn, ready to gun down anything that moved?

He stepped around Ruiz's body, moving toward the open bedroom doorway. He spotted the duffel bag near the closet. Kneeling beside it, Encizo cautiously opened the zipper, peering inside at the individual charges of C-4 plastique, each with its timer attached.

He lifted the charges out one at a time, removing detonator wires with the deft touch of an expert. When all of the bombs were disarmed, lined up on the floor in front of him like harmless lumps of clay, Encizo rocked back on his haunches and expelled a weary sigh.

No pounding on the door of the apartment yet, but he had pressed his luck as far as he dared. It was time to go. The call could wait until he found a telephone off the base, at which time he would send the CID to check in on Gregorio Ruiz and his bag of tricks.

There was no hurry now, at least with Encizo's end of the game. He could afford to catch his breath. As for the others...

He could only hope that they would still be breathing when the smoke cleared.

Gurabo
1425 hours

THE FIRST BLAST of gunfire had shocked Francisco Obregon out of his siesta, spilling him from his cot to a kneeling position on the plywood floor. He shook his head to clear it, reaching for the holster on his hip, remembering at the last moment that his gun belt was hanging from a wall peg above the cot.

He rose and turned to reach it, anxious questions tumbling through his mind like pieces of a puzzle scattered by a hurricane. A single shot or burst of fire might mean an accident, but he was listening to sounds of all-out combat now. The camp—their final, safest hideout—had been sniffed out by the enemy, and now Obregon's men were fighting for their lives.

He buckled on the web belt and retrieved his Smith & Wesson submachine gun from the floor beneath his cot. Obregon would have to reach the weapons hut for extra ammunition, but at the moment he was more concerned with escape. It would mean a mad dash to the compact car he had driven from San Juan, and from there a race to the nearest highway, eluding his pursuers who would surely be on foot.

How many of them were there? Obregon could tell nothing from the chaotic sounds of gunfire, and he moved toward the nearest window in a crouch, dropping prone as a bullet smashed the glass and whispered past his face, drilling the flimsy wall behind him. Panic caught him by the throat and tried to strangle him, but Obregon brought himself under control with an effort, crawling on his belly until he reached the wall below the window.

He risked a peek outside, recoiling from the sight of three dead soldiers sprawled on open ground, their lifeblood soaking into the dirt. Others were running aimlessly around the compound, firing their weapons at the tree line without a clear target in sight. In seconds flat, fear had erased months of training and indoctrination, turning the remnants of the ANI into undisciplined rabble.

Anger vied with Obregon's personal fear for control of his mind. It was a shameful thing to see his soldiers scrambling about like mindless peasants, even though he felt the urge to cut and run himself. Perhaps they needed an example, someone to remind them of the fact that they were members of a revolutionary strike force, pledged to sacrifice their lives to defend the cause.

But was Francisco Obregon the man to offer that example in his present state? His hands were trembling as they gripped the submachine gun, and his bladder suddenly felt full to bursting, as if it might let go any moment of its own accord. Simply stepping out of the bungalow would be a risk, much less trying to engage the unseen enemy, but Obregon was sick to death of running.

It was days now since he had really felt like a man, entitled to hold his head up proudly in the company of other soldiers. Betrayed by his woman and outmaneuvered by his enemies, he had watched his troops decimated as he fled like a thief in the night when his adversaries approached. His comrades might not understand the fear he felt inside, but Obregon knew well enough, and it was eating at him, nagging him to prove himself.

And if it cost him his life, at least his memory wouldn't be sullied by the taint of cowardice. Another generation of rebels would write songs about him someday, calling him a hero—and how could a son of Puerto Rican peasants come closer to immortality than that?

With new determination he approached the doorway, flicking off the safety of his Smith & Wesson subgun. In his mind he could already feel the sunlight on his face and smell the gun smoke drifting in the yard.

His time had come, and if it was the last time, he would take it like a man.

Obregon reached the door and whipped it open, smiling as he stepped outside.

Miami International Airport
1330 hours EST

THE FBI HAD TAGGED Raul Gutierrez more or less by accident. The call from Able Team on Friday afternoon had moved the Bureau to intensify surveillance on Hector Aguilar, and his rendezvous with Raul Gutierrez in suburban Coral Gables had been duly recorded, passed on to the special agent in charge of the Miami field office. From there the message made its way to Stony Man, and wheels began to turn.

"They're sure about this guy?" Lyons asked.

"Beyond a shadow," Blancanales replied. "They've tracked him in and out of Puerto Rico half a dozen times on diplomatic papers. Langley reckons we can double that, at least, on bogus passports."

"Any firm connection with the ANI?"

"I'm no believer in coincidence."

"I'll second that," said Gadgets Schwarz.

They stood on concourse B, a three-man island in the flowing stream of humanity, surrounded on every side by tourists dragging luggage, friends and family come to wel-

come travelers or see them off, airport employees in their
uniforms.

"They've cleared security already?"

"That's affirmative," Blancanales said. "Gate B7, waiting for Lufthansa outbound to Zurich. No hardware."

"Makes it easy," Lyons commented.

"Two on one?"

"It might not go that way."

"I don't mind going with you," Gadgets told him.

Lyons shook his head. "We'll need the coverage out here
if one of them gets past me."

"Fair enough."

Passing through the security checkpoint, Lyons emptied
his pockets of coins and keys, retrieving them on the other
side of the metal detector. No alarms sounded at his passing because he carried no firearms, a concession to the circumstances. What he did have was a six-inch dagger molded
from a sturdy polymer. Its blade was needle pointed, semi-
flexible and capable of being sharpened to a razor's edge.

Like now.

He moved along the concourse, counting off the gates
until he reached B7. Lyons recognized Hector Aguilar on
sight, pegging the dark Latino on his left as the target from
Havana. They were deep in conversation, leaning into each
other, Gutierrez wearing a smug half smile as he spoke.

The flight to Zurich wasn't scheduled to depart for another ninety minutes, but Gutierrez plainly preferred to do
his waiting at the airport rather than gambling on taxis and
traffic to make the deadline. Lyons counted seven more
early birds lounging in contoured plastic chairs; more travelers passed him coming and going, bound to various departure gates or deplaning from incoming flights.

Clearly Lyons couldn't take Gutierrez where he sat, much less both men together. The mechanics of disposal weren't insurmountable, but there were too many witnesses on hand. Lyons had been counting on a semipublic take out, but this was something else entirely.

He would have to wait.

Lyons picked out a seat for himself near B8, the no-smoking section, and settled in to watch his targets from the corner of his eye without appearing to observe them. Neither seemed to notice him, nor was there any reason why they should.

If he could only wait...

His mind was racing, sorting out potential problems with the set. Suppose Gutierrez didn't budge before the boarding call for his flight? By that time there would be a crowd around the gate, and Lyons would have lost his chance to make the tag. It would mean letting the Cuban go entirely or dispatching another agent to find him in Europe.

Unacceptable.

Lyons was steeling himself for a move on the spot when Gutierrez stood up, said something to Aguilar and struck off in the direction of the men's room.

Bingo!

The Able Team warrior gave the Cuban enough lead to make it look natural, trailing in his wake as if it were the most natural thing in the world. He would still have to worry about witnesses in the rest room, of course, but at least they would be screened from passersby.

He brushed through the swinging door, scanning the room at a glance. The urinals were unoccupied, and he stooped to check the open space beneath the stalls. One pair of shoes was visible, and Lyons recognized the cuffs of his target's beige slacks.

He dawdled at the mirror, combed his hair, hoping that no one else would enter while he waited. He could always wait them out, of course, but Gutierrez was another matter. If he emerged with another man in the room, Lyons would have to make an immediate decision—to kill or let him walk.

The toilet flushed, and Lyons moved to stand before the Cuban's stall. He reached inside his jacket and palmed the plastic dagger, holding it flat against his thigh with the point toward the floor.

Any moment now.

He heard the latch and stepped forward, ready when the metal door swung inward. Raul Gutierrez blinked in astonishment, tried to slam the door in self-defense, but Lyons shouldered through and hit him with a short left jab above the heart. The toilet caught Gutierrez behind the knees, and he tumbled backward, banging his head against tile, one arm thrown up before his face.

Lyons went under the arm with the dagger, shearing through the soft flesh below Raul's jaw and putting all his strength behind it, warm blood spurting out across his hand and wrist. Gutierrez stiffened, thrashing with his legs for just a moment, then he slumped back on the bowl, arms dangling at his sides.

The Able Team warrior left him there, closed the door to the stall behind him and spent a moment washing his hands. Outside he saw Hector Aguilar waiting where Gutierrez had left him, staring idly out a giant window toward the runway.

He would have to wait.

Lyons turned back toward the main concourse, walking with hands in his pockets, mingling with the passengers from an incoming British Airways flight. Blancanales and Schwarz were waiting for him at the checkpoint.

"Like that?" Schwarz asked.

"One down. We'll have to wait for Aguilar or let the Bureau pick him up."

"Let's give him to the Feds," Pol suggested.

A grin split Schwarz's face. "I'll make the call."

Gurabo
1435 hours AST

BOLAN SLAMMED a fresh magazine into his M-16, moving around the fire-gutted bungalow in a combat crouch. He counted eleven bodies in the clearing, all of them ANI troopers in khaki or olive drab fatigues, stained dark with the blood from their mortal wounds. Four of the six buildings were shattered or smoldering, two with their walls blown out flat on all sides like collapsed cardboard structures.

As the warrior watched, a grenade took out the communications bungalow, shrapnel punching jagged holes in the prefab walls, its door cartwheeling across the compound. The door was followed closely by a rag-doll figure, smoking as it hit the ground and crumpled in a boneless sprawl.

How many more? Was Obregon among the dead...or had he even come here in the first place?

Bolan was preparing for a break across the compound when he heard an engine revving somewhere close at hand. Behind the open mess hall? Bolan shifted position, half rising from his crouch as a Land Rover burst into view, fishtailing in the dust before its rear tires found traction and dug in, accelerating toward the narrow access road on Bolan's flank.

An automatic rifle raked the vehicle from the eastern perimeter, shattering glass on the passenger's side, but the Rover kept coming, accelerating into the approach. The Executioner narrowed his eyes, trying to make out the driver's face through a dusty windshield, stiffening as he recognized the snarling face of Francisco Obregon.

The M-203 launcher was loaded with a 40 mm high-explosive round, and Bolan used it now, firing from the hip at a range of twenty yards and closing. The HE can impacted on the Land Rover's grille and detonated with a crack of thunder, crumpling the vehicle's hood and slamming it backward into the windshield with force enough to star the glass.

Obregon lost control of the vehicle, veering off course and plowing into the wreckage of a grenade-shattered bungalow. The wounded engine died on impact. The Puerto Rican scrambled out the driver's side and dropped from sight behind the Rover, popping up long enough to loose a submachine-gun burst in Bolan's general direction.

The Executioner was already moving and responded with a burst of 5.56 mm tumblers that drilled through the passenger's door of the Rover, burning into the seats and dashboard.

Obregon tried another burst, closer this time, his bullets kicking up spurts of dust on Bolan's flank. The Executioner threw himself prone, lining up his next burst on instinct, slamming a half-dozen rounds into the Rover's right flank, finding the fuel tank and striking a spark.

A mushroom of flame blossomed under the vehicle, spreading rapidly, spilling into the wreckage of the bungalow. Bolan waited sixty seconds, and he was on his knees when Obregon erupted from the heart of the inferno, trailing a long cloak of fire behind him and flapping his arms.

Bolan dealt Obregon a mercy burst that lifted the man completely off his feet and punched him through an awkward airborne spin. He came down in a smoking heap, unmoving as the flames devoured his clothing and the flesh inside.

The Executioner rose to his feet and made another scan of the compound, spotting Katz and the others emerging from cover at various points. Besides the men of Phoenix Force, no one was moving in the camp. If not a clean sweep, it was the next best thing.

"We're running overtime," Katz told him, moving closer through a pall of drifting smoke.

"I'm done."

"We've got a call," James said. A red light pulsed on the walkie-talkie at his hip, signaling an incoming message without the normal blare of static that would put an enemy on guard. James raised the unit to his lips and keyed the transmission button.

"Phoenix One."

This time the caller's voice was audible, though faint with distance, carrying an undertone of static.

"Disengage when finished," came the word. "Gray lady down."

"Affirmative," James told the distant listener. "We copy."

"So." The single word from Katzenelenbogen said it all.

"I guess." The smile was irresistible, tugging at the corners of Bolan's mouth.

"It's a hard way to go, that," McCarter said. "The sub, I mean."

The Executioner responded with a shrug.

"Dead's dead," he answered, and began the long trek through the forest to their waiting cars.

EPILOGUE

Stony Man Farm
Sunday, 1300 hours EST

"A not-so-simple accident," Brognola said, his dark eyes circling the conference table, lingering over each face in turn. "The Navy's calling it a problem with the nuclear reactor, all hands lost. A tragedy. The good news is, they only had a special shakedown crew on board, testing some new electronics systems."

"Aguilar?" Carl Lyons asked.

"He's singing to the FBI right now. With any luck he just might roll up G-2's network on the gulf."

"Survivors from the ANI?" James asked.

"We can't be sure. If so, they're not about to call attention to themselves."

"Until the next time," Katzenelenbogen said.

Brognola spread his hands. "We take them as they come. Whoever might be left has lost their power base, supply lines, the whole command infrastructure. If they're not washed up, at least they're back to square one."

"And Camacho?" Schwarz inquired.

"Another unrelated accident. You hear about them all the time."

"That's a knock to the old Navy ego," Grimaldi suggested.

"Better some egg on the face than admissions of traitors in the ranks," Brognola countered.

"Right. I see your point."

"You've earned some R and R," Brognola said. "There's nothing critical right now. I wouldn't be surprised if we could spare a week or so."

"Is that with pay?" Gadgets asked, and laughter spread around the conference table like ripples in a pond.

It felt good, Bolan thought, to sit among friends and unwind. Until the next time, right.

And there would always be a next time in the hellgrounds, as long as savage man kept preying on his own kind for ideology or profit.

Bolan's eyes met those of Barbara Price across the table, and he read a message there. She told him that today could be enough, if they took full advantage of the time.

Tomorrow, the Executioner knew, would take care of itself.

Join Mack Bolan's latest mission in

THE TERROR TRILOGY

Beginning in June 1994, Gold Eagle brings
you another action-packed three-book in-line
continuity, the Terror Trilogy. Featured are
THE EXECUTIONER, ABLE TEAM and
PHOENIX FORCE as they battle neo-Nazis
and Arab terrorists to prevent war in the
Middle East.

Be sure to catch all the action of this gripping
trilogy, starting in June and continuing through
to August.

Available at your favorite retail outlet, or order
your copy now:

Book I:	JUNE	FIRE BURST (THE EXECUTIONER #186)	$3.50 U.S. $3.99 CAN.	☐
Book II:	JULY	CLEANSING FLAME (THE EXECUTIONER #187)	$3.50 U.S. $3.99 CAN.	☐
Book III:	AUGUST	INFERNO (352-page MACK BOLAN)	$4.99 U.S.	☐

Total amount	$_____
Plus 75¢ postage ($1.00 in Canada)	$_____
Canadian residents add applicable federal and provincial taxes	
Total payable	$_____

To order, please send this form, along with your name, address, zip or postal code,
and a check or money order for the total above, payable to Gold Eagle Books, to:

In the U.S.	In Canada
Gold Eagle Books	Gold Eagle Books
3010 Walden Ave.	P. O. Box 636
P. O. Box 9077	Fort Erie, Ontario
Buffalo, NY 14269-9077	L2A 5X3

TT94-2R

TAKE 'EM FREE

4 action-packed novels plus a mystery bonus

NO RISK

NO OBLIGATION TO BUY

SPECIAL LIMITED-TIME OFFER

Mail to: Gold Eagle Reader Service
3010 Walden Ave.
P.O. Box 1394
Buffalo, NY 14240-1394

YEAH! Rush me 4 FREE Gold Eagle novels and my FREE mystery gift. Then send me 4 brand-new novels every other month as they come off the presses. Bill me at the low price of just $14.80* for each shipment—a saving of 12% off the cover prices for all four books! There is NO extra charge for postage and handling! There is no minimum number of books I must buy. I can always cancel at any time simply by returning a shipment at your cost or by returning any shipping statement marked "cancel." Even if I never buy another book from Gold Eagle, the 4 free books and surprise gift are mine to keep forever.   164 BPM ANQZ

Name	(PLEASE PRINT)
Address	Apt. No.
City	State	Zip

Signature (if under 18, parent or guardian must sign)

* Terms and prices subject to change without notice. Sales tax applicable in NY. This offer is limited to one order per household and not valid to present subscribers. Offer not available in Canada.   GE-94

Adventure and suspense in the midst
of the new reality...

JAMES AXLER

DEATH LANDS®

Rider, Reaper

A peaceful interlude for Ryan Cawdor in the mountains of
New Mexico becomes a blood-soaked game of survival as Ryan's
idyll becomes a mission of revenge. His quarry on a cross-desert
manhunt is the General, a man who grimly prepares to destroy
his pursuers.

Hope died in the Deathlands, but the will to live goes on.

Available in August at your favorite retail outlet, or order your copy now by sending
your name, address, zip or postal code, along with a check or money order (please do
not send cash) for $4.99 for each book ordered, plus 75¢ for postage and handling
($1.00 in Canada), payable to Gold Eagle Books, to:

In the U.S.	In Canada
Gold Eagle Books	Gold Eagle Books
3010 Walden Ave.	P. O. Box 636
P. O. Box 9077	Fort Erie, Ontario
Buffalo, NY 14269-9077	L2A 5X3

Please specify book title with order.
Canadian residents add applicable federal and provincial taxes.

DL22

Don't miss the next installment of

THE Destroyer

Infernal Revenue
Created by
WARREN MURPHY
and RICHARD SAPIR

A fiendish artificial intelligence chip known as *Friend* boots up disaster for CURE....

Friend has covertly hijacked the new computer system at CURE and screws up the database so efficiently that both Remo and Chiun quit—just as *Friend* releases a stealth virus that will hold the world hostage to technoterrorism! Can a reluctant Remo and determined Chiun work to foil the greatest threat CURE has ever faced?

Look for it this September, wherever Gold Eagle books are sold.

Or order your copy now by sending your name, address, zip or postal code, along with a check or money order (please do not send cash) for $4.99 ($5.50 in Canada), plus 75¢ postage and handling ($1.00 in Canada), payable to Gold Eagle Books, to:

In the U.S.	In Canada
Gold Eagle Books	Gold Eagle Books
3010 Walden Ave.	P. O. Box 636
P. O. Box 9077	Fort Erie, Ontario
Buffalo, NY 14269-9077	L2A 5X3

Please specify book title with order.
Canadian residents add applicable federal and provincial taxes.

DEST96

Are you looking for more

DEATHLANDS®

by JAMES AXLER

Don't miss these stories by one of
Gold Eagle's most popular authors:

#63057	PILGRIMAGE TO HELL (1)	$4.99	☐
#63058	RED HOLOCAUST (2)	$4.99	☐
#63059	NEUTRON SOLSTICE (3)	$4.99	☐
#63060	CRATER LAKE (4)	$4.99	☐
#63061	HOMEWARD BOUND (5)	$4.99	☐
#62507	DECTRA CHAIN (7)	$3.95	☐
#62508	ICE AND FIRE (8)	$3.95	☐
#62512	LATITUDE ZERO (12)	$4.50	☐
#62513	SEEDLING (13)	$4.95	☐
#62515	CHILL FACTOR (15)	$4.99	☐
#62516	MOON FATE (16)	$4.99	☐
#62517	FURY'S PILGRIMS (17)	$4.99	☐
#62518	SHOCKSCAPE (18)	$4.99	☐
#62519	DEEP EMPIRE (19)	$4.99	☐

#63807	EARTHBLOOD #1	$4.99	☐

TOTAL AMOUNT	$
POSTAGE & HANDLING	$
($1.00 for one book, 50¢ for each additional)	
APPLICABLE TAXES*	$ _____
TOTAL PAYABLE	$ _____
(Send check or money order—please do not send cash)	

To order, complete this form and send it, along with a check or money order for the
total above, payable to Gold Eagle Books, to: **In the U.S.:** 3010 Walden Avenue,
P.O. Box 9077, Buffalo, NY 14269-9077; **In Canada:** P.O. Box 636, Fort Erie, Ontario,
L2A 5X3.

Name: _____

Address: _____ City: _____

State/Prov.: _____ Zip/Postal Code: _____

*New York residents remit applicable sales taxes
Canadian residents remit applicable GST and provincial taxes.

DLBACK3

**Don't miss out on the action in these titles featuring
THE EXECUTIONER®, ABLE TEAM® and PHOENIX FORCE®!**

SuperBolan

#61431 ONSLAUGHT $4.99 ☐
With his cover blown by a leak traceable to the highest levels of Russian security, Mack Bolan is forced to go solo, with Mafia hit men and cartel killers burning a trail of bullets and blood from Moscow to the Black Sea coast.

#61433 RAMPAGE $4.99 ☐
Rampant terrorism is sweeping through Europe as a fearless new force with a gruesome agenda turns the French Riviera into a killing ground.

Stony Man™

#61889 STONY MAN V $4.99 ☐
When an international drug machine declares war, Stony Man—Mack Bolan, Able Team and Phoenix Force—jumps into the heat of battle.

#61891 STONY MAN VII $4.99 ☐
Stony Man: America's most classified weapon—action-ready and lethal.

#61892 STONY MAN VIII $4.99 ☐
A power-hungry industrialist fuels anarchy in South America.

(limited quantities available on certain titles)

TOTAL AMOUNT	$
POSTAGE & HANDLING	$
($1.00 for one book, 50¢ for each additional)	
APPLICABLE TAXES*	$ _____
TOTAL PAYABLE	$ _____

(check or money order—please do not send cash)

To order, complete this form and send it, along with a check or money order for the total above, payable to Gold Eagle Books, to: **In the U.S.:** 3010 Walden Avenue, P.O. Box 9077, Buffalo, NY 14269-9077; **In Canada:** P.O. Box 636, Fort Erie, Ontario, L2A 5X3.

Name:_____
Address:_____ City:_____
State/Prov.:_____ Zip/Postal Code:_____

*New York residents remit applicable sales taxes.
 Canadian residents remit applicable GST and provincial taxes.

GEBACK6A